TOO CLOSE TO HOME

FINN ÓG

For the woman on the radio, and all like her.

BEFORE

Sam had watched an innocent man be removed from his home. Two known players flanked him. He'd called it in over the net and followed them to a block of flats. He heard the Scots accent of his gnarly little friend, Min, pick the party up inside the block. Min and his men had been embedded in the flats for weeks, listing through the walls. He heard his pal describe a bath being filled. They all knew what that meant. What they couldn't work out was why it was being allowed to happen.

Then they were ordered to absorb the sounds of the the interrogation of an innocent man. Sam's friend patched it through to the ops room. Min repeatedly asked for permission to intervene. He was repeatedly denied. They listened to the man break. They listened to the interrogators setting up a recording device. For his family, they said. So his family would understand what had happened. But Sam and Min knew the tortured man had not done a thing. He had not been the informer.

Sam listened from his car at the foot of the flats. He heard the fabricated confession, he heard the man describe a shame he could not possibly have felt. He heard the victim plead for his family, that they not be told he was an informer, that he had been killed for some other reason – he didn't want them saddled with the stigma of thinking their father was a tout. Which he wasn't - a fact Sam and Min's commanders seemed content to ignore.

Sam felt his secondment coming to an end as he unlocked his vehicle and made for the stairwell. He heard Min on the net now demanding permission to intervene. Sam's signal cut out as he wound up the concrete steps to the thirteenth floor. The first Min was aware that his buddy had left the vehicle was when he heard the door to the flat next door smash open. Min immediately cut the audio feed and ran to help.

It was too late. The lights had already flickered. Two hundred and forty volts had been dropped into the bath alongside the innocent man. Sam and Min did what needed to be done, the two others who had been in the flat with Min helped tidy up.

All four addressed the subsequent inquiry with total silence. They refused to answer any questions.

Their own interrogators were in a tricky position. They were asking why four of the best trained operatives in covert intelligence gathering had tried to save an innocent man's life. It was an odd position to take.

Stalemate.

So the four ops were punished with a cover-up and sent back to their home units. One to the airborne, one to signals, two to the marines. They sucked it up – they'd disobeyed orders - but they could live with it.

They left with skills that many years later, would come in handy.

1

Isla was buzzing. A little bundle of worry and excitement. Sam was struggling.

They debated the packed lunch. He stared at the lunchbox and dropped in a few extra treats, breathing deep and hard; then he heaved the brand-new bag full of sharpened colouring pencils and freshly covered books onto her back. For two months he had made notes about what she might need and of what her mother would have packed for her. A change of knick nocks, a bottle of water, a teddy, tissues. And wipes. Isla's mam never went outside the door without a bundle of moist bricks. Isla looked up at him with her beautiful big eyes and Sam dropped to his knees, gripping her in as her little arms tightened around his neck.

Eventually they climbed the little ladder out onto deck and they drove the dinghy ashore. Isla asked a million questions about what school would be like. She wasn't beginning as other kids had – dreadful circumstances had made her a late-starter, so primary three was where her formal schooling was beginning, after a few false starts. In her absence from education she had gathered skills no kid her age could have, but she'd learned about life in ways that Sam would have preferred she had not.

He cast her off in the playground and Isla turned to him with fear in her eyes. She wasn't used to being around lots of other kids, she wasn't used to being anywhere other than at his side – she was barely used to dry land. But his salty little sailor was tough, and when the teacher emerged, as planned, to take Isla under her wing – she went. Just as she started to climb the steps of the mobile classroom, Isla turned.

"Daddy, I'll be ok. Don't worry."

That choked Sam more than the departure. He nodded rapidly and turned into the wind before she could see his struggle.

Grim slapped his prodigy on the shoulder. He seldom made physical contact with anyone, so the nudge went a long way.

"Well done, son," he said to the youth, who didn't smile but beamed with pride at being selected and trusted to carry out the job.

Anthony. As names went it wasn't the worst but he yearned to be known as something else. Anthony was ordinary – a name among many in an estate where nobody was going anywhere. The best he could manage was Tone, but the options were few: Ant was rubbish and Tony too obvious. A name like Grim, though, that said a lot. That spoke authority, serious business, respect. Anthony wanted a name like his mentor. To be known only by that short name, a menacing name, a name that inspired respect – or at least fear.

"Well, get on then," Grim told him. "And remember, if you're scooped, we'll look after ye, so long as ye say fuck all."

The lad wouldn't utter a word. He was afraid of Grim but not of the police. Prison, if it came, would be a tattoo to be proud of in a slum where there was nothing to boast about. If the kid went to jail, he'd come out a man feared of nothing. In deeper, in harder and out of options but to keep going. Just as Grim wanted. Grim was clever that way. He could make men do things – inspire people, and inspiration was hard to come by in places where everyone's future was the same: the dole, benefits, a house in the same old hole.

Grim watched the lad get into the passenger seat of a waiting car and be driven off. Home for a kip before being delivered to the middle of nowhere.

Grim leaned in against the door frame. He didn't rationalise his own skill set but he was conscious of it. What he offered were prospects of a kind. Progression. He could make the local populace wary of a young man just by paying him some attention. That young man's shoulders would swell, his chest would barrel like a bouncer's and he'd become someone among the no ones. It created a hierarchy, and in return the young man would do whatever Grim bid.

Routine took a bit of getting used to. Sam had to install a washing machine on the boat – no fun when he watched the battery power drain like a sink. He even considered moving to dry land such was the mountain of washing school created. And Sam hadn't ironed since he'd left the navy. Gone were the days of the pair padding about the decks in bare feet and sawn-off jeans, hanging T-shirts and cut-offs on the rigging to dry in the breeze. With the exception of underwear, one outfit could last a week at sea. They had washed in a fresh-water rain barrel – body and clothes. But structure had brought chores and homework and tiredness and frustration.

Sam loved to watch Isla learn, but she was behind. He'd insisted she begin her education with kids her own age, determined that she wouldn't feel out of place, yet he doubted the wisdom of that decision every night as she struggled with sums and words and spelling, and so he read to her, long into the evenings, and with time and the odd tussle she spelt out the random words he selected to test her.

As time went on they settled into a pattern. She no longer rose with the dawn – she needed every minute of sleep she could get, and instead Sam sat alone on deck with tea as black as tar dealing with his demons and waiting for Isla's seven o'clock alarm. Then they'd recap tables and spellings as he fed her toast like a bullet belt into a machine gun before Isla struggled into the rigours of her school uniform. Isla hadn't had any real structure to her life since the day they'd decided to leave dry land and live aboard the cutter, yet every day at 8 a.m. they clambered through the cockpit, over the rails and into the dinghy. Ashore they'd climb silently into the van for the short drive to school.

And then Sam to his worry as the cash dried up and he fought the instinct to return to what he knew best.

Anthony couldn't swallow. His mother looked at him but didn't seem to care whether he ate or not. She didn't know it was his last night. She blew a little puff through her nose, turned away and went out onto the doorstep to finish her smoke.

Later, he wrestled around on top of his childhood mattress – full of sharp stabs and pinging springs. Eventually he rolled over and lifted the scrapbook his grandmother had kept. Page after page of gnarled card peeled back as he examined three days of newspaper cuttings. Three days in which his family's history had been written. It had been short, their involvement – but it gave them something to cling to. The death of his uncle was marked annually by a loyal but dwindling audience who marched to the spot of his obliteration. They laid wreaths and made speeches. Well, *a* speech these days, just the one, now that the family was no longer with the mainstream.

The scrapbook was poor, on reflection, as a shrine to a son. Mounted with Pritt Stick and slapped in without structure, the barracks stood amid the mess. Bullet strikes and ricochet marks, stains on the tarmac – which his grandmother had claimed was her son's blood draining into the street, but it was hard to tell in black and white.

In truth Anthony had long since lost interest in the story. Where once it had served as inspiration of a sort, it was now just a pedigree to which he could cling. "My uncle died for Ireland" didn't sound so good any more now that the war was over. His own motivation may have had its genesis in the event fifteen years before his birth, but it hadn't stuck. He was more interested in not being just another skinny little bastard in a forgotten town with nothing to do.

2

Sinead had called twice. He'd watched the phone light up and *Charity* appear – the affectionate nickname he'd always intended to edit. Sam's desire to answer was as strong as his determination not to. He hadn't heard from Sinead in an age – since he'd called to tell her she was safe and he was ok. "Getting away from things" was how he'd said they'd be for a while. He expected people to understand. The fact that father and daughter had put to sea with no course set should have surprised nobody.

Of course, he knew Sinead would find him if she needed to – her sister could see to that. That bolshie little bitch was good at her job, capable. In truth he liked the twin, in very small doses. She was testing. She had an opinion on everything and a mouth like a mower, churning up and cutting away at anything she disagreed with.

On Sinead's third attempt to get through Sam took the view that something was wrong – she was a sensitive type and not one to intrude on his time with Isla. Sam stared at the buzzing handset and decided that the time had come to take a call.

Grim was content he'd done all he could: a change of clothes at Primark to dump any devices the spooks might have managed to place on him, a departure from rushed conversations in cars that they now knew were ripped to hell and a stroll in a forest amid creaking trees with great dollops of rain creeping through the canopy.

He snapped and rustled for a full twenty minutes before anyone presented themselves. First came a man who in any other environment might have made an effective enough manager. They nodded at one another but said nothing; standing wiping the heavy droplets from their cheeks as they waited for the boss.

He made them stiffen for a full hour under the swaying shelter. Then, from nowhere, came that slow gait; his slim build testament to time spent hungry in a cell smeared with his own shit. But the darkness was inescapable. How someone so pale could exude such black intent was baffling. His aura was pure menace, born of utter hatred.

Nods all round then clipped conversation. There was a collective comfort, close to trust, in their shared experience at the pleasure of the queen. Their precautions, hard learned, felt impenetrable.

And yet still, someone caught every word.

"Ehm, how are things?"

Sam knew immediately that she needed something. Their conversations were riddled with complexity, subtlety, caution. What was unsaid was often more important than what was actually discussed. Sinead was forcing herself to start with a pleasantry otherwise she would have opened with "I just wanted to see how you both are".

"Grand," Sam replied. "You're not, though, I'd say." His tone urging her to cut to the chase.

"That obvious? Sam, I could really do with some help."

He exhaled. "Smashing and bashing, no doubt."

"No, not really."

"*Not really* might not crack it, Sinead. You know I'm not wanting that kind of work any more – it's too dangerous for Isla."

"This isn't ... it's, well, it's more straightforward – and it's good money," she added in a rush. "Cash job if you want it, and for you it's as handy as it comes."

Sam had heard this type of talk before from others in his select bunch of ex-clients. Invariably the soft jobs had usually ended in bruising or bloodshed. Sinead, however, had been the first employer of his new career, and his most trustworthy. She was also the only one who knew about his circumstances – his daughter, their way of life, their bereavement.

"Does it involve your sister?" he asked.

Sinead suppressed something that on a better day might have become a giggle. She knew how the two of them locked horns yet suffered from mutual, but well-concealed, professional admiration.

"Kind of. She's appearing as an expert at a trial."

"Oh? What type of trial?"

"The worst kind."

"So you want her minded."

"Not in a way that she would notice, if you follow me."

"That feisty little mare is well capable of looking after herself," Sam said, baulking at the thought of spending long periods in Áine's company.

There was silence at the other end and Sam somehow knew he had gone too far. This was the sister of a good friend – a very good friend. That was as far as Sam could allow the description to go. For now.

"Where's the trial?" he asked softly.

"Criminal Courts, here."

She meant Dublin, which was two hours from where he was and therefore a pain in the arse as Isla needed to be kept on the clock, no disturbances.

"The family – the parents of the victim, they were looking for a consultant, and, well, you can guess the rest."

Sam's shame dawned on him. Sinead's sister was a tech genius. She worked for all the big companies in Ireland, from local start-ups to the west coast multinationals. Well, she *had* worked for them – until Sam had enlisted her help with a job and got her blacklisted.

"Has Áine not worked since ..." He didn't want to say too much on the phone.

"No," Sinead replied, clipped and to the point.

"So she's, like, freelancing?"

"This is her first job in months. She's not impressed."

"But I thought she was in big demand?"

"Sam, that last thing ruined her reputation with Silicon Valley. They closed her right down. She's been going up the walls."

"She must hate me."

There was a pause, which was confirmation enough. "She wouldn't want you looking out for her anyway," Sinead said.

"How did she get this job then?"

"The family came to me looking for someone good, someone they could trust."

This was no surprise. Sinead had become the go-to person for the Irish media when it came to commentators on abuse, immigration, prostitution or the examples of online bullying that never seemed to go away. If he allowed himself to acknowledge it, her voice on the radio or appearance on the telly always made his mind wander into complicated territory.

"How long is the trial due to last?" Sam asked.

Sinead sensed the opening. "Three days. Starts next week but she'll need someone sooner than that. The bastard just got bail."

Sam knew immediately what case she was referring to. "I'm with you now," he said. "The bloke who groomed the special needs girl?"

"*Woman*," she corrected.

"How did he get bail if he was up for murder?"

"Haven't you heard about the prison crisis?"

"No."

"That fire in Portlaoise Prison led to some edict. Unless there's a threat of flight or reoffending, even the worst criminals are tagged and sent home. There's no space for scumbags in the cells."

"Would they not release a few thieves to find room for a murderer?"

"He's not a murderer yet. Innocent until—"

"He'll be found guilty, though, won't he?"

"I'd say so. The stuff Áine found was horrendous."

"What do you mean?"

"The cops weren't doing much but the family knew the answer lay in her computer and phone. Áine was brought in by the witness's folks to do the Guards' job for them. It was she who found all the messages hidden away in hard drives."

"Why couldn't the cops find it?"

"They said they couldn't crack the security, and the big boys refused to help. They went to the cloud people in the States and got knocked back, so they gave up."

"Seriously?"

"Didn't take Áine long, as you can imagine."

Sam had seen Áine at work. Her personal workspace at home was like ground control at NASA.

"But if the victim's dead, who's looking for protection – besides your sister?"

"That would be the witness – another woman. He abused her as well but she didn't say anything at the time. It was only when the dead woman's body turned up that she came forward and her folks came to me. That led to Áine, and now he's got bail and we're all shitting ourselves."

"If the witness had told someone earlier, could he have gone to jail before he killed the other woman?"

"Not that simple, Sam," Sinead said, evidently exhausted at the male take on such matters. "Even if she had spoken up, nobody would have listened."

"Why?"

"Cos the killer's got a respectable enough job and she's got, well, she's got issues."

"What sort of issues?"

"You'll understand when you see her."

Sam noted how Sinead was subtly assuming he was going to take the job.

"I think you'd better tell me the whole shebang now."

Sinead sighed. "She's tricky – the witness. She behaves like a child but she's in her thirties. There's no official diagnosis – you know, she hasn't officially got a lower mental age or anything. Her parents, they're well got, if you know what I mean. I don't think they'd want to think of her like that, you know, as having special needs. But she's not a normal adult – not to my mind anyway. She's like a really spoilt teenager."

"So how did he groom her? How did he get at her?"

"Same as the dead woman – phone, chat room. That's why Áine is key to the prosecution. She can draw direct comparisons between the dead woman he groomed and the surviving one."

"If she has special needs, what's she doing with a phone and a computer?"

"What planet are you on, Sam?" Sinead's frustration broke through. "You think that because she's got some mental health issues she's not entitled to have the same gadgets as everyone else?"

"Ok, sorry. I just don't want to be doing this kind of work any more."

"Is that a no?"

"Course not. I just don't know what to do with Isla. She's only started school and it's tough for her. She's two years behind and it's a struggle."

"It's only a week, Sam. Maybe ..."

Sam waited while Sinead wrestled with what she was about to say.

"Maybe I could mind her for you? Take her to school and whatever. Might be fun."

Sam was taken aback. It would mean Sinead having to come and stay on the boat – their space and their sanctuary. He found it confusing, conflicting.

Sinead filled the silence. "It's a bad idea."

"No, no, Sinead, it's not a bad idea. I just need to think about it if that's ok?"

"Of course, of course." Sinead was now on the back foot.

"And Sinead?"

"Yes?"

"If I do take this on, there's not a chance I'll be charging you, you know that."

"Well, I reckoned you'd be running low on funds, so I mentioned you to the father of the witness. It seemed to put him at ease and money's no object – they're worth megabucks."

The call ended and Sam stared at the floorboards that had once concealed his cash. The bilge of the boat was scarily empty.

And at that moment he heard an almighty crash from the shoreline nearby.

Anthony didn't know Belfast. Not at all. He'd only been to the city a few times shopping with his mother as a nipper, and then once at Christmas for the turning on of the lights – the one and only treat he could remember. His grandmother had been there too. It had ended as quickly as it had begun with the rattle and shove of buggies and a herd of humans filling and emptying the streets in a frenzy. Mr Tumble had twatted about on stage, much to Anthony's shame. At ten he was much too old for such entertainment. He'd been too short to see anything and too big to be hoisted aloft. A crap day, he had told his mother when they got home. Perhaps that's why she'd never bothered to take him anywhere since.

He got off the train at Central Station. It had been drilled into him that the address was a short walk from there, and he had been forced to memorise his instructions: cross the street, walk towards town, stop at the arch to the market, because nothing was to be written down. Not ever.

Anthony managed the first set of directions. His gaze lifted beyond the green wrought-iron fence to the stone-carved lettering: "St George's Market". Inside was a bustling mania, and a stench. At the far end fish men in white wellies were pushing brush shafts with wide rubber blades, swashing guts and swill towards the drains. Closer to the gate well-dressed women in plimsolls were dismantling stalls and rolling up paintings and prints.

Next set of directions: turn back the way you came, thirty feet, glass-fronted offices.

He was nervous but determined not to make a mistake and so he marked it out like Jim Hawkins pacing the steps to buried treasure. Looks like nothing, he thought, but then he'd been told not to lift his head, to avoid the CCTV cameras, and the gaze from under his hoodie was furtive.

His next job was to walk the route he would use to bring the car in, over and over. He had to walk it different ways from the motorway to the location in case of traffic or road closures or accidents. So he set to it.

"What the ...?"

Sam had tried hard to stop swearing. They called it the "fuck tape" back in the Marines and talked about taking the tape out before they went home on leave. In truth, it was more than just their language they had to watch when dipping back into civilian life, and today was no exception.

Sam marched straight at the man in the overalls and clutched him by the throat. "What were you thinking?"

The bloke stared at Sam, terrified. At six feet and sixteen stone the man was no soft touch, but Sam had come ashore and up the beach at such speed that his fury blew ahead of him. The man's rigger boots dangled off the ground as he choked out an apology.

"Hydraulic failure," was all he managed to grunt after Sam let him fall to examine the wreckage. Under a small boat lay the remains of his van. Isla's booster seat was crushed and Sam's throbbing temper gave him enough strength to wrench back a panel and retrieve her colouring books and blanket.

"You twat," he spat at the crane driver. "You've got a whole bloody yard to swing a boat and you decide to lift it over the only vehicle parked in the place." His incredulity made his voice summit in register. It was all he could do not to lace the driver with a kicking. But Sam was in the process of trying to remove himself from such temptations – to be normal, more measured. He breathed deep and ground his teeth.

"I'm really sorry, mate, I just didn't think the crane would pack up."

"It's knackered. What if my kid had been in that van?"

The driver looked at the blanket in his arms and the colourful books and shook his head in despair. Sam reckoned he'd got the message.

"Help me get this door open, I need the insurance docs."

3

"How was your day?"

"Really good." She beamed.

It was the first time he'd heard Isla say that.

"Why have you got my bike?"

"Cos we're going to cycle back to the boat today, darlin'."

"It's a long way, Daddy."

"Yes, but there's been an accident with the van."

"Did you have a crash?"

"No, wee love. Some eejit dropped a boat on it."

"How did they lift a boat over the van?"

"With a crane, darlin'."

"The great big crane?"

"Yes, the massive one."

"Is the van being mended?"

"No, darlin', the van can't be mended. It's going to the scrapyard."

"To the dump?"

"Uh-huh."

"But, Daddy, all my stuff is in the back!"

"It's ok, I took everything out, wee love, every last bit."

"Phew," she said.

They clambered onto the bikes and Sam took her aft quarter on the roads to force cars around her. Isla's little knees hammered up and down like a fiddler's elbow but she still needed a shove up the steeper inclines.

"Have you got much homework?"

Isla ignored the question as another popped into her head. "Can I go and play with Molly some day?"

Sam had heard her talk about Molly – who seemed to have a tall imagination unless it was Isla who had the imagination and was attributing strange factoids to her pal.

"We'll see. Where does she live?"

"Don't know," said Isla glumly.

"What's the matter?"

"*We'll see* means no."

"No, it doesn't," said Sam, trying to persuade himself that she was wrong.

Isla pedalled silently and slowly. Sam felt the guilt.

"You can go, wee love, soon. I promise."

Her little feet picked up pace and she cast a call over her shoulder. "Thank you, Daddy."

He smiled. "There's something I want to talk to you about."

Isla looked apprehensive but said nothing.

"It's quite important and you'll need to think about it."

They got into the dinghy and motored the short distance to where their boat, *Siân*, was moored – the most static she'd been for months. Below deck he made her get the books out and began fumbling around in the galley.

"Sketty bolognaise?"

"Yes, please. We're not going sailing again, are we?"

"What?"

"You said you want to talk about something. Do you want to leave Ireland again?"

"No, love," he said soothingly. "I was wondering how you'd feel about someone coming to mind you for a few days."

"Who?" Isla asked, interested. She hadn't been exposed to anyone other than her grandparents in years.

"A friend of mine – you met her once, very briefly."

"What's *very briefly*?"

"Quickly. You said hello to her once."

"I don't remember."

"She's really nice."

"Is she as old as you?"

"I'm not old, Isla."

"Yes, you are, Daddy."

"She's ..." Sam paused, unsure, "she's probably about the same age as me."

"Why do you not know what age your friend is?"

Sam had never thought about that before but some things are so important when you're wee.

"I think you'd like her."

"What's she called?"

"Sinead."

Isla's head was between the clutches of two colouring pencils. "Ok." She shrugged as if it were no big deal.

But to Sam it was closer to an ordeal.

Safe houses were hard to come by and Grim had few options. Sympathy for the struggle had waned significantly. The most effective operators were all in jail. Fundraising efforts were pathetic and they relied on smuggling and cigarettes these days or taxing criminals, so there was no money, which meant the families of those in prison were pretty pissed off. In the old days the movement would have supported them but there just wasn't the cash for that carry-on any more.

Morale was low, and households that had once harboured a regard for those prepared to keep fighting for a socialist united Republic of Ireland were scarce. Grim cast around for weeks for a place for the kid to stay. Eventually he found a family of diehards in a County Antrim seaside town, but he knew as well as anybody that diehards stood the greatest chance of being monitored. Beggars can't be choosers, he reasoned, and accepted the offer.

It niggled at him, though. The level of infiltration among the ranks was grating. The Brits always seemed one step ahead. All that the remaining republican groups could manage were small acts – incendiaries or shots fired. Such skirmishes got reasonable publicity, for sure, but they failed to capture any real attention or give the impression that there was still a movement worth joining and fighting for. They'd been forced to fashion small improvised devices, house them in plastic lunch boxes and attach them to vehicles using the magnets from stereo speakers.

There was no formal organisation. Disparate groups tried to follow one another's efforts to make it look like a campaign but it was hard work, especially when there was no coordination. As soon as approval was given for an attack, details somehow leaked out and the target car was suddenly inspected. Some of the devices didn't explode, which suggested tampering. Their organisation was leaky and they were all too aware of it.

The targets were usually peelers – police officers or prison guards. Above all, Grim and his comrades wanted to kill fellow Catholics who had joined up. The aim was to frighten other young Catholics away from any notion of joining the new police force and making the Police Service of Northern Ireland the enemy, as the old RUC had been. The PSNI was, in Grim's opinion, becoming far too acceptable to the Irish nationalist population north of the border. They needed an identifiable adversary now that the British military had withdrawn. Without an enemy, after all, there could be no war.

"I'll take the job."

"Really?" said Sinead, probing.

"But I might need a vehicle."

"Oh?"

"It's not important but I thought something was insured when it wasn't. It lapsed while we were at sea and I've been driving around for a month with no cover."

Sinead knew better than to tut. She waited.

"And I'd also like to take you up on your offer if that's still ok."

Sinead realised what a big deal this was and so tempered her pleasant surprise. "Great."

"If you're able to cover the cost of a hire car, then we're on. For three days."

"You could take my car when I come north?" Sinead suggested.

"You'll need it, I'm afraid, to take Isla to school. Our van is, well, flat-packed."

"No problem."

"How are you with boats?"

"I think I'm about to find out," she said brightly.

"I'll make sure she's tied up in a marina or at a pontoon or something.

"Ok," said Sinead. "It'll be fun. Girls together."

"It might well be," said Sam believing it as he watched Isla sleep.

Perhaps a change from looking at him all evening, every evening, would do her good.

It certainly wouldn't do him any.

If he couldn't sleep before, he certainly wasn't going to sleep now. Anthony wasn't used to the sound of the sea but he guessed it was close – although he wasn't allowed to find out for himself. It washed and crashed and roared every night as he waited for the car and minded his manners with the people downstairs in this small house.

He didn't quite understand what was going on. His hosts were an older couple and their son, who looked to be in his forties. None of them appeared to work. The son seemed odd. Stupid, Anthony concluded. He'd glimpsed an IRA tattoo on his upper arm, faded to the colour of seaweed, as he left the bathroom one morning. He also had some home-made inkings on his hands but Anthony never had the courage to look at them long enough to work out what they said. They gave him the impression the man had been to jail.

Anthony reckoned that might be why he'd been placed with this family. Every army needs its unquestioning foot soldiers and the son was probably one of them. Anthony observed the whole thing with interest – sponged it up. He decided he wouldn't become just another follower like the unemployed son with the grubby tattoos. He would be like Grim.

Sam got off the Enterprise train at Dublin's Connolly Station. He normally enjoyed travelling by train but he'd spent the whole journey worrying about Isla's quiet thoughtfulness. Would she think Sinead was there as part of a plan to introduce a mother figure? And if she did, might she be right?

The introduction had gone surprisingly well. Sam had rather anticipated a pushback from Isla – a bashful pleading with him to change his mind, but she hadn't kicked off. In fact, she hadn't seemed at all worried – which ought to have pleased him yet instead he found himself slightly deflated by her ambivalence towards his departure. He knew it was selfish; he understood that it was part of *his* neediness for her. He would miss her like mad, even if it was only for a few days.

Sinead, however, appeared to be a natural.

"Hello again, Isla." She had started with an uncharacteristic babble. "You won't remember me but we met when you guys got off the boat in Dungarvan. It was pouring rain that night and you were so hardy – you'd sailed such a long way."

"I remember," said Isla brightly. "You had yellow shoes on."

"Yes, I did!" said Sinead.

Well, fuck me, thought Sam.

"I *like* your dungarees," Sinead had rattled on, and the next thing Sam knew the two of them were looking at the dresses Isla had been drawing in her fashion-designer book.

He might as well have been abroad.

Out of shame the yard owner's son had driven him to the train. He'd also allowed Sam to tie the boat up to the pontoon to save Sinead from having to use the dinghy.

He left Dublin Connolly by the side entrance and headed west, allowing the twinkling chat of the chancer to fill his senses as he weaved his way through the market towards O'Connell Street. Sam reckoned it would take him forty-five minutes at a good pace to get to the courts. He loved the roguery of inner city Northside Dublin; everyone had a wise-crack, and comments to strangers were framed as instantly familiar.

At the complex he set about his recce. Parking was a night-mare – there were few options within sight line of the enormous round building but no shortage of traffic attendants. That meant if he hired a vehicle, he would have to keep it moving. Not ideal if he needed a quick extraction.

Across the road was a small garage selling cars and offering valeting. He tried the half-suited man behind the counter. "Any chance I could hire a car here?"

"No luck, buddy," the man said. "We're all about sellin' the yokes here."

"If I was to pay cash and leave a vehicle on the forecourt but have access to it in the case of an emergency, how would you feel about that?"

"Eh, what sort of emergency are we talkin' about here, buddy?"

Sam thought for a moment. It went against the grain for him to give anything away, but this job was more official than anything he'd been involved in since he'd left the navy, so what the hell.

"I'm looking after a witness in a trial across the road." He motioned at the courts.

"Like a bodyguard?"

"Pretty much."

"Are you, like, a Guard?"

"No, private hire."

"Right." The man was sceptical.

"I don't think I'll need the car. It's just in case I need to get her away in a hurry. But there's very little risk here, to be honest. I'm just building in contingencies."

"How long, and how much cash are we talking?" the man asked.

"A week. How much are you looking?"

"A grand," said the man.

"I can't even do half that," said Sam turning away. "But, listen, thanks for your time."

"What's the case?"

Sam turned back and summed it up. The story was all over the news anyway. "A bloke who groomed a special needs woman."

"Groomed, me hole," said the man, disgusted. "He raped and murdered her." He reached below the counter to a shelf that would have been at eye level when he sat. He lifted a picture frame and spoke as he held it facing himself.

"You're minding a witness for him or against him?"

"Against – for the prosecution."

"Then why aren't the Guards minding her?"

"It's complicated. Bit bizarre but the man got bail, so—"

"Read that, yeah," said the man before turning the picture towards Sam. "That's me girl there," he said. "Gorgeous, wha?"

Sam looked at the image of a teenager standing with the man in front of her, held by the arm by a woman who could have been her mother. The grip was affectionate but somehow firm.

"She's a special kid too," said the man. "So, yeah, ye can have the car, buddy, and I'll get you a fine fast yoke and I'll park it right there." He pointed to the traffic on-slip.

"Right," said Sam, rather taken aback. He had forgotten how, like Liverpudlians, many Dubs would give you the shirt off their backs no matter how little they had. He fished in his pocket to draw out some cash.

"No money, buddy," the man said. "Just look after your witness and send that bastard to Portlaoise."

"I don't really get the location," said Grim.

"Neither did I," said the manager, before his bald head tilted back with the pint and his thick neck chugged the beer down his throat.

The pub was one of the few places the pair thought they could talk. They were well enough known to be left well enough alone. This was a "no customers required" sort of establishment. A camera at the door threw up an image on a screen at the bar and a buzzer prevented entry until the bar person was satisfied that they knew the customer. In the past there had also been a cage but that had gone since the threat of attack had diminished.

"So what's there? Why's he so keen on that address?"

The manager sighed. "It's just an office."

"It's obviously not just an office." Grim looked at the manager who stared straight back, reluctant to elaborate. "Fuck's sake," he said, angry that his former cellmate was so reluctant to trust him with the information. There had always been grit between them because the boss was closer to the manager and the pair occasionally kept Grim out of the loop.

"If he finds out I told you, he'll not be happy."

"If you don't tell me, he'll need to find someone else to rear his chicks," said Grim.

It was understood that the boss couldn't incubate "volunteers" without his permanent security shadow ticking them off, one by one, like a skulking fox. Without the loyalty of the two men facing one another the boss would get nowhere – his pedigree as an unreformed republican was such that he couldn't brush his teeth without the Brits knowing about it, so he needed lieutenants who could get stuff done.

The manager waited a while, pouting gently as he thought.

"He thinks the office is where they're doing the donkey work for a future inquiry."

"Another one?"

"The whole nine yards – who did what, who knew what, what we did, what they did, collusion ..."

Grim snorted. Collusion. A word now woven into the fabric of the Northern Ireland conflict. A word to describe the flow of information from rogue members of the security forces to loyalist paramilitaries who hated the IRA. Bad cops and soldiers unable to beat the burden of proof had occasionally passed on the names, addresses, routines and movements of suspected IRA members. Such information was hungrily received by opposing gunmen loyal to the union with Britain. The outcome had been predictably bloody and frequently botched.

"Why would the boss want to destroy an inquiry? Sure, that's to our advantage – exposes the police and the Brits."

The manager's eyebrows raised in agreement. "That's what I thought too, but then he explained it – there is no good outcome for us. He says the office location is where they're poring through old records – the ones held here anyway. Others will be in London, he reckons."

Grim's face screwed up. "Looking for what?"

"IRA agents – touts. The boss thinks they have lists of who was working for the Brits all along."

Grim was incredulous. "Well, what's to lose? Again, that's good for us. If they show that the IRA was run by the Brits, then the peace process goes to hell in a handcart, dunnit?"

"If you take a simple view, it does. The boss doesn't see it that way."

"Well, how does the boss see it," said Grim, affronted at being thought of as dim.

"It's complicated. But aside from the political stuff he sees it as a chance to show them that we know where they work in secret, and that we have moles of our own. He reckons that will send a strong message to Whitehall that we are not to be fucked with."

"So how *does* he know about this location?"

"Sorting office, I'd say. He has a few people in there. They keep an eye out for specific names. When a letter arrives with a new address on it, they take a snap on their phone and pass it on later."

Grim thought for a moment. The boss knew the tricks from his time in IRA intelligence, before he broke rank over Sinn Féin's pursuit of the peace process.

"How did he know what names to look for?"

"Sure, that's easy," said the manager. "Who leads inquiries?"

Grim considered. There had been plenty of inquiries into matters connected to the Troubles. Many held in public. "Barristers, retired judges?"

"So he had his people keep an eye out for various names – especially the retired ones, especially the ones who sent him down or refused him bail."

"Right," said Grim, impressed but confused. "But how did he know that any of these people were working on collusion?"

"I'd only be guessing."

"Well, guess then," said Grim, increasingly irritated.

"Well, politicians have been calling for an inquiry into collusion for a long time, right?"

"Uh-huh."

"So the Brits are gonna want to make sure that whatever is in the records isn't too damaging, right?"

"Correct," conceded Grim.

"They want the story to favour them."

"I'm with you."

"So they're gonna do a bit of work to see how bad it's likely to be before they decide whether to give in and allow the inquiry or whether it's gonna dig up too much awkward shit."

Grim just nodded.

"They need to make sure that nobody finds out who the real informers in the IRA were, right?"

"In case they're close to the ones who made the peace deal," said Grim.

"Exactly. So what's the best way to do that?"

"Find the evidence first, destroy it, then call the inquiry?"

"Well, yeah," said the manager, "but more than that. What do they do about people who aren't on board the peace train – people like us and the boss, for example. If there are people out there still prepared to kill cops and blow stuff up, then isn't it in their interests to suggest that the likes of you, me and him were the informers?"

"Ok," muttered Grim, slowly understanding what the boss might be up to. "So he's worried they'll out him as a tout to protect the real informers?"

"They're dirty enough."

Grim shifted on his butt cheeks, a tightener. "I still don't see how he knew all this work was happening, though?"

"Well, there's more than one post office."

"What do you mean?"

"There's a mail service at Stormont, you know. Like a courier within the estate."

Grim didn't know that but it made sense. Stormont housed the local government assembly as well as a sprawling complex of civil service offices and thousands of staff.

"But this stuff is sensitive," Grim reasoned. "The Brits aren't going to let local politicians know about any of this until they're sure it won't be damaging to Downing Street?"

The manager sighed. "Correct. But it's not just local politicians inside Stormont Estate, is it?"

The penny dropped. "The NIO."

"The NIO," repeated the manager.

The Northern Ireland Office was the official residence of the Secretary of State, a member of the British Cabinet, who was a keeper of secrets and often at odds with local politicians. The secretary was privy to security information in a way that local politicians weren't. It was the secretary who was supposed to approve the bugging of suspects, who was briefed by Box – MI5, and military intelligence.

"So the boss has got someone in the NIO?"

"Dunno," said the manager. "But he somehow got information or saw documents out of the NIO. My guess is that he's just done the usual – had someone lift letters or something, some unassuming civilian who maybe gets them copied or whatever and puts them back. Or just steals them. Sure, post goes missing all the time."

"No, it doesn't," said Grim.

"Then maybe it just goes unanswered. I haven't a clue. But the point is – he knows, and he thinks taking out this office will leave a mark on the Brits."

"I'd say he's right," said Grim.

Sam had two people to mind, two locations, two problems. How could he look after Áine – who knew him by sight, and another woman he hadn't yet met without being in two places at once? Instead he focused on the threat, and for two days kept an eye on the accused from the driver's seat of a loaned Subaru with two hundred and eighty brake horsepower.

The man was called Delaney and his image was plastered all over the digital versions of the Irish papers. Sinead supplied the address and Sam simply sat outside his house – which the accused refused to leave. Sam saw his bathroom light go on, go off, the blinds go up and down, the TV flicker and the bins go out. Other than that, nobody came and nobody went. Sam reckoned he was probably afraid of a public backlash.

On the morning of the trial he finally felt able to abandon his vigil, got a shower at a swimming pool and walked the perimeter of the court, which backed onto Dublin's Phoenix Park. Nothing about this job was straightforward: the thoroughfare out the front was busy, there was a lot of traffic, four ways in and the tram stopped nearby. The footfall was substantial, and it would be hard for one man to keep all approaches covered. Sam didn't really consider the job to be high-risk, but then he didn't know a great deal about the accused. Despite a few secondments to various units during his time in the Special Boat Service, close protection had not been one.

He strolled past the foyer of the courthouse and through the doors into a massive marble atrium. The security detail at the door looked rough enough, but not necessarily sparkling. Big blokes with tools were fine for the wrestling matches that the courts inevitably witnessed – rival gangs descending on tiny rooms for cases of murder and assault, and heavies were also required to keep the travellers apart. Sam knew well that traveller gangs had unusually high levels of pain tolerance – they played with hatchets, chains and sawn-off shotguns and held a grudge like a baby on a balcony.

The space was vacuous. The sight lines were good, but, as ever, the risks lay not in the public spaces but in the wings. Sam wandered slowly to the allocated courtroom and took a look inside. Standard, surprisingly so for such a modern building. The seats were typically hard and built from timber and the bench looked traditional. There were two doors for the public, one for a jury and another for witnesses. Behind the bench was the door to the judge's chambers. Five entrances in all: a pain in the arse.

Then he went outside to look at the toilets. This had been his biggest concern. Assuming that the accused was able to groom and persuade women to do whatever he wanted, Sam reckoned that the risk was likely to come from a woman. There was no guessing how many others he'd manipulated – and what lengths such a person might go to to quell a witness statement being made. Sam's darker imaginings had a brainwashed devotee waiting in the jacks for Áine to powder her nose before attacking her. Áine was feisty, for sure, but there are few defences against a committed assassin with a knife or a needle. Any woman's handbag contained half a dozen instruments that could be used to kill or wound a person – all of which would be waved through security. On top of that, the accused would be sitting in the courtroom apparently unconnected to any such assault. No witness means no conviction.

Sam looked at his watch. One hour to go until the case was due to be called. He lifted his phone.

Poor reception.

"Hello," Sinead answered, dropping in and out.

"Hi, how are you both?"

"Grand, grand. Isla went off ok. She was happy. I can't get the light on in the main cabin, though."

The phone signal was rubbish, so he cut to it.

"I'll text you instructions, but, listen, I'm not happy about this. The place is exposed. We're going to have to tell Áine that I'm here to look after her. I need to stay close to her otherwise, well, it's too risky."

"She's never going to go for that, Sam."

"I'm not trying to worry you but this place isn't great."

"She thinks you're there to look after the other witness. I'll call her and see if I can get her to sit with them. I'll ring her now. I'll have to make it work."

He fired off three instructional texts to Sinead before she called him back.

"What did you tell her?"

"I told her you'd be there for Kaitlin."

"This is the heiress?"

"What?"

"The one who was groomed but survived."

"The heiress, yeah. Like I'm Charity."

Sam reddened. He hadn't realised Sinead had known his nickname for her. "That was before."

"Before what?"

"Before we became ..."

The silence was excruciating. There was no adequate description for what they had become. Sinead dug him out of his hole.

"Áine's not happy. I'll leave it at that."

"Ok," said Sam. "And Sinead?"

"Yeah?"

"Tell her to go to the toilet before she gets here and not to use the jacks in the court."

"Weird but ok."

They might have been twins but the fact that they'd shared a womb was the only similarity Sam could detect in Sinead and Áine. The former was caring, considerate, compassionate and fair; the latter was aggressive, abrasive, argumentative and alert. Always alert, like she was fully charged and never used up her reserves. He saw her arrive – her chin pulled back, her neck straight, ready for a ruck. Her walk was busy, her stride long; she was fizzing.

Sinead had obviously told her that Sam would be around for a few days.

"Áine." He nodded at her as she strode straight past him.

She declined to say anything. She had brought no notes and no folder. Everything she needed was probably stored in her mind. She was nothing if not smart. Sam would have considered her a genius were it not that she was such a bloody dose.

He turned to follow her at a distance.

"She's inside," Áine snapped over her shoulder. "I'd say you'd want to go and introduce yourself."

Lifts were shuttling up and down inside the atrium as the scales of justice began to swing for the day. Sam followed Áine's arse towards a small group of well-turned-out folk. There was a couple in their late sixties: he a pinstriped distracted sort, she a manicured fragrant type. They stood either side of a younger woman who chewed gum with her mouth open.

"John, this is Sam, your, well, heavy beef, I suppose," said Áine.

"Ah, yes, how are you?" the man said, offering his hand and gripping Sam as hard as he was able. "This is my wife, Julianne."

"How do you do?" she said, pure D4 – over-pronounced and presentational. She failed to proffer her paw, as if he was nought but an oily rag.

"And this is my daughter, Kaitlin."

Kaitlin looked every inch the heiress – too cool for school despite being in her thirties. Her mouth churned like a cow on grass while she stared at him.

Sam turned to the other suit. "I assume you're the brief?" he asked.

"Ehm, well, yes, I'm the state counsel, actually."

Sam never had much time for barristers, so he let the suit excuse himself and set about extracting some information from his employers.

"I know what Delaney looks like, but is there anything beyond the obvious to suggest that he might want to upset things? Has he been in touch?"

The father wanted to field the questions. "Kaitlin has been receiving messages from someone but we don't know who."

Sam turned to Áine as if to say, *Can you not find out who?*

He got a snort and a look away in response.

"Text messages?" Sam asked.

"Snaps," said Kaitlin.

"But you need to accept a friend request to receive a message on Snapchat, don't you?"

Áine leaned in and in a patronising tone said, "He can barely use a toaster, I'm afraid. Not very technical." She over-enunciated her consonants to let the family know she thought Sam was a nuisance.

"I accept the requests, then I realise it's him, then I get rid."

"You need to get rid of that phone," said her father.

"You can fuck off," she retorted.

"Kaitlin!" the mother hissed through clenched front teeth, the tendons on her neck making her look like a turkey.

"I'll need to see the messages," Sam said.

"They're all gone," she replied, with a look that said, *What are you going to do about it?*

"Well, what did they say?"

"Nuttin' much." Kaitlin cracked the gum between her palate and tongue.

"Are you sure they're from him?"

"Who else?" she said, her eyebrows raised in adolescent petulance.

Sam had been prepared for this, yet still found it disconcerting. She had the figure, the dress sense and laughter lines of a rich woman in her thirties, but she acted with less maturity than his seven-year-old.

"Here he comes," said Áine from his right.

Sam turned to see a familiar figure enter the foyer, with, presumably, his wife on his arm. He looked like he'd just been through an ordeal and Sam imagined the press photographers outside had tracked him all the way to the door. The man was dazed, probably from the flashbulbs, and the look on his face further exaggerated when he caught sight of Kaitlin and her family.

"Bastard!" the heiress shouted suddenly.

Sam noticed how her stare was more aimed at the woman at Delaney's side.

"Bastard! Fucker!"

Sam wondered if she had Tourette's.

"Kaitlin," her mother scolded again in a stage whisper. "You were warned not to do that!"

Security guards hustled over immediately and ushered the group towards a family room. The language out of the daughter on the way there was salty. When they sat down Sam laid out some ground rules.

"I'll be here at court with you each day."

"I'm sure you feel safer already, Kaitlin." Áine's head wobbled in sarcasm.

"If you get messages from the accused, you must tell me, and obviously report that to the court," he said. "You don't go anywhere without letting me know, and your mother can accompany you to the bathroom or anywhere I can't be with you."

Kaitlin looked at him slyly, and Sam imagined she was thinking of ways to test him as a pupil might test a new teacher.

"Thank you, Sam, for coming all the way from Belfast," said the father. "You come highly recommended." He looked to Áine, who raised her eyebrows but said nothing.

"Well, if you do what I say, hopefully there'll be no drama."

The door opened. "Court is about to sit," said an usher.

4

"Mark leaving Green 12, headed west, country bound."

The big white van had hooked up a fertiliser spreader in broad daylight. The team following the van knew it had been stolen from a remote farm in rural County Fermanagh. They had tracked the van across competing jurisdictions but when it had left the towns the Gazelle helicopter kicked in and followed it at a height beyond hearing range. Occasionally vehicles rotated in and out checking progress as directed from above until the van came to a stop. A single operator watched at a distance as the spreader was lifted into the back of the van by two men, the vehicle's open doors revealing a mechanical grinder and what looked like sandbags. The operator called in what she had seen, the helicopter confirmed receipt and the van was topped and tailed all the way to Donegal.

"They're baking a cake," the operator said.

"Stealing the ingredients," confirmed the Gazelle.

"Contrary to what you may have read in the papers or seen in the media," the brief – now attired in ridiculous headwear pontificated – "the accused is not a wholesome family man with a fine job and a love of country sports. We shall show, over the coming days, how his pleasures are derived from altogether more darker pursuits. How he has, in fact, used a genial persona to manipulate vulnerable women to engage in," he paused for effect, "unusual sexual activity with elements of dominance and coercion and that he did – in the case of Anne Seeley – a vulnerable woman – take the very life from her."

Sam watched the jury hang on every word the barrister said and boggled at his persistent use of impenetrable language. It struck him that the court system was full of such parodies – the unwashed sitting in conscripted judgement of facts delivered by over-educated buffoons who have little sense of how real lives are lived. He had once witnessed the sentencing of a street alcoholic for theft. The judge had leaned forward in his robe and wig and told the man how he must in future limit his drinking to a sherry before lunch. Sam had actually laughed aloud. The homeless bloke had wrinkled his arterial tributary of a nose.

The state counsel continued to baffle the jury with long sentences.

"We shall endeavour to demonstrate how the accused harnessed the power of information technology to captivate his victims, ingratiate himself on wholly false pretences and upon the premise of *assisting* his victims in their ailments discharge the most heinous and gruesome fantasies upon them."

Sam looked to his left. The heiress and her parents appeared every bit as gripped by the performance as the jury. Beyond them at least Áine had the wit to wear an expression of incredulity. She somehow sensed his gaze and turned. For the briefest of moments they shared a look that conveyed that they were both on the same page about the court's charade before Áine remembered she detested Sam and turned back to the counsel's theatrics. Still, it was a moment – a gentle sanding of the rough edges.

Sam zoned out a little. The barrister reminded him of some of the worst officers he had encountered overseas. He had been a marine, which was one thing, and the Marines had its fair share of arseholes, for sure, but for the most part the brass were solid, well-meaning and tough leaders with a bit of sense. He couldn't say the same of his experience of army officers. Their sense of entitlement, their basking in superiority and their insistence on recognition of rank at every opportunity had irritated Sam and got him into trouble. Nearly. The barrister made him think about a regimental arsehole he'd met in Iraq in a makeshift officers' mess. It was before he'd been disciplined, and as such he was still SBS without a uniform and operating largely at will. His unit had shuffled in under darkness and all he had wanted for his men was a bit of kip and to stock up on water. If they came across a bit of extra ammunition, Sam wasn't averse to pilfering from the regulars who tended to spray most of it up walls in any case.

He'd heard the army captain blustering orders around the little camp, which was poorly secured and badly kept: do this, do that, don't be so silly. The usual piffle of poor leadership. The officer hadn't even introduced himself to Sam's ragtag of unwashed arrivals. Sam had quietly suggested to his team that they get their heads down wherever they could, but was overheard by the captain, a man of a similar age to Sam. He had evidently deduced from Sam not barking his orders that he was an NCO, a non-commissioned officer, at best. He'd probably also heard the Northern Ireland accent. When the two men crossed paths twenty minutes later, the captain immediately turned to Sam with a demand.

"Make a cup of tea, there. Two sugars."

As introductions went, it wasn't ideal. If the captain had

even said please, the situation could have been markedly different.

"Try that again," Sam had said, knowing in his heart that things had already gone too far. His little unit had been working days and nights on end. They were exhausted and he wasn't best disposed to such demands, even when well-rested.

"Tea," the captain had said slowly, using his tongue, teeth and a widened mouth to enunciate as clearly as possible. Theatrical – like the barrister.

Sam responded in kind – clear and concise. "Away and fuck yourself."

"Well, haven't you just made an enormous mistake," sang the captain, who rose to approach Sam.

"Sit down, son," Sam said, not even looking at the man but knowing how it was all going to end.

"Son?" said the captain. "How dare you!"

Sam knew exactly how close the Rupert was without even looking at him. He decided he'd give the man one more chance but hoped he wouldn't take it.

"You'd be wise not to come closer."

"Who on earth do you think you are!" bellowed the captain placing an arm on Sam's shoulder.

Sam span with the encouragement and before anyone knew anything the captain's nose was plastered up his face and he was panting on the dry dirt floor.

"Ch-charge," was all the shocked captain managed to say.

"Sir," said Sam.

"What?" said the captain, eyes streaming and blood gushing.

"Charge, sir."

"Left it a bit late, you foolish fucking buffoon," said the captain, still stunned by what had happened. "Do you realise what you have done?"

"I'm more aware of the situation than you are, captain."

"What?" spat the Rupert, blood spattering out with his disbelief.

"You shall address me as 'Sir'," Sam said slowly, mocking the captain, "and you shall apologise."

The dawning was a delight as the captain finally registered his miscalculation. He had two black eyes to take back to his troops and no explanation other than he went into a tent with an unidentified special ops bloke and emerged without his dignity, a tooth and a straight nose.

Sam's gaze fell back to the curly wig on the barrister. He appeared to be closing, his cloak swooshing and swaying as his sheaf of papers was brandished towards the jury.

"You must brace yourselves for some disturbing testimony." He lowered his tone for gravitas. "For this is a serious case with the most serious of outcomes."

Sam looked at the accused, passive in the dock. The woman at his side was a wreck. Then he looked at the heiress, who was chewing her lip and looking anxious. Then he looked at Áine, who looked like she might kill dead things, and he resolved to pay more attention from that point on.

Anthony fidgeted, paced, he even did some press-ups. There was no TV and he had no phone. He had to get out – just for a while.

"Where you goin'?" said the son, as Anthony made for the front door.

"Just gonna take a walk along the beach."

"Not supposed to."

"I know," he replied, looking at the man in his slippers and a wife beater above tracksuit bottoms. He reeked. "But it's been four days."

"Pish," said the man.

"What?"

"Four days is pish," he repeated. "Wait till you've done fourteen years."

Anthony understood what he was being told: tighten up. If you can't sit in a room for four days, what chance have you of doing jail time?

"That what you did?"

"And the rest," the man replied.

"What for?"

"Possession, then a killin', but it wasn't me."

"So why d'ye go down?"

"Forensics. Had lifted the weapon for the boy that done it, then handled it after to put it away again. They done me on the ballistics and the residue."

"How did they catch you?"

"Boy that did the shooting was a tout."

"You went down for the fella that actually did the shooting?"

"Aye."

"Fuck me. You can't have been happy about that."

The living room door opened onto the hall and the mother emerged. "That's enough now. Come on in, son. *Pointless* is comin' on soon."

"Right y'are," he said and walked past her.

The mother closed the door behind her son and stared at Anthony.

"He got injured, in the jail." She tapped her temple. "Screws beat him after a fight on one of the wings."

"Did they?"

"He'll not be going back, ok? So nobody's to know you're here, y'understand? You're not to go out. If you go out, you don't come back, ok?"

"Ok," said Anthony.

"You can come in and watch a bit of telly if you want, but we'll have to pull the curtains."

"Ok," said Anthony. "Did he really do fourteen years?"

"He did," she said. "Man and boy. And now he's like a boy all over again. So my advice to you is – whatever you're doing – don't get caught."

The morning was moderately more interesting to Sam as two Garda divers described how they had recovered the body of Ann Seeley. An angler, who made a brief appearance in the dock, confirmed that a day's fishing on a lower-than-usual Lough Derg had produced no fish and one handbag – the contents of which betrayed its owner. The fisherman immediately recognised the name on a library card as that of a missing woman who had been in the news a month before. He called the Guards who, two days later, recovered the corpse.

"What was your impression of the body when you recovered it?"

Sam tuned in.

"Well, it was fairly manky," said the guard, unchecked, before he corrected himself. "I mean, like, it had been down there for some time, you know?"

The barrister floundered as someone in the courtroom sobbed, and Sam turned to see an elderly couple consoling an older woman – the dead woman's mother, he presumed. Sam stared at the callous guard who didn't know where to look.

"Is there anything else you would like to convey about Miss Seeley's remains?" the exasperated barrister tried again.

"She was weighted down," he babbled, "with dumb-bell rings."

"Dumb-bell rings?"

"For, like, on an Olympic weights bar. The yokes like big

saucers you put on the ends to make them heavier."

The barrister then referred to exhibits that were shown to the jury and displayed on a large screen for the court to see. The guard confirmed that the weights were the ones that had weighted down Ann Seeley's body.

Next, forensics and a pathologist took turns describing in nauseating detail what the woman had gone through. Sam's attention turned to the older woman, and he willed her friends to take her from the court rather than have her hear what had been done to her daughter. Then he looked for a long time at the accused who sat utterly passive without a glint of emotion.

Lunchtime recess was a silent affair during which the heiress rocked in her seat and ate nothing while her parents gazed into the distance in mild shock. The case turned to Ann Seeley's personality. Vulnerable and kind were the themes, as witness after witness described an impressionable, caring woman with an affection for children and small animals. Sam noted that Ann's mother hadn't returned after lunch and he found himself wishing she was present for the testimony that was, in effect, a tribute to her daughter.

At four o'clock the prosecution suggested to the judge that they'd done a day's work, which caught Sam on the hop. Tomorrow, said the brief, they would focus on the technology that had led the police to the accused. The judge seemed keen to get to the sherry, and so everyone stood as he swept out like a Hollywood movie star.

As they filed out Sam kept an eye on the accused and on Áine, but there was a quietness about the departure. Nobody, Sam guessed, believed the man was innocent, and that, he reasoned, meant that the greatest danger to Áine and the heiress was in the hours before they gave evidence. Which meant a few tough hours for Sam.

Grim hated his encounters with the boss. There was just no warmth to him at all; he was cruel to the core. His eyes were stone dead and his pallor made him look sick, yet his wiry frame was fit. He had a habit of twisting the unruly ends of his beard, which made it possible for him to speak without anyone ever properly noticing his lips move. His voice was soft, and he never used one more word than was necessary.

"The mix?"

"They've got everything they need and they're in location."

"Car?"

"Sorted. We have it months now. Nobody's actively looking for it. It's been modified – suspension lifted, so nobody'll identify it as laden."

"Routes?"

"All recced. The kid's been well versed."

"Comms?"

"Comms?" Grim's neck tightened.

"Yes," said the boss, neither annoyed nor angry, yet somehow still menacing.

"Eh, well, we thought no comms cos of the tracking. Just a briefing – delivered already, then get the car to the kid."

"Simple as that."

Grim couldn't make up his mind if he was being asked a question or being commended. The boss just stared at him. Eventually he stuttered a reply – just to fill the vacuum.

"Not saying it's simple, just keep moving parts to a minimum. Reduce liabilities, you know."

"Not simple, then?" the boss said, hushed, and Grim nearly shit himself.

The boss blinked slowly and turned his head away while keeping his eyes fixed on Grim's. Eventually the eyes rotated to align with his head and he walked away in his curious gait.

Grim was deeply relieved to see the back of him.

Sam couldn't cover two bases, and certainly not two as far removed as those of Áine and the heiress. Áine and her twin shared a flat in the Liberties which was, in part, due to Sinead's sensibilities. Combined, the pair could have afforded more, but it didn't feel right to Sinead to be away from the people for whom she worked. The heiress lived with her folks in a Georgian three-storey in the leafy and loaded Southside suburb of Ballsbridge. Sam had to find a way of bringing them all under one roof, so he had a quiet word in the ear of the brief.

"You'll be talking to the women tonight?" Sam nodded at Áine and the heiress gathered in a huddle in the atrium outside the court.

"Eh, no, as a matter of fact."

"I think you should. I need them to be persuaded to stay in one place tonight."

"Really? Why?"

"Well, you want them both to give evidence tomorrow, don't you?"

"Yes, of course."

"And yer man's not on remand, is he?" Sam nodded at the accused who was looking around for his wife.

"No, he's free to go home," confirmed the barrister.

"Then probably best they're looked after. And there's two of them and one of me, so if they're in one place, that's handier."

"Well, I really don't think there's any actual risk—"

"I really don't give a bollocks for the risk assessment of a lawyer in a wig, sunshine. Just you make sure those two women are at the same address tonight and not at different ends of the city, and I'll make sure they're both here and happy in the morning."

The barrister stiffened and tried to summon the courage to remonstrate. "This is not the north of Ireland," he stuttered.

"And this is not a fucking debate," Sam said calmly. "Just tell them you'll call in about ten tonight, leave it till eleven and I'll make sure Áine has a bed in Ballsbridge."

Sam was used to people doing as he asked.

"Fine," said the barrister uncertainly, and scuttled off under his curly toupee to convey the bad news.

Then it was Sam's turn.

"You ok?" he asked Áine as she passed.

"Yeah," she said, which felt like an opening. Any time she didn't tell him to F off was a bonus.

"Tough listen for you."

"That's nothing compared to what I've read in his messages to her," she replied as she kept walking.

Sam kept pace.

"The brief says you've a late-night prep session."

"Yeah? Where?"

"Ballsbridge."

"Oh, mega."

"Look, Áine, why don't you stay in Ballsbridge tonight?"

"So you can protect me?" she mocked, stopping.

"Áine, I don't have the skills or intelligence you have. I don't have any way of making up for the mess I caused when you lost your job. But I can do this ... and I owe your sister – and I owe you. And he's a dangerous bastard and you're about to send him to jail for the rest of his life. So what do you reckon? One night. I'll be around and then you're shot of me."

She glared at him for a solid minute.

"Sinead sent you for me, didn't she? This isn't about them at all, is it?" She nodded to the heiress and her folks.

Sam said nothing. Áine eventually wilted under the weight of her sister's concern.

"The *only* reason I'm doing this is because they live in a fucking mansion and I will probably have my own bathroom. Now, you can drive me to the flat and I'll get some clothes."

Sam was relieved not to have to spend another night in a car outside the Delaney's house. He told Áine to wait where she was and went to get the Subaru, content that he had finally managed to do something helpful for Sinead.

"I'm quite sure there is nothing to worry about." The barrister mustered a little bit of bravado as he hurried down the ornate hall in the Ballsbridge mansion. Sam had waited for the briefing to finish before he locked down the house for the night. He held the enormous Georgian door open as the barrister turned on the step to speak his learned mind again but Sam closed the door in his face.

Something caught his eye as he did so. He moved to one of two front reception rooms and, keeping the light off, took a look outside. The street was wide, littered with superior SUVs, Land Rover Discoveries fit for a horse stud and low, sleek BMWs and Audis. There were also thunderous trunky trees lining the plush street like a guard of honour – plenty of cover for anyone wishing to remain concealed. Sam opened the door to the marble-floored hall, allowing sight and sound lines between the front door and back, and remained in position for almost an hour. He could just make out the sound of water running and toilets flushing as the household retired for the night.

Eventually he pulled up an armchair and sat in the shadows, gazing through the full-length window. He allowed himself to doze, waking to take a good look around whenever the nod of his head stirred him. Hours passed as he stiffened into a right angle, the silence of the house and the travel catching up with him.

And then she was there, staring through the window, right in front of him.

5

Nothing was what it seemed, but then nobody in the unit expected it to be. Each member understood that the team was made up of people with very different interests. There were the military bods who did the scary stuff, there were the bosses who fought a lot, there were the techs who handled all the sneaky-beaky kit and there were the intelligence types who watched and listened and ultimately pulled the strings – or the plug.

Libby was a chosen name. No reason. She watched the monitors in the briefing room. It was like gazing out onto peaceful countryside. She had seen the men enter the shed and had a fair idea what they were doing in there. The operations officer came in behind her but said nothing. He was the senior rank on the base but had no control over her. Having a spook in the team was part of the deal: his guys and girls gathered the information and Libby interpreted it – along with whatever else her colleagues in other units fed in. Of course there was a puppet master somewhere, with one eye on politics and one on security – that was just the way the thing worked.

"Good signal," she commented for lack of anything else to say.

"They've done well. Hard to make everything so clear given how desolate the place is."

"How long do you think we can keep them in the field?"

"Long as it takes," he said. "We can leave them food drops if necessary. Question for me is – how long do you think they'll *need* to be in there?"

Libby looked at him squarely. "I haven't been given that information as yet."

The operations officer knew there was no point in asking anything else. Even if Libby did know, she probably wouldn't tell him.

Sam wasn't easily startled but a bolt of alarm gripped his neck and shot down his spine.

She was just standing there, frumpy and silent, watching him. He got the impression she'd been there for a long time, just waiting for him to stir. And when he did, she hadn't flinched. Utterly disconcerting – utterly eerie – utterly fascinating.

Sam recognised her immediately. He stood up and looked beyond her, searching for her husband. He had no choice – if she stayed where she was, just staring like a zombie, she would unnerve the neighbours or even the inhabitants of the house and he wouldn't have done his job. If he went out to her, she could attack and he would have to deal with her, and hurting a woman was an unattractive proposition. A street full of neighbours watching made it even less so. She could also be a decoy for the husband. If she caused a commotion at the front, maybe he would try to slip in the back. He weighed it in seconds and decided.

He closed the curtains in her face, entered the hall, opened the front door and wedged it to prevent anyone sliding in and locking him out, took five paces and grabbed the woman by the arm and hauled her into the porch before closing the door again. He considered masking her mouth to keep her silent but she hadn't so much as yelped – compliant and resigned as if she was used to manual handling.

He took her into the room that moments ago she'd been watching him sleep in and sat her in the armchair. She was cold to the touch – like she'd been outside for hours. She was dressed only in a light rain mac, a flowery old-fashioned skirt and blouse and sensible shoes. The attire was fit for a woman twenty years her senior.

"Who else is outside?" Sam whispered forcefully.

The woman's quizzical gaze rose to meet his.

"Nobody?" she said, more of a question than a statement.

"Why are you here?"

"To help," she said absently.

"What do you mean?"

"To warn this young woman," she said with a vacancy that suggested she was medicated.

Sam assumed she was talking about the heiress. "Warn her about what? How dangerous your husband is?"

The woman's eyes had dilated and found interest in the soft focus of a middle distance.

"There is that," the woman said with a curious mixture of confidence and carelessness.

"You're not making any sense."

"No, I don't suppose I am, really."

"What do you want?"

"May I see her?"

Sam noted the woman's manner of speech: refined, pronounced, educated.

"Who?"

"The little tart with the chewing gum."

The woman rotated her head to find Sam with another stare. It took him aback – she was clearly loopy loo.

"I'm not going to let you see her." Sam looked at her, baffled.

"Why?" asked the woman, genuinely surprised.

"Because you're married to the man who groomed her," said Sam.

"Oh, I don't want a conversation."

"Then what do you want?"

"I want to *warn* her."

"I think she already knows how dangerous he is," said Sam, bordering on incredulous.

"But I don't want to warn her to stay safe," said the woman. "I want to tell the little bitch to stay away from him."

The chat with the mother kept Anthony awake. Could he really live in a cell if this all went wrong? Maybe that's what had made her son such a weirdo skulking about the place in his slippers. Anthony looked at the four walls of the bedroom and decided to break the rules and open a curtain. He needed to look at *something*, and it was dark after all. Who would notice at four o'clock in the morning?

He drew the heavy material back a little and then pulled the bed over towards the window to allow him to rest his arse on the mattress and his elbows on the moist windowsill. It was pretty dark, just as it had been when he arrived, but as to where he was, he still didn't know what town he was in.

Anthony cracked the window open a fraction and could hear the sea. He could smell it, he thought, on the breeze. He rested his face on his folded wrists and listened to the waves wash up, his eyes smarting a little from the salty wind. And then he heard the front door ease open and closed below him.

He froze for a second, afraid that shutting the window and curtains would betray him. He watched as a body padded down the short path to the little gate and sat back instinctively, somehow convinced that the person would look up and see him watching.

There were houses on either side of the wide road, but the lighting was poor and it was hard to tell. By the time Anthony eventually mustered the courage to lean forward a little, he had lost track of the person's progress. Then he caught sight of a single red light down the road to his left, as if a driver had touched their car's brake light. The light illuminated the walker in the gloom and, bent at the hip, they appeared to talk to someone in the vehicle before the back door of the car was opened. No interior light came on, though, preventing any view of the occupants.

Shit-scared, Anthony reached up and quietly pulled the window handle towards him, silently slicing off the sea breeze. He gently drew the curtain back across the window, but fear made him leave his bed where it was. A few minutes later he heard the gate open and shut, then the front door. Alert but with his eyes crushed closed, he lay and listened as he half heard half imagined the weight on the stairs and the shuffle past his bedroom door.

Sam propelled the wife into the street, her mouth open and angry before a calm descended over her and she moulded her glare into a menacing smile. She turned slowly and began an overly dignified walk into the shadows. Sam watched until she vanished; her soft, sensible shoes giving no clue as to her progress.

He returned to the armchair and found himself reluctant to open the curtains again. The woman's manner had been singularly unsettling. Bombed out of her mind, he thought – yet alert and smart and deliberately provocative. Sam wished the husband, Delaney, had come instead – then at least he could have bust his head. The woman, though, was either a clever ruse or a jealous foray by a scorned wife. Perhaps she had chosen to take her husband's infidelity out on the other woman? What was clear was that Loopy Loo was evidently not all there, and the bits that remained were the scary bits. Sam reckoned she was potentially as dangerous as her husband.

He decided that he'd talk it through with the father in the morning. Even when the husband went to jail, she could still pose a risk. The old man's wealth might be put to good use in securing a minder for the heiress. If he got her a bodyguard, Sam could get back north with a clean conscience.

The boss smiled at the irony as he clocked his shadow. He knew it was her because he knew the town and he knew she didn't live in it. She was well-turned-out this time: deep-purple woollen skirt, suede boots, grey top. She drank her tea and steadfastly refused to look his way. They had known he was coming, of course, because they had a rip in his house. They had heard him arrange to meet his wife there and, sure, it gave him an interest to watch them watching him. It was easy really. He was so well known that everyone glanced guiltily at him. He was used to that. Fame – or notoriety, perhaps. His name and bad things were twisted together like the wreckage of an air strike. But the ones who didn't steal scared looks in his direction were those who weren't afraid. They were the reconnaissance unit – or whatever that regiment was called this week. They didn't fear him – they hated him, and they were properly trained, and they were carrying.

He ordered a coffee from a terrified waitress and he sat still

and composed – as he had learned to do in his cell. The fifty-
something drew out her teapot for as long as she could before
having to order more. And they danced together, she and he,
without touching, or looking, but intimate and knowing nonetheless.

Sam glanced across the court at Loopy Loo dressed just as she
had been the night before, hair unwashed and bunched in a
bun. She sat passive in the gallery, looking like she'd got more
sleep than he had. After a few moments she seemed to sense
him looking at her and she turned her head towards him.
There was no acknowledgement. Her expression reminded
him of a film he'd seen about the liberation of Belsen – she
was there, but not there at all. Sam wrote it off as pharma-
ceutical.

The heiress was called to the stand, where she affirmed
rather than swore.

Sam turned his attention to the accused. Delaney was
looking with interest at the heiress, as if curious. Slowly and
deliberately he stretched out an arm and gripped the wooden
banister before him. He looked relaxed, confident even, as he
performed an almost-silent drum roll with the fingers of his
right hand and the timber. The heiress looked straight up at
him before the barrister held court.

"Could you please explain how you met Mr Delaney?"

"Online."

"The internet is a big place. Could you be, perhaps, a little
more specific?"

"No."

Nobody spoke, yet there was noise as people shifted in their
seats and shuffled in surprise. Sam felt Áine stiffen to his left. In
the row in front the mother shot a look at the father.

"Ehm ... it would be most useful if you told us where exactly you met the accused. Was it a chat room?"

"Leading, judge," the defence interrupted.

"Quite," said the judge.

The barrister nodded his acquiescence. "Please, in your own words, describe the online relationship."

"No," she said, turning to look at the accused.

Delaney smiled, Loopy Loo looked spaced out, the barrister looked stunned. The heiress' mother shook her head in bewilderment and her father just stared straight ahead as if this sort of disruptive behaviour didn't come as a complete shock.

"This is somewhat irregular," the barrister bumbled – more for the jury than the witness. "We need to know how and when you met. Could you please characterise your relationship with Mr Delaney for the court?"

The brief turned to the gathered with his hands held out and a quizzical look on his face as if to say, *Not my fault. Not what we planned.*

"It's none of the court's business," said the heiress evenly, without affectation or emotion.

"You are a witness called by the prosecution, young woman," the judge piped up. "Please answer the questions posed."

"You can fuck off," said the heiress to the judge.

Sam caught Delaney smirking, the judge reeling and then a whole series of events led to the heiress being found in contempt of court. Journalists bustled out of their overcrowded press box to file copy on the extraordinary turn of events, and the hearing was adjourned.

Grim answered the knock at the door to a scabby teenager with a face like a painter's radio.

"Call for you," he said, then turned away.

Grim was immediately agitated. He followed the youth out onto the road and across to a house in the next block. Inside, a phone sat on the edge of a sofa. Grim had an arrangement with the teenager's mum – monthly payments to keep the landline connected.

"Hello?" he said. It could only be one of a small clutch of people.

"My money's about to run out. Ye'll have to call me back."

Grim looked around and clicked his fingers impatiently at the youth; air scribbling a gesture that resulted in an IKEA pencil being produced. No paper, so he wrote on the door frame. The woman rattled out a number. Grim hung up and dialled back.

"There are next to no call boxes left, you know," she began.

"Where are ye?" he said, concerned about being compromised.

"Don't worry, I took the train to Coleraine."

"You're in a call box?"

"Aye."

"What's wrong?"

"It's been three weeks. I want to know what's happening."

"It could be another three weeks. You know how this works."

The woman bristled at being admonished by a younger man – for whom she was doing a favour.

"What you need to understand is that this will *not* be another three weeks. He's a strange one. I don't like him."

Grim wondered who the strange one really was.

"You said he can't leave the house, and he can't even come down to watch the telly during the day cos the curtains are open. I'm fed up having a stranger in the house, so you need to hurry up."

"Doesn't work like that."

"Well, you may find him somewhere else, then."

"Look, there is nowhere else. I'll see what's happening, but you might have to hang on for a while more."

"Look, son, your card's marked. Get on with it or get him out."

Grim threw the handset onto the sofa and was about to leave when impulsiveness took over. He snatched the phone up again and walked to the adjoining kitchen door to find the youth standing by the sink.

"Get yourself out for fifteen minutes. Anyone else in the house?"

"Nah," he said, making to leave through the back door.

Grim dialled a number from memory. A few estates away, a similar process had begun. A woman answered, Grim told her to go and get *him* and then there was a long wait. Fifteen minutes later, the boss came on the line.

"Yes," he said, so quietly that Grim wasn't absolutely sure it was actually him.

"Is that you?"

"Yes."

"I'm sorry, but I've a problem with the digs for the young fella. How much longer do you think?"

"You rang me about accommodation issues?" If anything, the boss's register had fallen.

"I don't want to be bothering you with my end—"

"Yet you are."

"I'm in danger of losing goodwill here – these people are hard to find."

"What's that got to do with me?"

"Nothing, it's just, she's wondering about timing. You know, how much longer?"

"And she expects us to tell her that?"

"It would be useful, you know, in keeping her on board."

"You need to find a way to ensure she stays on board."

"Aye, ok." Grim wilted under the menace. "Sorry."

Áine stepped into the breach.

Sam watched her sassy walk to the witness box as the barrister outlined to the judge how he had been compelled to "reassess the prosecution schedule in light of unforeseen events".

The judge didn't seem to give a bollocks.

Áine affirmed and confirmed her details and the brief got stuck in.

"Could you please tell the court what your area of expertise is?"

"You could say I'm a software engineer but I have a background in counter invasive cybercrime – or hacking, to you, and database interrogation and taxonomy security for blue-chip companies. I've worked for many of the Californian and West Coast multinationals."

"Can you explain what happened on the night of the seventeenth of November last?"

"I was approached through a third party to examine a tablet and smartphone to see whether I could establish if its owner had been in contact with Mr Delaney, the accused."

Áine was momentarily distracted by the defence lawyers who began whispering between themselves and sharing pages from lever arch files.

"And who owned the devices you examined?"

"Ann Seeley."

"Now deceased. And were you able to determine if Ann Seeley had been in contact with Mr Delaney?"

"I was," said Áine, with a stern countenance.

"Tell us what you found, please."

"I found some of the sickest conversations I've ever read."

"Objection," said the defence barrister.

The judge leaned forward. "Please just stick to the facts. There is no requirement for opinion. The jury will disregard that last statement."

"Sorry," said Áine, although Sam suspected she knew exactly what she was doing.

"Please outline who the contact was between and what the content of the discussions were."

"The conversations had been deleted, but deletion only goes so far. If you think about it as a series of steps, it's like walking through the countryside - you can go back and scrub out your footprints, but a sniffer dog can easily follow where you went."

"In this case you were the sniffer dog." The brief was plunging off script, he apparently couldn't resist.

Áine didn't seem to like that. "Well, I found the stuff."

"Which was?"

"All the messages between Delaney and Ann Seeley."

"Were they encrypted?"

"No, just deleted. If they'd been accessed through any other means – like an external device, they would have had end-to-end, but not on the device from which they were sent or received, which was what I had."

"End-to-end?"

"Encryption. So, like, if the Guards were trying to crack the conversations remotely, they would have struggled. The likes of the NSA in America or GCHQ in Cheltenham, England, could probably decipher it all pretty quickly, but I don't know if the skills are here in Ireland in the public sector."

"But they exist in the private sector?"

"Oh, yeah," she said. "Teenagers in bedrooms with enough time on their hands could pick it apart eventually. But, sure, I didn't have to – I was handed the devices. And once I cracked the logins and passwords ... it was all pretty straightforward."

The barrister looked mildly distracted and Sam noticed the defence team bristling with excitement as they flipped through pages, looking for something. The prosecution brief became more unnerved by their commotion as he continued.

"Tell us about the conversations – without, if you don't mind, your opinion on what was said."

"Sure," said Áine, composing herself. "Well, the accused – Mr Delaney – he began politely in a chat room back in the June sort of reaching out to Ann Seeley and getting to know her."

The prosecution pushed a button on a laptop somewhere and large screens either side of the judge glowed in ignition as the messages were pumped up in pixels. Each juror had a screen of their own.

"Pause, if you will, while the court reads what was written."

Áine sat passively as everyone in the room read.

Hello. How are you? My name is Laney.

Hi, Laney. I'm Ann. Where are you?

Ireland. You?

Yay. I'm in Ireland too. Close to Lough Derg, Co. Tipperary. Why are you here on this site?

Felling low. Like most people. Thinking about the future. Thinking about no future. You know the score.

I do, Ann.

The brief eventually broke the silence. "What sort of a chat room was this?"

"It's a suicide site," Áine said, "for those thinking about ending their lives."

Suddenly there was no noise in the courtroom. For the first time Delaney sat stony-faced and stared straight ahead.

"Please continue with what you found."

"Well, that's it for the first contact, which is confusing because the conversation didn't come to a natural end – nor was there any direction to move it to another platform."

"Another platform?"

"Like, a different provider – to get off the chat room and onto a commercial messaging app."

"Yet you did find the pair on such a provider later?"

"Yes," said Áine.

The screens flicked between pieces of evidence as a more mainstream interface appeared.

"So this is a messenger-type system where messages are supposed to vanish as soon as they are read and the conversation is closed down."

"But you have been able to access it?"

"Yes. I used to work for the company that made it, so I'm familiar with the code and its back doors."

"Back doors?"

"Yeah, like, no system is totally foolproof. Every keystroke on every computer is most likely traceable if you know how to go about it. I'm not saying that it applies everywhere, all the time, but on this interface there is a way to get into the back end."

"And what did you find there?"

"Well, there was a conversation between Ann Seeley and Delaney and in it he's talking about chaining her up and raping her."

There was a collective intake of breath from the courtroom. The message flickered up onto the screens.

Áine, perhaps through discomfort, ploughed ahead. "And she seemed to be agreeable to that, so long as he agreed to do what they had discussed."

"And do you know what that was?"

"For that you need to go onto another platform where they used end-to-end—"

"Encryption?" said the barrister, all part of the act.

"Yeah," said Áine. "You can see here that Delaney asked if Ann would let him put her out of her pain."

"What does that mean?"

"Well, what does a vet say when he puts a dog down?" Áine snapped at him.

"Is there any evidence to suggest that he meant assisting her in suicide?"

"There is a message further on." She looked at a solicitor in the middle of the courtroom. "Scroll to August eleventh."

The messages rolled through on the screen, and then there was a pause.

I can end this for you if you'll let me. I can snuff out all that pain.

The barrister turned to the court and theatrically repeated the phrase, emphasising the second sentence.

"Snuff out your pain. In common parlance, what is your understanding of the word *snuff*?" he asked Áine.

"Objection!" called the defence. "The witness is not a linguistics expert."

"But she is an internet expert," said the brief. "I can reframe the question, judge."

The judge nodded cautiously.

"In the online world," the brief had his eyes closed, as if searching for a safe way to pose the question, "what meaning is attached to the word *snuff*?"

"To kill someone during sex on camera," said Áine matter-of-factly.

"To kill someone during sex on camera," repeated the brief for the jury's benefit.

And yet the defence team didn't look concerned. They looked smug.

The boss and his wife went for a walk down by the lough. The droning noise of dredgers digging up sand from beneath the surface pleased him; background noise was always welcome.

She wore a scarf; he had a ski buff. Both were pulled up over their chins to just below the nose, despite the autumn warmth.

"Try to remember every word now. Don't just summarise what he said."

"Ok," she replied, chastised and a little bit angry.

"It's important."

"I know."

"Keep your voice low."

"Sorry."

"Well?"

"He said there is a separate room and that's where the material of interest is. He said there needs to be fire in this room and it needs to look like the bomb caused it."

"Did he say where it is?"

"He said the back of the building, third floor. He says there is more paperwork coming."

"Right. That it?"

"No. He said the room is being kept secure from staff and only the chair has access. Thought that was weird."

"He means the chairman."

"Oh," she said, feeling stupid.

"Did he say anything about timings?"

"He said, *tell him soon*. He's posh, isn't he?"

"You'd be wise to forget that fact."

She stiffened slightly. "I'll not remember any of it, you know that."

His grunt was enough to keep the pressure on her. "Anything you're forgetting to tell me?"

"That was it. Word for word," she said, desperate for an acknowledgement that she had performed well.

She got nothing.

Lunch was a silent affair. The parents of the heiress pushed soup around a bowl and said very little, embarrassed by the time and money their daughter appeared intent on wasting. A crown solicitor sidled over and informed them it was unlikely the heiress would be kept in the cells overnight. The judge, according to the lawyer, recognised that there were special circumstances – the mention of which sent the mother into red-rimmed anguish.

Forty-five minutes later they were back in the courtroom, Áine was ready for battle and the brief was about to reveal some of the most twisted behaviour ever to be heard in the Irish courts.

"Judge, if we may, we would like to make an application." The defence barrister was unexpectedly speaking for the first time since his opening appeal for the jury to keep an open mind.

"Oh?" said the judge.

"Yes, perhaps a moment in chambers?"

And they swooshed out, like batmen in their capes, with folders under their wings.

One whole hour later the courtroom was called to rise as the judge returned, his face like a slapped ass. Something was badly wrong.

"Judge," began the defence counsel, "we apply for the dismissal of the case against Mr Delaney on the basis that the spine of the prosecution case is established on material illegally obtained."

Áine turned to Sam, her eyes on springs.

"Go on," said the judge, like a teacher at parents' night.

"We submit that the information contained on the devices purportedly owned by Ann Seeley was private and obtained without a warrant. Passwords were circumvented without the necessary paperwork being completed or permissions granted by a member of the judiciary, and the searches were, in effect, illegal."

"What say the prosecution?" The judge rotated to his left knowing very well what the prosecution had to say – the whole thing had been thrashed out in chambers beforehand.

"While there is significant circumstantial evidence in this case, and corroboration from a witness now in contempt of court, there is no escaping the fact that the weight of the evidence against Mr Delaney was contained on the devices alluded to in this morning's evidence."

The judge spoke to the prosecution again. "And why, at this late hour, has there been no acknowledgement that the proper procedures for obtaining this information were not adhered to?" said the judge for the sake of the optics and the journalists scribbling furiously in the press benches. The judge was covering his ass: *not my fault.*

"Judge, how the information had been obtained was not known to us at the time of discovery. We had rather assumed that the third-party approach to the hacking witness—"

"The internet expert," corrected the prosecution barrister.

The defence ignored the clarification and let the allegation linger.

"—had come from the Gardai. Instead, it transpires that the *expert* was engaged by the parents of a witness who is now in the cells and who appears intent on not giving evidence. This case, judge, is built on sand. The devices of the dead woman were handed over by her mother to the parents of said witness. A series of undisclosed streams of evidence – improperly obtained, that besmirch my client and amount to little more than character assassination and titillation of the public through the press. We move to dismiss."

The judge turned again to the forlorn prosecution brief, whose wig hung in despair as he spoke.

"On consideration that the evidence given is not what we

had anticipated, we request that the charges be left on the books."

Sam didn't know exactly what that meant but assumed that the pompous barrister was asking for a second chance to try again at a later date.

"Denied. I see no option but to dismiss the charges against Mr Delaney." The judge turned his attention to the man in the dock. "You are free to go."

There was clamour in the court as hacks bolted to their feet and a little man from the wings emerged to ask everyone to stand – which was unnecessary as most people were up anyway, and the judge exited without dignity or respect.

Sam watched Delaney intently. He wore a knowing but not an elated smile, and held out his hand to his lead defence barrister. Sam was surprised to see the SC decline to shake Delaney's hand. The whole counsel team would be out of pocket in the absence of a long, lucrative trial, but Sam sensed that they also knew that they had just unleashed an unstable psychopath on society.

The case had collapsed in a blur and Sam struggled to rationalise why. Something didn't seem right, though. But that was that. I can go home – job done, he thought.

6

"Sinead's gonna be so disappointed," said Áine.

It was the first time Sam had noticed Áine – the hard one, the bolshie, brash and brazen sibling – longing for the regard of her softer sister.

"She'll be proud of you. She always is. You're a gobby little bitch, but she knows you have a heart of gold. Even I know it."

Sam wasn't given to long, soothing plámás.

"Thank you," said Áine quietly, not looking him in the eye.

The pair stared out to the water, the surfing distraction sparing a mountain of awkward moments.

"He'll eventually get what he deserves."

"Well, perhaps he should be helped on his way," Áine quickly shot back, and the suggestion hung in the air like slurry in summer. Both knew that Sam's past was riddled with such despatches.

They'd had a fraught few hours. Sam had been forced to bundle Áine and the heiress out of court through a press pack four deep. He despised the fact that his face would be on the front cover of half a dozen newspapers in the morning, on the telly that night and in the Sundays again. They would show the shot as archive in years to come. It unnerved him and flew in the face of everything he tried to avoid.

But it *had* been unavoidable. The press had swarmed and shouted. It was undignified and distressing. Sam's arms had swept snappers aside to get the heiress through and in the direction of the car with Áine following in their wake. The press had realised that Sam planned to cross the road with the women, and on two occasions he'd had to yank the dangling straps of cameras, forcing them to the ground and the operators to the pavements to examine the damage.

"You'll get charged with assault," Áine had hissed.

"I'll be back in the north by teatime," said Sam. "They'll hardly extradite me for that."

The heiress had sat in the back, Áine in the front, as Sam wove through Dublin headed for the tree-lined street into which the previous night, Loopy Loo had managed to vanish. When they got there they realised they had yet another battle on their hands. The smarter members of the media had deployed to the point of arrival rather than departure. Sam didn't want to leave Áine in the car while he delivered the heiress, nor did he want to drag the sister of his close friend through a press pack twice, so he took a detour, double-parked and whipped the heiress through the rear of the house.

"You're not leaving?" the father had said.

"I've got to get Áine back, John. I was here to help you until the case was over," Sam panted.

"Yes, but..."

The father, John, was evidently distressed. He stood, hopeless, in the hallway of his grand manor looking like a frail, afraid old man. Sam relented.

"John, I doubt anyone thought Delaney would walk, but I can't be here indefinitely – I've a wee girl to look after. Look, I'll give you another night, but you need to start hunting for security, ok?"

The father brightened. "Yes, yes, Sam, thank you. One more night. That will give me time to make arrangements. Thank you."

And then they were Northside again, over the Liffey and looking for a place to stall until the hacks hit their deadlines and gave up on the idea of staking out Áine's flat. Sam followed old tracks and headed for Clontarf, the beach and the sea. They pulled in on Bull Island; the wind and swirl of the sand had kept all but the hardiest golfers away. Sam didn't ask, he simply opened his door and Áine followed. They leaned against the breeze, hands deep in pockets, as kitesurfers skimmed about, their vibrant propulsion dipping and drawing, pulling them forward.

"S'pose you can do that?" Áine asked distractedly.

"Badly," Sam conceded. "Clears the head totally."

Áine just stared at the spectacle, moderately impressed by what the kids were able to do with just a board and a half-balloon.

"I don't get what she was at," Áine said eventually.

Sam knew she was referring to the heiress.

"Was she on board when the barrister was briefing you?"

"Completely," Áine said. "She was up for giving evidence. She was so cross that he had turned up with the wife. She hated him – I thought she did anyway."

Sam mulled the wisdom of telling Áine about Loopy Loo's night visit but decided it might be more frightening than informative.

"He seems to still have some sort of hold over her."

"I dunno how," Áine said with disgust. "If you'd seen what he wrote to her, it was ..."

"What?" Sam pressed gently.

"Depraved."

"How?"

"The stuff he was asking her to do. Like, it might have been sexual – in a way – but it was, like, harmful. Physically harmful."

Sam didn't want the details. Such things always made him think of Isla and the people out there who might hurt her. "It's one thing talking about it on a computer, but it's another to actually do it. I thought the heiress was all talk."

Áine looked at him quizzically, as if he had misunderstood what the whole thing was about. "You know she never met him?"

"What?" Sam said, utterly confused.

"He was getting her to, like, perform for him," she said.

Sam just looked at her, totally blank.

"She would video herself doing the stuff for him using the camera on her phone or tablet. Then they would talk about what they would do *when* they met."

"But they didn't actually get together?"

"No. At least I don't think so. I found no evidence of it anyway."

"I just assumed she knew him."

"She did know him. They talked for hours and days."

"That's not the same as meeting someone."

"You might not think it's not the same but she did, and it looks to me like she had, like, fallen in love with him or something because she could have said enough in court to put the bastard away for life."

"He met Ann Seeley, though, if he managed to murder her."

"That twisted fucker killed her alright, but he only actually met her once."

"Serious?"

"Serious. He talked to her for months – same story. How are ye? Lovely to be chattin' to ye. How have ye been? Then, like, how are ye sleepin'? How's the dark moments? Can I help ye with the sadness? Do you want to talk in the night when you need it?"

"Sounds like he understood both women quite well."

"He picked them. Like, he deliberately went on to that suicide group to find vulnerable people. And he chose women who lived close so he could get to them. Then he worked and worked his way into their minds, and then he offered to help them with the ultimate gift."

Sam stared at a kid carving a short wave and asked a question he didn't really want the answer to. "Which was what?"

"To help them with their suicide. With Ann Seeley it got to the point that she was pleading with him to do it. She was seriously fucked up and he just made it worse. Stick this in here for me, do that for me, tie yourself up. One night he watched her for twelve hours, shackled to her own bed. Then he drove ten miles to a phone box and called the Guards and they went and released her. He's a fucking mentalist."

Sam blew breath through pursed lips and stared straight ahead. Áine turned to look at him and sensed she had said enough.

"Anyway, he's out now, and I fucked up."

"You didn't."

And she knew he meant it.

The operations officer called Libby's room and she made it to the briefing suite within three minutes.

"The X-rays are in the shed," he said by way of greeting.

"They must be about to move – it's too early for anything else." She looked at the digital clock on the wall: 0300 hours.

"We should have put a camera in the shed," said the ops officer.

"The dogs would have gone wild. We know what they're doing in there anyway."

"But we don't know how big it is."

"Does that matter?"

The ops officer didn't know whether it mattered or not because he didn't know what the overall plan was, so they just stared at the screens as the shed doors opened and a car was pushed out. A burst came through on the radio.

"Eyes left."

The ops in the dugout were directing the techs back at the base. Libby watched the images on the screens judder as the night-vision camera hunted for focus. Two people had entered the yard and were walking towards the shed doors. The camera panned with them.

"The driver?" Libby asked.

"Maybe."

One of the men got into the driver's side of the car. The other went into the shed. The car pulled away, not turning on its lights until it reached the end of the farm's lane. Then a van emerged from the shed and followed the same process. The van manoeuvred around the car, flicked on its lights – which came as a blast of white on the screen, then increased its speed down the road. The car stayed where it was, lights extinguished.

"Scout vehicle," Libby said. "Is the Gazelle up?"

"In the air now. We don't know where the car's going, do we?" he asked Libby.

"Let's see," was all she said.

He didn't know whether she knew or not. He tried not to care.

Floppy feet and a twisty run. A frenzied little bundle of excitement hurtled up the pontoon towards Sam. She leapt unquestioningly upwards, her little arms clamping his neck. Sam closed his eyes and savoured the moment. Such greetings wouldn't last forever – nor would his back withstand the gesture; Isla was growing like bracken.

When he opened his eyes he could see Sinead through his daughter's hair. She was standing nervously on the pontoon, her hand on the guard rail of the boat. He held on to his daughter for a few more moments.

"How are you, wee lamb?"

"Good," was all she said.

"How did you get on with Sinead?" he whispered. "Did you have fun?"

"I luffed it," he heard her say.

"You loved me being away?"

"No, Daddy, I luffed having fun with Sinead, but I luff having you home more."

That wouldn't last forever either, so he was happy to take it all in. He wandered towards Sinead with his barnacle still attached.

"Someone's been missing you," she said smiling.

Sam lifted his chin slightly from Isla's shoulder. "She has just told me she loved the last few days."

"She wasn't on her own," said Sinead. "We had great craic."

"Thank you so much, Sinead."

"How's Áine?"

"She's ok. She's worried she's let you down, though."

"What?" said Sinead, almost angry at the notion.

"Why did Áine let you down?" Isla earwigged into the conversation.

"Never you mind, nosey little lady. Jump on board and we'll be down in a minute."

"Aw-wuh."

"Go on, Isla. Two minutes."

Isla huffed off. "Just two minutes," she mimicked mockingly.

Sam's body made a move and then stiffened – he didn't

know whether to hug Sinead. He never knew. Hugging didn't come easy. He'd had female friends who double cheek kissed incessantly on nights out and random meetings. They did the rounds with everyone but left him lipstick free. Now that Shannon was gone his cuddles were for Isla. It wasn't that he didn't want to hug anyone else – he just didn't know how to.

"Cup of tea?" She threw him a lifebelt.

"Maybe something stronger?"

"Not for me. I'd better get back to Áine tonight if she's in bad shape."

Sam tried to ignore the stirring of disappointment in him.

Sinead skipped over the guard rail and down the companionway like she'd been sailing all her life.

"How did you sleep? The rocking can be hard to get used to."

"Like a baby," she said.

Sam looked around. The galley was pristine, just as he'd left it. Nothing had changed except for a few new paper and card creations made by Isla, with obvious adult assistance.

"She's gutted at the result of the trial. And ..." He paused.

"What?" said Sinead, pouring from the whistling kettle.

"Well, he's out now, so you both have to take care. It maybe wouldn't do any harm to get offside for a while – a holiday or whatever."

"I'm way ahead of you," she said. "I booked us a week in Majorca. Cheap as chips."

"And she was ok, Isla?"

"She was good as gold, Sam. You have a little gem there. I *luffed* it, too."

Sam could see she was genuinely happy with her time spent with Isla.

When she left she spared him the difficulty and put out her hand. Sam shook it gently, his eyes saying more than his mouth.

"Thank you, Sinead. Really."

"Don't be daft. You were doing me a favour minding Áine."

"Let's look at your flat security again when you're back."

"Oh-kay," said Sinead in a deep voice, mocking his deliberate deflection.

Sam closed his eyes in realisation.

"Don't worry – you're right. Come down and we'll sort it."

"Have a nice holiday."

Sinead turned slowly and moved away. He almost called after her, but then didn't – couldn't. He watched her all the way to the top of the marina. He wanted her to turn and he didn't want her to turn.

He went down below. "Where did she sleep?" he asked Isla.

Sam had made his bed up for Sinead, expecting her to use it.

"In my bottom bunk," Isla said. "Why?"

"No reason," Sam replied absently.

He wasn't sure what to make of that or how he felt about it. But it was confusing nonetheless.

Not once in the weeks Anthony had been cooped up in the room had anyone knocked on his door.

He looked at the old radio alarm clock, its red digits glowing fiercely. Five fifteen in the morning. He panicked that he'd been caught observing the late-night liaison, so he just lay in the bed, seized.

The door cracked open. "Get up. You're wanted for a wee walk."

He could just make out the slimy green kelp on the son's arm as it held the door. Anthony's heart battered hard. This is it, he thought. They're gonna take me out and do me.

The son just stood there, unsure whether Anthony had

woken. "You need to get up and come with me. You need to hurry up."

Anthony had no choice. He swung his legs out of bed, socks still on – the house was bloody freezing. He reached out for his hoodie and pulled on his jeans and trainers.

They crept across the landing and Anthony noticed the parents' door open a fraction – the darkness concealing whoever was looking out. He somehow knew it was the mother.

The son pulled on a jacket and they left the house. Anthony's alarm increased when the son stepped over the gate with a movement that looked like second nature - leaving Anthony wondering whether he had actually watched someone else creep out at night.

"Where are we going?" he managed.

"Down to the front," whispered the son. "No talking."

They walked downhill for what felt like a mile; the noise of the sea building with every few feet. They turned a corner and walked up a slope. Anthony could make out movement at the harbour wall, creaking, and an unusual tapping noise.

The son stopped. "We'll stand over here," he said, motioning to a concrete structure with a pitched roof.

"What's happening?" Anthony asked.

"Your car's on its way."

"We're doing it now?" After such a long and unexpected wait Anthony found himself suddenly reluctant despite his desperation to escape the house and his crusty clothes.

"Doubt it," was all the son said.

Anthony could hear a vehicle approach, heavy. Within a minute a van pulled up and stopped.

"That's it," said the son.

"What? I was told a car. I've never driv a van before."

The son shrugged and gently shook his head.

The driver's window rolled down. "Hello?"

The son stepped forward. "Here," he said.

"How am I supposed to get in there? There's gippo bars," a country-sounding voice whispered.

Anthony and the son stepped forward to look at the height-restricting barrier designed to prevent traveller families setting up a caravan site beside the harbour.

"Oh, right. There's another car park higher up," he offered.

"Fuck sake. You walk up there and I'll swing round," growled the man, who drove up hill.

The son beckoned Anthony follow him but Anthony refused to go.

"I'm not going anywhere in that van," he said.

The son stared at him, shrugged again and stomped off up the hill.

Anthony debated running. If he took off, they'd get him for sure – he had no money and no idea where he was. What was the van for? There had been no mention of a van. And where was Grim?

"Fuck's wrong with you?" The van driver somehow appeared at full height, right in front of Anthony. He was enormous, clothed in black with a woolly hat pulled down to meet what might have been a beard, but Anthony couldn't make much out in the gloom.

"Nothin', nothin'."

"C'mon well," said the man turning and leaving Anthony no choice but to follow.

Suddenly it just didn't feel like he was about to be slotted.

They walked fifty feet and the man told Anthony to get into the passenger seat of the van while the man climbed into the driver's side. There was no sign of the son.

"I've never driv a van before," Anthony began to turn towards the driver.

"Don't look at me," the man growled.

Anthony's eyes shot forward where the morning light was slowly lifting the veil on his surroundings. He could just make out some rocks and the outline of a few boats. "Sorry," he muttered.

"There's a motor coming – a Ford Mondeo. Ye know the kind?"

The man's accent was alien to Anthony. It was northern and southern all at the same time.

"No," he confessed.

"Ye know a Ford?"

"Yes."

"She's a saloon."

"Right."

The man could see this wasn't helping Anthony.

"Silver."

"Ok, ok," he said, eager to please.

"Key start, but y'need to mind y'erself, for it's the key that sets things in motion, y'understand?"

"Uh-huh."

"D'ye understand or d'ye not?"

"No," Anthony confessed.

The man sighed. "Ye start a car ordinary like this."

The man's accent was confusing Anthony. Some words were garbled together into one phrase and others were almost spelt out. Anthony eyes followed the man's hand from the top of the wheel to the ignition, where he clicked the key two notches.

"The next one turns her over, ok?"

"Ok." He could hear his voice shaking.

"But when ye get this other motor, and ye have her in place, ye have to kick the key the other way, see?" The man rotated the key anticlockwise. "Ye will need to turn the wheel a wee hair just to get her to click into place." The man's hand wiggled the steering wheel a tiny fraction.

"Ok," Anthony said.

"Right, so," said the man as a car approached.

It passed their little car park and turned into the area where

Anthony and the son had stood. The pair sat in silence for few minutes and Anthony could feel the man staring at him. Still he hadn't the courage to look up from the dash.

"There's another fella coming," the man said. "Don't be looking at him either."

"Ok," said Anthony.

"Ye just get out when he arrives and head back to your digs."

Anthony began to panic again. He was only a short walk from the house but he'd been so on edge by events that he had no idea where he was in relation to the house. He flinched as the passenger door opened and he glanced to his left in fear before remembering he wasn't to look at the new arrival.

"Ok, on your way, son," said the new man – who sounded just like the first.

Anthony climbed down from the cab, eyes to the floor.

"Yer motor's down below," said the second man. "Key's under the front wheel arch, nearside, wedged in the spring."

Anthony didn't follow but wasn't about to say so.

"Know what y'er about, then?"

Anthony stared at the ground and said nothing.

"D'ye understand everything?"

Anthony just nodded, noticing that the second man was wearing grey surgical gloves.

"Speak up now, son, if there's something y'er not right with."

The man had detected his uncertainty but Anthony was too scared to say that he didn't really understand any of it. Instead he deflected.

"I don't know where the house is," he muttered.

"Ye wha?" said the first man.

"Where I'm staying. It's the first time I've been out. I don't know how to get back."

"Fuck me," said the first man.

"Well, we don't know where it is," said the second man. "How did ye get here?"

"There was someone with him," confirmed the van driver.

"Well, where're they?"

"Good question," said the van man.

"Look, son, we've been here too long as t'is. Ye'll ha'ta find y'er way back yersel'. We can't help ye wi' that."

Anthony nodded. He just wanted the men gone and his embarrassment to end.

"Good luck ta ye," said the second man, who hauled himself into the cab in Anthony's place. The van growled to life and pulled off.

Anthony turned to the pier below, now exposed in the grey dawn. He thought for a few moments – if he got going he might identify the small gate before most of the neighbours woke.

7

"Why have you lifted up all the floorboards, Daddy?" Isla looked at the mess. The boat looked completely different when stripped back. "Will I get the screwdrivers?"

She was a handy wee woman to have around. She could identify tools and understood how they worked. Like a surgical assistant, but oilier.

"I was looking for something. I was going to have it all back in place by the time you finished school but I ran out of time."

In truth, he had only confirmed what he already knew: there was no money left in the bilge. It had been worth a shot, though. At one stage he had acquired so much cash that a sealed cellophane bag could well have gone missing or been washed into another underfloor compartment by the movement of the boat under sail.

But, no, every last note was gone. He sat and thought about the tens of thousands he and Isla had managed to burn through. They'd decoupled from society after Shannon's murder, sailed through the Med, round Ireland, round Scotland, footering about France and west coastal Europe. Sam hadn't thought twice about the spend – it felt almost justified. They had been hurt, wronged, aggrieved; they had a chasmic hole in their lives and, as such, money seemed pointless. Pointless, at least, to be frugal with. They had eaten out, gone on trips and treats, anything that allowed Isla to smile again – if even for a short while. He craved that happiness in her. It was like a ketamine blast to the sternum – it didn't take the pain away, but it made him care just a little less, for a little while.

They'd stayed in marinas instead of swinging on anchor. It was more comfortable and easier with a small child in tow – but it was also more expensive. They'd done Disneyland Paris twice, gone on adventures and stayed in the odd hotel. It broke up the long sails and the nights of cards and reading stories from books. And he'd kept *Siân*, their boat, in pristine order, no expense spared.

Of course, the cash had been ill-gotten in a way. He had amassed it while working for Sinead or his little friend Fran, liberating prostitutes, trafficking victims and even seafarers from slavery and captivity. Cash was easy come by in such settings. Unsuspecting and incapacitated pimps, jailers and ships' officers often had bundles of money lying around. He had lifted the spoils as justification for the risks he was taking – if caught the consequences were the clink or the crematorium.

There had been well over a hundred thousand euros at one point. He'd spent a quarter of it on the boat, given a quarter to a Libyan woman and her daughter to set them up for a new life in Ireland and fluttered through the rest with Isla. He sat, still and silent, a niggling and unattractive proposition knocking around his head. He lifted the laptop and tapped in "benefits Northern Ireland".

Sam had never claimed. Not one penny. But then he hadn't paid taxes since he'd left the Marines. He looked at the requirements: talk of National Insurance contributions, employment history, address details and skills. It was far from encouraging.

The navy had presumably paid his Insurance stamps, but he'd worked off book ever since and his abilities were in leading men at sea or in the sand. Not ideal. He had no idea how he could begin to explain keeping a child for two years with no visible means of income. It could open a bag of snakes if he finally declared himself and asked for state help. Then he looked at what he was entitled to, which confirmed for him the futility of it all. He could earn more scraping boats.

And so he'd clambered over the side of *Siân* and walked ashore where he accosted the sheepish boatyard owner.

"You need a hand," Sam stated rather than asked.

"With what?" the yardman asked nervously.

"Here, in the boatyard. You flat-packed my van and I can't afford to pay for it. I need a job – you need help. I know what I'm doing, so ..." He left the implication hanging with a shrug.

"Ehm ... well, yeah. You ... you want to work for me?"

"Not really," said Sam. "But yeah."

The yard was close to Isla's school, the boat was tied to its pontoon and it suited just fine. Working in the boatyard meant he'd be able to drop off and collect Isla from school.

"Right," said the yard owner surprised. "Not sure what I can pay you, though. And the work's, like—"

"I know the work. I did it for long enough. I can rig, do hull repairs, fix sails, most stuff."

"What I have is cleaning and polishing, driving the crane—"

"Well, I can do that better than you can obviously."

The man's chest swelled in irritation. "What would you be looking?"

"Twenty an hour."

"I couldn't even pay you half that." The yardman almost sniggered.

Sam gave him that look – the Halloween face, Shannon had called it. When looking out he felt it to be little more than a blank stare, but she'd explained that when he deployed it, recipients felt the reaper had arrived.

"Maybe I could give you half that."

"I'll start in the morning. Six o'clock."

"I don't start till ... ok, six o'clock. I'll leave a list of stuff on the door of the shed."

"That'll do well."

Sam stomped back to the boat having just interviewed himself, negotiated his own salary and dictated his working conditions.

———

"Wanna take a stroll?"

The boss looked at his wife. He knew what that meant: someone had called the council offices she cleaned. She was always on the same floor at the same time every day. Any one of the phones could ring and she would answer provided she was alone. Very occasionally an overenthusiastic worker appeared before seven o'clock and she would ignore the phone, which would be picked up by the keen employee: "Hello, hello, hello," only for the handset to be replaced. When that happened she was forced to wait until the following day to collect the message for her husband.

The boss stopped to stare across the expanse of the lough. On a good day they could see three of the six occupied counties: Tyrone, Derry and Antrim. His native Armagh had always been a blight on Britain's landscape – a matter of considerable pride to him. His county and its unruliness had proved a major handling and he wanted to keep it that way.

"So what's he said?"

"There's a delivery due at the location. You are to understand that there must be fire and all floors are to be destroyed."

"*I am to understand?*" He ground his teeth. "Patronising bastard."

"I'm just telling you what he said."

The boss mused upon the desire to shoot messengers.

"Next time he rings tell the fucker there'll be fire."

The yard owner was a handless prick. Sam kicked off two hours before Isla woke every morning. At eight he got her up, made them both breakfast, took her to school and was back on the tools by nine – at which point Handless started his lack-adaisical day. Most of Sam's time was spent fixing the half-assed botched jobs his new boss carried out. He knew the yard owner felt undermined, that he was being upwardly managed, but the man didn't have the capacity to deal with someone like Sam. Handless almost fell into a sort of rhythm whereby he consulted Sam on how to carry out jobs, Sam then patiently spelt out directions only to berate the boss for not having listened when he made a bollocks of it. This went on for a while coupled with the boat owner praising Sam's standard of work, which only served to irritate Handless even more. Instead of harnessing cheap and skilled labour, he grew to resent it.

About three weeks in Handless kindled a kind of bravado and started leaving deliberately shitty jobs on the clipboard in the shed for Sam. It was the tone of the writing on the shitlist than annoyed Sam more than anything.

1. Get the big schooner scraped back to the gel. Make sure.
2. Clear the toilet and replace pipes and Jubilee clips.
3. Bail all dinghies in yard and turn over.
4. Sand back yawl topsides. Needs done by end of day.

Sam raised an eyebrow as he read the note. They both knew that the sanding job would take three days in itself – six if Handless was to do it. Sam realised that his time in the yard was drawing to a close. It had been inevitable, really – nobody likes to be undermined. Sam decided to see how their first conversation of the day went before doing anything rash – he needed to keep the pontoon space.

By dinner time they had agreed to part ways. The owner had been snippy all day, so at six Sam took it head-on.

"Would you prefer to work alone?"

"What?" the owner said, unprepared for confrontation.

"We both know you're not happy with this arrangement. I think my work is good but you might not. If you want to work on your own, just say."

"Well, it's just, you know—"

"Yes or no?"

The owner floundered around, nervous, not wanting to give up the opportunity to slip back into uselessness. "I don't want to be working the sort of hours you're working."

"You don't need to," said Sam, curious that that was an issue. "You own the place."

"My father owns the place. He sees you working at six and finishing at six. I know you take Isla to and from school for two hours every day but that's still ten hours every day and—"

"So you'd prefer I go?"

"Your work is good, Sam, it's just …"

Handless was on the back foot and scared of directness. His MO was to leave his irritation in notes on the clipboard.

"Can I keep the berth?"

"What?"

"On the pontoon – can I keep the berth?"

"Of course."

"If I do you a turn when you need it, instead of every day, can I have the berth for free?"

The son was staring at an offer that suited him very well.

"Eh, well, yeah."

"Right, well, then, I'll finish up, and if you need a hand, you give me a shout. And I keep the berth and just pay for electric. Agreed?"

"Ok," said the son, feeling like he had just struck gold. "But, you know, maybe don't mention this to my dad. Maybe you could say you got another job."

"Fine by me," said Sam, having cut a deal that would reduce their overheads while his income was down.

"Right, then," said the son.

Sam turned tail and wondered, as he walked, what the hell he was going to do next.

Libby was at a loss. It gave the ops officer a tingle of contentment.

"So they've just left it there?"

"Yes."

They were looking at a harbour that was becoming increasingly shrouded by fog rolling in from the sea.

"Ok. We need to get boots down and we need to track the van."

"Your call. Do we keep the Gazelle on the car or track the van?"

"Car until we get eyes on, then the heli can go for the van. We've a fair idea where it's headed anyway. The priority needs to be the laden vehicle. Agreed?"

"Makes sense," said the ops officer, who turned to ready a team for deployment.

"Shit," Libby muttered, her hands raised to her chin, fingers tapping her temple. She had expected the car to be removed straight away. Instead, she had watched the youth get into the

van, the car arrive and the youth dismount and wander
aimlessly through the town. It was not the scenario she had
been building in her head. She lifted her phone to relay events
up the chain.

To her superior it came as no surprise at all.

Sam had often wondered how the rain always came just as the
water tanks began to suck air. Shannon, he imagined. Shannon
looking out for us – minding us.

He was dozing. He'd been working out what their
minimum viable income each week needed to be: ninety
pounds. That meant a deficit each week of exactly ninety
pounds. The buzz entered his dream – the clippers in the
barbers at the NAAFI. And then his eyes sprang open and he
located the handset just in time to see *Charity* disappear.
Because of a thing, as yet unidentified and certainly unspoken,
she never rang just for a chat.

His mind was now restless and remained so until a voice
message bleeped through: "Hi, Sam, maybe give me a call back?
I have a proposal for you – a job proposal." She rushed to
clarify her words and then groaned. Sam tapped the button to
return the call – no point in her agonising.

"You know what I meant," she said immediately upon
answering.

"I know," said Sam laughing gently. Humour the antidote to
difficult conversations.

"So how is Isla?"

"She's grand, thanks for asking. How are you?"

"Ok, actually." Sinead sounded chirpy.

"Oh?" said Sam, interested in her high spirits.

"Yeah, we're looking at a new flat by the river – amazing
views. Quite exciting, really."

"Sounds posh," said Sam, knowing the twins wouldn't move away from inner city working-class Dublin without cause. It would grate on their social sensibilities.

"A housing association came looking to turn our block into a shelter," she explained, which immediately made sense. "And, well, you know ..."

"You do enough for people, Sinead. You deserve a bit of comfort. You get paid pittance for the hours you do – and get less thanks for it. Don't begrudge yourself a view of the Liffey."

"Thank you, Sam."

"How's Áine?"

"Buzzin'," she said. "I've never seen her so businesslike. She's designing her workspace and study, she's pricing some sort of cabling and satellite kit. I think she's actually delighted to spend some of that incredible money she used to earn."

Sam's cheek twitched at *used to*.

"Anyway," Sinead began to babble, "I've a job for you if you're interested?"

"Funnily enough," said Sam, looking to the sky and imagining the hand of his wife squeezing his neck.

"Hear me out now – it's not a bodyguard job."

"Just as well," said Sam. "Most people who need bodyguards actually need to be shot."

"Not this one. You know her, actually."

"Áine again?"

"No," Sinead said. "I believe you call her *the heiress*."

"Right. Is Delaney back on the scene?"

"Dunno. I think the parents had her under house arrest since the trial, but she's kicked off and they've agreed to let her go on holiday with some friends."

"From house arrest to a holiday – that's a bit of a gear change."

"The father says he can't keep her cooped up forever, and

given that it's abroad he's more relaxed about it – provided I can persuade you to go along."

"Ah, Sinead, I'm not a nanny."

"You wouldn't be," she said. "He's looking for someone who can keep an eye on her without her knowing."

"Right," he said.

"I'd say you could do that."

There was a time, thought Sam, when that was all I did. "How long?"

"What?"

"How long's the holiday?"

"Ten days. Name your price."

"Ten grand," Sam joked.

"I'll tell him."

"Serious?"

"Well, he can afford it, and he asked for you specifically. Let's see what he says."

"Should have said twenty."

"Try it if you like."

Sam did the sums, rounding his and Isla's weekly subsistence figure up to one hundred pounds. Twenty grand would let them live frugally for two hundred weeks, nearly four years.

"Ok, tell him twenty grand plus expenses." Sam thought the ask was mad but Sinead took it in her stride.

"You might need to give a little."

"I'd be happy to negotiate." He chuckled. "He'll never pay that sort of cash."

"He might if you're prepared to tell him a bit about your background."

Sam mulled that for a moment. Not attractive, but neither was the dole. "You can tell him."

"I can't tell him what I don't know."

Sam was silent again for a beat.

"Do you not know?"

"Not really. I guess a lot."

"Let me think about that, but in the meantime you can give him the basics if you think it would bring in the big bucks."

"Spell out the basics, just so I have it straight what you want me to say."

"Special forces. Would that do?"

"It's not much," she said, "but I can try."

"Marine, lots of deployments, then Special Boat Service. All between us."

"Grand, so. I'll let you know."

A stirring of excitement bubbled in Sam's shoulders. "Thanks, Sinead."

"Don't thank me yet – you haven't heard the best bit."

"She's going to Yemen?"

"No, *eejit*. This is, like, your happy place. Full of boats. She's going to Venice."

"We have people watching these 24-7," the ops officer told Libby.

"I know."

"You've been staring at those screens for hours. We'll tell you if anyone moves."

She longed to offload her anxiety but such discussion was discouraged. Two wings of the security estate working together but not always to the same end. She would love this experienced man's opinion on leaving that car sitting there. The prize, of course, was great – he could deliver the whole cell to the police, but that had never been her modus operandi before. Spooks never formed part of the evidence chain and securing convictions wasn't the priority. Libby's job was to gather the intel and feed it into the machine.

She had joined – well, been recruited, to keep people safe,

to stop attacks wherever possible, and yet here she was staring at a major risk and all she could do was watch. If something went wrong, would she be able to sit and stonewall? *Yeah, I knew it was there. No, I didn't just do nothing – I monitored it around the clock.*

And then she watched in horror as someone approached the car.

"Oh, Daddy, I have a note for you from Molly's mummy. She wants me to go for a sleepover!"

Isla's excitement glistened. It gave Sam pleasure and pause.

"Where does Molly live?"

"Oh, can I go, Daddy, please?"

"Where does she live?" asked Sam again.

If he said yes, it would be the first time since her mother's death that Isla would be in the care of someone he didn't know. And a sleepover too. It was a big test for Isla herself. He suspected the idea of it was more appealing than the reality.

"Don't know," was all Isla said, her voice sinking with the realisation that she might not be allowed to go. She may have been only seven but she understood her father's instincts and his determination to keep her close.

Isla rooted in her bag for the note. Sam read the invite, tapped Molly's mother's number into his phone and told Isla to change out of her uniform. As the phone rang he resolved to avoid interrogating the woman. As ever, he had naturally picked up on the routines of others as they dropped their children to school – almost unconsciously mapping who belonged to who, what vehicle they drove and who their partners were. He didn't know anyone's name but he made finely tuned assumptions about their likely occupations, style of parenting and even their inclinations. He'd seen Molly's mum often and his loose impression had been good. She said hello in passing, which was more than some did, and she was attentive to her daughter.

Of course, everyone knew who Sam was. He and Isla had returned to the town where his wife had been murdered, and in a small community no such event goes without gossip, particularly when you choose to live on a boat instead of a house, you've got an unidentified background and no apparent job.

"Hello?"

"Hello, my name's Sam, Isla's my daughter. She gave me the note you sent home. Thanks very much for asking her."

"Hello, hello," she said, perhaps surprised he had called so quickly. "Thanks for getting back to me. You know what kids are like – on at you all the time to ask." She laughed nervously but Sam felt her warmth of character, which just made things more difficult.

"I'm sorry, I didn't get your name."

"Ah, what a dope. I mustn't have put it on the note. I'm Sally – Sal." She laughed again for no reason.

"Well, thank you, Sal. Isla's pretty excited, but I'm not sure she's quite ready for all that." Sam struggled to express himself properly.

"I totally understand," Sal said graciously, "I'm not sure Molly is either, and, you know, that long away from home, it's … a lot."

"Oh, right, I thought it was just a sleepover?"

"Oh," she said, her tone dropping. "Sorry, again – I wasn't clear in the note." She laughed with increasing unease. "We were actually wondering if Isla would like to come to our holiday home for a few days at half-term?"

"Right," Sam said, a little more sternly than he had intended.

"It's no problem if it doesn't suit, honestly, Sam. It's just they've been talking together and, well, I sort of gave in and asked. Sorry."

Sam imagined she was gnawing her lip in anticipation.

"No, no." Sam tried to put her at ease. "It's just, well, I don't know if you know but Isla's been through quite a lot ..." His gaze rose from the floor as the door to Isla's cabin cracked open and his half-dressed daughter looked out with pleading puppy eyes. She silently mouthed "please". Sam turned away and gestured impatiently to close the door.

"To be honest, I did know that, Sam."

Sam had often caught the glances of the mums sitting in each other's cars at drop off watching him walk past. He knew they'd be talking – it was natural. And there would be gossip too: *Wonder what he does all day?*

Sam sighed. "Ehm, where's the holiday house?"

"It's right beside the beach in Ballycastle. They'd have a ball. I'm sure Isla likes the sea – of course she does, of course she does."

Sam could almost see Sal shake her head at the stupidity of her comment.

"Well, Sal," said Sam, lowering his voice as a countermeasure to alert little ears. "Isla's never been on a sleepover before. She's doing well but, you know, night-time hasn't always been easy for her, and this is two nights, which is a lot."

"Oh," she groaned, "we were actually thinking of three nights."

Sam was silent for a few moments. "I've kind of lost track – when is half-term?" He pretended not to know, trying to buy time, even though he was staring at the calendar.

"They get a half-day Friday fortnight."

"Sal, I'm sorry, I've to go overseas for a job. I'll not even be in the country then if she wants to come home or anything."

"Look, honestly, it was only an idea. Please don't think any more about it. I had just promised Molly I'd ask. Really, it's no bother. We can get them together for a play date at some stage instead without a sleepover."

"I'm really sorry," he said. And then he sensed, rather than heard, Isla crying behind the door. He cracked it open a bit to see her little body turned away from him on the bed, her loneliness drawing him back to the despair he'd tried so hard to beat. "Can you let me think about it?" he said into the handset.

Libby had her own separate secure line to her boss in Belfast.

"We've just had a community cop approach the vehicle and stick a ticket on it," she imparted with exasperation.

"Well, it has been there for rather a long time," he said.

"I just ... I don't see the logic of letting it sit there."

"Of course you do."

"Ok, I see the logic, but I don't see the justification."

"You let me worry about that," he said patronisingly.

"It's not a built-up area but there's a lot of people around at times."

"This thing was made by one of their best engineers."

"Was it?"

"Yes. I think you need to calm down somewhat."

"I didn't know that."

"I know you didn't."

"How do you know that?"

The man just snorted condescendingly. She hated him in that moment. He may have made her, but she loathed him. She resented the way he treated her – as a little girl. She despised his superior tone, his willingness to play with lives as part of some greater game.

She stared at the images relayed by two covert cameras deployed by the ops team. There were two cars in the area, too, each equipped with their own cameras and microphones. The ops officer had seen risk enough to withdraw *them* to a safe distance, so the logic of just leaving the vehicle in situ didn't withstand scrutiny. She placed her head in her hands, exhausted, frustrated, disgusted. But when her head lifted again things were so much worse.

A harbour authority van had pulled up and a woman in a high-vis vest was on her knees at the front of the vehicle attaching a wheel clamp.

8

S am looked out of place in the plush confines of the Royal Dublin Society. He had, rather stubbornly, refused to dress for the occasion despite being told they were dining in the private members' area. He'd arrived ahead of time and found his name had been left at the door.

"Very good, sir," said a manager-type, who was suited and shoed to sparkling perfection. "My name is Robert. I'll be looking after you today."

Sam was shown to a table and Robert almost asked for his jacket before realising he didn't have anything other than the shell fleece he'd arrived in.

Sinead came next. Sam rose to meet her, a familiar nervousness creeping over him.

"Hi," was all she said, drawing in her own chair before Robert had a chance to.

"Sparkling water, please." Robert took his direction and withdrew. "He's just behind me," she whispered conspiratorially. "He didn't baulk at the money."

Sam smiled and Sinead smiled back – a roguish grin

creeping across her gentle face, and then she rose at Sam's prompt as the father of the heiress approached.

"Sam, Sinead, lovely to see you again." The old man's hand stretched out, careful to greet Sinead first – ever the gent. "How have you been?"

"Grand, thanks," Sinead said.

"Good, good," said Sam.

The father sat down and reclined in his seat, then leaned forward and began with an apology. "Regrettably I won't be able to stay for lunch after all. I have an issue with one of my execs – potentially a nasty business. But please do enjoy the menu. I've told Robert to make sure everything goes on my tab."

"That's not necessary," Sinead said.

"Not at all, not at all," he waved her politeness aside. "Least I can do given that you travelled all the way down from the north to thrash this out."

"How can I help?" asked Sam, curious as to how the father would frame the conversation.

"Well, my daughter – as you know – is taking a holiday and I want to know she is safe. You have been impressive in the past, so I asked Sinead to gauge your interest."

"I really didn't have much to do last time."

"On the contrary, Sam, I know what you did. You got her in and out of court, you protected her from the press, you stayed that extra night with us when you were needed elsewhere and," he paused, "you also dealt with our night visitor."

That came as a surprise to Sam who had no idea anyone had been aware of Loopy Loo's nocturnal arrival.

The father noticed Sam's expression. "I do not sleep well, Sam, not at all. So, you see, anything that puts my mind at ease is worth paying for, even to the tune you have requested."

Sam resisted the urge to offer some sort of leeway and decided to wait and see how the negotiation played out.

"I propose to pay your fee and can offer one hundred and fifty euros per day in expenses, subject to a few caveats. How does that sound?"

"Depends on the caveats."

"My daughter must not – and I mean *must not*, be aware you are there."

"No problem."

"Can you be sure of that?"

"Yes," said Sam without hesitation.

The father looked at him for a long moment, then shifted uncomfortably before beginning his next piece of prepared speech. "I do not know a great deal about you despite having asked." He gestured at Sinead who smiled sheepishly. "I have the bare bones of your background, which in itself is reassuring, but I do not suppose you are going to supply references."

Sam just looked back at him offering nothing. The father's lips flattened and he nodded gently as if he had expected as much.

"However," he glanced at Sinead, "you come with an absolute and unequivocal recommendation."

"Well, that's good to know," Sam said.

"So how would you like to be paid?"

Sam hadn't thought that through, so he decided to characterise his answer as a joke. "Can you do cash?" he said smiling.

"If cash is required, cash can be got, but if you want it today, it will have to be euros, I'm afraid."

"That's ok, I can wait. You come highly recommended." Sam twitched his head just short of a wink.

The father grinned. "Touché."

"What about flights?" Sinead inquired, trying to take the conversation away from money.

"If agreeable, I would like you to be on the same plane there and back, Sam. My PA can help with the details." He pulled out a slim notepad and began writing. He tore off a page and handed it to Sam.

"That's grand. And thank you."

"No, no, really, thank you, Sam. I know she will be well-looked-after. Now, have you any questions for me?"

"Has he been in touch?"

"You mean the murderous cretin? No, not to my knowledge, and I very much hope that will remain the case."

"So why the need for protection?"

The father sighed, sat back for a moment and became a little dreamy as he looked away. "Because she is my little girl, Sam. She may be a handful, she may despise me at times, but she is all I care about, and because all I can do is invest in her safety. Nothing else seems to do any good. Nothing at all." He was lost in thought for a while before he leaned out of his chair to speak with enthusiasm. "I can thoroughly recommend the linguine, and don't be afraid to tuck in a napkin at the neck," he said, before looking at Sam's lack of suit and tie and quietly admonishing himself. "Anyway, we'll see that the details are looked after, and thank you again." He rose, there were handshakes all round, and the father was off.

Sinead looked at Sam. Sam looked at Sinead.

"So," she said.

"That was a breeze." He shook his head.

"You're obviously worth it," she said, then blushed. "He thinks so anyway."

There was a silence and then Sinead felt the need to correct her own correction. "Not just him, like, other people too. You make them feel safe."

"Like who?" Sam said.

"Like me," she said, looking away.

A familiar awkwardness descended over them. Neither knew how to change course. Sam tapped the arm of his chair and Sinead gazed around the room watching anyone but him.

"The specials today are shoulder of lamb and hake on a bed of colcannon with asparagus, and the soup is parsnip with Mumbai spices." Robert saved them as he handed out menus.

"Oh, I don't know if ..." Sinead stole a glance at Sam to see if he was for staying.

"That sounds very nice," he said. "Can I get a pint of stout, please?"

"Certainly, sir. I'll leave you to decide."

Sinead reverted to people watching, unable to hold his eye. From her throwaway thoughts she muttered a question. "How *can* you be sure?"

Sam panicked a little, fearing she was finally steering towards the rocks he had so far managed to steer clear of.

"Sure of what?" he asked nervously.

"That she won't know you're there."

Ordinarily Sam wouldn't get into detail about his past, but this wasn't an ordinary situation – and he was desperate not to get into the obvious alternative. "I spent some time doing work like this, you know, back in the old job."

"But I thought you were a marine, well, special forces or whatever?"

"There were secondments."

"What does that *mean*?" she stressed, somehow frustrated at how little she knew about him. She looked away again. "Like, I wouldn't have told him anything more about your background, but, to be honest, when he asked I realised that, actually, I don't *know* anything."

"You know more than most."

"Well, maybe that's just not enough, Sam," she said, her face set firm in profile; frustration taking her as close to anger as he had ever witnessed.

"Well, what would you like to know?"

"Like, what *did* you do? Maybe you can't say – or just prefer not to, like, me."

Sam paused briefly, suddenly realising she wasn't hungry for information, she was desperate to be allowed in. "I trust you, Sinead, totally and utterly."

She looked up at him under her fringe. "Do you?"

"Yes," he responded, surprised she had to ask. "I trusted you with Isla. That's - that's all I have?"

"Ok," she shrugged, as if not altogether convinced.

"Look," he whispered, "I *was* special forces for a while, but in that time there were these – opportunities - to join other teams."

"Close protection?"

"No, well, yes, but I never did any of that. I always kinda thought—

"People who need protecting often need shot."

Sinead could never be accused of not listening to what he said, but then he could never be accused of saying a whole lot.

"There was a unit, or units, that did surveillance work."

Sam petered out as his pint arrived. Sinead was still smarting a little. There was no smoke, but there were embers. He found himself filling the silence.

"We were a rabble of different skill sets based all over the country."

"Which country?"

"Northern Ireland," he said, again surprised.

"Oh." It was her turn to be blindsided.

"We kept track of known characters, drew up lists of associations, monitored their comms and movements, mapped out their networks. That sort of thing."

"What did your rabble look like?"

"Well, there were all sorts of ops – operatives – that's what they called us, actually. Such-and-such op and such-and-such-op."

"So you were Sam op?"

"No, you took on a name. You weren't supposed to know

anyone else you were working with. It was all a bit convoluted. The only one I knew was someone from my own group. He was deployed with me. That was irregular."

"Right," she said baffled.

"There were intelligence folk. They weren't called op, they were called spook—"

"Like Sinead spook?"

"Exactly. And signals teams and mechanics. They were techs and spanners."

"Bit weird."

"They built our vehicles and rigged covert cameras around our AORs – our areas of operation. People didn't know the half of what we were able to see."

"And where was this?"

"In the north."

"Yeah, I get that, but, like, the whole country?"

"Pretty much. There were different DETs for different areas."

"Different what?"

"DETs, detachments. That's just what they were called. Each detachment was made up of a boss and ops, and we were deployed to keep an eye on people or arms movements or whatever. And if we got wind of a planned attack, we'd dig in and wait and then let the plods make arrests. We hardly ever engaged anyone but we were there in case the police made a bollocks of it."

"What were you, like, hiding in ditches or what?"

"Ditches were glamorous. In dumps sometimes – landfill sites. Once I had to go to the tropo clinic after three weeks under rotting bin bags."

"What's the tropo clinic?"

"It's where you have a drip feed of penicillin to get rid of diseases."

"Glamorous, indeed."

"Some of it was fun. There was a lot of drinking back then when things went right, but when they went wrong – they went really, badly wrong."

"How?"

"People died."

"Right," she breathed in.

"But the point is, we could get so close, like, within earshot – almost all the time, and the mark never knew we were there."

"How?"

"We were just really well-trained. And we were rigged to the hilt. We'd the best of kit – the techies were smart guys. Our cars were specially designed for us – armoured doors and floors and seats, and they had cameras and mics and it was all fed back in real time long before that was ever possible in the commercial world. The techs hid cameras all over the place – not the CCTV ones you can see in any city, covert units, hidden away, so when the mark reckoned he or she was clear of all the cameras they knew about, we were actually right in their faces in housing estates and even in their homes."

"You put cameras in their houses?"

"Sometimes, but we didn't really need to. We had rips in there and lumps on their cars, so we could hear almost everything."

"How was that legal?"

"None of it was legal. We weren't even supposed to be in-country. We were deniable, totally and utterly. Nothing we recorded ever went to court or to the cops or anything. We were there just to protect lives and stop bombings or shootings or attacks or whatever. We did the graft then handed over to the police who made the arrests and started the prosecutions. They had to find their own evidence, so we always tried to arrange it in such a way that the marks got caught in the act."

"What can I get you?" Robert had returned.

"I'll have the lamb, please," Sinead said, distracted by Sam's sudden openness and not keen on the deviation.

"Fish, thank you," Sam said, "and another pint. Sure, will you have a drink?"

"Go on, then. I'll have a glass of Malbec if you have it."

"Certainly." Robert retracted as if he'd laid a wreath at the Cenotaph.

"So you did a bit of breaking and entering?"

"All the ops were pretty handy at that – even the foot-handed paras."

"Parachute Regiment?"

"Yeah. We always had good banter with the airbornes. They're tough enough, but they're not subtle."

"No, they're not," remarked Sinead.

Everyone in Ireland knew what the paratroopers had done on Bloody Sunday. Thirteen dead on the streets of Derry. A key moment in a thirty-year conflict.

"So you were after the IRA?"

"Kind of, but that was changing as I was there. There was a period when the Provos almost became the good guys – which sounds weird but that's how it seemed. The nutters who came next were more our focus – where we were based anyway."

"Who? Loyalists?"

"Sometimes, but it was mainly the dissies – the dissidents. The ones who broke away from the main IRA and started up their own gangs. The Real IRA, The Continuity IRA, the I-can't-believe-it's-not-the-Real-IRA IRA. There were dozens of them."

"So how did you deal with that?"

"Same score – we got all over them. The spooks, we had at least one spook at all times in our DET – they worked at turning them, and we worked at watching the others."

"Turning, you mean persuading them to become inform-ers? Touts, like?"

"Yeah, although I imagine the persuasion was pretty blunt."

"How did they do it?"

"Honestly? I don't know. But I'd say the usual three things – sex, money and power. If someone was shagging someone they shouldn't have been, they were ripe for turning. Same if they had a wee problem betting on the dogs or if they'd fallen out with someone more senior, then they might have a gripe and be worth a punt. But that wasn't my area."

"So how do you know it happened?"

Sam paused for the first time, thinking about how far to go. It would be awkward to stop now. He had found himself curiously willing to tell Sinead things he'd never spoken about before.

"It was kind of obvious some of the people we were watching were actually assets and it could be infuriating. Say we had someone digging up a bunch of explosives and say they were ten feet in front of us. I mean, literally, ten feet, and we had been waiting on them for days – a week even, and we were about to call in the TCG—"

"Wait." Sinead held up her hand. "TCG?"

"The police, like a tasking coordination. There was also a tactical support group – cops in boiler suits and balaclavas with all the heavy kit and helmets basically."

"Ok."

"So there were times when the spook – who was part of our team, remember, called the whole thing off."

"How?"

"Well, she or he might be back at base watching the whole thing on the feeds—"

"The feeds?"

"The images we were sending back, the pictures – video or audio."

"Ok."

"And if the wrong person turned up where they weren't

expected, the spook wouldn't want their source to be lifted. You see?"

"But if the source was arrested, would it not give them more protection? Within their own organisation, I mean?"

"Who knows what games the spooks were playing. I could never work it out. It was – sometimes - it was just wrong. That bit did for me in the end. They were moving chess pieces while we were shitting in doggie bags and drinking out of puddles."

"Lovely imagery, Sam."

"You did ask."

"I wasn't really expecting you to answer, though."

"I know you weren't."

She looked at him, happy that he had confided in her. "Do you miss all that?"

"Shitting in plastic bags?"

"Yeah, cool stuff like that."

"I miss the rush of removing someone who wants to kill innocent people. I miss the total physical effort required to do some of the stuff we did at sea. But there are bits I will never miss – things that were done that will stay with me, and, to be honest, I haven't paid for it all yet – although I've definitely paid for some."

"I know you have," she said softly.

"How do you know?"

"I can see it, Sam."

"I know you can," he conceded, the drink washing away walls as he stared at the confessional collar of his pint. He twisted the glass.

"The lamb for you, madam," said Robert.

Sam could have kissed him for his intervention.

"And the hake. Now, can I fetch you anything else?"

"One more pint and another one of those, please." Sam pointed at Sinead's wine.

"What do we do about this?"

The operations officer had materialised at Libby's back. Most of the team were giving her a wide berth.

"Well, if we remove the clamp, someone will probably notice and ask why."

"If you don't, then the car is stuck there."

"I'm not too proud to ask for advice," she said without looking at her colleague. She trusted him and needed his experience.

"Reason it out," the opso said. "The car has to move at some point. The young lad who we think is going to drive it can't even find his way home, so he's probably not going to be able to bust a clamp off."

"Agreed." She sighed.

"So it has to come off. The question then is when?"

"Ok. We wait till we get the nod that it's all going ahead."

The ops officer spoke quietly so nobody else would hear. "It's your call but it might just be worth thinking about the plan if nothing happens soon. The next step is they'll send a pickup to tow it. Then things become extremely dangerous."

Libby shivered. She hadn't thought of that. "Thanks, I appreciate it," she said.

9

"Thank you, thank you, thank you, thank you, you're the best!"

Isla was dancing a jig on the pontoon – hugging him once, pogoing, then hugging him again. She hurtled into babble and preparation.

Sinead had persuaded him in the end. Women need women, she'd said. They need to talk about stuff you cannot ever understand.

The Malbec had turned black on her lips and teeth, but she'd had that many she was almost beyond caring. He was as full as an egg – his drinking days long behind him and his threshold low.

"I can take her when she's back." Sinead had become uncharacteristically ebullient with the grape. "Sure, we'll have right craic, me and her. She's gas."

Sam had noodled the idea around his fuddled head and apparently agreed. It had all seemed so sensible and straight-forward. Sinead had followed it up with a confirmation text the next evening – which he knew was, in part, a means of communication and a test to see if anything had been said in the fog of drink that could damage their friendship. Or relationship. Or whatever it was that they had.

It still troubled Sam that he wouldn't be on hand if Isla got distressed. The Venice job was getting in the way of that. He had occasionally imagined what it would be like when she started to get out and about more. He'd always thought he'd get her a wee Nokia with a speed dial and he'd just jump in the van and go get her if she wanted. Ideally with this trip he'd have booked a B&B close by and maybe kept an eye at a distance.

But Sinead had told him to get real. The booze had inspired a dismissiveness in her and she'd berated him for being too clingy. It had grated because he knew she was right. There had been talk of loosening apron strings and other such bullshit sayings that Sam had deliberately ignored. Isla was seven, not seventeen.

Even so, an agreement was reached. Sam would take Isla to meet Molly's folks and they would go on holiday for a few days. Then Sinead would collect her and they would stay on the boat where close to normal life would resume until Sam returned.

Molly, it transpired, lived in a mansion. Isla lived on a boat. Each kid thought the other's life was cool, apparently. The driveway was crunchy as the car Sam had borrowed from the yard owner's son announced its arrival between perfectly planted trees.

"Hello!" he'd heard from behind as a broad, low-sized lady emerged from a hole in a hedge. "I'm just sorting the dogs," she explained, her handshake revealing a firm grip.

"Nice to meet you," Sam said.

"Lovely to meet you. We hear so much about Isla," Sal said, staring at his daughter's back as she and Molly tore off towards the house.

"She's very lucky to be taken on holiday. We must return the treat at some point," said Sam. "How is Molly with boats?"

"I'd say she'd be excited, although we've never done any sailing or anything like that."

Sal seemed pretty laid-back. Sam felt he could grow to like her.

"So you're off yourself?"

"Yes. I'll be gone until the end of next week, but a friend of mine will collect Isla if that's ok? She and Isla are pals and she sometimes looks after her while I'm away."

"Are you overseas often?"

"Not really, not any more," Sam said absently.

"Of course, of course," Sal said, nodding sagely, and Sam realised that she thought she'd put her foot in it.

"Oh, it's ok. I didn't mean—"

"No, no, of course."

Neither of them clarified anything, yet everyone seemed to understand.

"I know it's a big move, first holiday and all that, without mum or dad," Sal said and visibly cringed. "Sorry."

Then the kids emerged from the stately front door carrying Molly's Trunki suitcase between them.

Sam shook his head – no apology required. "Don't worry, Sal, honestly."

Molly's mum tightened her lips in sympathy and tilted her head towards her shoulder. She reached out as if to touch Sam's arm and then thought better of it. "I'm not going to pretend I understand – I couldn't possibly, but in my work I do have some experience of this sort of thing. The first sign of any distress and I'll call you. I promise. And we'll take good care of her."

"Thanks, Sal. What line of work are you in?"

"I'm a paediatrician at the Royal."

Her profession gave him some comfort. He'd heard of the Children's Hospital at the Royal – a remarkable place by all accounts. He looked at her and nodded.

"Here's my friend's number by the way. Sinead. She lives in

Dublin, but any problems at all and she'll get on the road. Otherwise she'll meet you here in a few days when you get back." His gaze fell to Isla, who was fizzing with anticipation on Molly's arm. He slung her bag out from the back seat. "Alright, wee lamb, you have a great time." Isla nearly hopped into her father's arms, delighted at being released. He whispered in her ear and he hugged her. "You ask Molly's mum to call me any time, ok? About anything, you hear me?"

"Yes, Daddy."

"I love you so much."

"I luff you," she whispered back.

This is what it's like to go crazy.

Anthony sat on the floor and stared at nothing. He'd stopped going down to the television in the evenings – he couldn't stick the smell. They all drank some stinking tar-like liquid from mugs at night. They also watched ridiculous old repeats and had competitions to see who could remember whodunnit from the first time they'd seen the shows – detective stories, weak mysteries. He couldn't stand listening to the old bloke wheeze. They masked him up to an oxygen tank every now and then. It made him think of his mother's chain-smoking.

Instead, he lay on the pink floor and stared at the ceiling, going quietly insane. His resentment at what he'd been asked to do grew and grew. He berated himself for listening to Grim. Anthony couldn't believe he was actually craving the freedom of his tired little town, the cycle track under the bridges, the abandoned factories forgotten by all but those who lived there. At least the disused industrial plots had provided a place to go and sit unseen. He even missed the lough, the shore, the odd swim.

He suddenly realised he'd been scratching at the wall for ages and looked in shock at the little pile of dust scored along the pink carpet. *Who has pink carpet?* He scooped up the dust but had nowhere to put it. It was still daylight outside, but he had no choice. He fumbled the curtain and pushed aside the blind, spilling dust down the condensation on the window-pane. He got the latch levered up and threw the dust into the air. He heard a noise from below and in panic quickly slammed the window shut, replacing everything as it had been. Almost. Save for the mess.

He heard footsteps on the stairs and grabbed all he could of the mortar left on the carpet, irrationally terrified.

The mother stood there staring at him. "What are you doing with the window?"

"Nothing."

"Have you been looking out that window?"

"No," he said, like an eight-year-old.

The mother tore across the room and whipped back the blind, pushing Anthony behind her to conceal him. Dust had caught across both the inside and outside of the pane.

"What's that? What have you been doing?"

"Nothing," he repeated, disgusted that this old woman was scaring him.

"On the floor – what's that? What have you been doing?"

She crouched down towards him. He could smell her age.

"What's in your hand? Have you been looking out the window again?"

She knew. How did she know?

"Move!"

Anthony reluctantly stepped forward and heard the mother gasp.

"What – have – you – done? What's happened the wall?"

He just looked at her, silent, embarrassed. He was back in school cowering before a teacher, terrified.

"Open your hand!"

Then he gathered his courage, remembering what he was there for. He hadn't gone through all that risk and crappy training just to be spoken to like this by some pensioner. "Never you mind," he said, growing in confidence.

"What did you say? What did you say to me in my own house?"

"Never you bloody mind, you old bitch!"

She jabbed forward grabbing his wrist but he twisted free with ease.

"What is it!" she yelled, incandescent now with rage.

"You wanna know?" he shouted, and threw what was left of the mortar dust in her face.

She stood eerily still, shocked, livid, resolute. Her voice dropped. "You'll regret that. Oh, yes, you will. You – will – regret – that."

And she turned and walked slowly out, leaving the door wide open.

Sam's outlook was foul long before the three o'clock alarm went off, and it didn't improve as he hurtled south to Dublin Airport. He thought back to the last few occasions he'd been there. Not ideal. Most of his visits had been to deposit vulnerable women he'd *liberated* from brothels for Sinead. Occasionally he had dropped off seafarers for Fran. On one occasion a girl's pimp had pulled up at the drop-off point and tried to take her back. Sam had been forced to fight hard, which had undoubtedly resulted in his face being recorded on a CCTV database. When Ireland eventually adopted wholesale facial recognition technology he'd be screwed. All in all, Dublin Airport wasn't his favourite place.

Underlying his foul mood was that he wasn't looking

forward to the job ahead. He had been many things in the past but a childminder wasn't one of them. Nor could he pretend he was without prejudice; he knew he was predisposed to a disregard for the ignorant wealthy, and the heiress fell into that category. She may be undiagnosed as daft, but she was certainly aware of her status in society.

He watched her file through the priority section at security while the oily rags like him wove around the pillared tapes. He took some pleasure in finding her on the far side, queuing like everyone else and huffing petulantly as she was directed by a hardy Dubliner to bag up her private ablution solutions. The little security woman might have been from the rebel Liberties. Her voice travelled like the wind as she commanded the heiress to deposit her rash cream in the bin as it was much too large for the plastic bag she'd neglected to bring.

On board he could see her up front. Her roots delicately dyed – not a single trace of nature. Her head was permanently turned towards her companions, but Sam was pleased to have been spared their chat. It would be a long ten days.

Still, at least there would be boats.

"I want him gone."

Grim knew immediately who was calling and who she wanted gone.

"Where are you calling from?"

"Never you mind. Just get this wee shit out of my house."

"What's happened?" Grim asked, now significantly alarmed.

"He's crossed the line," was all she would say. "You get up here and you take him away."

"That's not possible," said Grim, hardening his tone.

"If you're not here by tomorrow night, you can collect him on the street. That's it. Done. Finished."

She hung up.

Oul' wagon, thought Grim, worried about where – in her temper – she had made the call from. He had no other safe houses. He hadn't the balls to ring the boss and explain. He considered looping in the manager – him being a resourceful type, but he wasn't happy about that either; they had deliberately separated the risk so that nobody knew the elements of the other's responsibility. It was a means of avoiding compromise if one of them turned out to be a tout. Nice to be trusted, he had thought, when the manager suggested it. The boss seemed reluctant at first – Grim just put that down to control freakery, but he had come round in the end.

There were too many wee issues with this one. He'd get out if he was able, but it wasn't that simple. Nobody resigned from this game – they went to jail or were interred.

So he went for a walk to chat to the manager.

———

Sam clambered into a river taxi, hard on the expenses tab but he couldn't lose the heiress on the first trip of the first day.

Following her and her friends had, so far, proved easy enough. They were so self-absorbed that they had no notion of the people around them. The only worry was the constant preening of one of the three women, who whipped out a pocket mirror every five minutes or so to check her hair or make-up. Sam was genuinely astonished by the speed and frequency with which she checked her reflection. Worryingly, she also used her phone for the same purpose, under the inadequate guise of taking selfies. Sam was forced to meander out of the background of each shot every time she fished for her phone.

Sam peered over the raised bow as the old, inefficient taxi

pushed water before it. Instead of enjoying the astonishing views of an unusual environment as his boat carved in the wake of the women's, he found himself doubting his decision to have gone there at all. What if Isla screamed in the night? Her friend would think she was a baby. Maybe she wouldn't be asked back.

He knew he'd too easily followed old tracks back to work that may not stretch his muscles, but would at least let him use hard-learned skills. He desperately wanted to change himself into a man who didn't need intrigue or challenge to make him feel alive – but doubted whether he actually had it in him.

———

"We're going to take the clamp off." Libby was suddenly very sure of herself.

"Just like that?" the ops officer said, sarcasm creeping in.

"Yep, as soon as it's dark and quiet enough."

"Why the rush?"

"Because I'm told the wee lad might be on the move soon."

"So my team have to risk their safety to cut off a wheel clamp that realistically could be replaced by some traffic attendant tomorrow?"

"I think that's unlikely. There's no reason for anyone to approach the vehicle again – the local police know it's been ticketed and the red coats know it's clamped. Unless they have hawk eyes they'll not be near it for a few days. Hopefully this thing will all be over by then."

"Ok," said the ops officer. "It's about time this thing went off."

Careful what you wish for, thought Libby.

———

"This is going to be awkward."

"Really?" sniggered Sinead.

He'd called her from an iPhone 6 supplied by the heiress's father and begrudgingly installed with gadgetry by Áine.

"You're going to have to ask the father for money. I can't keep up with the heiress."

"Why, is she partying already?"

"She got in a Lexus at the airport. Not a crappy wee taxi – a Lexus. It drove her little harem about fifty feet – they obviously couldn't walk in their candlestick heels, and then they got into a river taxi."

"Sounds right up your street."

"It cost two hundred euros."

"Go way!"

"Have you ever been to Venice before?"

"Nope."

"Well, neither have I and I'll not be here again."

"Where is she now?"

"In a hotel. It's one of those places where the room keys are actual heavy keys that they hang on hooks in reception, so I've already been into her room and pinged a camera in there. I just hope she doesn't get jiggy with some Italian bloke later."

"Jiggy?"

"Romantic."

"Well, I'm sure you can switch the camera off, Sam."

"Yeah, but this is the really awkward bit. I was just told to keep her out of trouble. Now I'm thinking – does that mean keeping other people out of her bed?"

"So long as it looks consensual, I don't see what you can do about it," Sinead said.

"Well, how will I know that if the camera's off?"

"That's what you're being paid the big bucks for, Sam. Use your judgement."

"I'm not a bodyguard, especially not for posh totty. I can tag them, no problem – I've stuck a lump in her handbag – but I can't be in and out of designer boutiques. I'd look like I was there to rob the place."

"You look just fine, Sam," Sinead said, and they had one of those quiet moments where he almost returned the compliment but couldn't quite manage it.

"Anyway, will you ask him?"

"If you can watch his daughter shagging an Italian? I'd say the answer will be no."

"Expenses. Will you tell him this is gonna cost a bit more? And can he send me an advance through you? This whole thing could get out of hand and I want to make sure Isla's lunch money is coming out ok."

"Is it really that tight?"

"Well, I haven't worked in a while. Nothing that paid me anyway."

"Don't worry, I'll get it sorted. He won't care, so long as his kid is ok."

"Thanks, Sinead."

"And Sam?"

"Yes?"

"Seriously, jiggy?" She laughed.

"Feck away off."

10

"Standby, standby."

The ops officer looked up in amazement as one of the key figures on his watch list walked across the screen. Hagan. He drew up the file on his tablet: known as the manager, a people person, a fixer, sharp dresser. The opso looked up at the sports jacket and thought he caught the glint of a cufflink at the man's wrist.

"You'll never guess who just showed up on scene," said the former SAS trooper who was tracking the new arrival.

"Paul Hagan," said the opso.

"Affirmative."

The opso was stunned. The chief of staff of the highest-risk dissident republican group operating in Northern Ireland within metres of a live operation. Hagan vanished into a doorway. "They must be running short on foot soldiers."

"Affirmative."

"What's his status?"

"Licking an ice cream."

"Serious?"

"Affirmative. Mint chocolate chip."

There was a small shake of excitement through the ops room as those gathered wondered if a serious hitter was about to compromise himself. They all knew the dissies were light on bodies but it would be a significant sign of weakness if Hagan were to drive the vehicle.

Libby arrived breathless. "Just as well we removed the clamp."

"It was a good call, Libby." The opso pressed the transmitter. "Can you get images to us?"

The screens flickered and from a concealed camera in the trooper's car the manager could clearly be seen sucking on a cone.

"Bizarre," said the opso.

Libby leaned across to talk into the mic. "How long's he been on location?"

"Only caught him heading into Mauds," said the trooper. "Didn't see him arrive but it can't be long. Less than ten minutes anyway."

"Has he looked at the vehicle?"

"Mauds is close to it, twenty-five metres. Can't say if he's had a proper look yet. Not since I got eyes on anyway."

Libby and the opso looked at each other pensively. Surprises were exciting – but they were also dangerous.

The beach was littered with huts that spoilt Sam's view of the heiress and her pals, which didn't matter because he could hear them. How they managed to witter on endlessly about celebrity, fashion, make-up and films astonished him.

The girls had hired one of the thousands of huts lining the seaward-facing side of Venice. It brought a welcome fresh Adriatic breeze rather than the moderately pungent waft from the canal network on the lagoon side.

Sam had found a way through the rear of a neighbouring hut where he sat on beach furniture and allowed the women to numb his brain. At least on the beach they were containable, and he'd grown to like the island of Lido.

The women had snapped and posted as much as they'd talked and bitched. He heard the faux shutter of their phones make incessant captures and imagined them pouting and plunging to give lift in their bikinis while sucking in from their cheeks – no such thing as a double chin on Instagram. Then they read the comments – mostly from "such a bitch" as far as Sam could make out. When there were compliments the commentator was needy; when the commentator was less than generous they were sworn up and down Venice.

Not once did they swim, which suited Sam just fine stretched out on a lounger in the warmth, his charge within feet of him and no idea he was there.

"We need to seize that camera," Libby said.

The manager hadn't spotted the snapper, yet Libby and the operations officer could see him clearly on the trooper's covert car cam relayed fifty miles in real time and technicolor.

"What's he photographing? Is he following Hagan?"

The opso got on the radio. "Where did the photographer come from?"

"He's been here for a while," said the trooper. "He seems to be doing some sort of shoot for the harbour or ferry or something. He's a commercial and portrait sort – it's written on the side of his van."

"Get the name," said Libby.

"What's the problem?" asked the opso.

"There's more than likely a suspect vehicle in his shots, and now there's a leading dissident with an ice cream a few feet away from said vehicle. That's the problem."

The operations officer understood what she was saying. It created a trail, and the snapper could well have accidental shots of one of their own team.

"How do you want the camera taken? Not best to leave it and get it later?"

"Probably," Libby conceded. "Maybe just get the address and we'll steal his kit and camera cards overnight."

"Ok," said the opso and relayed the message to his two ops on the ground.

They stared at the screen for a while watching the manager finish his cone, look around the harbour and stroll away. A message came through the radio network.

"I don't think he knows which vehicle it is," said the trooper.

"Really?" said the opso.

"He hasn't once looked at it – or any other car for that matter. It's as if he doesn't know it's there."

The opso looked to Libby. "Could that be the case?"

"S'pose it's possible."

"Where's he headed?"

"Up the hill," came the trooper. "I could follow on foot. Suggest you send a car too."

The opso was torn. He didn't want to deploy both sets of eyes away from the suspect vehicle. He also didn't want his op stranded if the manager hopped into a waiting car. "Negative. Follow in vehicle. Keep second eyes on the Ford."

"Received."

Libby and the opso watched the trooper's car move gently out of its space and turn up the hill. They could just make out the manager about a hundred yards ahead. The trooper pulled in and let him proceed up the straight road.

"He's going to the safe house," Libby said.

"Looks like it."

"Why would someone as senior as him compromise himself like that? Surely they'd have sent someone else?"

The opso just shook his head in bewilderment.

"They must be confident they're clear of surveillance," Libby reasoned aloud.

"He's stopping," said the trooper.

They looked up. Sure enough, the manager had turned and appeared to be about to stretch his legs on the way back down the hill.

"What is going on?" Libby whispered. "What are you up to, Hagan?"

Sam was drinking too much coffee; he could feel it in his heart, which was working much too hard for the energy he was expending. But to secure a seat in a public place purchases had to be made, and he had long since learned that espresso was the best option. Water meant he was laden with a groaning bladder, and that made a mess of the three Fs: fleet of foot, prepared for flight and able to fight – three requirements in Sam's line of work. Boxing on a full bladder was never advisable.

The witless women tottered around endlessly as if they were on day release. They'd taxied a walkable distance from the Excelsior Hotel – where they'd been star-spotting, to the ferry terminal where they'd travelled with the unwashed to the main island of San Marco. It was a pleasant place for Sam to operate – absolutely wedged static with tourists. He'd watched as skulled out protestors on gondolas blew whistles and waved flags at an enormous cruise ship. They appeared to be telling it to go home but he couldn't be sure whether they were environmentalists or whether they had simply had enough of the city's tourism.

Eventually the women came to rest in a huddle of excitement beside a shopfront on a side street. It was no ordinary shop – they appeared to be on the cusp of being branded. Sam plonked his arse down at a small table close by and ordered as the women made their selections from the window menu. One appeared to dare the other, and he again thought of their arrested development, their childlike carry-on.

Sam debated for a moment. How would he feel if in years to come Isla came home with a tattoo? He rather liked the heiress's father. The old boy had suffered, he could see that. Sam brought out his phone and dialled.

"Hi."

"What about a tattoo?"

"No, thanks, don't like them," Sinead said.

"She's about to get a tattoo."

"Ha ha! And I suppose you think she shouldn't. You're such a prude, Sam."

He shook off the jibe, knowing it was accurate.

"Well, should she? Her da's paying me to look after her. If it was me—"

"Yeah, well, what can you do about it?"

"I'd say I could stop it alright if it was a good enough idea."

"It's not."

"So what do I say when she comes home with a dolphin on her chest?"

"Ooh, is that what she's going for?"

"I can see a man stencilling it on with a pen as we speak."

"Her father would probably say, 'Why the hell did you get that done?'."

"And what would he say to me?"

"Why the hell did you let her get that done?"

"That's kinda my question."

"Well, how do you stop it without her knowing you're there?"

"So, I *am* to stop it?"

"I dunno. Maybe. Your call."

"In the years I've known you this is the least helpful you've ever been."

She laughed. "Nothing's easy when it comes to women."

"Don't tell me," he said, "ask me. I'll talk to you later. I've a wee job to do."

"Fuddy-duddy."

Sam passed by the parlour window to see one of the friends being stencilled with exactly the same design as the heiress. No imagination at all, he thought.

Time was short. He squeezed down a bin-jammed alley into a lane that ran along the back of the terrace. It was just about wide enough for his shoulders and it stank. He realised that the buildings had been designed as houses and converted later, so he was forced to flip out his phone and, against his better judgement, allow Google to identify his location. He soothed his conscience thinking it didn't really matter – the phone was an expensive burner notched down to expenses and therefore not traceable to him. Still, it grated.

From the satellite image he could tell when he was at the back of the tattoo parlour. Quickly he found what he was looking for – a manhole cover in the cobbles half concealed by a bin. He wondered what the hell he was doing. If he failed, Sinead would know about it when she saw Flipper staring at her from the heiress's cleavage. He didn't really fancy that.

So with a busted broom shaft he levered an electric conduit up and out of the manhole. He used the edge of the opening to bounce the shortened stick under his weight and was exceptionally pleased to feel an eventual give in the cable, as if ends had parted. He decided he could do no more, threw the shaft away, replaced the cover and dragged a bin over the top. He could hear a commotion behind, so he slipped through to the right and out onto a new street, conscious that his hands were filthy with fish waste. In due course he doubled back on himself to resume the seat he had vacated ten minutes earlier, peeling a few napkins out of a small metal dispenser. The waiter emerged with his hands held apologetically aloft.

"Another espresso?" Sam suggested.

"Sorry, we have problem," said the waiter. "Is problem with barista machine and ..." He opened and closed his hand above his head, struggling for the right word.

"The lights?"

Light, light, yes. Sorry, we must close."

"Ok," said Sam. "No worries."

He peeled off ten euros while watching the women emerge from the parlour, their heads shaking, trying to cover their felt-tipped chests. He composed a text: *No tattoos today*. He hit send. The phone buzzed back immediately and he smiled as he read: *Grumpy old fart*.

"ICI female approaching."

"Who is she?" Libby asked.

"Dunno," said the opso.

"Not a happy bunny," remarked the trooper.

The trooper edged his car closer and Libby got a proper view of the woman marching across the street to join the manager. Her face was indeed like a slapped arse.

"That's the owner of the safe house, where the kid is staying."

"This is all a bit odd, Libby."

"I know," she muttered distractedly.

They watched the manager attempt to walk the woman into a stroll in the gentle sun, but the woman was having none of it. She had clearly come out looking for a row. Libby and the opso watched as the manager gestured for her to keep the volume down, his palms flat towards the ground, basketball style, as he looked furtively around.

The operations manager asked the trooper, "Can you get sound?"

They watched the screens as the car moved again, the cameras realigned and the engine was killed. Although scratchy, they could just make out what was being said.

"Not tomorrow, not the next day, not next week. You tell that man that that little gobshite is to be out of my house today," she shouted.

The manager spoke clearly and calmly trying to placate the woman. "It will only be a few more days now. I understand, honestly I do, it's never easy having a stranger in the house, and he's a young fella and he's out of his comfort zone, so as a gesture for your trouble we'll double the allowance."

"You don't seem to hear what I'm telling you. You forget I was in Armagh and on the drip before you were even out of nappies. Now that sack of sticks is to be gone by this evenin'. Y'understand?"

The opso looked at the spook.

"Armagh?" Libby said.

"The women's jail. She looks about the right age."

"So she's the connection – not her son?"

"I don't know. You haven't told us anything about this part of the set-up," the opso said exasperated.

Libby realised she would be best to share a little. "The safe house, it seems, is just up that road. There's a couple in their late sixties living there with their son – who did two stretches for PIRA. They took in a kid by agreement with a person of interest. We think the kid is going to transport the car."

"So you thought that because the couple's son did time for the IRA they'd used his place for the safe house, but you didn't check out his parents?"

"I guess we didn't," Libby conceded, confused by the oversight.

"What's the son's name?"

"Liam Walsh. He looks pretty small-time, to be honest."

The opso nodded to one of the analysts who banged the name into the database.

"Four years for possession, then life for murder."

"We checked – he was more of an accessory. He handled the weapon afterwards but went down for the lot."

"Anything about his mother in there?"

"Nothing showing," said the analyst.

Libby sighed a little. "Father?"

"Nope."

"Model her face," the opso barked, now frustrated.

The analyst took a profile grab from the image being relayed by the trooper and they waited as his computer churned away.

"This isn't a choice, Deirdre," they heard the manager's voice harden. "You know how this thing works. You do your bit, we reimburse you what we can."

"Deirdre," the opso barked at the analysts. "Check known republicans in their sixties and seventies called Deirdre."

"I've done my bloody bit, more than," the older woman growled.

"This is getting serious." The manager tried to change tack, tried to lay down the law. "You know the score now."

"Are you seriously threatening me?" she hissed, seething. "I'll show you how serious this is, you little prick."

With that she marched off across the road, up the hill and into the house. The manager looked livid as he turned down the hill. Doing so he looked directly at the camera, his clenched jaw falling open as anger gave way to panic. His pace quickened and he began to trot down the pavement.

"He's clocked me," said the trooper, but everyone at base had seen it already.

The opso sighed and closed his eyes.

"Deirdre Rushe," said an excited analyst. "Face match confirmed. Six life sentences in 1973. Part of a bombing campaign at military bases in England."

There was silence in the room for a few moments.

"How did we miss that?" the opso snapped.

"Maybe we didn't," Libby muttered quietly. "Maybe we just weren't told."

The opso looked at Libby and could see she was heaving back anger. Perhaps she was going native, he thought. Such comments with implicit criticism of her own branch of the operation were not common.

Then the power play was set aside as another major problem presented itself.

He couldn't wait any longer. He dialled Sal and closed his eyes in the hope that she would answer.

"Hi, Sam," she chattered happily. "Unfortunately the girls have just gone for ice cream. They're having a ball."

"Ah, that's great. What's the weather been like?"

"Good, good, you know Northern Ireland, but it's grand for autumn and they have their wee wetsuits and the sun's out. There's not a lot of heat in it, though – sure, you know yourself. How are things ... there?"

Sal had never inquired as to where Sam was headed. What he looked like often deterred people from asking.

"Aye, no bother," he said. "Is she behaving?"

"She's great. A lovely young woman, honestly. They're getting along well together, they really are."

"Right, well, that's grand. I'll maybe try later, then – or tomorrow?"

"Any time, Sam, any time at all. They'll be back in about twenty minutes if you want to give it a go then?"

Sam looked up and saw the heiress's two friends walk out of their hotel. The heiress was nowhere to be seen.

"It might have to be later if that's ok?"

"That's grand, Sam. After dinner will be fine."

"Thanks a million, Sal." Sam drifted off a little as the call ended and he wondered where the women were going and where the heiress was.

He picked up his phone and logged into the web hosting service that the camera in her room was feeding to. There was an inevitable delay. He could see there was sixty per cent left on the battery assembly, which would get him through tonight and the next before he would need to replace anything. The image came through in moments and he was moderately alarmed to find there was nobody in the heiress's room. He could see that the bathroom door was closed, so he kept the image up for a few minutes hoping she would emerge.

Worried, he popped the phone in his pocket and decided to take a stroll through the hotel lobby in case she was having a drink there, but a quick tour proved fruitless. He went back outside and waited for the 4G to send and receive, and relaxed, momentarily, as steam bellowed from the now ajar bathroom door, and the heiress in a towel and turban pottered around the room. He protected her dignity, stuffed the phone away and took a walk.

———

"Get two bikes on the road."

The compromised trooper had already been told to extract.

The motorcycles were fitted with cameras and bikers never looked out of place on the north coast of Northern Ireland.

"What about the heli?" Libby asked. It wasn't her call to deploy hardware but she had a plummeting feeling about how things had gone.

"We can follow the manager on overt cameras. He's probably just going home," said the operations officer.

"Maybe we should lift him – before he can tell anyone else?"

"Send the plods in?"

Libby thought for a moment. She would need authorisation for that.

The opso was strangely reassuring. "He's experienced. He'll not do anything on the phone – he'll not want to place himself there. We've got breathing space because he'll want to relay any message face to face."

"We've only got eyes on the suspect vehicle now and nothing on the safe house."

The opso hesitated. "What are your concerns around the safe house?"

"I don't know – but then I wasn't aware Deirdre Rushe lived there."

"Right," said the opso. "Put the Gazelle up."

An alarm sounded and an analyst went through the motions of sending coordinates to the pilots. Five minutes later they heard the Gazelle's blades begin to turn and Libby relaxed just a fraction. She knew the heli would be overhead in a matter of minutes.

"Where are you sending it?"

"Harbour, ideally, then I'll release the car to the safe house."

"Ok."

It made sense. Even though the heli could operate effectively above hearing distance, it did no harm to keep it coastal where a helicopter was more likely to circle rather than a residential address.

"Coffee," barked the opso. "And get some food in here, please."

Libby agreed they were in for a long haul. The manager's arrival had unnerved everyone.

Ten minutes later a camera operator wearing a headset confirmed he was getting images from the Gazelle. He punched them up onto the screen on the left. The aerial view began to settle, and the opso ordered the car at the harbour to move towards the safe house for a drive-by and then circle back for a lay-up. Libby watched the car manoeuvre out of the spot it had been in for a few hours and tracked with it up the hill at a slow speed. As it passed the address she had reason to swear.

The door to the safe house opened and the young man stumbled out – not as if he'd been pushed but certainly as if he'd been told to clear off. He looked behind him in anger just short of defiance, stepped over the gate and stomped off.

"Get round again and pick him up," the opso ordered. "And where are the bloody bikes?"

"ETA fifteen minutes," came a cool head from the computer monitors.

"You're making me nervous," the opso whispered to Libby.

"I don't know what's going on," she said. "Just feels wrong."

"It does," was all he said back under his breath.

11

Sam sauntered back towards the hotel after half an hour, which was an hour too early. Eventually he flicked on the camera feed to find the heiress sweeping up a clutch bag, assessing her paintwork in the mirror and making for the door. Must be a special night, he thought, and readied himself for a follow to wherever she was planning to meet her friends.

The other women had headed left in the general direction of the Excelsior Hotel – their chosen holiday haunt, but the heiress emerged and crossed the road to a swanky-looking restaurant at the water's edge. Sam assumed her friends would join her in due course.

The location, however, was problematic. There were shrubs and bushes along the roadside that prevented him getting a sense of where she was sitting. The only clear view, in fact, was from the water, but he had no boat. He decided to wait for her friends to come back and then realised that she hadn't been carrying her tiny shiny handbag, which meant she no longer carried the tracker. Deprived of the means to find her if she did go AWOL, he looked around for height to try to get eyes on what she was doing, but aside from her own Hotel Riviera there was nothing overlooking the restaurant.

So Sam walked straight into the lobby and up the stairs, looking for a way to get onto a second-floor balcony that over-looked the street. The little veranda was empty, and he reck-oned the worst that could happen was that a waiter would appear and ask him what he wanted to drink. Once in position he relaxed when he found the back of her head and shoulders lounging against wicker outdoor furniture. She was sucking a tall cocktail through a straw two hundred metres away. Not ideal, but as close as Sam could manage.

It took another half hour of waiting, but eventually the heiress was joined at her table. Her arms extended upwards, hands out-turned in delight, as Ann Seeley's killer bent down to give her a kiss.

"Where is he?" Libby whispered.

The bikes were snarling around the streets hunting for the kid and the images were being relayed back with break up to the monitors in the ops room. The Gazelle was transmitting the harbour view with the car park and the roof of the suspect car clearly visible.

"Standby," came a muffled voice on the radio network. One of the bike ops could be heard but he was moving too fast for his image to get through consistently. And then it popped up in pixelated boxes, a young man with his back to the camera. "That him?" the same voice asked over the net.

"Affirmative," said Libby. "Is he walking funny?"

"He does seem to be," said the opso. "Lactic acid build-up maybe? How long's he been cooped up in there?"

Libby knew the opso was fishing for information she hadn't yet volunteered, so she opted to say nothing. They watched him gradually iron out the stiffness in his limbs as he hammered around the town aimlessly. Various camera angles were offered between the two bikes that moved around him.

"Is he talking to himself?" the opso asked.

"He's muttering. Looks raging," Libby replied.

"I don't think he knows what to do. She's obviously chucked him out, and the manager's just scarpered."

"Seems that way," Libby said, deep in thought.

"If he's as cross as he looks, he could be ripe for turning. Maybe bring him in, be nice to him for a while, get him to tell us what's going on?"

The thought had crossed Libby's mind. Any informer was an asset, but that wasn't her decision to make.

The opso was suddenly full of helpful suggestions. "We could secure the car, hand it over to the engineers and it would still be a success. We get a tout, a major find, and everyone stays safe."

"Let me make a call," Libby said.

***

Sam could make out lobster. The pink shells were tilted in display by two waiting staff as they approached the table, all part of some opulent act to make everyone feel special.

He had no choice but to sit still. If he waded in and split them up, there would be claws everywhere and the heiress's father would be compromised as a snooper. Sam wrestled with the notion of calling her father to fill him in but decided that things might get messy and the fewer people who knew about the presence of a murderer on a Venetian island the better.

Where Delaney had sprung from Sam had no idea, but it was obviously all part of some well-plotted plan. Though how she had coaxed her friends into becoming complicit in the deceit was confusing. Surely no proper friend would support a dirty weekend with a murderer?

Drinks were delivered with incredible regularity and there was dessert with sparklers, then they strolled twenty feet to the railings to look out over Venice as the sun set. He could see their heads coming together often – kissing like teenagers. Sam watched with resignation. He should have realised this encounter was a possibility – and he wondered whether the father had guessed as much. Why send Sam to mind his kid if there was no real risk?

Eventually the pair rose and arm in arm they bundled out of the open-air restaurant into the street where they had a long, lingering kiss and seemed to settle on a destination. He watched as Delaney steered the heiress towards a restaurant pontoon and shouted to one of the sleek white river taxis.

Sam sprang to his feet and bounded round into the hallway and down the stairs. He crossed a small roundabout and blasted over another road just in time to see the varnished transom of the boat dip into the water as the driver opened the throttle. He hunted around for another taxi to follow but the dock was silent. The only noise came from the street behind him and the boat that was streaking into the distance.

Anthony swore the old bitch up and down every street he walked. She said she'd demanded Grim come and see him and Grim had obviously refused. He'd lay on a bed for almost a month and nobody had given a bollocks. He'd done what had been asked of him and still it wasn't enough. That old woman was a hard, wrinkled witch, he thought.

Worse still, he was embarrassed. Treated like a child, thrown out, just as his mother had done a few times. "If you can't live by my rules, you can live somewhere else." He'd always gone back to his mum – he'd had no choice, no money, no friends worth talking about, no options. But there was no way he was going to go back to that old tart.

He had believed in Grim – that the man would help him rise through the ranks. All hope and respect was gone now. Anthony's loyalty turned to deeper hatred with every step. He wanted to hurt Grim but had no idea where to start. He hunted for signs to tell him where the hell he was ambling about, growing angrier. And then the first pang of despair came as he realised it was late in the day and he had nowhere to sleep, no money for a taxi or a bus, no food and no water.

And then he remembered that he did have one thing.

Sam ran beyond the ferry terminal. He had no idea where Delaney was staying, no idea where the river taxi was taking them, no idea what to do next. He watched the stern light on the taxi fade among the thousands of lights now illuminating San Marco until eventually a boat stuttered past and he yelled at it to come in.

"Taxi?" the smoking helmsman inquired.

"Yes, taxi," said Sam, incredulous. "What did you think I wanted?"

He kicked the gunwale away from the pontoon just before he stepped aboard and turned to the driver. "I need you to go as fast as you can. I will pay, ok?"

"Ok," said the driver, moderately amused by Sam's urgency.

"See that light? Of another taxi? I need you to go there, fast, ok? Flat out."

"Ok." The driver shrugged but seemed in no hurry to turn the boat and make pursuit.

"Look, hurry up, this is serious. I need you to go quickly." Sam's voice fell and the driver seemed to get the message, gunning reverse and revving the engine into forward as the stern wave caught her.

"Faster, please," Sam said.

"I not see this light," shouted the driver over the drone of the engine, shaking his head as if Sam's request was pointless.

In truth, Sam couldn't see it any more either.

Libby used the secure line and was met with a bark.

"What is it?"

"I need to make you aware of developments."

"Well?"

"At 1600 a known head turned up in the town just metres from the suspect vehicle."

"Who?"

"Paul Hagan."

There was a silence for a moment.

"Hagan, the manager?"

"Yes."

"Ok."

Libby could imagine the wheels turning.

"That all?"

"No. Hagan approached the safe house, but before he got there a woman came out to him."

"From the safe house?" Her superior sounded mildly alarmed.

"Yes."

"Did you ... identify this woman?"

"Yes," said Libby proudly. "She is Deirdre Rushe, a former Provisional IRA member who—"

"I know who Deirdre Rushe is!" snapped her superior.

"Sorry," she said softly.

"Do others in the DET know her identity?"

"Yes," she said, confused. She sensed this was not good news.

"So what happened between the manager and Rushe?"

"They had an argument and he tried to persuade her to keep the kid in the safe house, but she was livid and threw him out."

"Threw the kid out?"

"Yes."

"Where is he now then?"

"Just walking around the town talking to himself."

"Not good, Libby."

She waited for direction, but all she could hear was a hand tapping a desk. To fill the silence she resorted to desperation. "We could capitalise on this maybe? Lift him – turn him? Send in the engineers? That would be a result, wouldn't it?" she ventured, clutching at someone else's ideas despite her reservations.

"Not the smartest suggestion I've ever heard," he said, and her heart sank.

She was always worried that one bad move could lead to her judgement being questioned and an end to her progress.

"Stay on the kid and keep me in the loop. Every turn. I may want patched in at some point."

Libby left the call utterly despondent, convinced her career was over.

Her superior lifted a different phone.

They docked in San Marco, Sam dispensing notes like confetti upon the taxi driver. He stepped ashore tempted to start running but reminded himself to assess, to put himself in their shoes. They were drunk, they were evidently amorous and carefree. Where would they go? Sam assumed it would be to

Delaney's hotel – wherever that was, but perhaps they'd decided on another drink. Maybe he wanted her so pissed that he could do whatever he wanted.

Sam walked around the open-air bars, combing each for a drunk Irish couple. It was still warm, so he looked outside along the entire length of the quay – which took exactly one hundred minutes, then he started scouting indoors. Three hours after he'd lost them, and now deeply concerned, he stood by the water's edge and closed his eyes.

What would Delaney do? Sam struggled to put his head in the space of a psychopath. If Delaney wanted to do sick shit, he'd hardly do it in his own hotel room, Sam reasoned. A dead woman in his own room? No, if he was going to kill her, Sam bet he'd take her someplace with no association to him. The easiest way would be to make sure there was no body found. Plenty of water in Venice – maybe he was going to drown her. Then, of course, maybe he didn't want to kill her at all.

Sam looked at his watch. Three hours twenty minutes. "Think," he said aloud, trying to calm his mind. "*Think*."

Then, with urgency, he produced his phone and patched into the web host, entering his password. And there she was lying back on her own bed, in her own hotel room, elbows angled, head propped up at the shoulders staring at Delaney – whose back was to the camera. His hand was raised, like he was taking the oath of office. She was transfixed, as if it was some kind of ceremony.

And Sam was miles away, on the wrong island, separated from his charge by water.

Anthony turned suddenly, a moderate warmth creeping into him. He still didn't know where he was, but he knew where he was going.

Libby and the opso watched his about-turn.

"What's he at?" she said to nobody, knowing in her heart exactly where he was going.

"Get one of the bikes to the bottom of the town ready to pick him up," ordered the opso.

The temperature in the room cracked up a notch as a dozen eyes flickered between the Gazelle's feed and those of the bikes.

Libby left the room to report in.

Sam began to run east along the quay, unsure of where exactly he was going. He couldn't see any taxis, and in any case he hadn't brought enough cash to pay for one. The passenger ferry was slow, still it was an option, but he needed something more direct – something faster. He looked at Lido Island and his trot broke into a canter along the ancient quay. He skirted the edge of temporary fencing erected around a landing point for superyachts. Some had security guards outside, others appeared to be shrouded in darkness. A notion coursed through his mind and then he dismissed it – getting arrested would help nobody.

He ran close to the edge giving himself a view of the water below – hoping to spot a boat tied up and easy to pinch. There was nothing. Then ahead he noticed movement on the seaward side of one of the massive private boats surrounded in fencing. Was it a temporary pontoon? He kept running until desperation made up his mind. He hoped the iPhone in his pocket was as water resistant as advertised and dived gracefully into the water.

He pulled hard beneath the surface; long, hauling strokes with enormous kicks to keep him submerged and drive him forward. He couldn't see a thing but when he reached the surface he found himself a lot shorter than he had hoped for.

Still, he was close enough to see a tender bobbing merrily against a retractable walkway of steps. It wasn't the sort of thing the yacht's owner was likely to travel in, more of a crew work-boat for cleaning the hull and windows.

The yacht itself wasn't in darkness but he couldn't see anyone on watch. The breeze puffed gently offshore, so he quietly breaststroked to the rubber dinghy and paused, listening for any movement. When satisfied, he hauled himself over the side and lay in the solid part of the boat for a few moments untying the bowline knot that held the painter, and then he made his profile as low as possible as the little boat began to drift from the big one. He wanted to start the engine and get going but forced himself to wait until he was as far out of earshot as possible: one hundred metres, one fifty, two hundred. When sure that none of the city lights were casting a beam over him, he leaned back and looked at the outboard, quickly identifying the fuel line and tracing the electrical starter cable to the console.

No keys.

He went back to the engine, ripped the electric start off the side of the hood, isolated the positive connection inside a discarded rubber glove that had been lying in the hull and pulled the manual rip cord. The engine shuddered to life first time and Sam increased the revs gently by easing a lever at the side of the hood forward. Because of its design the boat didn't have a manual steering arm, so he set the engine in the centre and guided it by leaning the boat from side to side. He kept his eyes on the superyacht for a while but nothing seemed to stir. Pleased, he just kept going, increasing the speed and revs as he moved further away.

Anthony went as far as he could and took a wrong turn by a

golf course, which brought him alongside a beach – a fair distance from the harbour. It was getting cold and kids were being told to gather their stuff and come on. There was moaning on the breeze, which irritated him. He had never been taken to the beach – not ever.

He trudged back in the direction he had come. It took him another twenty minutes to get to the harbour, where he glanced around before crouching by the Ford and looking under the wheel arch. He stuck his arm in, got it covered in rust and muck, and tried to remember what the man had said. It wasn't driver's side – was it? He tried the back wheel, then stood and walked around the car before kneeling by the passenger-side tyre, feeling around instead of looking. At last his fingers caught something in the taut metal spring. The key – wedged, as described – between the hoops of the suspension. He whipped it out and let himself in via the nearest door.

Sam didn't want to waste any time but he didn't want to leave the stolen tender in plain sight either. He turned the boat and motored a short distance away from the hotel, turning into a canal at the first opportunity. Up ahead was a small walkway with steps up from the water, so he lashed the boat to a lacing eye, skipped over a short fence and walked quickly over the bridge. He fired up the phone. Delaney could be seen clearly now lying beside the heiress – who appeared to be falling asleep, wrapped in his arms. His head rested against hers.

Sam walked it through. He'd bust down the door, grab Delaney, deal with him and extract. Which would have been fine but for the fact that Sam stepped off the walkway straight into the brawny arms of two police officers.

"Whoa," said the opso, suddenly on edge at what the kid had done. "Pull the bikes back to at least one hundred metres. Let's swap them out now for cars, please, and get a van in the area too."

Libby came into the operations room and looked immediately up to the screens. "He's in the car?" The encroaching darkness prevented her seeing clearly.

"Yes. I think our safe moment of arrest has probably passed," said the opso. Not quite *I told you so*, but not generous either.

Libby ignored it. "He's in the passenger seat?"

"Yes," confirmed the opso.

"Ok," she said, curious.

"We need to think about a cordon," the opso muttered. "What do the higher powers say?"

"Let's see," she said, which was sufficiently ambiguous. In fact, all her superior had done was listen and hang up. She knew her boss would have patched himself in by now – watching with them, watching the kid, listening to everything.

———

Sam couldn't understand the officers. He assumed he'd been stopped for stealing the dinghy but neither police officer so much as looked towards the boat at his back. He'd dried off a lot, but his shirt and jeans were still sticking to his body, which wasn't lost on the cops.

"I don't know what you're saying," he kept repeating.

Eventually one of the cops relented and attempted a little English. "No in water," he said, shaking a finger at Sam.

"What?"

"No on bridge."

"You wha?"

Sam was astonished to see them produce a plastic cable tie and attempt to loop it over one of his wrists.

"Don't do that," he said, offering them advice. "Seriously, please don't be silly. Don't be doing that."

He wrestled his arm free and the other policeman actually placed his hand on his sidearm. Sam couldn't believe what was happening.

"Look, there's somewhere I need to be right now, and I'm sorry for whatever it is I've done but I can't let you stick that thing on me."

"Is no swim here," said the cop again, and it crossed Sam's mind that he might be being lifted because they thought he'd been in the canal. "Bridge," the cop nodded with his head, "is private."

"The bridge is private," Sam repeated, flabbergasted that such minor misdemeanours were sufficient cause to be banged up.

"*Si*." The cop elongated his confirmation and took another step towards Sam.

He had no choice. When the cop again reached for his wrist, Sam used the momentum to take the officer's arm at the elbow and leaned back on both feet – falling to his arse while spinning the cop into the canal behind him. Sam rolled to his front and onto his feet and ran towards the second cop, who had panicked and drawn his Beretta. Sam could see from his stricken face that the man had no intention of firing his weapon, so he simply stuck his shoulder into his chest and knocked him flat before taking off through a series of small gardens. He leapt a fence and then had to climb a gate, and realised that he should have stayed on the other side of the canal where there was an actual road. It did make him wonder where the cops had sprung from.

As he rustled through hedges and around garden furniture, he heard windows opening above him, and then shouts as people were roused from their evening routines. By the time he got as far as the road, he could hear sirens coming from the direction he wanted to go, so he was forced to take off up a narrow street full of poorly parked cars – away from the heiress's hotel and deeper into the island of Lido.

Anthony sat with his hands tucked under his armpits; the car key between his legs. He found himself thinking of his mum and whether she was wondering where he was. Probably not. She might have reported him missing, but she might not. They had grown exhausted of one another – he of her submission to a life of fags, TV and cheap wine, and she of his restlessness, his willingness to get involved with what she saw simply as a bunch of older, manipulative criminals.

They hardly spoke these days. When he came in she just looked blankly at him before he went upstairs. They went through the motions: she heated oven grub for him every night, he mostly ate it; she washed his clothes, he wore them. Yet suddenly, in the car seat in the cold, he missed her.

The car smelt faintly of the gardening section at the back of the general stores near his estate. He often went there to buy compost for the weed he and a pal used to grow in the attic – but that was before he had joined Grim's group. All that was forbidden now. He remembered ordering the seeds, checking them every day under the cellophane as it condensed like the window of the car in which he sat. He breathed in and, eventually, drifted off to sleep.

The secure line went off for the third time that night. Libby's superior was the only one left in his building.

"Hello."

"Hello. Well, he seems to be asleep."

"In the vehicle," he remarked, conveying an unusual hint of bewilderment.

"I suppose he has nowhere else to go, and it's autumn and it's cold."

"Leave him."

"Do we ... need to maybe think of a cordon?"

"Not a wonderfully intelligent suggestion."

"Sorry, I just—"

"The whole point is to see where they're taking it and who else is involved," her boss snapped back. "In the grand scheme of things it doesn't really change the goal – does it?"

"No, I suppose it doesn't," said Libby.

"Erecting a cordon would demonstrate that we knew it was there."

"Yes, of course," she said, admonished and embarrassed, yet grateful for the cover of the decision being taken from her.

"Let's see what he does next."

"Ok. Thank you."

It was a small island, so Sam had no idea where all the police were coming from, but they were swarming the streets. He realised, with reluctance, that the darkest areas of Lido were the canals themselves. The middle of the waterways were lit by the street lights well enough to allow taxis and gondolas to proceed safely, but at the edges of the water's surface – in the few feet beneath where people walked and drove – there was enough shadow to keep concealed.

Slowly Sam lowered himself back into the water and gently made his way by fastening his fingers between the foundation blocks of the city.

Within minutes he realised that the police were afloat too. The first hint came with a sweeping yellow light. He could see its track hit a wall – telling him that a boat was coming around a corner. He could hear its engine rise and falter and presumed that the police were methodically checking every nook and cranny of the canal walls.

He turned and swam hard for a few moments until he came to a small day boat tied to the wall. It had a canvas cover drawn over it, which he debated clambering beneath but chose instead to use the hull's V shape to his advantage. From the bow he worked his way back between the boat and the wall, ducking under the inflatable fenders that protected the boat from the stone. Then, without straining the mooring lines too tightly, he wedged his shoulders between the hull and the wall – the gunwale of the boat almost completely concealing his head from anyone searching on foot, while the space at the waterline allowed his shoulders to do the work of the fenders and rest between the fibreglass and the bank.

He braced as the police vessel puttered towards him, the yellow sweep meticulous, the natter and communication sounding professional. The beam came to rest on his hiding place and he could hear the engine slow. Officers deliberated and then he exhaled deeply as the wash of the police boat buffeted the day sailor sideways, compressing his ribcage. The police came alongside and began using torches to examine the small craft. Then Sam heard the tearing of Velcro as they ripped open the access points in the boat's cover. He could hear the thunk and clatter of their torches through the hull when they peered beneath the tarpaulin. After about five minutes they seemed satisfied that nobody was hiding in the boat and he heard them sticking the fur teeth of the Velcro back together before finally moving off.

Sam remained where he was, conscious that his body temperature would continue to slowly drop but reasonably confident that the canal was above ten degrees, and he knew he could stick it out for a good while. He'd been trained for exactly this type of hardship.

Twenty minutes later a second patrol boat came along, this time with a white light and not as thorough. Sam knew this crew would realise that another boat had already covered this route, but it didn't stop them hovering alongside Sam's boat for a few heart-stopping minutes before driving on.

And all of this was costing the heiress time and, potentially, her life.

12

"What the fuck is going on?"

The boss was astonished that this contact had called on the estate phone. "What do you mean?" He gently placed aside his alarm and listened.

"Your chief of staff has just appeared in the town."

The boss thought for a moment. This meant all sorts of things. "What town?" he said, knowing full well what town the contact meant.

"Let's not."

"Ok," said the boss slowly.

"The kid's in the car. Why's the kid in the car?"

The boss had no answer but his proclivity for silence was useful in such circumstances.

"The place isn't ready. The papers aren't even there yet."

The boss just breathed down the line, computing.

"Can he take direction in the car?"

The boss waited a full ten seconds then said, "No."

"What sort of shitshow are you running? Has your use expired?"

"Did you just ring to tear me a new one?" the boss asked eventually.

"I may as well have, given how little you seem to know about your own people."

"You leave my people to me," he said softly and gently cradled the handset. He could not recall ever having been so angry.

By dawn Sam could almost hear his own body shaking. He was creating ripples on the surface. There hadn't been a foot or water patrol in well over an hour, and he had to assume that the police had moved their attention elsewhere. The last thing he wanted was to be climbing out of the canal just as the locals were climbing out of bed.

He emerged, shook like a Labrador and tried a gentle jog in an attempt to get his limbs functioning – but was restricted by his jeans.

The Hotel Riviera was just a few hundred yards away. He crept down the towpath, past his own stolen dinghy, which remained undisturbed, and crossed a wider footpath. Less than five minutes later he was knocking, painfully, on the door of the hotel; his chilled knuckles just about sufficiently defrosted to begin sending signals to his brain again. An old man rose grindingly from an armchair close to the door. The well-dressed gent pressed a button and admitted Sam, who thanked him and strode straight for the stairs opposite. If the old guy had any queries about Sam's residency – or indeed his wet clothes – he didn't pose them.

Two floors up Sam placed his feet at an angle and one shoulder against the door while his left hand pressed down on the ornate handle – no point in battling two lock bolts when one would do. He crouched a little at the knee and summoned all the explosive power he could find, engaged his glutes and lats and forced the door up and in.

It didn't take long for the dry old timber to begin to crack. Kicking a door in is always noisy, slow and often unsuccessful; bits of frames give way before locks or shims, but Sam knew that steady pressure in the right place was likely to reap better results, and the heiress's door opened with minimal noise.

He could hear a scuffle inside and turned around a separating wall to find Delaney scampering to his feet, dressed as he had been the night before. Sam wheeled to find the heiress tied, face up, to the bed. Her hands and feet appeared to be bound under the frame itself by a mixture of her own belts and clothes. She looked disturbingly peaceful and initially Sam thought she was dead until her eyes pulled focus to follow him. Then her gaze rotated to Delaney – who was trying to work out how to get out of the room.

Sam instinctively went to the heiress, tearing the belt that was forcing her arms over her head. As he did so Delaney scampered past his back. Sam turned and reached out to grab him but his blood was flowing too slowly, his muscles were contracted and his joints chilled stiff. Delaney managed to make it out the door. The belt came away in Sam's hand, which left him stumbling backwards and baffled, and he suddenly realised that the heiress could free herself if she so wished, which only served to confuse him further.

He put it down to some sort of kinky shit and instead grabbed the hidden camera from the light fitting and took off after Delaney.

Anthony's jaw chattered loudly with the cold. He kept thinking about that smiling weirdo who always sat at the back of meetings and said nothing. Anthony had seen him from the window

– sure what did it matter at that stage? The old woman already hated him, so he could look out all he wanted. He'd seen them argue, the weirdo and the woman, and whatever they'd said the result was that he'd been chucked out on the street.

Through the condensation he could make out movement – people walking towards a building. It looked like an ice cream shop but it was probably serving food too. Anthony was starving but he had no money. Grim hadn't even given him a tenner. He was foundered, angry and he felt like crying, which shamed him. He was supposed to be doing a big job and instead he was sitting in a freezing car with no cash, watching families go for breakfast. He wanted breakfast in a café. He wanted to hurt Grim so much. He hated that bastard.

He thought about shooting him, but he didn't know where the guns were hidden. He thought about setting his house on fire. Then he thought about the car he was in. This car was important. It had been delivered, at night, by country boggers. It was to be taken to a very specific place. It could have weapons in it for all he knew, so Grim wouldn't want it anywhere near him. Anthony reckoned that might be a good plan – drive the car to Grim's house and leave it right outside. That would tighten the fucker. Then Anthony might ring the cops and tell them – he might even post the key through Grim's letter box.

Anthony brightened at the notion, unsure as to whether he actually had the balls to see it through, but then he remembered that cars have heaters.

"Ambulance!" Sam shouted to the old man as he skidded through the lobby. "Room 212, get an ambulance!"

The old man looked astonished but nodded and made for the reception desk as Sam threw himself out the door. He caught sight of Delaney's white shirt rounding a corner close to the restaurant he'd eaten in the night before. Sam took off after him, but when he reached the corner he could see Delaney running towards a group of police, huddled and probably very pissed off after a night of fruitless hunting for a night-swimming tourist. Sam cut immediately right. He crossed the bridge he'd walked over less than ten minutes previously and had an idea. If Delaney was headed east, Sam could avoid the cops and still track him in parallel, by boat. And sitting, eager as a puppy for a walk, was the very tender he had stolen from the superyacht.

Once outside the canal network Sam motored quietly in the open lagoon, the morning light still not entirely exposing him. As each block of housing passed by he could make out Delaney in the pool of the street lamps, walking east while regularly checking his rear oblivious that Sam was watching him.

Block after block came between Sam and his view of Delaney. Wherever he was going it felt like only a matter of time before Sam would have to get out of the boat and chase him again.

And then as the red rim of the new day cracked over Italy, Sam got his first break of the week: Delaney turned towards him. His attention was over his shoulder, looking for Sam at his rear, not expecting him to be afloat, right in front of him.

Libby couldn't stand at rest. She felt the full weight of the opso's stare.

"I'm waiting for direction from Belfast," she said.

The opso didn't respond, which was almost more irritating than it would have been if he had.

Libby couldn't say any more – she knew her superior could hear them and see the feeds, but it was a one-way arrangement.

What is he going to do? she thought. What would I do in his shoes?

"If he'd been left a phone in the car, he'd probably have used it by now," she reasoned aloud. "We have a working assumption that he has had no communication with anyone else. We don't believe he is working to any original plan. He appears to have been thrown out of the safe house and, therefore, he's unpredictable. If the car moves, we follow."

The opso turned to her now and spoke for the first time in over an hour. "We follow a laden vehicle in traffic?"

"We do. We see where it's going."

"Your call," was all the opso said, but it sounded like, "Your fault."

———

Delaney made a track like a sailmaker's stitch – his weave dictated by his aft-turned head – paranoid, afraid, desperate. Sam watched him intently, content to drift on the tideless lagoon, happy to see where Delaney would land.

He stuttered around some trees, oblivious to Sam's presence, and then began to pat his hip pockets, his chest and his arse. Sam assumed he was searching for his phone and when he raised his head to the sky it seemed reasonable to assume that he had left it at the heiress's hotel. Delaney paused momentarily, debating what to do next. Then he noticed a small pontoon with a walkway from the road. Sam immediately knew what he was thinking – he'd get a river taxi off the island of Lido. Easy-peasy.

Sam gently opened the throttle on his stolen dinghy and made sure he got there first. He came alongside the pontoon, his back turned to the walkway, holding a cleat to keep the boat stationary.

The gloom had all but lifted to reveal a small island, about one hundred metres away. It looked abandoned – no lights burned on it – only the dawn had revealed its presence.

"Señor?" he heard at his back.

Sam sat still and waited.

"S'cusé?" Delaney evidently had no Italian.

Sam kept his back turned and used his free hand to beckon Delaney aboard. Easy-peasy.

Espadrilles was all he could think as he caught Delaney's step from the corner of his eye. Sam despised espadrilles and the people who wore them. His quarry wobbled to sit on one of the inflated tanks behind him and only when settled did he lift his head to look at his driver.

"Hello, Delaney," Sam said with a genuine smile, delighted to take the fare.

"You want pancakes?" Sal asked the girls.

"Can I have Nutella on them?" Molly asked.

"Chocolate, for breakfast?"

"Please, Mummy."

"Ok. Isla, what would you like?"

"Sausies and toast. Please."

"You've very good manners, Isla."

"Thank you," Isla said, in the voice of Shaggy from *Scooby Doo*.

Sal laughed. She was enjoying Isla's company, as was Molly. They played contentedly – often just drawing or cutting things out. And they were hardy too; plunging in the waves for longer than Sal really thought sensible, but they never seemed to feel the chill.

Sal ordered and then wondered about Isla's dad. He hadn't called back as he'd promised. She didn't know the man, but that somehow didn't strike her as being like him. She couldn't help bundling a little nosiness into concern.

"Isla, what's your daddy doing? Do you think he would mind if we rang him so you could speak to him?"

"No," was all she replied, which wasn't entirely what Sal wanted.

She couldn't help being curious. "What does he work at?"

"He works on boats," Isla said.

"Oh? Abroad?"

"What's abroad?"

"Overseas – in a different country."

"Sometimes we sail to other countries," Isla said.

"Do you?" Sal said, surprised. "Where?"

"Everywhere. Round the world. Once we rescued people from the sea and brought them to Ireland."

Sal dismissed the comment as fanciful seven-year-old witter. "So when your daddy goes away, does he work on boats?"

"Yes," said Isla, but it was clear to Sal that Isla didn't know and probably hadn't thought about it before.

"I thought he was in the army or something," said Sal, knowing she was probing too far.

Isla said nothing.

"Maybe not," Sal drifted, cross at herself for having listened to gossip and for her conceited intrusion. "He just, sort of, looks like that. Anyway, would you like to ring him?"

"Can I?" Isla's little face brightened.

"Here." Sal fumbled in her bag for her phone, her thumb slipping around the screen to release it, and then hit recent calls and dialled.

Isla placed the handset to her ear and waited and waited. Eventually she began to speak, watched by Sal and Molly. "Hi, Daddy, it's Isla. Hope you're ok. Love you." She was about to return the phone to Sal's outstretched hand when a thought hit her and she whipped it back, turning to try and grab some privacy. "Oh, Daddy, were you in the army? Love you." She hung up.

Sal scrunched her eyes in shame as the sausages arrived.

Some people get so scared that they actually can't move. It doesn't happen often but when it does life for an assailant becomes incredibly simple. Such was the reaction of Delaney as he stared at Sam, mouth slightly open, his mind hopping hurdles, ears pinned back like a hare caught in lamplight.

Sam had let go of the cleat as soon as the espadrilles had landed in the dinghy, and by the time everything had registered with Delaney they'd drifted more than six feet from the jetty. Sam gently opened the throttle as Delaney stared, agape, unmoving. Sam stared back, alert to sudden movements – a dive for the tide or an attack, but Delaney plainly didn't have the wherewithal. Sam felt no need to talk but he did think as abductions went it was remarkably straightforward. Easy-peasy.

Within two minutes he had rounded the nearby island and found an old landing point on the lagoon side, shielded from the shore of Lido.

It was only when he stepped ashore that Delaney spoke. "You're not going to leave me here, are you?"

"Looks like a nice place," remarked Sam, who reckoned if Delaney simply thought he was to be abandoned it might make the next fifteen minutes easier.

"But, it's … the plague island."

Sam hesitated. "It's what?"

"It's where they sent the lepers and the plague victims to die."

"When?"

"During the plague." Delaney was regaining his composure.

"Silly boy," Sam remarked from the small landing quay.

"What?" Delaney was sitting in the dinghy, apparently unable or unwilling to move.

"To google a place you intend to commit murder," he said. "Leaves a trail for police."

"Commit murder?"

"Let's not mess about, Delaney. You had that girl tied up and ready to be your next victim. You're a woo-woo and you're sick."

"I was helping her."

"Helping her to die."

"That's what she wants."

"Look, Delaney, I've been trailing her for days. She's happy with her mindless mates. There's nothing wrong with her – apart from being a bit dim."

"She's troubled, in pain." Delaney was beginning to adopt an air of intellectual superiority.

"Get out of the dinghy, Delaney."

Delaney sat where he was, defiant and attempting to take the lead in the negotiations. "You can't possibly understand ..."

"You can't swim, can you?" Sam whispered through Delaney's pontificating.

"What a woman like that is going through ..."

Sam reached down and grabbed the rope that ran around the dinghy. He straightened his back, lifted the side of the boat high into the air and deposited Delaney deep into the lagoon. There was a sputtering and a slapping when he bobbed to the surface, his hands patting the water pointlessly as he tried to find a way to stay afloat. Sam whipped the dinghy up onto the bank and took one of the oars from its holder. He turned the blade flat and gave Delaney a hefty slap on the head with it.

"Please," was all Delaney could manage.

Sam rested the blade on his shoulder, but as Delaney made a grab for it he applied his weight to the pole and levered the flailing man under. He held him there for twenty seconds, then let him pop up. As he did so he felt a vibration from his pocket. He ignored it but marvelled for a moment in appreciation of a phone that had survived so many hours submersion.

Delaney began to plead and Sam dunked him again.

When he came up he asked, "Is she drugged?"

"What?" Delaney managed.

Sam rested the blade on Delaney's shoulder to stop it slipping off his juddering head and dunked him again. Third time lucky, he thought.

"No!" Delaney spat when he surfaced.

"So why didn't she move?"

Delaney lashed around. He wouldn't be able to keep it up for long. "She wanted to die. I was helping them."

"How many were there?" asked Sam, never having considered that there may have been more.

"Just two," Delaney said, but Sam couldn't work out whether he was lying or not – there was too much splutter to make sense of it.

"So how did you get her to lie sedated for you when she could easily have freed herself on the bed?"

"Because she wanted it – I was helping her, you idiot."

That earned Delaney a good long lungful of lagoon water. It took him a few bokes to clear it when Sam eventually raised the oar.

"She's hypnotised," Delaney pleaded, coughing.

Sam almost laughed at his own stupidity. Of course. "That's how you got her to change her evidence," he stated.

Down Delaney went.

Sam was deep in thought now as his mark began to drown in front of him. A question occurred. He rose the oar. "Your funny tapping on the bench of the dock, that was your trigger to put her in a trance?"

But Delaney was a lost cause, now only surfacing momentarily. Sam looked around at the island. It was overgrown, forgotten perhaps. A leper colony – fitting, he thought. He looked at Delaney and debated letting him flounder, but he had more questions and didn't want a body to be discovered floating – there were too many boats around. Man's not a donkey, he thought. Why carry him when he can crawl?

Sam proffered the oar and Delaney used the last of his energy to grab it. Sam pulled him to the bank and rolled him onto land where he heaved and barked, croaking out brown spume.

Sam talked absently. "So Loopy Loo – she's hypnotised too. That's why she's such a dope."

Delaney managed a confused look.

"Your wife," Sam explained.

Delaney said nothing, because he couldn't. Sam helped him clear the last by kicking him hard in the stomach.

"Were there others, Delaney?" Sam crouched to his ear. "Last chance before you go back in the drink."

"One more," Delaney admitted with a heavy breath.

"What was her name?"

"Audrey," said Delaney.

"Audrey *what*?" said Sam, frustrated.

"Kavanagh."

"Ok, Delaney, on your hands and knees, then. Let's see where the lepers lived."

Sam looked at the crawling mass and took a little pleasure that his espadrilles had floated off.

"Snapper's back," came a rasp over the radio net.

"What's he doing?" Libby's exhaustion had set her on edge.

"Dawn shot of the harbour, looks like."

"Brilliant," said Libby flatly. "What about the kid. What's he doing?"

"You can see what he's doing," clipped the opso in similar humour.

"He's getting out – look. Why's he getting out of the car?"

"Piss, maybe?"

"He's going round the front."

"Uh-huh," said the opso drily.

"Shit, he's going to get in the driver's side. He's going to drive off."

The opso shook himself and began barking. "Standby, everyone, ready for a follow." He took his hand off the transmitter and turned to the woman directing the helicopter. "Get the Gazelle in the air."

The whole team heard the signal. The aircraft would be up in fewer than eight minutes.

"Where's he going?" Libby muttered.

Sam wedged open the old barn door to an enormous red-brick building. He put his foot to Delaney's arse and propelled him through it. It was pitch-black inside. He pulled out the phone, now down to thirteen per cent battery, and swiped the light on. The walls tunnelled ahead into darkness in perfect symmetry, like a railway track at dusk. What an incredibly dark place to end your days, he thought; lepers and the dying lining the edges, moaning and pleading for mercy, flashed through his mind. It would have been like a field hospital after a major attack, but merciless to the agony.

"You can't leave me here," Delaney said, almost as incredulous as Sam was at the notion that he shouldn't.

He beat Delaney into the dry building, sweeping ahead with the torch to get his bearings before switching off the light to preserve power.

Delaney began to moan, suddenly very afraid.

Sam just hit him with the oar and kept him moving.

"What are you going to do with me?"

"Keep crawling," was all he said, but Sam still didn't really know.

Anthony sat in the driver's seat and with his new sense of purpose set about playing with the heater to get himself warm enough to drive. He twisted the dial to red, flicked the selector to chest level and put the key in the ignition.

Then he stopped. What had the culchie said? Turn the key a weird way. Yeah. Free the steering lock – had he said that? Was it backwards? Turn the key backwards. Yeah.

Anthony turned the key backwards.

He jiggled the wheel.

Free.

Then he turned the key forward to start the engine and the heater fan.

And he ended up in the café after all.

Libby stared at the monitors unable to speak.

Every op in the room sat motionless.

The screen flickered. Then the image came back, utterly altered in a split second.

The opso kicked in – calm, professional, thinking fast. "Extract, extract, extract. Slowly. Return to base."

"We should help," Libby whispered.

"Over to civilian staff now," the opso said quietly in her ear. "We need to get the fuck out. You know that."

"Ambulances," she said.

"Not from us," the opso said. "We were not there," he said firmly.

"No," she said, still in shock.

"Get the heli back before it gets anywhere near that town," he barked to his team.

Sam snapped the light back on and was surprised at how far into the building they had come. The phone shone in Delaney's utterly bewildered face. He was almost choking with the fear, staring up but unable to see Sam beyond the glare. Sam turned a little to see what was around them: a solid dirt and dust floor, brick walls, timber rafters, pitched roof. No furniture, nothing left behind. An appalling vacuous museum to the dead. He ran the beam along the base of the walls, but aside from an odd loose brick and pigeon shit, there wasn't even anything to fasten Delaney to. He had expected rings in the walls to manacle the writhing in their agony, but there was no frames, there was no infrastructure. He flicked off the light to preserve battery, shrouding them again in darkness.

Then his phone lit up by itself – an alert. He would have ignored it but for one word that stood out: Ballycastle.

What?

He tapped the banner, which launched a news app in Italian. He could make out four more words.

Esplosione. Irlanda del Nord.

Sam's heart stopped.

His gaze fell to the writhing hateful bastard beneath him.

He paused, motionless. All breathing space evaporated. Things needed to happen fast. Sam couldn't afford to leave DNA – he hadn't actually laid a hand on Delaney and now he couldn't. There was no time. Then the Tetris blocks arranged themselves and removed the bumps. He took ten paces.

13

"**R**ain," he explained. "Got soaked." Sam wasn't given to explanations but he had to persuade the official to let him on the plane, sodden as his passport was.

The chaos of Marco Polo Airport might work in his favour. Had he been entering Italy, there would have been trouble. Because he was leaving, he represented the departure of a potential problem. Sam accepted the proffered moist booklet and turned, half expecting to be called back.

The phone buzzed in his pocket as he hunted for a shop to buy a mobile charger, but he was in serious danger of missing the gate closure. His stride became a run as he heard his name over the tannoy. There was no choice. He had to get home.

"What about the snapper?" Libby said absently.

The opso turned to her. "We'll get his images later – like we agreed. A break-in."

"I think we should tidy-up sooner. That photographer's got a different story now."

The opso stared at her for a moment. "Fuck, Libby, I want my team out of there."

"So do I, but I don't want them on some batch of before-and-after images."

The image feeds back to the DET were down. The recordings had been deliberately stopped, and the analysts were in the process of preparing everything for disposal should the police, at some later stage, come looking for evidence. Nothing would be worse than an accusation that a security team had been watching a bomb vehicle for days yet had done nothing.

The opso was blind. He lifted his radio. "We need to deal with the photographer. See to it that the camera is disabled and the contents removed."

"Copied. I can deal." Car two.

The opso didn't respond. Libby closed her eyes.

"Is there any chance I could borrow your phone?"

The broad woman turned to look at Sam. She was barely able to manoeuvre in the tight seat. He was wedged between her at the aisle and another woman at the window. They appeared unamused at having a pungent, slightly damp wide-shouldered bloke deposited between them. The woman stared for a second and then looked back at Facebook, choosing to ignore him.

Sam's anger hit the bell. "I wouldn't ask if it wasn't important. My phone has died and my kid, at home, is in trouble. Now, can I borrow it – please? I'll pay you whatever you want."

The woman concentrated on keeping her head forward, staring at the screen, determined to ignore him. Sam couldn't believe it. His arms began a familiar tremor, his chest and upper back swelled, and his brain battled to keep him in check. They hadn't even taken off yet and getting removed from the plane before it was airborne would defeat all purpose.

"Will you just look up the bomb in Ballycastle for me?" he tried instead. "See if anyone's injured?"

The woman's eyes widened in alarm and she reached up to press the buzzer for the attendant. As she did so the plane began to move forward and Sam could see the hostesses moving to the front.

"Cabin crew, seats for take-off," the captain announced.

Keep your counsel, Sam told himself. Deal with it when we're in the air.

The woman put her phone away as if it were plated in platinum, and Sam pushed back hard into his chair, his limbs humming with the desire to move; his body constrained and confined to a tube for the next few hours while his daughter ...

He drove his mind away from what could have happened. He thought instead of what he was leaving behind him in Venice. He prayed. Over and over. He pleaded for forgiveness, yet felt no remorse. Was this his just deserts?

He wondered what the authorities would make of the burning boat slowly sinking not far from the airport dock. It had been scrappy, his extraction, but he didn't care. Nothing was important any more other than getting home to Isla. He willed the plane to take-off. Get me to Ireland, he prayed. Please let me get to Ireland before they add it up and turn this yoke back. Arrest me in Ireland if you're going to arrest me at all.

And finally the nose lifted, with the woman still pressing her buzzer again and again. They were up and Sam was relieved, and he was terrified.

The operative performed a slow circle around the town and

came back to rest one hundred metres from the harbour. He could hear the sirens encroaching on the outskirts – he had little time. One last scan of the facia boards of houses and buildings to locate CCTV and private cameras, one more tick along the doors to register who has smart visualised doorbells and then he was out of the vehicle striding at pace towards the harbour's edge.

All the time he kept the snapper in sight while scanning left and right for witnesses or observers. But the wounded were too distracted to pay any attention.

The photographer had his eye to the viewfinder, oblivious to what was going on behind him. It suggested he had always been portrait rather than press – a change from the hardened snappers the operative was familiar with who were alert to everything.

A tap on the shoulder nearly sprang him out of his shirt. He'd been out of his depth as it was, unsure of the decency of recording shredded survivors with their underwear exposed. The operative said nothing but put out his hand, gesturing with four wagging fingers to hand over the kit.

The snapper looked at him, unable to decide what to do. The operative made the gesture again and the photographer acceded – looping the strap from around his neck and giving the stranger his work tools. The operative deftly tilted the body, slid the card cover, extracted the camera's memory and tossed the unit itself into the sea.

"What the f—" the snapper began.

The operative had been practising his Northern Ireland accent, even though he was from Luton. "Have a bit of respect," he said.

The snapper just stared. Then his hands fell to his sides in resignation – like he agreed with the operative, who turned and made his way back to the car, and then back to north DET.

"Yes, madam?" The flight attendant was irritated to be summoned so soon after take-off.

"Can I speak to you alone?" said Sam's neighbour.

He couldn't place her accent.

"No, madam, the captain has not yet switched off the seat-belt sign."

"This man," she gestured at Sam, still insistent on not looking at him, "tried to take my phone from me."

The attendant turned to Sam, querying eyes, slightly shocked.

"I did not," he said, somewhat surprised. "I asked if I could *borrow* her phone. I have an emergency at home and my phone is flat."

"Is not possible to use telephone on the aircraft," said the Italian attendant.

"Would it be possible to charge this for me, please?" Sam attempted to make good out of bad. "It really is the most serious emergency."

"Can I move seats?" asked the rude woman.

"No," snapped the attendant. She had seen something in Sam's eyes. "There is no vacancy."

She held out her hand to Sam, who placed the handset into it. She then reached to extinguish the call light on the panel above the lady's head and withdrew.

Sam sat back, still twitching, but knowing he had done all he could for the moment. Then he got another shock as the passenger on the other side leaned across him and spoke to the rude woman.

"You're some oul' wagon," she said, pure West Cork. "Sure, the man only wanted to borrow your phone. May you get help when ye need it." She leaned back.

The rude woman closed her eyes with utter determination, and Sam didn't know what to say. His ally filled the vacuum.

"I'd give ye me own phone if I had one but I hate the bloody t'ings," she said.

"Thank you," he muttered. "Appreciate it."

"No bother," she said. "'Tis the last time I go on holiday with that one," she nodded her head sideways.

Sinead hit the radio, then the steering wheel and swore at the traffic on Dublin's North Wall Quay. Stationary, she waited for the clock on the dash to click to the hour, and then cursed the Angelus because it set the news back by a minute, and then decided to use the holy reflection to place her request with the Almighty.

"Please, God, let Isla be alive. Please, God, let her be safe and well. Please, Jesus Christ, let that child not have been anywhere near that bloody bomb. Sorry, Lord, for swearing."

She hit the dial button again as the bells tolled, but Sam's phone went straight to answering machine – as it had the thirty times since she'd first heard the headlines. Then the chimes gave way to the sig tune and a man began to speak.

"It's believed at least ten people have been injured in an explosion in Northern Ireland. Although the cause of the blast is unclear, there is a heavy police presence in the County Antrim town of Ballycastle. Here's Grainne Whelan of our northern staff."

Sinead began to creep along, fixated on the bumper in front.

"Early reports, as yet unconfirmed, suggest the explosion occurred in or near a car close to the harbour in the seaside town, at around nine thirty this morning. Multiple ambulances from Causeway Hospital in Coleraine, as well as Antrim Area

Hospital and now Belfast, have been despatched. Eyewitnesses contacted by RTÉ say that a number of people have been injured, some seriously. Although the cause of the explosion is, as yet, unconfirmed, the possible involvement of dissident republicans will be one initial line of inquiry. The threat level remains at severe in Northern Ireland, and a number of dissident groups continue to plan and launch attacks aimed mainly at members of the security forces."

Sinead inched forward, willing the left turn towards the tolls, the Port Tunnel, and the road north.

"All staff involved in this operation, whether on the ground or in the ops room, will be granted exceptional leave for one week."

"What?" Libby looked at the opso, who ignored her as he addressed his team, arranged around him in plastic chairs.

"This op did not happen. We were not there."

Libby was stunned, yet somehow not surprised. Her head rotated gently, her gaze unable to rest on anything or anyone.

"All recordings shall be expunged, all imagery removed and destroyed. The techs will ensure that all on-board cameras are either wiped or disabled. All inventory must reflect a BAU status for the last five days – routine ops, no locations. See to it that the external cameras show us leaving, re-log the correct vehicles and assign them to alternative duties. I don't want some smart-arse lawyer or barrister tearing our logbooks to pieces in court. Understood?"

There was a murmur of agreement around the room.

"Questions?"

"How soon do you want us off base?" one of the spanners spoke up. "There's a fair bit of work in getting plates reassigned and hardware off the bikes and vehicles, and the van will need dealt with too."

"Make it shiny. Absolutely everything must be cleansed beyond finding or get them destroyed. The logs must be meticulous. You know the score – we've done it before. No cop – no matter how senior or how good – can come in here and find any discrepancy. Then you go on leave – not before."

"Surely the cops won't get access?" Libby asked.

"Don't bet on anything," said the opso, his seasoning as a leader beginning to show. "We take nothing for granted. Nothing. Ok, get to it."

The chairs scraped back and the wiping work began.

Sam was on his feet as soon as the light went off, and he took the opportunity to stand on a bloated toe as he made his way up the aisle.

"Sorry to hassle you, but did you get a chance to charge that phone for me?"

The attendant had seen him coming and presented him with the iPhone. He pressed the button and nodded as the screen came to life.

"You have no idea how grateful I am," he said to her.

She smiled as he banged in the six numbers and hit Sal's number. He stood into the alcove by the still-closed cabin door and heard the tone go straight to answering machine. His hands fell to his side and he hit his head back off the plastic divide. The unit vibrated constantly but it took a moment for him to realise that messages were coming through, and with trepidation he began to swipe and scroll.

Sinead. Missed calls. Twenty-nine of them. He tapped.

"Excuse me, sir, we need to access the walkway and open the door."

Sam shuffled aside waiting for the connection.

"Where are ye?" she sounded frantic.

"Just landed in Dublin."

"Oh, right," she replied, suddenly unsure. "Have ye heard any, ehm, news today, like?"

"I know there was a bomb in Ballycastle, that's all I know. What's going on, Sinead?"

"I don't know much, I've been trying to call the number…"

"Are there injuries?" He was talking firmly, not in the mood for soft soap.

"Some."

"How many?"

"Ten … at least."

Sam shook the fear from his mind to allow the practical to kick in. "And where are you?"

"On the way. GPS says I'll be at Ballycastle in forty minutes. How are you going to—"

"I'll hire a car or get a taxi – I don't know yet. I'm still on the plane. I can't get through to Molly's mam."

"Neither can I. Look, just cos Sal isn't answering doesn't mean—"

"Yes, it does," Sam said.

There was no other reason a woman in good order wouldn't answer her phone.

"I was thinking, maybe they jam the signal, you know, if a bomb goes off."

"She's a doctor, Sinead, and she's a parent. She'll know the importance of getting a message to me. Even if the signal's blocked, she'd have found a way if she was able."

There was silence on the other end. There was no answer that would help.

"Call me the minute you arrive. Please."

"I will."

The techs and spanners couldn't even call in reinforcements. The fewer people who knew what was going on, the better. So they worked an assembly line, rolling under the van, the vehicles, inspecting them from their pits and raising the bikes on the lifts. Once taken apart, the covert kit was handed to the tech who made sure the logbook was amended for each and every item. This was then signed off and the device was cleared. Of course, for some of the equipment a transfer of data from the unit to a computer was required, so – rather than increase the audit trail – such items were put on a shelf for disposal. At the end of the afternoon they would be crushed and incinerated and all record of their existence removed. That part was relatively easy – all the techs had kit squirrelled away, unaccounted for, unlisted and unknown. They knew how to do what needed to be done – no questions, no hesitation.

<hr />

"I'm here."

"What do you see?"

"I don't want to say, Sam."

"Say, Sinead. Just tell me exactly what you see. Don't hold back."

The taxi driver beside him didn't know what was going on but the fare would be massive. Half of it had been paid in cash, there was an agreed hundred euro by the gearstick for speeding fines, and he'd been shown another three hundred he would receive as a bonus so long as he didn't let the car go under one hundred and forty kilometres an hour in the south and ninety miles per hour in the north.

"There's mess everywhere. Like, the walls of some buildings are pretty badly damaged, the windows are all smashed. I can't get very close, there's police tape and cops everywhere. No ambulances. They must have all gone."

"Is there blood?"

There was silence for a moment.

"Yes, Sam, there's blood."

"Where?"

"Outside what was a coffee shop."

Sam closed his eyes and tried to remember the last voice-mail he'd received from Isla. He was sure there had been a coffee grinder sound in the background.

"Describe the restaurant."

Sinead was unnerved by his cold delivery, his commands.

"It's ... it's a whole mess, Sam," her voice cracked and shook. "There's glass inside and outside, the tables are mangled. There's bandages – oh, Sam, there are bandages and big plasters everywhere. Sam, I don't want to be telling you this – I don't know where they are. They might not even have been anywhere near here." She began to cry.

Sam's focus wilted a little. He wanted the information – he needed the information, but he couldn't ask her for any more. "Sinead, listen to me, please, listen to me carefully."

He could hear her sobbing had muffled as if she'd moved the phone away from her ear.

"Sinead!"

"Yeah," she croaked.

"Try to get a cop. Try to get a cop to talk to me. Explain who I am and give him the phone."

"Ok," she said, moderate relief entering her voice.

He heard her crackle and stumble around a little, and then he could just about make out her pleading with someone.

"Please can you help me? I've a man on the phone – he's on the way. His daughter could have been here and we can't find her."

"His daughter was here – at the harbour?"

"Maybe, we don't know. But we can't get her. We don't know how to find her."

"What age is she?"

"Seven. Isla. Isla Ireland."

There was ear-splitting silence. Sam imagined the man checking notes or turning away to speak into the chest mic on his radio.

"What's happening, Sinead?"

But Sinead wasn't listening. He suppressed an urge to shout down the line at her. Then he could hear her muted talking over the din of the taxi.

"She was here on holiday, with her friend Molly. Molly's mother is Sal. Sally."

There was a crackle on the line.

"Sam?"

"Yes?" he choked.

"What's Sally's second name? What's Molly's surname?"

Sam began to shake his head. "Fuck, Sinead, I don't know. I can't remember. Fuck. I can't remember."

He couldn't believe he didn't have that vital piece of information. In that moment he felt every ounce of incompetence of his past bear down on him. Of all the negligence, this seemed his greatest.

"We don't know. Well, now is hardly the time, is it, officer?" he heard her say. "The man's daughter is missing. Now where can he find some information?"

More battering and rumbling and then she spoke into the phone. "We have to go to the hospital, Sam."

"Does he think she's in the hospital?"

"If she's not there, then that's good news. All the injured are at the hospital."

"Can you go? Now?"

"Yes, but there's a problem."

"What?" Sam's heart was hammering.

"They don't know which hospital."

"Like – how many are there?"

"The most badly injured have been taken to Belfast."

Sam turned to the taxi driver. "Take me to Belfast."

Sinead heard the order. "Sam, we don't even know if they're—"

"*I know*, Sinead."

"How?" She was pleading now.

"I don't know how, but I know. I'll go to Belfast, you go to ... I don't know – you go to the closest one, and then the next closest one. Go now. Please, Sinead."

Grim was late to the party. He'd been shopping at an outdoor outlet mall with his wife. He didn't carry a mobile phone because he didn't see the point in telling the Brits where he was all the time.

He stared at the television in the living room of his own home. He was in his slippers and he was smoking a cigarette. A suited young reporter was telling the national news how much was unknown about what had happened.

There was one soothing piece of information, though: the driver of an at-present unidentified car that had been close to the centre of the explosion was believed to have died.

Well, thought Grim, at least that was something.

He put on his shoes, wrote down the number of his preferred solicitor, loaded up with three boxes of fags and waited to be arrested.

"They're not here."

"Where are you?"

"Coleraine. Causeway Hospital."

"You're sure."

"There is no woman with children."

"Are there children?"

"One. Not Isla."

"Could it be Molly?"

"No. It's a boy. That's all I know."

"Are there dead there?"

Sinead paused. "Yes. But I think it's an adult."

"You think?"

"They won't tell me anything about the dead person but I know it's only one."

"So it could be Molly's mum?"

"I don't think so. I'm thinking it was whomever was in the car."

"What do you know about the car?"

"They're saying here that it was the bomb – that the bomb was in the car – a car bomb."

"And why do you think the dead person in your hospital was in the car?"

"'Cos it's not a body, as such. I spoke to one of the orderlies outside. She said it's, you know ..."

"Pieces."

Silence.

"Ok, next one."

"Leaving now."

Although neither knew it, the manager passed Sam at that moment heading south. He hadn't been quite so slow on the uptake as Grim and had packed a bag and made for the border as soon as news had broken.

"Where are you going?" His wife had found him rooting in the wardrobe.

"Free State," he'd replied over his shoulder.

"Prick," she'd spat. "There was wee uns injured in that y'know."

"Not here," he'd rounded on her, his finger pointing to the ceiling, performing a tiny circle. He stared hard at her, imploring, warning.

She didn't care. "If you had a hand in that," she pointed back at him, "don't come back."

He leaned in towards her, neck out, teeth gritted in a whisper. "Wasn't supposed to happen like that."

"Aye, well, it did. Now fuck off to yer Free State."

She'd gone downstairs and he'd gone to the car. He cursed the fact that he'd helped Grim out – that he'd been to Ballycastle the day before. He thought about his destination and doubted whether he'd be back this time.

"Where're we for?"

Sam turned to the taxi driver and wondered himself. Which hospital would be on intake – would it matter? They'd go to the Royal, wouldn't they? Trauma experts. Troubles experts. Gunshot specialists.

"The Royal."

"Where's that?"

"West. West Belfast. Come off the motorway in a couple of miles."

"This all to do with that bomb, is it?" asked the driver with sympathy.

"Aye."

"You've someone missin'?"

"Yes," said Sam.

"Y'er daughter, is it?"

"Yes."

"Fuck, brother, I am sorry to hear that. I'm sure she'll

turn up."

"Come off up here, turn left at the roundabout and the entrance is on the right. It's like a warren in here. I don't know exactly where A & E is."

"We'll find it, buddy, don't worry."

Sam began to shake. For the first time in his life he thought he was about to cry in fear. His legs extended in the footwell and he pressed his back and hips into the seat with such force that it jumped a click. The driver looked round at him momentarily, and was about to say something soothing, which might have been a very bad move, when the phone rang.

"Sinead," he said, eyes staring ahead, jaw trembling, his hand shaking.

"She's here, Sam."

"Alive?"

"Alive."

"Injured?"

"Scrapes." She broke down.

"Only scrapes?"

"Yes, yes, yes, Sam." She was breathing through her nose. "Cuts and scrapes."

"What else, Sinead. What is it?" He could hear her gulping and choking. "Sinead, tell me what it is. Just get it out." He listened to her distress while navigating with hand signals for the driver: *we're not stopping.*

"It's Molly. She's gone."

Sam blinked hard, breathing through his nose. "Does Isla know?"

"I don't know. I don't know."

"Sal?"

"ICU. In Belfast. Critical."

"Ok," he said, the tears now hammering down his cheeks. "Ok. Thank you. Thank God. Can she talk?"

"I don't know. I can see her. She's in a bed through a

window, but I can't talk to her. I'm not related – they won't let me." With that Sinead completely broke down, convulsing.

"Thank you, Sinead. Thank you so much. I'll be there as soon as I can. I'll be there soon."

14

T hree weeks.

It took three weeks for them to determine that Molly's mum wouldn't be able to attend the funeral. She was still on a ventilator at the hospital where she worked, oblivious that her husband was having to bury their child.

Sam didn't want Isla there. He refused to allow that memory to remain with her. Perhaps that was the wrong decision, but it didn't feel like it.

He went. He watched a child be buried in the pursuit of an Ireland that wasn't one inch closer to birth as a result of her death.

He made his way slowly back to the boat. He knew he was heading for a shutdown – his mind going dark, shutters banging closed, all peripheral vision blinded. The worst of it was, he didn't care – he craved the focus that was coming his way. Perhaps, in preparation, that was why he had insisted Sinead stay with them.

"You need your space," she'd said.

"Maybe. But this might be best for Isla. I don't know why,"

he'd replied, and refused to rationalise his request further than that. "But if you need to get back, honestly, it's no problem."

"No, not at all, of course I'll stay. But you have to tell me as soon as you want me to go. You need to promise me that."

"I will, honestly."

Isla was scanned. She was prodded and paraded around, observed closely by doctors, new and old. A steel line of stethoscopes. Unbelievably, she'd walked out the hospital door two days after she'd been wheeled in.

Sam refused to think beyond thanks that his child, who had been sitting opposite her friend, had survived while her friend had died. He was not at all sure he had the capacity to deal with all this again – the repair, the shock, the constant scare and worry for his little girl. Was it a message? Was it his fault – payback for his past?

It was easier to imagine the former, so he allowed his weakness to gradually creep over him, his rage to build. It came easier than the alternative.

The manager took a dander around the village most mornings, breathing in the sea air and stretching his legs. Then turned and strolled through the few red-brick rows to a teahouse with which he was becoming accustomed.

Greenore was a port town on the edge of Carlingford Lough – nicely forgotten – its streets embroidered with doily windows and well-swept steps. At fifty, Hagan brought the average age down by half.

The cups in the tearoom were ancient and cracked with deep brown crazing in keeping with its beige backstory. There was a museum of sorts, quirky old stuff on the walls, a fridge from the seventies with sweets from the nineties.

It was a place of gossip and rumour, where a twitch of a net curtain was enough to set the news on fire. So the manager got out front and centre with his own story, targeting those who would talk before an alternative could be created for him.

His days were spent in idle irritation reading the local rags and staring at the old curved screen in his room. Then, when it got dark, he took another turn as far as the ferry terminal, such as it was. He stood bent at the railings and stared across the lough to the north, a separate country. Gradually the notion crept in that he would never be able to return there unless by virtue of extradition, which itself seemed inevitable. The blinking lights of an occupied territory made him maudlin, and he slowly rose and ambled back to his digs.

And he waited.

Isla was back in Sam's cabin at night. It just worked out that way – nothing said. He simply found her moving that direction when he told her it was bedtime; he had no objection. Sinead took Isla's cabin and for a week they lived like that, saying not very much but going for walks and watching movies. Every now and then Sam cast off and they motored round the islands, sitting in the cockpit, looking out more than in. He wanted the salt air to tire his daughter so that she might get through the night. Sinead made lots of tea and Isla drank half cups.

He was back to watching her flickering in her sleep. He read endlessly about counselling – where to get it and how; the different types – behavioural, eye movement, mindfulness; and the symptoms – depression, abnormal behaviour. None were a fit for what Isla had been through or how she appeared to be dealing with her pain. Post-traumatic was the closest, but what about bereavement – and how do you deal with that twice? Isla would never get over the murder of her mother, Sam was sure, but to endure the horror and mindlessness of what had happened to Molly overwhelmed him, as he was sure it would her, eventually.

He got up and went above, leaving the window cracked so that he would hear Isla if she moved. In the table he found a bottle of Pusser's Rum: gunpowder-proof. He sucked the cork out as quietly as he could manage, but he got caught.

"Share a splash?" He poured a liberal amber measure into a heavy tumbler and handed it to her. "Careful with that."

The dark liquid caught Sinead by surprise nonetheless, tears welled in her eyes and she caught a cough. She waited to recover, pulling Isla's duvet tighter around her shoulders.

"We are so silent," she said, at last.

"I know."

"I feel like I'm intruding."

"Why?"

"I think you might talk more if I wasn't here."

Sam didn't know what to say to that, so there was yet more silence for a while as the heat slipped down their necks like diesel to an engine and they waited for it to ease their dialogue.

He poured again, then spoke. "I think she needs to talk to a professional."

"Agreed."

"I think we need to start that soon. PTSD is no joke."

Sinead noted the *we*. "She's been through so much. I really don't know how she's still so, like, brilliant."

"She's like her mam," Sam said absently, and the comment hung between them, but not uneasily, which was strange.

They drank and Sam heeled the bottle again.

"Will I leave you off – maybe tomorrow?" she asked softly.

Sam looked at her. He wanted to speak, but couldn't.

"I think it's maybe best I give ye some space. But I'll be around, any time ye need."

He closed his eyes and nodded slowly.

"They know."

"Sorry?" Libby wasn't apologising, she was confused.

"The MIT team is looking into the bomb."

"I wasn't sure if it would go to major investigations or stay within branch."

Old units had new names, but old hands had old references. Special Branch had been replaced with Crime Ops and its ground teams with a letter and number, but the spooks still called it what it was – a unit going its own direction. Both knew that Special Branch wasn't really an investigative unit, it was more about gathering intelligence – and where it suited, preventing crime. The Police Service of Northern Ireland had a high-ranking senior who liaised with MI5, but it was hard for Libby to imagine that the sharing of information was fulsome or done with good grace.

"How clean is your house?" Her superior seemed relaxed given the stakes.

"We're tidy. It's the opso's gig to square everything away, really, and I can see they've been working hard on it."

"And the paper trail – the bookings and logs? That's the type of thing a QC is likely to go for. You know how they love a file full of documents."

Libby was familiar with the forensic comb of those at the bar. Caped crusaders in ridiculous headgear poking and nipping at any detail overlooked. Inconsistency was the ally of any barrister; the ammunition with which to fire doubt into a courtroom. Doubt led to quashed convictions and embarrassment for security folks.

"Everything is in order, but I'll have another walk through with the ops officer."

"Soon, Libby."

"What do they know?"

Her superior was quiet for a moment, then she heard him sigh. "They know who was behind the attack."

That came as a relief. "So they don't know we were watching them?"

"As things stand that is not an issue that has been raised."

"That's ... odd, is it not?"

"They're busy. In time they may make an assumption."

"Then they'll come looking for evidence."

"Of which there ought to be none."

"Understood."

"They have made one request, though."

"Yes?"

"They want the suspects placed under surveillance."

Libby paused, struck by the irony. "Who do they want specifically?"

"Curiously, they have a shortlist, and I imagine you may know where to find these people."

Libby could detect a smugness on the encrypted line.

"They'll want the boss watched," Libby said. "Have they got the other names?"

"They think they do, and they're not wide of the mark, to be fair. They want the man Grim, they want the manager, they want the mother of the bomber – although I cannot see the advantage frankly, and they want a handful of has-beens who have nothing to do with anything."

"So, as we were, really."

"Better. If they think we are keeping an eye on them, then they won't deploy their own."

"Yes, of course."

"So let's see how it all shakes out, Libby. Everything up to this point destroyed. Everything from this point on logged meticulously, please."

"Understood."

Sam became increasingly uncomfortable with Isla's apparent indifference. He could detect very little adjustment in her state of mind. After a quiet week, in which she had said nothing, she appeared to revert to her old self – playing, chatting – she even laughed on one occasion. Sam was inclined to throw an arm around her, to expect her to visit in the night, but she had taken back to her own cabin at bedtime, and to reading again, and drawing.

He should have been happy about it, yet he found it disturbing. Surely she should be grieving or bottling it all up, he thought. Why are there no signs of trauma? The time had come.

"Right, wee love, we need to have a talk."

"Ok."

"You've had a terrible time."

"I don't want to talk about it, Daddy," she replied immediately.

"It's so hard for someone your age to see something like that."

Silence.

"And you've been through too much already."

"You mean Mammy," she said, a little too matter-of-factly for his liking.

"Yes, I mean Mammy."

"Daddy, I don't want to talk about it."

The soft scratch of a felt tip on paper.

For the first time ever, he had no idea what was going on in her head. "I want for you to talk to someone properly – so that they can take all the bad stuff out of your head."

She looked up at him then, straight in the eye.

"I don't have bad stuff in my head. I only have the nice memories of Mammy."

That took Sam by surprise. "Well, that's brilliant, wee lamb, but you've also been through a terrible thing."

"The bomb."

Sam was struggling with her directness. "Eh, yeah, the bomb. And, like, Molly."

"I just do the same with Molly as I do with Mam. I just remember the good things and stuff."

"But it might not always be like that."

"Why?"

"Well, in the future you might remember the bad stuff too."

"You shouldn't remind me of that, Daddy," she scolded him.

"I'm not trying to remind you of it, darlin'. I'm just trying to make sure it doesn't do you any harm."

"But if I don't think about it, then it won't do me harm."

Sam stared at her, lost as to how to work around her logic.

"You don't always get a choice of what you think about, Isla."

"I do. If I'm thinking about bad stuff, I just say, 'Get out,' and then I think about fun stuff instead."

Sam shook his head a little. It was like reasoning with her mother – he was ten steps behind before they even started moving. "Well, I'd like you to talk to a person to make sure your mind is going to be ok."

"Where is Sinead, Daddy?"

"She had to go back to work."

"Did you send her away?"

"No, Isla," he said, surprised. "Why would you think that?"

She just shrugged.

He felt himself getting slightly prickly at the suggestion but wasn't sure why. He got up and made for the companionway having achieved next to nothing.

"Do I have to go?" she said to his back.

He knew she wouldn't have lifted her head from the drawing. "Yes, wee love. I think it's for the best."

At five o'clock in the morning a small tactical support convoy split in two. The front half stayed on the dual carriageway, the other rolled towards a housing estate. The timing was ideal – any wee scallies keen on starting trouble were asleep, and the boys in boiler suits could make their snatches and extract before a petrol bomb was poured.

Grim had waited for hours, smoking and thinking, running through the motions of how to distract himself during interview, zoning out the officers who would question him. Eventually he had taken his thoughts to bed.

There would be an effort to turn him – he expected that. They would try to kick him around for a while, then some unidentified character would come in – calmer and more confident. There would be a dance of sorts: this new arrival would do a lot of looking, spend a lot of time silent, then drop what they imagined to be a killer line – "You've an interesting browsing history," or some such shite. Grim had learned to ignore them in just the same way as the ordinary peelers. He'd pick something on the wall or door over their shoulder and hold it for as long as he was able. "You never fancy getting out of here, away from all this? Can be arranged – new life, maybe in the sun?" He knew it was nearly over when they started getting on to money; the last roll, the final effort to tip him into betrayal.

Their problem was he had no closet full of perversions. Beyond his willingness to kill for political gain, his mind was largely clear of sick pursuits and there was no lever to lean on. And he had no desire to leave Ireland – to take the money and relocate to what he knew would be an equally awful housing estate in the north of England where the people would be less inclined to welcome him and where he would be utterly dependent upon increasingly disinterested handlers.

Grim's motivations were concentrated in revenge and politics and those were hard commitments to crack. In the absence
of sexual deviance or a serious gambling addiction, there wasn't
much the Brits could do to flick his switch.

They may have knocked – but if they had it was deliberately
soft, before the frame was beaten through in two taps. He heard
them come in and leapt to get his trousers on before they
dragged him into the street in his trunks. He hated when they
did that – exposing his skinny, long white legs to the neighbours. He had just zipped when a bottle-green baseball hat
appeared at the door and he was swivelled and pinned forward
onto the bed, cuffed, elbowed and dragged down the stairs. His
wife had simply rolled over.

Outside, he was content to see the neighbours opening
their curtains and lifting their blinds to investigate the heavy
rumble of police Land Rovers. He was bare-chested, his broad
shoulders and upper body a marked contrast to his pathetic
little legs. He remembered reading the words of Joseph
Goebbels: "If we cannot be respected, we can at least be
feared."

The boss, on the other hand, had to put on a show. It was
expected. A man of his stature couldn't be taken quietly – that
simply wouldn't do. He was lifted out in his pants by four large
men, kicking and swinging. He still had his socks on.

Two young lads emerged in support and starting clodding
stones at the TSG cops, pinging the windscreen of the armoured
Land Rover. The driver simply lifted the grill. The boss was
bucked in the back like the carcass of a cow, his pale body flopping
around under the boots of the officers as they pretended to hold
him still for the journey to Antrim's Serious Crime Suite. There he
would be given a telly-tubby forensic suit and left to freeze in a cell
for hours while they waited for his brief to get out of bed.

They didn't bother trying to pick up the manager – the

Guards had pinged him in a village over the border in the Irish Republic. The Major Investigations Team would start the extradition process in due course.

"Isla thinks I sent you away."

"Why?"

"Dunno. I was trying to have the counselling talk."

"Ah, Sam, I'm sorry."

"Not your fault. Just, well, odd – you know, the way she interprets things."

"How do you mean?"

"I don't know, just that she thinks I would send you away. That's so wide of the mark."

"I think that's a compliment?"

"So do I."

Sam shook his head at how quickly their conversations could become complicated.

Sinead rescued the confusion. "There's someone wants to see you."

"Hardly your sister?" Sam couldn't really think of anyone else.

"No. Well, not that she doesn't want to see you—"

"Don't worry, I know I'll never be a favourite of Áine's."

"She likes you more than she realises."

"Aye. Who then?"

"The father."

"Who?"

"Kaitlin's dad. The heiress, as you call her."

"Shit."

"Why *shit*?" Sinead said warily. "You never told me how it ended in Venice."

"Scrappy – not for the phone, to be honest, but I left her safe. Have you heard how she is?"

"Well, I know she's back in Dublin – he told me that much."

"Did he say what he wants? Is he, like, angry?"

"Why would he be angry if you left her safe?"

"She had a visitor out there."

Sinead was silent for a moment while the cogs meshed. "You're joking?"

"He didn't mention that?"

"I don't even know if he knows about it."

"How was he – did he come to see you or what?"

"He was concerned."

"About what?"

"About you, Sam. He knew what happened."

"How?"

"I told him."

"Right. So why did he come to see you?"

"He didn't – not at first. He rang and asked how you were, I filled him in. I sort of assumed you'd have told him, but then I realised you hadn't … sorry."

"Wasn't really a priority."

"Of course. The funny thing is, he did come to see me after that. He said he'd heard the thing on the radio and he wants to see you."

"What thing on the radio?"

"Molly's mum – the interview – he heard it."

"What? She's in intensive care."

"Sam, how long's it been since you listened to the news?" Sinead asked, bewildered.

"Few days," he said. "I don't really want Isla hearing anything, and I'm sort of not wanting to hear anything myself."

Sinead paused, deliberating.

"Sal's come round, Sam. She's done an interview. It's every-where. It's—"

"What?"

"D'ye know what? I think maybe you're right. I think you might be better off not listening to it."

It was Sam's turn to say nothing for a while. Then something occurred to him. "I should go and see her."

"Maybe."

"When does the father want to see me?"

"He didn't say."

"Do you think he'd come here? I'm not that keen on leaving Isla."

"You could bring her to Dublin – get off the boat for a while. I could mind her – take her out. If, you know, you'd be happy with that."

"Can I just make one thing clear?"

"Yes."

"I did not send you away."

She laughed, a little relieved. "Sure, I know that."

"A day out for her is a good idea. I could take her on the train – I still don't have a van. And the father hasn't paid me yet, if he's ever going to."

"Well, I'm looking forward to hearing what went on over there."

"Don't be," he said. "It was—"

"Scrappy," she repeated.

The police had dissident arrests down to a fine art; the plan was to make them all suspicious of one another. By staggering releases and letting the most unlikely detainees go free first, the cops could sow doubt into the heads of their comrades. Dissident republicans knew that their ranks had been infiltrated, that Special Branch, the spooks and probably even military intelligence had all pocketed a slice of their membership.

Equally, the dissies knew there was next to nothing they could do about it. Every now and again, if they felt there was enough evidence of someone passing information to the security forces, they would shoot one of their own – plug him in a pub or rattle off a shotgun through a living room window.

The cops knew that and played on it.

First to be released was the boss. Amid muted fanfare and cheering he was spirited from the Serious Crime Suite, a clutch of tracksuits and trainers surrounding him as he was led away to a waiting car.

Grim they kept, in the hope he would believe he'd been thrown to the courts by his master. That, it was hoped, would fracture loyalty and foster suspicion. Which it did. By day three, an extension obtained, Grim was tiring of hovering over a hole to shit, of his puke-encrusted mattress and of the freezing cold cell. He'd had his hair sampled, his prints taken, his image recorded – and he was still in a dust suit. The bed blankets were little more than rubber-backed bathmats, and the peelers had refused to give him anything to read. He was going bingo. He'd asked for a shower, yet to be granted, and was on his sixth snack box of chicken legs and chips. His guts would never hold out to that type of feeding.

Of course, the custody sergeant had taken great delight in keeping his hatch flap open as the boss was paraded past. Grim hadn't been able to contain his curiosity when a day later he posed the question he knew he ought not to.

"Where was he going?

"Who?" the custody sergeant asked, knowing full well who was being referred to.

"The bloke who was arrested same night as me," Grim said, trying to keep the charade together.

"Oh, your old pal? He was released, sure."

"So when are you going to release me?"

"Sure, why would you be released?"

"Well, why was he released?"

"Ah, now," was all he got, and the flap was flipped shut.

Talking was fine so long as it wasn't on tape, he tried to console himself. Yet he was pissed off at having said anything. That was not the plan.

Isla took Sam's hand on the platform and they waited for the train. On impulse he'd bought them first-class tickets. Might be fun, he thought. Treat her a little bit, get her a posh breakfast and a complimentary glass of orange juice served by a bloke in a waistcoat.

"Where are we going?" she asked as she buzzed her enormous seat between recline and upright.

"Well, you're going shopping with your pal. The one I *didn't* send away, little lady."

"Sinead?" she said excitedly.

"Yes. She's going to take you round Dublin for a while. Dublin's much bigger than Belfast, with lots of big shops and stuff on the streets."

"Thank you, Daddy," she said, the kindling of a glow in her cheeks.

Toast and sausages devoured, he pulled out her Kindle and entered the Wi-Fi code. "Now, you can chill and watch this for a while. I've got to listen to something before my meeting."

"Who are you meeting?"

"A man about a job."

"Are you going away again?" she asked, immediately alarmed.

"No, wee love, I'm not going away."

She stared at him with a look that said, "I've heard that before." At least it felt that way to Sam. Eventually she pulled her feet into the enormous seat and drifted into a world of making stuff with discarded rubbish.

Sam pulled on his headphones, braced himself and hit play on the programme he'd downloaded to his phone.

"Five weeks have passed since a car bomb, believed to have been left by dissident republicans, took the lives of eight people, including two children. Despite multiple arrests, nobody has been charged with the attack in the County Antrim seaside town of Ballycastle. One of the children who died was seven-year-old Molly Black. She was having breakfast with her mother and a friend in a café close by when the device went off. Her mother Sal, a consultant paediatrician, was left in a critical condition – and tragically was on life support when her daughter's funeral took place. Thankfully, she is recovering from her physical injuries, and our reporter Niamh Cullen has been speaking to her in her hospital room in Belfast. I warn you, this is not an easy listen, folks, but it is an important one."

Sam hit the pause button and looked out the window for a while. Then he looked at Isla, engrossed, and carried on.

"It was just a normal morning," Sal began. *"The kids wanted to go to the beach and I was out of bread, so I decided to treat them and we went to the wee café down by the harbour. We'd go in there for ice cream in the evenings sometimes, but we'd never been there for breakfast before and it just seemed like a normal thing to do."*

"You were on holidays, weren't you?" said the reporter.

"Yeah. We'd be there quite often. It's nice, you know. Molly loved the beach and she had a wee pal with her and they were just having a ball."

Sam looked across at her wee pal and wondered what the hell her wee head was really making of all she'd seen.

"It's, it's not the type of place you'd expect to be targeted in an attack, is it?"

"Not at all. I mean, you don't really think anywhere's a target any more, do you? You kind of think all that's behind us, that the peace process did its job. So, you know, it was just such a total shock."

"*Do you remember anything of what happened?*"

"*I remember the girls getting their food, and I had a coffee and a scone, and we were just chatting, you know? And then there was this enormous gust of wind. There wasn't any noise, though, which is still strange to me. Just this blast of wind. And I was reaching for Molly and then that's all. That's everything.*"

"*You were unconscious for more than three weeks.*"

Sam chewed the inside of his cheek, astonished at Sal's composure.

"*Can you tell me what happened when you came round?*"

"*My husband was sitting roughly where you're sitting. He was upset, you know. They'd been bringing me round deliberately, so he knew I was probably about to wake up. And he knew he would have to tell me.*"

There was a pause, then the reporter did her job.

"*Tell you what?*"

There was a long pause, then Sal's voice broke. "*Tell me Molly was gone. That my wee girl was dead.*"

Now, I want you to stop any time you like. If you want to stop, please just let me know and we'll switch the recorder off."

"*I want people to know what these things do, Niamh. Don't stop it.*"

Sam hit pause again, covered his eyes and gave thanks that he hadn't had to go through what Sal was going through.

"Daddy, what's wrong?"

"Nothing, wee love, watch your programme," he said.

"Are you sad?"

"I've just a pain in my back."

He hit play again.

"*Did you understand what was happening?*"

"*Yeah,*" Sal said, "*I knew immediately. The whole thing was plain to me as soon as I opened my eyes. I looked at my husband, and I remembered the gust of wind, and I think I just knew it had been a bomb. I don't know how.*"

"Tell us about Molly if you feel able, Sal."

"You can't sum up seven years in a radio interview. You know, it's every moment of a life that makes a person, and she was so quirky. And she loved to be around quirky people too. She was full of nonsense and ideas, and she was just so lovely."

Sam could see Sal's tears, her throat heavy with phlegm and the shake in her delivery threatening to shut her down.

"Take your time, Sal."

"Every parent has the right to see their child grow up. I work in the Children's Hospital and I see sick kids every day. And I see their parents. I thought I knew how hard it was for them to see the most precious thing in the world to them in pain and sometimes slipping away. But now I know. Now I know myself what it is to lose a child, and I am so sad, and I am so angry – what right had they to take my daughter from me? What put it in their heads that the death of my daughter was somehow worth something to them? I put – we put so much into raising her, and she was so lovely – she was so loving and kind, and they took all that from us, and I just don't understand what they got out of it. I just don't see how her death, how her obliteration – 'cos that's what they did to her ..."

Sam had to stop the playback as Sal convulsed. He held back his own tears and refused to look at Isla, who was shooting him tiny concerned looks over the top of her screen.

He decided he'd had enough, for now anyway. He didn't need to hear any more to decide what needed to happen next.

15

P olice requests for close observation were a pain in the arse for the opso; it meant that everything had to be done by the book. Day-to-day the DET's role was to gather and prevent – gather information, prevent atrocities. Putting together evidence packs was usually not a priority.

Yet when the police came knocking to make surveillance requests, not only was the DET obliged to carry those out, but it needed to record the whole thing in a way that would be acceptable and irreproachable in a court of law, which meant second-guessing barristers, which meant doing everything utterly within the confines of the Investigatory Powers Act. If they strayed beyond that, they needed to make damn sure nobody could find out, which meant second-chairing all footage before it was handed over. This inevitably slowed everything up and made the opso even more irritable than usual.

Of course, his team didn't stop intercepting calls and communications – regardless of whether the Secretary of State had signed them off – as was the legal requirement. They just wiped the transmissions after they had got what they needed.

And they didn't stop listening to all the cute little devices they had placed in the bathrooms and bedrooms and sheds and beds throughout their area – but they were careful about any transcriptions made and had to be sure that they couldn't fall into the wrong hands – the police.

There was one convenience, though. Previously the DET wasn't supposed to be watching Grim, his boss or the manager. The official request to do so, however, gave the opso a certain degree of cover to operate. Where before they'd had to dodge the cops as well as their targets, now at least one headache had been removed. For the moment they were official.

"Excuse me?"

"Your host has requested you leave your phone with me," said Robert, who Sam remembered from last time.

"Have you got his phone too?" Sam wasn't particularly happy about the arrangement because Isla was loose on the streets of Dublin and he wanted to be reachable.

"I do," was all Robert said.

Sam began to wonder if Robert was more than a waiter but handed over the handset anyway.

"He has reserved a private room for you both." Robert gestured to a heavy varnished door.

"Ok," said Sam. "Do you want me to knock too?"

"That won't be necessary, sir."

"Sam's fine."

"Sam, he's expecting you."

Robert ducked and departed and Sam turned the hefty handle.

"Come in please, Sam," said the father.

"How are you, John?"

"Very well, very well, but how are you?"

Sam tilted his head. "So-so."

"Of course. And Isla?"

"Ehm, I don't know, is the truth, John. She's, well, she's surprisingly good as it happens. Scratch the surface, though, who knows?"

"It will take time, lots of time, Sam."

"What about, ehm, Kaitlin?"

"Heartbroken, thank God."

"So you know?"

"Know what?"

"About Delaney?"

"What about Delaney?" The old man bristled, panic setting in immediately.

Sam just looked at him for a long while, deliberating. He hadn't prepared for this conversation and he should have. "How much do you know about Venice?"

"I know what Kaitlin's friends told me. I fund their extravagance, you see, and they fill me in on a few details."

"Risky," said Sam.

"Better than having no idea what's going on," the father replied.

"What did they tell you exactly?"

"That she had a date and that it went wrong – and that's why she's so contrary."

"Did they know who the date was with?"

The father's forehead creased. "I assumed it was someone she met out there."

Sam shook his head slowly. "We're confident this is private in here?"

"Yes," said the father, increasingly agitated. "Absolutely."

"She met Delaney."

Sam couldn't have done more damage if he'd punched the old man.

"How?"

"In a restaurant."

"I mean, how was he able to travel?"

"He's a free man."

"Yes, but—"

"He was clearly there by arrangement."

"How the hell?" The father's worry was morphing into anger.

"Let's take a walk, John," Sam said, gesturing to the air as if it were contaminated.

They left the Royal Dublin Society in silence, crossed the road outside and made their way to the river. Strolling along Beatty's Avenue and onto a walkway towards the Liffey, the father's desperation for information became apparent.

"What did you do?"

"I'm not going to get into that, John, but it's over. They won't meet again."

"You're sure?"

"As eggs are eggs."

"She's safe?"

"She's safe from him. Hundred per cent."

"Is he ...?"

Sam nodded.

The father thought for a while. "Thank you."

Sam said nothing.

"He had a terrible hold over her," the father said, distant now, consumed by his thoughts.

"It was hypnotism, believe it or not."

"What?"

"He had her hypnotised – that's what he did to her in court. He locked her in. That's why she turned in the witness box. I'd say he was good at it. He also killed another woman. I was hoping you'd take the name and, I dunno, maybe do something about it, but you need to keep me out of it entirely."

Sam turned to look at the old gent and realised he was

being too matter of fact with him, hitting him with too much rough information in one go.

The father looked distraught. "Who was she?"

"He said her name was Audrey Kavanagh."

"You spoke to him – to Delaney?" the old man paused to look up at Sam.

"I'm really not going to elaborate on that, John – it's of no use to anyone, but I believe the name of the girl is accurate."

The father was bemused, which turned to pensiveness. "I'll ... look into it, I suppose," he said. "Sam, you said she was safe from *him*, but is she safe – generally?"

"Look, John, this isn't my area of expertise but I have a daughter and if she were in the same position, I would want to know, so I'll tell you what I know – only you'll need someone smarter than me to work it out, ok?"

"Yes, Sam, please tell me all you can."

"This is going to be hard to listen to."

"Go on, Sam, please." They began walking again, two swans puttered past.

"I think she had arranged for him to help her take her life."

The father's eyes began to swim. "Suicide?" he croaked.

"I think so. I assume he talked her into it – that he made her feel like he was helping her do it. That it was, like, a favour – or some bizarre act of love or something."

The father remained silent for a long while before speaking again. "Does Kaitlin know what happened to him?"

"All she knows is that he took off. Far as I know, she thinks he got chased out of a hotel room."

"Did she see you?"

"It was all pretty quick, but it's entirely possible."

"Her friends didn't mention any of this."

"They weren't with her. They were probably off spending your money in an expensive champagne bar."

"I want to know more but I don't want to know more," the father said.

"All you need to know is she needs help, and that she's safe from Delaney. I can promise that absolutely."

"Thank you, Sam."

"You're grand."

"What about your daughter?"

"She needs help too. I'm working on that."

"I hope you don't mind but Sinead has filled me in on your background."

Sam said nothing, unsure of how he felt about that.

The father pattered on. "If I can, if you would permit me, I would like to help you."

"You're paying me, sure – you're paying me well. That's a help."

"I heard that lady's interview."

Sam nodded but said nothing.

"It was incredibly moving."

"It was."

"We all deserve to live our lives without fear of things like that happening, Sam."

"Well, you'll not find me disagreeing with that."

"So what I'm trying to say is, you have a daughter, I have a daughter. You have kept my girl safe. If there is anything I can do to keep your girl safe, then I would gladly repay the debt – regardless of our financial arrangement."

"I'm not really following you, John?" Sam turned to the old man.

"I'm saying, this country has had enough of that business – the violence, the killing."

"You're right about that."

"I think I have some small insight, Sam. I think that if you were to need any assistance, financially, or, perhaps ... logisti-cally, then I am at your disposal – as it were."

Sam strolled on for a while. "Might take you up on that, John."

———

"Where did these come from?" Libby barked accusingly at the opso but knew it wasn't his fault.

He peered at the iPad she was holding. "Before shots?"

"Before shots," she repeated, then swiped through a series of images. "After shots."

"The snapper," said the opso.

"There was nobody else there – unless you're selling our surveillance images to the press?"

The opso just gave her a look.

"Your operative was supposed to have destroyed the camera cards."

"He did."

"How do you know?"

"Because he does what I tell him to, and because he does what he says he'll do."

Libby knew that. The opso had his team's back, their loyalty and their respect. They wouldn't bullshit him.

"Well, we need to know where they came from."

"From the angles, I can see that they came from that snapper. That was where he was standing." The opso pointed at the screen. "And there – that's the right angle for looking across at the café. It was him."

"How?"

"Wi-Fi, or data. He must have been sending the images back in real time – immediately."

"A commercial photographer? I thought it was just the press pack and the paparazzi who carried on like that."

"Can't see any other explanation."

"Me either," she said.

"Does it matter? I mean, I can't see any of our team in shot."

"Well, we don't know what other shots he took," Libby said. "There could be a whole slate of them being emailed to media outlets all over the world."

"It's probably too late for a break-in."

"If he reports a break-in, that will get the police interested and make things a whole lot worse. Who knows what they'll find on his hard drives."

"You might just need to let it play out. That's the problem with this gig, Libby. You can control a lot – but not everything. When something really is beyond your control, it really is."

"Beyond control," Libby repeated the phrase. She'd heard it before but had never felt it quite so keenly.

Sinead had walked the little legs off Isla, from which were now dangling two sparkling white new trainers. They were a brand, apparently. Sam didn't know which, but he suspected they had been very expensive, and that Sinead had blown a week's wages on his daughter. Her enormous seat was swamped by glossy-looking paper bags with unnecessarily elaborate handles. He watched her try to stay awake as the train gently sprang and swayed her asleep.

Sam was distracted by what the father had said, his determination to assist. It occurred to Sam that while it had been rooted in what had happened to Isla, it also had something to do with what the father had heard Sal say on the radio. He knew he had no choice. He lifted his phone and pressed play.

"Please don't feel you need to describe—" the reporter said.

"I want to," Sal said. "People need to know what they did to her tiny body. They need to know that as long as these brave freedom fighters are out there, anybody's child could be next. They need to know that the doctors tried to refuse my husband see his child *because of what they did to her, what that device did to her. They need to know that my husband was determined to see his baby girl, and that he wanted to hold her – he wanted to hug her, and I wish so very much that I was able to hug her. But what he hugged were just bits of her. What they left of our beautiful baby were laid out on a table. He couldn't even hold her hand—"*

"Sal, Sal, you really don't need to—"

"People won't want to hear this, I know. I know. But I believe with all my heart that they should, and then – for those who might have an inkling of regard for what those heroes did, they might think again. For my child – our child, was buried in bits."

"Would you like to take a break, Sal?"

"No, I'd like you to broadcast what I've said. I'd like you to have the courage that the people who took Molly from us did not have – to face the people of Ireland, of Northern Ireland, and to say to them this is the price. It's not those mighty men who made that bomb that were carried to their graves in pieces – it was our beautiful child – and it has achieved absolutely nothing. And if they have children, maybe they'll look at them and think, what in all sense was I doing? Now, I don't expect them to hand themselves in – I don't expect that they'll ever be caught, but, please God, will they think before they plan anything like that again, for whatever their intention – whatever purpose they set out with, all they did was massacre children."

The reporter was silent for a second, evidently wavering as to how to manage this powerful, eloquent, grieving woman.

"You yourself were really badly injured."

"So were a dozen others." Sal dismissed the deviation.

"You may not walk again," the reporter pressed, which came as news to Sam.

"Honestly, I don't care," Sal said, and Sam knew she meant it. *"They took Molly, and with Molly everything else has gone. Nothing can come to any good now, you see. They removed all the point of life, of living, of working."*

"In time—" tried the reporter.

"In time nothing," whispered Sal, with an almost-silent conviction. *"You may think, 'She is grieving,' and you would be right, but I know – I know with all my heart that our lives are finished now. There is no good. They tore our child to pieces, they extinguished such a beautiful life, and, in a way, we will die with her."*

And Sam felt everything the father had felt, and probably more.

Eventually Grim was bailed. But not before he got the visit from a bloke making a half-arsed attempt to sign him up.

"Your comrades appear to be abandoning you. Why are they all at home when you're still here?"

Grim just stared at the spook, in his suit, in his cell.

"The big boss, he's drinking tea with his wife. The manager, he's having a wee holiday by the sea. And you're here. Why is that now?"

Grim knew not to reply. To say anything was to give them an in. He knew he needed to bide his time and wait for the spook to accept the inevitable: Grim wasn't for turning. Not just because of his commitment to the cause. Everything the suit said had a certain resonance, the begrudgery, the confusion. When you're on your own in a cell for days all sorts of notions and contortions enter the head, all sorts of mysteries and fantasies. The lack of outside makes the inside quite a murky place to inhabit. No, Grim was not for turning because Grim didn't want to be shot in the back of the head and have his naked body dumped on waste ground, with his skinny white legs on show for everyone to see.

The opso watched the manager on the monitor.

"Range is amazing," Libby commented absently.

"Camera's on a boat."

"Really?"

"Our friends in east DET, they're getting him from Carlingford Lough. To him it just looks like a fishing boat."

"So it's in Irish waters?"

"S'pose it is. Hard to be absolutely sure, though." He smiled. If he'd a metal filling it would have glinted.

"I assume the police will try to extradite him?"

"Unfortunately."

"Unfortunately?" Libby was surprised.

"Was a time when we'd have snatched him."

"Old war stories?"

The opso bristled. "Old but good."

"Go on, then," she goaded him.

"Stopped bombing in Belfast for months once with one snatch."

"How?"

"Sent a single operative across the border."

"To do what?"

"Beat the shit out of the IRA's quartermaster."

"How did that stop the bombing?"

"Cos the operative dumped him on the northern side and he got lifted. Between his injuries and his accusations and his trial and whatnot, he was in the system for a very long time."

"And that was enough?"

"He was the only one who knew where the gear was – the Semtex, the guns. They were paranoid – more suspicious than this lot." He nodded at the image of the manager. "If only one person knew where the toys were, then only one person could get blamed if we found their weapons dumps. Was clever enough. They kept their quartermaster over the border, out of reach, until we sent one lunatic across in his hiking boots to bring him and leave him like a sack of shit on the wrong side of the line. When he popped up in our jurisdiction, the towns went quiet."

"You want to do that with the manager?"

"I would *love* to do that with the manager."

"Different times," said Libby. "The Irish government are our friends now."

"Shame that," said the opso, watching the manager take his constitutional, down by the coast, free as a bird.

Sam's distraction wasn't lost on Isla. He was given to blundering about with a grumpy, almost-aggressive demeanour when he didn't know where to start a job that needed doing. He knew it would come to him, but he needed a nick from which to open a cut.

He no longer had the necessary information at his fingertips. In the navy, or the various secondments he had taken, intelligence had been plentiful. Now, the first thing he had to do was find out who was who, but to make inquiries would expose his interest and attract unnecessary attention.

He had first-hand knowledge of what would be going on in the background. Whatever his old unit was now called, it would be all over his targets, watching – undetected and undetectable, which meant any intervention by him would be noticed, and logged and lead, probably, to his own incarceration. Which would totally defeat the purpose and draw him away from Isla entirely. Sam knew what would happen if he went about it without due care and attention to detail.

Yet he never really doubted that it had to be done. There was just not enough grey in the matter. Isla could have been Molly. He could be Sal. The people who killed Isla's pal couldn't be reasoned with.

"Daddy, what's wrong?" he heard her say.

"What do you mean?"

"You seem cross."

"I'm just thinking."

"What about?"

"Nothing you need to worry about, wee lamb."

"Maybe we should go sailing," she said.

Sam turned to look at her properly. In the absence of any other thread to pull, and desperate for progress of any kind, he nodded. "That's a good idea, little lady. Let's do that."

The opso was bored. Libby was bored. There was nothing doing.

The screens showed routine – no deviation from the ordinary. For the operatives in the field, it was spine-seizing stuff sitting in cars with not enough walking. The only team that was enjoying itself was the eastern unit, which got to play at fishing for a few days.

"They grumbling much?" Libby asked.

The opso looked at her. "They don't complain, but they're pissed off."

"How long are you going to keep the original team on leave?"

"Long as I can."

Libby nodded. "The snapper's images are a problem. If the cops come asking questions, probably best your team isn't here to answer them."

The opso noted the distinction being drawn. It was 'our' team when the going was good, but the spooks had a habit of creeping to a distance when the shit hit the fan. He said nothing.

"So we have no eyes or audio on the Ballycastle family – the old girl and her son?"

"No need. Far as we know the cops have no notion of them or the role they played. Best just let that lie. If we start poking around, it only draws attention."

"Agreed."

"Sticks in the throat, though," the opso said.

"It does," Libby said, thinking of Deirdre Rushe. She'd been through the older woman's file since the bombing. A committed republican, Rushe had a hefty back catalogue of involvement in death – some military targets – and much collateral damage. "You ever get tired of this?" she asked the opso softly.

He shrugged a little. "I've been watching this lot for years now. It's strange, you know – to see them evolve and regroup, then fall out with each other. Every now and again, they get one over on us – they get something away, and while that makes me mad it gives me enough to keep going."

"When you were in the field – before you ran the show, did you never get tempted to take a few of them out?"

"Every day. Loyalists, republicans, paedos, rapists – we had them all at various times. But you know the score – the intelligence was more valuable than the satisfaction of killing a bad bastard. It's a long game. That's just the way it is."

"But these are the dregs," she said, nodding at the screen. "The paramilitaries *you* were following would have been better organised, they'd have replaced anyone you took out in a heartbeat. This lot," she pointed at an image of Grim standing at his back door smoking, "they don't have the numbers in their ranks to replace."

"Maybe there is a certain logic to what you're suggesting."

"I'm not suggesting anything."

Libby looked at Grim on the screen, then tracked across to the boss's front door, then to an image of Anthony's mother sitting in front of the television. The quadrant in the bottom corner of the huge screen was blank. No image of the manager, for the moment.

"You're right. If this lot were taken out, they would struggle to replace them. But that's the call you spooks make – not me. And those days are over."

16

"Hello, I just wanted to thank you properly for all the stuff you got Isla – far too much, but she's delighted with it. Anyway, hope everything's ok with you. Take care."

Sam ended the voicemail and took an armful of mainsheet. He could see Isla's new trainers tapping away below, dangling a few feet off the floor. He knew she'd have her new yellow headphones on, the ones covered with emojis, that Sinead had bought her.

They'd been sailing for about six hours and the going was good. *Siân* heeled just short of making him want to reduce canvas. He looked at the paper chart and wondered what to do next.

Sam had no firm plan, beyond returning to the scene. It was a process he had established over time: if in doubt, go there and something may present itself. It had often worked in the past. When things seemed desperate or hopeless, he frequently resolved it at site.

The phone buzzed in the inside of his sailing jacket, and his ears warmed a little at the name on the screen.

"That was quick."

"Ah, sure, you know."

"Get you at a bad time?"

"It's grand now. Was just seeing to a woman in the usual state."

"Trafficked?"

"Roma. Not for sex – to beg and get into benefit fraud. There's a gang being run, cross-border, actually. If ever you wanted to go back to the old gig, there's plenty to be looking at."

"Aye, right."

"You know I'm not asking."

"I do."

"How's my little butty?"

"She hasn't taken those shoes off, or those headphones, since you last saw her."

"Two weeks in the same trainers could be pretty whiffy on a boat. You sound like you're at sea?"

"We're off the coast and heading north for a few days. Change of scenery."

"Anywhere nice?"

"Thought we'd go to Glenarm for a start. Maybe take a skip over to Gigha at some stage."

"In Scotland?"

"Yeah."

"How far is that?"

"A day, maybe less. Depends what way the wind blows."

"What's in Gigha?"

"It's got tropical gardens because it's on the Gulf Stream, and warm waters come up from America. And it's got the best fish restaurant on the planet."

"Serious?"

"Only about a hundred people live there, but you want to taste the food in that place."

"Sounds lovely."

"Wanna come?"

"Now?"

"If you leave Dublin now, you could be aboard and get some kip before we set sail. Or we could just leave the day after or the day after that. I don't care."

"You don't care what?"

"I don't care when we leave."

"Oh, good. Ok, then. Sure, as you say, why not?"

Libby lifted the internal line and hit speed dial. "We have a problem."

"Oh?" said the opso, moderately interested despite the sinister suggestion. His mind had been so numbed by their task that something, even something awkward, was preferable to constant pointless surveillance.

"Seems the police have identified one of our vehicles."

"Doubt that," said the opso, sceptical. "How?"

"They have the snapper's shots."

"Come to the ops room."

It took Libby three minutes to cross from her secure office to the opso's command area.

"You're sure they're not just kite-flying?"

"No, I'm not sure," said Libby. "But whether they've correctly ID'd us or not, they've managed to get a formal request approved."

The opso's head see-sawed. "Well, at least we're prepared."

"To give them nothing. But we haven't prepared to give them *something*."

"Why would we give them anything?"

"Cos if they *have* correctly identified a vehicle that's ours, or an operative of ours, we need to explain what we were doing there shortly before a bomb went off."

"Yeah, well, let's see if they've actually identified one of ours."

"No," said Libby firmly. "Let's assume that they have and work out what we say when they come to see us."

"They're coming to see us?"

"They're sending Laurel and Hardy."

One member of the Police Liaison Team was short and stocky, the other was tall and thin – and they were no dozers.

"What do you want to say?"

"I won't say anything because I'll not be talking to them."

"Course not," said the opso, mildly annoyed that rank was being pulled. Libby had every authority to be absent when the police arrived, but the opso ran the show and the teams and so he would have to do the talking.

"Ok, so what would your bosses in the soft shoes like me to say to the cops?"

"If they do have something and if we can't deny it, then we need a story. Something plausible as to what we were doing there."

"Like what?"

"Like watching something other than a car bomb," said Libby sarcastically.

"Like. What?" he said slowly, with anger.

"How about," Libby's eyebrows rose and her lips pinched in a knowing smirk, "we give them the old woman?"

"Ah," said the opso, the proposition gathering appeal. "Under what guise?"

"Well, we get around the not-sharing issue by saying we were monitoring her for something else."

"We weren't monitoring her at all – we didn't even know she was there."

"And if *we* didn't, then they very probably didn't either. So we skew it all to her."

"How?"

"Can we say we do a periodic round-up of all the old hands – where they are, what they're up to?"

"She's a very old hand. Will they buy it that we just take a notion to tag someone for a while?"

"Depends what we come up with. Are there others we could lash together a monitoring file on?"

"Others of her vintage?"

"We'd need that probably – otherwise it's just too coincidental."

"We can certainly cobble together a few reports, but they would all be old mainstreamers – Provisional IRA types."

"Well, she was a Provisional. Once."

"Yes."

"So?" said Libby.

"So how long have we got?"

"Hour and a half."

"We can do that," said the opso.

Isla took Sam's hand as they made their way up the pontoon to the shower block.

"Think we might have a visitor for a few days," he said, hoping to please her.

"Who?"

"Guess."

"Ehm, can I have a clue?"

"Nope."

"Molly's mummy?"

That came as a total surprise.

"No, darlin', Molly's mummy isn't well enough to come visit. She's doing much better, though."

"How do you know?"

"I heard her on the radio."

"Why was she on the radio?"

"She was talking to the news."

"Why?"

"About, you know, what happened."

Isla went quiet. Sam let that breathe between them for a moment, then used the awkwardness to deal with another matter.

"I'd like you to speak to a person, not now, but at some stage – a professional person, just to make sure you're ok and getting better too."

"But I wasn't hurt."

"I know."

"Daddy?" she said in a way that told him she was ready to ask a big question.

"Yes, wee love?"

"Why was I not hurt?"

"It's a good question, wee love, but, honestly, I don't know. It's a miracle, and I am so grateful for it."

"Why did Molly get killed and her mummy get in hospital and I wasn't even very bruised or cut?"

"That's just the way it happens sometimes. It's just ... luck. And, you know, very bad luck."

"I think it was Mammy," she said.

Sam froze, there on the pontoon. He'd stopped walking and yet his heart rate increased. "What do you mean, Isla?"

"I think it was Mammy protecting me from heaven."

Sam took a deep breath. "I think you could be right, wee love. If she can protect you, she will. I know that for sure."

"Is that who's visiting?"

Sam began to panic a little, confused. "No, darlin', Mammy can't visit. You know that."

"Not Mammy, Daddy. The person to talk to me – the sessional?"

Sam's heart rate began to recover. "Professional," he stammered. "It's a professional I want you to see. But, no, I'm not talking about a counsellor. I'm talking about someone else."

"What's a counsellor?"

"Doesn't matter, darlin'. That's for later. The person who's coming is Sinead," he rattled, sorry now that he had tried to surprise her at all.

"Oh, ok." She shrugged.

"Is that not good news?"

"Yeah," she said, in a way that was neither here nor there.

He began to worry that talk of her mam combined with a visit from Sinead was an extra confusion in a messy mix. They reached the door and Sam turned practical as a means to escape his own muddled thoughts.

"I'm gonna sit out here in the lobby – just outside the door. You can go in and have your shower after I switch it on and make sure it's not too hot, and when you're done you can dry your hair in there too while I have my shower. Ok?"

"Ok."

He set the water temperature, laid out fresh clothes and her towel, then closed the door to give her some space. He sat in the spacious reception area with his head in his hands. She always took her time when, contrary to life on the boat, water supply was plentiful.

He'd been listening to the splash and slosh of water for about five minutes when the main door opened and a huge framed picture came through the gap. Sam rose to hold the door open to help the struggling man get the picture through without damaging it.

"Thanks, buddy," he said. "You're not sticking around for two minutes, are you? I've got to hang this bad boy."

Sam looked at the image. It must have been ten feet wide. "You were gonna put that up by yourself?"

"Mate, that's only the start of the hassle these bloody pictures have caused me," the man said.

Between them they took an end and raised it against the wall. The man marked the corners with a pencil, then they dropped the image down again. He opened the door and retrieved a cordless drill and plastic fixing pads. Sam held out his hand and took the pads while the man bored the holes.

"You could get a job, mate. I've six more of these to do."

"It's a cracking shot," Sam said, looking at the inflated image of the marina outside.

"Council job. Pays well. Part of a tourism drive for the north coast. We could do with it, given what's happened."

Sam said nothing, suddenly hoping Isla would stay in the shower.

"I was in Ballycastle that day, you know," he said, a dark look descending over his face. "Took a load of shots too. Spent two days there, actually, but I won't be putting any of them up any time soon."

"You were there the day of the explosion?" Sam was taken aback.

"Right at the harbour – framed the shot just like this one."

"And have you, like ..." Sam nearly said "blown it up", then corrected himself, "enlarged it too?"

"Yeah. I didn't enlarge the one of the bomb, like, obviously – just one of the shots from the day before. The police came and took all my hard drives. I've only the canvas now. Thankfully I had these off to the printers before they took my kit."

"You don't have it here, do you?"

"In the van. I've to hang the Portrush one next."

"Mind if I have a look?"

"C'mon ahead," said the man, as he nudged the hanging harbour on its new anchors.

"I can't – my wee girl's in the shower room. I don't want to leave her."

"Van's only at the door here."

Sam faltered for a moment.

"Look, never worry, you stand at the door and I'll slide it out. You wanna see the Ballycastle one?"

"Please," said Sam.

"Why?" said the man, suddenly curious.

"My dad was from Ballycastle," Sam lied. "He might like a picture like that."

The man shrugged and Sam held the door as the bloke gathered up his bits and went out. Sam could hear a van door slide open and wrestling and swearing followed before another ten-foot frame was dragged out. Sam placed his foot against the door and peered over a railing at the image.

"Don't suppose you'd sell it, would you?"

"No bloody use to me now," said the man. "Fifty quid, you can have it. They're usually two hundred."

"Can you take it off the frame and roll it?"

"Aye, it's just stapled."

Sam's heart raced as he scanned the picture while the man pinged the fastenings off with a small penknife.

"You know what, mate?" the man said as he handed the roll over the railing and accepted Sam's cash. "That's the first bit of luck I've had in weeks. See the day after I took that shot – the day of the bomb? Some goon came up to me, tore the camera cards out of my Canon and bucked the whole lot in the harbour." The man shook his head in wonder at the memory.

"Did you not try to stop him?" Sam asked, half expecting the answer he received.

"He wasn't the sort of boy you'd argue with – fit as two trouts. Anyway, thanks for your help. Hope yer da likes the shot."

Sam went back inside and called Isla to get out of the shower. He unrolled the canvas and scanned it again.

And then, confirmation of what he thought he'd seen on first inspection. There, as sure as he could possibly be, was someone he had once been deeply familiar with – a man he had followed by way of routine. Once a Charlie One, a mark, a person of interest, and here he was holding an ice cream in a seaside town just a day before the car behind him blew up.

———

Laurel and Hardy sat at a wonky desk in the grubby reception room, leafed through the files then looked up at the opso.

"So where's the video?"

"What video?"

"You sent your teams in to watch Deirdre Rushe and you didn't take video?"

Laurel had been sceptical before they'd started the conversation, and this revelation wasn't helping.

"There was no need for video – it wasn't an operation – it was just a check-in. See if she's moving about and if so, to where. It was just for a file update."

"And that's what you were doing there? That day of all days."

"Well, you can see from the file that we've been there plenty of days before. Nothing scheduled to it. Just good use of downtime. Practise as much as anything."

Laurel kept reading and flicking while Hardy stared at the opso. "You'll appreciate it's a bit of a swallow."

"Why? This is what we're supposed to do – check known people."

"Even if they've been out of the picture for years?"

The opso just shrugged.

"And when were you going to tell us you were in Ballycastle on that day?"

"We had no reason to. What we were doing wasn't connected to the bombing."

"But it's not you that's investigating the bombing, is it?" said Laurel, now angry. "That's for us to work out."

"Were you aware Deirdre Rushe was even living there?" the opso challenged the cop.

Laurel said nothing, which said everything.

The opso pressed on. "Look, if you think there's a connection – we don't see it, but you could lift her and see what shakes out of it."

"And you've nothing else?"

"Can I just remind you both that you still haven't volunteered what you have that placed us in Ballycastle."

Hardy sharpened his stare and Laurel raised his head, a cunning look creeping across his face.

"We have a witness statement from a photographer who says he was attacked by a man shortly after the bomb went off."

"So?" said the opso, his core contracting.

"So we wondered why someone would do that."

"Attack a photographer?" said the opso.

"Destroy evidence."

"What evidence? How?"

"By chucking it in the harbour."

"They chucked him in the harbour?" said the opso, hoping to blow smoke around.

But Laurel hadn't arrived in a bubble. "His kit."

"Have you recovered it?"

"What?" asked Laurel, wily.

"His camera."

"He's still got his camera – or, rather, we now have his camera."

The opso sighed impatiently. "Look, you're going to have to elaborate, fellas."

"You see it just as well as I see it," said Laurel. "You were at the harbour."

"What makes you think that?" said the opso, choosing his lack of outright denial carefully.

"Cos the boy that chucked the camera sounds just like one

of your outfit – he had a gammy accent, a pair of gloves on him, was fit looking and because I know, same as you know, that you're not telling me what I need to know," said Laurel. As he stood he slapped the paper file against his leg and turned to leave.

The opso stared at the two cops' backs and wished it had gone better.

The hull tapped twice and Isla's eyes lit up with more excitement than Sam had expected.

"Knock knock!"

"Go and see who's there," Sam said to her.

"I know who it is, Daddy." Her little trainers scampered up the companionway.

"Hello, me butty!" he heard Sinead say.

Sam whipped up the kettle, popped the whistler on the end and sparked the gas.

"Y'er welcome back," he said, turning to meet her. They hugged, which wasn't as awkward as it might have been, and he took her bag.

"So what's the plan, skipper?"

"Well, the weather looks good to leave tomorrow morning if that suits you. How long before you have to go back to work?"

"I've got four whole days if I want them."

"Come and see my stuff in my cabin." Isla took Sinead's arm, keen to show her how she had hung and arranged the gifts from Dublin.

"I'll put on the dinner," Sam said as they closed the door to him.

It was half an hour before they emerged. After dinner Sinead looked wrecked.

"Long drive?"

"Longer than I remember," she said distractedly, bringing them both back to the bomb. "She seems to be doing really well, Sam."

He could hear Isla's iPad prattling away behind the cabin door. "We had a shaky moment earlier on, but, yeah, she seems pretty good to me. But, then, that's a worry too, that she might be just bottling it up, you know?"

"I've been asking about a counsellor."

"A sessional?"

"A what?"

"I told her I wanted her to see a professional, and she asked me what a sessional was."

Sinead laughed. "What did she say?"

"She didn't say anything – she didn't say no. So ..."

"Well, the advice I've been given is to hold off. You can get into that stuff too soon and our people say kids need months to process trauma before counselling can be of use."

"Ok, how many months?"

"I've got a meeting with someone next week. I'll know more then."

"Thanks a million."

"What time do we cast off?"

"Five. Latest. You ladies lie on, though. I'll start off."

"You like the mornings."

"I do. It's peaceful. You're wrecked."

"I really am. I might go to the *leaba*."

"Get her to turn off that iPad."

"She's grand," Sinead said. "I could sleep through a hurricane tonight."

Which was music to Sam's ears.

An hour after that, and with no sound from inside the girls' cabin, he lowered the little RIB into the water from the back of the big boat. He pushed off, paddled her for fifty feet and at the breakwater started the engine.

"Look, it went ok," said Libby. "They got nothing, and they have nothing."

"You think?" asked the opso. "It's not one of your team who's been reported for assault."

"He didn't say assault."

"Could be criminal damage," said the opso.

"If they had an image of your op, then we might have an issue, but it seems pretty clear to me that there is no image."

"They'll be crawling CCTV in the surrounding area trying to pick him out. They might find the bikes, or the other car – or worse."

"Worse, how?"

"The Gazelle."

Libby had thought of little else. Explaining the Gazelle's presence in the airspace above Ballycastle would be difficult. She had relayed her concerns to her superior who had told her to keep him informed. "*If* they ask, tell them it was a comms check."

"They'll not buy that."

"They'll have to suck up whatever we tell them." Libby hardened her resolve.

The opso shrugged. "Whatever you say, Libby."

17

He didn't really know what he was looking for but his gut told him it would be useful to go. He'd never been to Ballycastle before and so the large, silent Rathlin Island ferry confused him in the darkness – its outline didn't look like a fishing boat. When he finally twigged what it was he gave it a wide berth in case there was CCTV on board to monitor passengers. Not that he intended to cause any trouble.

He took the little bruce anchor and wedged it among enormous rocks outside the harbour so that nobody would see his boat, and climbed onto the breakwater, stumbling and slipping his way onto the outer wall. He crouched to ensure he wouldn't be skylined against the murky horizon – imagining customs would be alive to the prospect of arrivals, although there was nothing but the sound of slapping halyards against aluminium masts.

It had taken him two hours to get there from Glenarm – the tide was against him, and he knew that with two hours back he had little time to look around. He found the spot he reckoned the photographer had stood and looked at the harbour. Then he rotated slowly, taking everything in – the car park, the marina, the dark gaping hole where the bomb vehicle had once been.

Slowly and with more trepidation than he had expected of himself, he made his way towards the café. The odd tail of plastic police tape still stuck out from knots tugged tight. Sam drew an aluminium gate anchored in a heavy plastic bases towards him a little and stepped inside. Under foot there was still debris and he could just make out the remnants of forensic kit.

He turned behind one tipped-up table and looked to where the window had been. Slowly the impact of what had happened crept back into him. He felt he was standing where Molly had died, opposite her mother, beside her friend. He could see the crater left by the car, yet if he took one step to the left – where he imagined Isla had been, it was obscured by a cavity concrete wall. That's why my child is still alive, he thought. The difference of two feet. He moved before his emotions could slow him, but as he did so he caught a flicker of blue light.

He immediately froze, knowing that movement in the dark was greater exposure than a silhouette. Then the light disappeared. He hunted for a way out of the café, assuming that someone had spotted him and called the police. He crept towards the kitchen and found a door – key still in the lock – to the backyard. There he hoisted himself easily over a seven-foot wall and dropped to the road outside.

The blue light was coming nowhere near him but he heard doors slamming and a commotion, so he walked uphill, curious. He watched reflections; glass was always a great way of betraying people, particularly where there were vehicles parked at all angles. Further into the town he caught sight of headlights – static, in the small window of a house door. He turned heel and made his way around the block, and within minutes he heard muttering, more doors closing then some sort of struggle. He rounded a corner, now looking downhill, before retreating again immediately. Three police cars, one armoured Land Rover and at least ten officers filled the top end of the street. He took ten steps into the unlit side of the street and watched from a distance as the cops – some dressed in tactical support kit, removed an old woman, an old man on oxygen, trundling his cylinder behind him, and then a middle-aged bloke from a house. There was hostility towards the police and Sam strained to hear, hoping they'd be read their rights in the street, but was quickly disappointed. The three were shoved into cars with more force than their age might have warranted – which made its own suggestion – and were driven off. The TSG team then set about conducting a search that Sam watched with interest, quietly crossing the road and taking in the house and its surroundings.

"There's nothing of interest in there," one of the gloved officers said to another. "She has no documentation apart from house insurance. None of them seems to even have phone bills – no sign of any mobiles, nothing."

"Have you lifted the floorboards?"

"We can do if you want."

"You know her background. If there's bomb-making equipment, it's not going to be sitting in a press in the living room, is it?"

"Sarge," said the first officer, adequately berated.

Sam moved away, looked at his watch and realised he was out of time. He made his way back to the harbour, got in the RIB and started the two-hour haul back to Glenarm. The boat bucked and revved hard as it bounced and bashed over the waves of a growing sea, but with concentration he kept her upright.

When he got back to *Siân* he cut the engine and stepped quietly aboard, winding the RIB up onto the davits as quietly as he could. Then he crept across the cockpit, slid the hatch of the companionway and received a shock.

"Good morning." Sinead was bundled up in a duvet waiting on him.

"Hi," he said as brightly as he was able. "What are you doing up?"

"To be honest, I'm sitting here wondering whether I was invited on this trip as a friend, or whether I'm just here as a babysitter to allow you to do whatever you've been off doing."

Her tone was as hard as he had ever heard her speak. His heart sank.

"No," he said, although suddenly he wasn't sure. "We asked you because we wanted you to come."

"*We* wanted me to come, or *you* wanted me to come?"

"We did. I did. Both?" Sam struggled.

"Do you want me here?" Sinead asked.

"Of course," he said. "I didn't want you to leave last time."

That seemed to take her by surprise and she softened. "Really?"

"Really."

"Why didn't you say?"

"I ... fuck, Sinead, I don't know. I'm not good at this stuff."

"What stuff?"

"Explaining things. Friendship, I guess."

"Friendship," she repeated, tired, frustrated.

"Relationships."

"Is this a relationship, Sam?"

He just stared at her hopelessly, unable to get any further.

"You're right, Sam, you're really not good at this stuff."

She turned with her duvet and went back to her cabin.

———

Sam didn't know what to do. He debated whether Sinead might

be more cross if he cast off and left, but she hadn't said she wasn't coming. The plan had been to leave at five o'clock and she hadn't appeared. If she gets up and wants me to take her back, we'll fight the tide and return, he thought. The option saddened him when he thought about it, so he stopped thinking about it and hoisted the mainsail.

Three hours later he was flagging. He'd watched Cushendall and the Glens of Antrim glow in the dawn then fall to the horizon as they pushed nautical miles under the waterline.

He'd not recognised the old couple or the younger man. They were geriatrics – the older couple, at least, yet there they were clearly being arrested in connection with the explosion. He checked his phone every few minutes that he had service to see if there were any news reports on the arrests, but it was still much too early for a solicitor to tip off a reporter. Eventually their identities would leak out, which might give him some time to try and repair the issue in front of him.

"Coffee?" Sinead was dressed, and apparently not surprised that they were offshore.

"Love one, please," he said.

She nodded and disappeared again. A few minutes later he heard the whistle and prepared himself for whatever he was due. She came on deck and handed him his covered mug and took a sip from her own.

"How far have we gone?"

"Twenty miles-ish."

"And how far is it to this wonderful restaurant?"

"Same again," he said. "I was worried you might not want to go."

"Were you really?" she said and looked straight at him.

"Yes."

Then her face softened and something short of a smile crept in as she turned away. "I'd cross the Atlantic with you two," she said, "never mind the Irish Sea."

And then she was below, and soon there was the smell of rashers cooking and he was relieved he hadn't told her they were actually crossing the North Channel.

Libby's superior never paid visits, yet she found him sitting in her chair in her secure quarters on the edge of the DET's area of the base.

"Oh," she gasped. Nobody but her occupied that wing of the building, built as it had been for more of her type during busier times.

He looked up from her handwritten notes, evidently enraged. "You gave the police something?"

"Yes, I kind of had to. Is there a problem?" Her voice began to croak a little.

"There is a problem," he said softly, which was even more disconcerting.

"We had to offer them something insignificant to explain why we were in Ballycastle."

"So, in your wisdom, you handed them the safe house?"

"We handed them an old-timer – largely removed from the whole thing."

"And how would you know how removed she is?"

Libby remained quiet for a moment. She hadn't really considered Deirdre Rushe to be key to this at all. Her file had ended almost a decade previously, and so handing her over hadn't seemed a problem. "Well, I looked her up and there were no updates on record, so I assumed she was old vintage?"

"Old vintage is often the most valuable."

"She's an asset?"

"She's not a person I want lying in a police cell with her emphysemic husband sucking on an oxygen mask and her imbecile son crying like a child about going back to jail!"

The superior's outburst was enough to quell the questions rocketing around Libby's head. "Sorry," she said sincerely. "The police liaison pair were coming and it seemed like a quick way to deviate their interest."

"Stall, Libby. Never act in haste. You should have put them off, not spun some reactive scheme. You need to be playing the pieces – not the plods."

"Understood. Of course. Sorry. How can we fix this?"

"What do they have on us?"

"To place us there?"

"In Ballycastle, yes."

"Very little. One of the ops approached the photographer and disposed of his camera cards."

"On the day itself?"

"Immediately after the explosion."

"So he could pass as an angered citizen?"

"They seem pretty convinced he was ours."

"And you handed them Deirdre Rushe on the strength of that? That they seem 'pretty convinced'?"

"Now you say it like that, I can see what a mistake it was."

"You cannot imagine what a mistake it was, Libby, but what's done is done. Now we must wait for Rushe to be released, and then give her some peace. If you tag her, or are requested to by the police, make it exceptionally loose. I do not want that woman upset any further."

Libby couldn't help but be curious at her superior's turn of phrase, but she knew better than to open her mouth again.

"Ok, it's pretty good," Sinead said as she finished the seafood platter she'd shared with Isla.

"It's really nice. I luff it," Isla chipped in.

Sam chugged a rum and felt as content as he had in a long

while. He looked at his little girl, completely at ease, and put up his hand to request a refill from the bar. Sinead poured another glass of wine.

"Can I go to the toilet?"

"Course."

Sinead waited until Isla had opened the door, then the warmth of the alcohol and the rustic surroundings gave her enough confidence to pose the question. "So you gonna tell me where you were last night?"

Sam deliberated a little, then thought – what the hell, I didn't kill anyone. "I went to the scene."

"Oh," she replied, genuinely surprised and then instantly guilty. "Oh, Sam, I'm sorry."

"Why?"

"Well, I just assumed you were, you know, working or something."

He thought for a moment. "You've nothing to be sorry for."

"I can ... understand, I guess, why going there was important. I'd forgotten you hadn't been there at the time."

"You saw it in the aftermath. That must have been rough."

"I was scared, for Isla. The rest of it just kinda went by in a frenzy."

"Thank you for what you did. It was ..."

"Don't be daft. But how was it – for you – seeing it?"

"Fine." Sam shrugged. "It's done now."

"You're tired," she said.

"Good tired," he replied. "In good company."

And she realised that was about as much as she could hope for just now.

"What's the plan tomorrow?"

"You want to see the gardens? Apparently they're beautiful."

"Yeah. Not really your thing, though, I'd imagine."

"I might go for a swim. It's pretty clear up round here – the water, like."

After three courses they headed down the single pontoon and Sam poured two powerful nightcaps as Isla got ready for bed. And then they were back where they'd been a few weeks before, sitting in the saloon, drinking strong rum, loosening their tongues.

"That unit you worked in."

"Uh-huh," Sam said, unsure as to why that should feature in Sinead's thinking.

"Is it still going now? I mean, is it supposed to operate in peace time?"

"It wasn't really supposed to operate back then. At least not the way it did, I reckon."

"But intelligence gathering was official, wasn't it?"

"Ah, yeah, but there was some blurring of the edges."

"So is it still going?"

"I'd say so, but it'll be even further under the radar now."

"And have you any friends left in it?"

"I don't know," said Sam honestly. "Why?"

"Just wondering, you know, they might be, like ... helpful."

Sam looked at her for a long while but didn't feel the need to clarify what she meant, opting to take her comment as a kind of endorsement.

"The DET isn't the type of organisation you could find out about. If someone was still in it – or back in it, which is more likely cos the secondments were mostly time-limited, there wouldn't be any way to find out. That's if it is actually still working at all."

"But you said it was?"

"I said it probably was. I can't see them giving up that sort of gathering capability."

"Gathering?"

"Information, movements, intel. The stuff we could do back then would make your skin crawl. I'd say the stuff they can do now with digital tech would probably blow both our minds."

"Probably should zip it then." Sinead slurred a little as she smiled but closed her lips to run a finger and thumb across them.

Still, it was comforting to know she had worked him out and wasn't cross about it.

Deirdre Rushe lay in her cell; an old woman crouching to her hands and knees to lie on a rubber mat, worried for her husband, terrified for her son.

The old man on oxygen was taken to a private room at Causeway Hospital where a police officer sat outside as he sucked on his bottle and watched his telly. The son was visibly upset at being back in a cell but was just about smart enough to remember to keep quiet.

And then the questioning stopped and without explanation they were released. The cops even ordered them taxis.

The opso handed Libby a tablet. "Demand from the police. Note the tone."

She looked at the call sheet: direct close observation of Deirdre Rushe and her son.

The opso's eyebrows knitted together. "They don't direct us, Libby, they request."

"We'll just need to wear this for a while. And we also need to make the watch more relaxed than usual – Deirdre Rushe is not a threat."

"How do you know that?"

Libby tilted her head a little. "You know better than to ask me that."

It did nothing to improve the opso's mood. "We're just the

oily rags, Libby. We're here at your command," he said and walked off.

Sam had plenty of time to think as they crossed the North Channel. Plied with coffee and grub he was joined at the helm, on occasion, by Sinead. They didn't say much, but the sea wasn't uncomfortable and the sun went down in a blaze of red, promising a good dawn. The instruments blinked from white light to red, and he showed her how to read the radar.

"So when we get back, you've got a day to relax. You might need it if you stay up all night."

"I'll go to bed soon, but I'd like to see the sunrise."

"I'll give you a call. It won't seem like long, though."

"Do you ever sleep?"

Sam ignored the question and posed one of his own. "How would you feel if I went to the scene again – when we get back."

"I'm sure I'm not supposed to ask why."

Sam shrugged in the dusk, but he didn't know whether she'd seen it.

"Fine," she said, but not in a it's-fine-but-it-isn't-really-fine-at-all sort of way.

"Thanks, Sinead."

The boat sliced on and Sinead eventually got up to go below. "You'll wake me – before sunrise?"

"I might even make the coffee."

Only one hack had been tipped off about the release. She called for comment but received none as the old woman and her half-daft son scuttled into the house, heads down. The curtains remained drawn from the night they'd been picked up.

Shortly afterwards an ambulance pulled up and the husband was aided to the front door by a paramedic.

Deirdre wondered how she would even manage to get a pint of milk if the journalist stayed outside. She had no friends in the town and she couldn't expect anything better than hostility from here on in. She had no doubt they would have to move house, yet again. That made her think of the man who had asked her to put the rangy youth up in her home. And she hated him.

Her husband looked badly shaken. She sat him down, slipped his feet into his slippers and made black tea. With wet eyes she stroked his wizened cheek, smoothing it with her thumb, sorry for all she had put him through over her fifty years as an activist. He bubbled and sucked as she went upstairs to turn on their electric blanket. She found a man sitting on the bed. Dressed oddly in black.

"Say nothing, step inside, close the door."

The opso stared at the screen and sighed.

"Right, pull back."

"Received," came over the net.

He turned to Libby. "We should at least have put a rip in the house."

Libby just shrugged. She couldn't disagree. It would have been standard to listen to what was being said in the home of someone arrested for involvement in a bombing. But her superior had been clear: loose watch, and only if requested by the police. She may never know for sure but everything indicated that Deirdre Rushe was more than an ageing old activist.

The old woman froze, yet evidently saw little point in screaming or running outside into the hands of a hostile reporter. She managed to get a hold of her emotions and gradually became calmer than he could have hoped for – taking him in, running him down from shaven head to wide shoulders, rubber suited head to foot.

"How long have you been here?" she said.

"Not long," he replied, curious as to why she hadn't first asked *who* he was.

"You lot said we'd be out sooner."

At which point the mist cleared a little and something told Sam he'd misunderstood.

"So what now?" she said.

"Sit down." Sam stalled, motioning to the bed, rationalising what was going on.

"You want to what – debrief me?" she nearly snarled.

Sam thought that was as good a proposal as any given that this was not going as he'd anticipated.

"Talk me through it," he hedged.

"I wanted rid of him." She shrugged. "So I went to Coleraine and called Grim and told him – get this kid out of my house."

"Why?" Sam was confused as to why she was talking so freely. Who did she think he was?

"He was a sulky little twerp, scratching at the walls, and I couldn't trust him. I caught him one night – looking out."

"Looking at what?"

"He saw me going to the car to talk to your lot."

Sam trod softly lest he messed up this unexpected opportunity. "Go on," he ventured, offering nothing, hoping for everything.

"Grim flew off the handle and sent that sleeked little shit in his place."

Bingo, thought Sam, and took a risk. "The manager?"

"Useless git. He just told me to hang on. I thought he was here to take the kid away. I'd changed my mind – I do not need this shit any more. I have a dying husband to look after – and you lot promised you'd get him the best of care and I am yet to see it."

She's an informer, thought Sam. Someone turned her.

"Then what?"

"Then I threw the lad out, and, sure, you know the rest. He's dead, God rest him."

"Tell me anyway. I need the details."

"Well, I don't know the rest, do I?" she rounded on him. "He obviously went to a car at the harbour and managed to trigger a device!"

She was angry now. Sam thought this stone-cold killer might cry.

"So what was the target?"

Her eyes sharpened and her head took a tiny move to the right, suspicion falling over her face like a shroud.

"Did you know what he was here to do?" Sam gave it a last gasp, knowing he'd lost her.

"Who are you?" She got up suddenly, reaching for the door.

"Who do you think I am?" He rose and slammed the door shut, conscious it would lead to interest from below.

She wrestled a bit but he caught her and manoeuvred her face down onto the bed, taking her arm behind her.

"That's your son downstairs," he growled in her ear.

"You leave him be," she managed to wheeze. "He's not wise and he's no threat to anyone."

"He's a dead man if you don't answer the next set of questions quickly and honestly."

She panted heavily and Sam could feel how brittle the old woman was in his gloved hands.

"What was the plan?" he barked.

"I don't know – you'd need to ask Grim or Hagan."

"Where can I find this Grim?"

"Who are you?" she asked again, defiant.

"You wanna keep your son and husband breathing, you tell me what I need to know right now."

"Creaghan," she spluttered as he twisted her wrist.

"Crayon?" he repeated, angry and conscious of noise and time.

"It's an estate."

"Derry?"

"Craigavon."

"Number?"

"Don't know," she gasped as the door opened behind them, a pause, then the son rushed in.

Sam let go of the tiny wrist and used the momentum of his turn to uppercut the approaching man who was unconscious before he hit the floor. His slippered feet actually caught air as he rose with the punch, his head smashing against a small desk on the way down.

"Leave him alone!" Rushe cried.

"Where was the bomb for?"

"What?" she sobbed.

"What was the target?"

"I wouldn't know that. I was just putting the boy up!" She stared at her son.

"Who made it? Who made the bomb?"

"Have you—"

"He's not dead – not yet. Who made the bomb?"

"You'd need to ask Grim."

Sam heard a door open downstairs, followed by a pant and a shuffle.

"Deirdre?" came a hoarse whisper, barely audible through the open door.

"You mention this visit to anyone, I'll come back and finish him," he pointed to the prostate son on the floor, "and the oul fella will choke to death without his bottle."

"Just get out," she growled, pushing past him to kneel at her son. "Get out!"

"Deirdre?" The voice at the foot of the stairs was weakening.

Sam rolled a balaclava down his face. The old woman rose to speak to her husband, but as she did so her ankle gave way and she stumbled round the door frame and plummeted down the stairs.

"Fuck," Sam said quietly, and went down after her.

The old man had one blue-veined hand wrapped around a medical-issue banister, the other clutching his mask as he heaved air into him and stared at his wife, bundled at his feet. His eyes opened in amazement as Sam, all in black, came down after her.

"You ... killed her," the old guy heaved, stunned.

Sam looked at her and had to agree that she did look rather dead, twisted upon herself, but he didn't have time to give it thought. He reached down and popped the tube off the old man's bottle and lifted the gas from its wheels. The convulsions followed quickly as Sam made his way back the way he'd come in, cylinder under his arm. He'd wait for four o'clock, dead hour, to extract past his former friends and the curiously loose surveillance he'd watched them put in place.

18

"What the fuck is going on?"

Two visits in one week. Not good. Libby looked at her superior and opted for honesty. "I ... thought maybe you were here to tell me?"

"What?"

"Well, you said withdraw, loose watch, nothing intrusive, so I thought—"

"You thought *we* did this?"

"No, no," she stumbled, meaning, yes, of course that's what I thought. She could see he was seething.

"Just how loose a watch was it that you couldn't see someone enter a house in a lit street with nobody else around?" he shouted.

"I don't know," she stammered. She'd never heard him raise his voice before.

"Two people dead, another straight out of jail and into hospital with a shattered jaw. This is great work, Libby," he spat, starting to walk around her room.

"I, honestly, I couldn't have imagined—"

"She was one of the best assets we ever had. One of *the* most senior. Now she's dead because of this fucking two-bit operation, and we have no idea who killed her!"

"Is it definitely murder?"

"It's worse – it *looks* almost like an accident. Whoever did this is either very lucky or very forensically aware."

"What does the post-mortem say?"

"Trauma to the arms, upper back and shoulder – which we might be able to blame on the cops during the arrest. That might get us away from the idea that she was pushed down the stairs, but the son's shattered face is hard to bloody explain, isn't it?"

"What's he saying?"

"What? What!" the superior screamed. "He's not saying anything! His jaw's in twenty bloody pieces!"

Libby shook her head in despair. "Where does this leave us?"

"A dead asset, a suffocated geriatric with a mysteriously missing oxygen bottle and a halfwit with a busted face, all within hours of being released from custody. That's pretty much where we're at."

"Can we blame loyalists? Locals? A local backlash!" She leapt at the notion.

"We," he lowered his voice, "we, Libby, will say nothing. We will not manage this. We will allow this to become a problem for the police."

"But we were supposed to be watching the house."

"That's for the opso to sort out with the cops."

"But it was us," Libby shortened her steps, careful not to upset her superior any further by saying "you", "that ordered a loose watch."

"Convey to the operations officer, Libby, that it is vital that that information is not passed on to the police."

Libby nodded and turned to face her second bollocking of the morning.

"Job on the safe house."

Unaccustomed as Grim was to compliments from the boss, he knew better than to bullshit him. "How do you mean?"

"Old Rushe – the tidy-up."

"Sorry, I'm not following you."

"Deirdre Rushe getting dead. Wasn't you?"

"No," said Grim, astonished. "When? I thought they'd released her?"

"And then this morning she's dead. Not you, then. Well, that's a shame. Thought you'd finally managed to do something right." The boss looked witheringly at Grim.

"Where's the manager?" Grim looked for a diversion.

"Not coming."

"Why?"

"Done a runner across the border."

"To where?"

"Usual, I'd say."

The three had met plenty of times on the shores of Carlingford Lough or in the hills and woods above it; hopeful of sufficient cover to avoid detection, confident that the Republic's surveillance techniques weren't as sophisticated as those of the British.

"Was she murdered?"

"I assumed so. Now, I dunno."

"Suicide?"

The boss shrugged. "Still, suits well enough. Gives you a layer of protection anyway even if it wasn't you."

"What about the engineer – has he been lifted?"

"Don't know," said the boss.

"That's the weak link, far as I can see."

"Weak how?" The boss's cold eyes rotated almost mechanically to stare at his number two.

"Well, the engineer could lead back to you," Grim ventured, suddenly unsure.

"You let me worry about that."

"Sorry."

"So what have the cops got?" the boss asked.

"Well, they can link me to the kid in the car, but that's all, far as I can see. My solicitor says there's no sign of surveillance evidence."

"They'll have surveillance," the boss grunted. "Be sure of that. But what'll they get from that?"

"Well, I was never in Ballycastle," Grim replied, but neglected to mention that the manager had been pressured into going.

"Ok, let's see. They'll want us to do a bit of time, no matter what. I'd expect a spell on remand."

Grim had anticipated as much. If prosecutors couldn't prove anything, they could at least offer charges of some sort in an attempt to take the pair off the streets until the case collapsed.

The opso stood like a DJ in a nightclub with one headphone pressed to his ear listening to the exchange between Grim and the boss. They hadn't killed the old girl, then.

The watch may have been loose, but to have failed to spot anyone entering or leaving the house was strange. They had no idea how two people had died under their noses without even a whimper.

"I want every word from that pair," he snapped.

"We've got them well covered," the operator confirmed.

Listening devices had been placed in the clothing of both Grim and the boss during their arrest. While they were in jail operatives had been deployed to their respective wardrobes to secrete further fully-charged units to coats, boots, shoes and buttons. It was as lavish an outlay as the DET had committed in years, and unless the pair met in a swimming pool in their Speedos, the opso was confident he would be able to patch in. He was happy with that, but less happy at the visitors he saw approach the perimeter gate on the monitor. He sighed and hit an intercom button.

"Let Laurel and Hardy in. Give them a brew and tell Libby they're here. I'll meet them in a conference room."

He set out on the five-minute walk. Libby caught him up on the way.

"It wasn't us, apparently."

"Don't talk shite." The opso was too exhausted to get angry.

"Really. It genuinely wasn't us. Up the chain – they're livid."

"They're livid that an old Provo is dead?"

"Livid that we didn't see anyone go in or out."

The opso stopped in his tracks. "Can I just remind you, Libby, that it was your team who demanded a loose watch."

"I know. I know."

"So it wasn't Grim, and it wasn't the boss. And you say it wasn't your crowd. So nobody did it, apparently. They just died all by themselves."

Libby said nothing – she had nothing to say.

"What do I say to this pair?" The opso started marching again. "This has put my team tight in it, Libby."

"I'm really sorry. What if ..."

"What?"

"What if I come in with you?"

"You'd be prepared to do that?"

"It's not fair that you take the heat for something I did."

The opso relented a little. "I know it's not *you*, Libby. I know there are people pulling the strings."

"But I can help put it right. You'd need to introduce me as one of your team, though. Best they don't know who I work for."

"You sure? What are you gonna say?"

"I have an idea," she said as they buzzed the gate. "Bear with me."

The gate opened and they crossed a short hallway to enter the conference suite. There stood the short one, while the tall one sat, fingers locked into one another on the desk in front of him. Nobody said hello.

"Big problem," Hardy eventually muttered – which was unusual given that Laurel usually did the talking.

The opso looked at Libby, who breathed in deep and began. "We've reviewed what we have. I'm afraid there's not much."

Laurel spat out a sarcastic laugh and arched his back into the rear of his chair. "Here we go."

"And who are you?" asked Hardy.

"She's my best analyst," said the opso.

"We were on location from when the first party arrived at the address on release from custody," Libby pressed on.

"Not before?" Hardy's tone was flat.

"Not before," Libby confirmed.

"When did you become aware of an incident?"

"We were monitoring the phone line. We knew of the emergency call same time as you. Although, as you know, there was no speech on the call on account of the—"

"Shattered jaw," Laurel interjected. "Do you expect me to believe that you didn't place a listening device in the house?"

"We didn't," said the opso.

"Why?" asked Laurel, not believing a word of it.

"Because we've been tied up getting your lot information on surveillance we don't have in relation to a bomb attack we knew nothing about," the opso barked back, managing to summon indignant anger despite lying through his teeth.

"This is beyond a joke," Laurel said. "I'm supposed to go back to the MIT team and tell them that the request we made," he gestured between himself and Hardy, "to have a watch placed on this family has resulted in two of them dead and not a peep was heard of any of it?"

"You asked for a watch, we put a watch in place – we monitored their phone."

"Sure, *we* could have done that!" Laurel shouted, exasperated. "You're supposed to bring an extra layer of sophistication to the whole thing!"

The opso looked at Libby.

She put out her hands and offered her spiel. "Listen, lads."

"Lads, now, is it?" Hardy's tone didn't waver.

"We can't give you what we don't have, and, I'm sorry, but we don't have anyone coming to or leaving the property. We just don't."

"We'll want the pictures, assuming you have some this time," Laurel nipped.

"You can have them." Libby looked to the opso, who nodded. "But it makes us wonder, is this whole thing a bit simpler than it seems?"

"What d'ye mean?" Hardy asked.

"Well, if we don't have anyone going in or leaving, could it not be that the son did it?"

The two men stared perplexed at Libby and the opso resisted the temptation to do the same.

She pushed on. "He's angry at being arrested, right? He turns on the mother, maybe they have a fight, and she hits him."

"That old crow couldn't break a man's jaw."

"Unless she hit him with the oxygen cylinder."

Laurel's head was shaking.

"She hits him, smashes his jaw, and in the struggle he pushes her down the stairs."

"So where's the bottle?" Hardy answered flatly.

"That's your job." Libby was keen to turn the tables. "You tell us. We're not experts in investigations."

"You're not experts in anything, far as I can see," Laurel growled.

"You've a man suffocated, right?" Libby pressed on.

"Uh-huh," Hardy agreed.

"Maybe that happened cos she took the bottle from the husband and hit the son, and he pushed her before the bottle could be reattached."

"All good," said Laurel, "except for one thing. Son's been interviewed in hospital and he wrote down his answers. He says there was a man there – hard-looking nut. Dressed like a space-man, he says. Waiting on them. Which makes me think, that's the second time some bloke who looks like an undercover bod has been spotted in that town. Which then makes me think you lot are giving us the fucking runaround. Which makes my boss think that your team needs investigated."

Messy, thought the opso, who could feel himself rinsed, rung and about to be hung on a washing line by everyone around him. And all because of a missing oxygen bottle.

The bottle had been essential.

Sam had predicted a very tight watch on their home. On his previous visit – darting around in the dark, he'd noted the split-level roofs of the semi-detached houses. The old girl's neighbour had upstairs window conversions, as well as a little pile of post in the porch behind the glass door. All Sam reckoned he needed was a gas-powered life jacket, maybe the cylinder from a foghorn as backup and his drysuit, which he'd washed down thoroughly. The suit, sealed at the neck, wrists and feet prevented hair, sweat or clothing matter from falling anywhere.

It was also pitch-black on his return visit, so he made his way to the house unnoticed. A hop onto a wheelie bin took him to the rear return of a gently sloping roof and to the cheap

Velux-alterative window. Carefully he fed the life jacket material between the seal and the sill and, when satisfied, he triggered the gas canister to blow the double hook locks to the side, leaving them unbroken and him free to roll in. The plan was to leave no hint at all that there had been a break-in.

All had gone far too smoothly as he stood in the silent house, confident the neighbours were on holiday. He'd been removing the roof-space hatch when he heard a car pull up. He froze and waited, then heard the groans of a stretch from a long drive and the trundle of a trolley suitcase.

Sam strode back to the window and reluctantly closed it again. Gathering his bits, he quickly stuffed them behind the heavy waterproof zip of his suit and chinned himself up into the attic. He replaced the timber square just as someone started up the stairs.

"Oh, it's damp up here, David," he heard a woman call behind her.

"Well, it's been a month. Open the windows for a minute," a man shouted.

"Too cold!"

"It's ok, I'll put the heating on for a while."

"You forgot to lock them, David!"

"What?"

"This one wasn't locked!" she shouted.

"Sorry. The key's in the bedside cabinet!"

Not good news. Sam waited. He heard the hum of a boiler come on, and twenty minutes later the windows began slamming shut, one after the other. Then the locks were turned.

When the woman was back downstairs he used the clanking of heating pipes and the creak of a warming house to cover his crawl through to the target house, only to find a partition wall had been built right up to the rafter. He rested on his knees for a moment and questioned whether luck was stacked against him. Outside were some of the best-trained special operatives in the British Isles, as well as what appeared to be a reporter. Meanwhile, he was locked in a roof space of two occupied semis and had a wall to dismantle without any tools.

Gently he extracted the foghorn canister and tried scraping the mortar from between the bricks with the nozzle. Accidentally, the air escaped and blew the old sand–cement mix out easily. He kept going until the first brick was loose and set it down gently. One after another he pulled the blocks off until the gas was finished and he had just enough room to climb into the next opening. He felt his way lightly, occasionally flicking on his head torch to confirm he wasn't about to plummet through the plasterboard. Ten feet to the hatch took thirty minutes to navigate. He listened intently. Nothing. He lifted it gently, lowered himself down, crossed a tight landing and sat on a bed in a room with a pink carpet. And waited.

The extraction had been more difficult. Sam was rusty. That two, possibly three, people had died required greater attention to detail than he had afforded on the way into the house. There would be a proper forensic investigation, so covering tracks was essential. He also knew that outside was a team who would apply more than usual effort to establish what had happened.

He left through the ceiling, abandoning hope of replacing the brickwork – there would be no means of establishing when the party wall had been dismantled. Then he lugged the canister, with great care, back to the neighbours' house, comforted by the snoring of one of its inhabitants. He checked the through-ceiling fittings for light from below and, satisfied, began his descent into the house. He balanced on the canister to replace the attic hatch, wobbling worryingly as he met the ground again, pausing for any indication of movement. Then, down the stairs to the back door – there was no way his luck would stretch to him retrieving the window keys from a bedside cabinet no matter how soundly the couple slept. There he unlocked it from the inside and once again placed the flat bladder of the life jacket carefully between the sliding bolts of the lock. On the outside he attached the air to the inlet and inflated the life jacket to ram the lock bolts back into place, then deflated it again as he pulled it free. Ten steps across the backyard brought him to a hedgerow over which he and the bottle went. The house behind stood silent as he made his way past their bins and onto a parallel street.

Down the hill he went, taking a joining street to check on his former colleagues – still sitting in their car apparently unaware of any excitement. It would take a very careful police investigation to establish a means of entry or departure. Content, he went back to the RIB and made his way to Glenarm.

The three of them woke late the next day, the salt air and the motion of the boat having put them properly out. Sinead made breakfast with an efficiency of movement, as if she'd battered around a cramped galley all her life. Pancakes, at Isla's request – flour everywhere.

And then, inevitably, the parting, but it wasn't an awkward affair.

"Right so, I'd better hit south," she'd said.

Isla looked up in surprise. "Why?"

"Because I have to go back to work and you lads have to sail home. I assume you're headed back?"

"Yeah," Sam said. "School, Isla. We've got to get back to normal at some stage."

"But you said you wanted me to go to the sessional?"

Any port in a storm, Sam thought. "A professional," Sam said. "A counsellor."

"I used to see a sessional," Sinead said, unexpectedly.

Sam paused and listened.

"Why?" said Isla, straight out with it.

"To help me with things in my head that were keeping me awake at night."

"What things?"

"Things from the past," was as far as she went. "Not for sharing with anyone except the sessional. You know, wee secret things."

Sam didn't want to pry but felt awkward ignoring her effort to encourage Isla. "Did it help?"

"It really, really did," she said brightly, still looking at Isla. "I sleep really well now."

"I sleep ok," said Isla.

"Tell me about it, snorey head," Sinead said.

They walked Sinead up the pontoon to her car, Isla carrying a small bag, Sam a larger one that weighed a tonne. He didn't ask what was in it.

"Thank you for a lovely trip." She bent down to give Isla a cuddle. "And thank you, Sam, for asking me. If you ever need a crew again, you know where I be."

He stepped forward and she fell into his embrace with ease. They lingered there for a few moments longer than they ever had before, his arms tightening around her ribcage. She, surprised at first, reciprocated with a strong grasp. Then the moment faded and with a gentle regret they dropped apart. And she was gone. Again. And Isla and Sam went to sea.

The opso went for a long walk. He'd been putting in the hours in front of the bank of screens, constantly looking up, neck crooked, watching, waiting. He needed to look down for a while, to look around at the beautiful scenery over Magilligan Beach, Lough Foyle and beyond.

Yet the exercise failed to lift the fog. All the way up he stewed. Every fall of a foot and stab of his stick slammed into the head of whoever pulled Libby's strings. It wasn't Libby's fault, but the opso had been around long enough to know

when it was his turn to get screwed over. He'd seen it before –
previous operators blamed and disciplined while the faceless
walked away without even being questioned.

He'd really grown to like Libby, to admire her, but knew she
didn't have the flying time to stand up to the suit who'd visited
her quarters. The opso had seen him coming on the cameras
and understood that his arrival spelt bad news for him. The
soft-shoe brigade only ever turned up when the wheels were
about to fall off – and they always ensured that their own
agency never got the blame.

He had taken altitude to breathe the air and stretch his
muscles, yet the higher he got the more indignant he became;
frustrated that a thirty-year career in the military was about to
end with indignity – probably discharge. That would impact
his ability to score one of those well-paid security advisor posi-
tions on civvy street.

He should have got out years ago, with his mates, he
thought. Do ten years, maybe even fifteen, and offski. Yet he'd
hung on because at the time he felt it was worth it. He'd got a
kick out of crushing terrorists, of preventing them making real
on their plans. His drive dated back to the seventies when he'd
been robbed of a father by an unidentified insurgent.

The opso had worked for promotion to ensure he stayed in
the DET. For many bereaved in the province Northern Ireland
held nothing but hostile thoughts, but he had grown to love the
countryside and the peace of the hills around the base. The
ability to leave a town or city and within minutes be in the hills
– hiking, walking, camping, never ceased to amaze him. He had
all but made the place his home, rarely heading back to Liverpool on leave. Instead he took to the mountains, north or south
– often against protocol, and as peace broke out across the
country he engaged more frequently with the natives and he
found he liked them.

When the bomb had detonated in Ballycastle he'd felt a

real shock of failure. During the daily violence, some disasters were inevitable, but they'd become accustomed to success in recent years. Now, his position as a faceless protector of the people he met had been plunged into confusion. How had they let that car sit there? Why hadn't they sent in the engineers in the alley cats to deal with it?

He had failed to speak up and make his case. All that time spent being a hard-ass with his team, running a tight ship of disciplined and skilled operatives, had dashed against the rocks of that harbour. It could have been prevented if Libby's lot had allowed it. The people who had made the bomb and placed it there could have been apprehended and the device defused – yet games were being played, for some unfathomable reason.

And now he was going to get the blame. The DET were characterised as the failing strong-arm of a security wing that was increasingly seeking technical alternatives to old surveillance challenges. It was political and financial as much as it was about sanction, he realised. And worst of all, the people who made the thing – the bomb, and the people who took it there – they were free to do it all over again.

Grim always assumed he was monitored. Not that he could see anyone, he didn't expect to – but the Brits had been at it for long enough. They'd managed to turn so many in the movement – even the most committed republicans had been persuaded or forced to change sides. Grim knew that couldn't have happened without boots on the ground watching every weakness and predisposition play out.

He had no desire to go back to jail; that wasn't the way it was supposed to work. At his age he expected the young bucks to get caught – like it had been when he was a junior. He'd done his time and risen in stature as a result. He'd been full of courage and commitment back then, game for absolutely anything, and he'd hung on every word of the old hands. They'd coaxed and educated him on the wings, in the cages, in the classrooms. It was incredible to be a part of the struggle back then – all men together for a common cause. The lines of command were clear, there had been respect and awe and determination. He missed it more than he cared to admit.

The ceasefires had changed all that. The peace process had drawn the leadership into bureaucracy and administration, slipping ever more distant from the values and aspirations that had pulled him in. He'd watched those old heads get well-paid jobs as community leaders or in fabricated businesses funded by the state they had tried to destroy. Many were elected to Stormont – the seat of political power that they had once sought to annihilate. They'd forgotten about the grunts in the sticks, outside the big towns. In east Tyrone, parts of south Armagh, Fermanagh, Craigavon, Lurgan. He and his type had become little more than an annoyance – branded traitors to a movement that had sold out. And it filled him with absolute rage. How dare they brand him a traitor when it was them who had abandoned the struggle and forgotten their patriot dead? There were men and women pirouetting in their plots at what was happening above their heads. This was not what his friends and family had died for; they hadn't gone to jail to allow those brave men in suits to take full wages and forget about the goal of a socialist and united Irish Republic.

And yet here he stood, an also-ran, with a boss who didn't trust him and a comrade who'd scarpered across the border. He looked at the wrought angle iron to which the name of his estate had recently been tacked, and realised they had been defeated. Totally and utterly beaten by a cunning force that had adapted from military engagement to an altogether more devious warfare – turning them against one another, blowing them up from within.

He hated the manager for running away. He felt abandoned, ashamed and even afraid of returning to a jail in which camaraderie was no longer present. The prison wings were filled with flailing, fading inked limbs of a war fought and willingly abandoned in favour of simpler lives, raising families and paying the bills.

Grim's regret almost brought him to tears, not for the kid who had been obliterated in the car or the lives that had been shattered by what he had helped create, but for himself.

Sam stared straight through him.

"He's on the move."

The opso turned to the bank of screens and peered over the shoulder of the woman tasked with monitoring Grim.

"Ok, can we get a camera on him?"

"Tricky. He's still in the estate. We have a remote covert in the waste ground to the south, so it depends what way he goes."

"Bring it up."

A second monitor flickered and a dew-dripping blade of grass came into focus. The woman turned the knob on top of a joystick and the lens pulled to sharpen a distant image of the open entrance to Grim's estate.

"That's not him," the opso said, noting a broad figure walking into shot.

"No," agreed the woman, staring at the GPS tracker attached to Grim's clothing, "but he's headed that way. That bloke's just a random."

"Keep on him," said the opso. "Maybe it's a meet."

The woman shrugged and kept both screens live. They watched Grim's progress as the random man – head covered by a beanie, chin by a buff, walked out of frame.

"He's gone," said the woman. "Here's the mark."

Grim entered the right side of the screen and paused, staring, it seemed, at a street sign. At least it would have been a street sign had it not recently been removed.

"What's he doing?" the opso said.

"Staring," said the woman.

"Where's the random – did they make contact?"

"Can't tell. If they did, it was only in passing – the mark's signal didn't pause."

There was a low growl from the opso.

"The mark is just standing there," the woman said.

"I can see that, thank you," he replied, dry as a bronchial hack.

"Weird," came the analysis.

"Insightful," muttered the opso. "Rotate the remote camera and locate that randomer if you can."

The woman jostled her joystick and the camera juddered and panned. "He's coming back," she said surprised.

The opso couldn't help being interested in this new presence, although he knew that it was more in hope than expectation. "Get a car on standby. I want that person identified."

"Do you want the car to follow the mark or the randomer?" the woman asked.

"Get another vehicle into the area," said the opso, following his gut. "We have Grim covered by the GPS tracker for the moment, so put the car on the random."

"Ok," said the woman in a doubtful tone that the opso tried to ignore.

Both men began to move in opposite directions and a few minutes later the random bloke appeared on a third monitor. The opso was intrigued. The man was clearly fit – his shoulders were broad and his gait betrayed his agility; he didn't pound the pavement so much as spring along it. Yet he was moving slower than he appeared able for, suggesting he was seeking something.

"I want a face match," said the opso. "Get the op on his tail to give me a frontal shot."

The monitor went to black for a few moments as the car in which the camera was concealed moved location. When it flicked back to vision, the image was relayed from a rear-view unit mounted in the boot through the number plate. The car was still moving, as was the random man.

"Where's he going?" muttered the opso.

"I don't think he knows," said the woman.

It was true that the man appeared to be looking around him, his footfall at times uncertain. And then, with a flick of his heel, he skipped onto a small wall and over into a rough patch of wasteland.

"Shit," said the opso. "See if the car can get round to the other side of that park or whatever it is."

The screen went blank again and the operations room fell silent waiting for a signal. Seven whole minutes elapsed before a picture was offered again.

"Is that him?" The woman leaned forward towards the monitor as if proximity would improve her understanding.

"Affirmative," crackled over the net.

The man was leaning into a white van and taking off his coat.

"Can you offer a facial?" the woman said into the mic.

The camera adjusted as the random bloke climbed into the cab of the van and removed his hat, then the buff around his neck. The image was very poor until he turned with his elbow raised to wipe condensation from the side window and at that moment the opso's neck stiffened and his jaw tightened.

"Is that enough for a match?" the woman asked the colleague beside her, who took a screen grab.

"Forget about it," the opso said suddenly. "He's nobody. Get back on the mark. Send the car to find him."

The woman turned to peer at him.

"Now! I want to know where the mark is," the opso growled.

The woman shrugged and turned back to her computer. The opso turned and left the room. He was done with Libby's superiors. At the top of Binevenagh Mountain he'd decided that if he was to be forced out as a fall guy, it wouldn't be before the bomb team got its dues. Regret and guilt could kill a man – wear him away and grind his mind. He would not follow his colleagues into that state of distress. Whatever lurking long game Libby's superiors were playing was of no interest to him. It had failed when the bomb exploded, but he would not.

Libby's senior was sufficiently self-aware to realise that he suffered from a superiority complex, but well versed in the affliction he was comfortable with that. What he wasn't comfortable with was an official historical inquiry looking into the dealings of the security services.

The added irritation was that there was nobody left to blame. He alone had given assurances to London that he would "sort things". The goal was clear: remove any and all incriminating documentation that may betray the extent to which Britain infiltrated, controlled and manipulated paramilitaries to do its will. Just as problematic was the constant suspicion that intelligence chiefs had turned a blind eye when agents within all the paramilitary outfits had attended, directed or actively taken part in torture, murder and atrocity. No current members could be tarnished. The dead could be blamed, but with reluctance. Best it just went away.

Which is what he had arranged, and what had failed. The bomb had been designed to destroy the inquiry's offices when the incriminating documentation arrived there. Its premature detonation had ruined that. The simple response would be to try again – a fire or an explosion ought to do the trick, yet it screamed of unprofessionalism. Coupled with that was his annoyance that so many people now knew of his – or Box's, interest in monitoring an explosive-laden vehicle. He had confidence in his ability to control covert military surveillance units, but in every organisation there were defectors and even those whose conscience got the better of them.

The documentation was about to be delivered to Belfast from London. Buried in there, and subject to inevitable unearthing by overeager and overpaid barristers, were papers that hinted – at the very least – of who the service had in their pockets all along. No names, of course, but indications of seniority. Were such information to be exposed, a jigsaw could be easily assembled by assiduous investigators that would not only show that his unit was aware of heinous acts at the point of planning – and did little to prevent them taking place, but also – and more worryingly in his view – that the peace deal brokered between Britain and the insurgents, had, in fact, been drawn between Britain and people who, in effect, were in Britain's pocket. It could prove to be the first peace deal signed on both sides of the table by the same side.

The superior could nobble the inquiry's chairman – almost anyone could be compromised, but it was unlikely to have the desired result. His instinct, as ever, was to make it someone else's problem; to weigh pressure upon someone to remove or destroy the papers, but the chairman wasn't hands-on enough to achieve that.

So he decided to go low-rent. At the heart of any court's legal proceedings is a clerk – a qualified and able lawyer. The inquiry's clerk had access, she had impeccable credentials and a rather ambitious air about her. She would become his way in and out of this debacle. He would forget all about the Ballycastle bomb for it was no longer anything to do with him.

19

S am saw the car as his crooked elbow painted a wide
stroke in the condensation.

"Fuck," he said out loud.

He had no doubt what it was – the vehicle had turned
rear-to, a manoeuvre Sam had performed himself a hundred
times. It allowed the op in the car to aim a camera at him
while monitoring the framing from his device in the front
without the mark being able to see him doing it. Sam
whipped up the hat and buff and put them back on, aware
that it was probably too late. They'd almost certainly got
something of his face already, which was the worst possible
outcome. If they had him on camera, he would need an
explanation as to why he was there – and, worse, he wouldn't
be able to do what he wanted to do anywhere near that
location.

But the DET's presence did have one advantage: it meant he
was in the right area. They wouldn't have been following him –
they had no reason to, and he'd hired the van using cash, so
there was no paper trail. He was certain he hadn't been picked
up in Ballycastle during the incident with the old woman and

her family. So the DET had obviously picked him up while they were watching someone else.

He started the engine and pulled off, watching for the follow, but none came. He began to wonder whether he'd been paranoid. Perhaps it was just a car with a man in it? Perhaps he was waiting on waste ground for a dalliance with a woman, or a man?

Yet Sam knew. It was DET. The careful positioning in the middle of nowhere, the pointlessness of turning away like that, the subtle weight of the vehicle on the suspension – it was all indicative of a car laden with armour and kit. Which suggested again to Sam that he'd been right: they'd been watching someone else when they picked him up. And that suggested Grim was close.

As he drove he picked through what he'd seen. All he'd had was the name of the estate – he refused to use Google Maps to confirm it because that would place him in the vicinity. He'd parked the van, made his way through the grass and soil and rubbish of the waste ground, rounded the corner onto a main road and wound his way into the estate. Most of the cul-de-sacs still had street signs, but none of them sounded remotely like the name given to him by the old woman, so he'd kept going, deeper into the warren, until he happened upon a signpost where the name was removed. That felt promising. The IRA used to do that.

He'd passed a bloke who had given him a wary look before stopping to stare at the street sign, but Sam had carried on. He had no idea which house might contain the Grim character, so he had turned and walked out again – wary of loitering. As he'd left he caught sight of the man ambling away in the distance before making his own way back as he had come, through the waste ground to the van.

So far, so unclear. What was it that had caused them to become interested in him? Had he been warm? Like that kid's game, had he been closer than he realised to the man he was seeking?

Sam strained to remember the face. They had passed one another, hadn't they, before the man stared at the sign? Which explained the DET's sudden interest – they had probably wondered whether they'd made contact, which in turn suggested there was no operative in the cul-de-sac itself. Interesting.

He needed confirmation. A billboard for a garage lit up the price of its fuel, so he prepared to turn off. He pulled his hat down but dropped the buff for fear of looking like a bank robber and strolled to the newspaper stand. He lifted a bunch of Sunday tabloids and hoped for the best, paying with cash and getting back into the van. He peeled through the rags looking for talk of dissidents or the bombing – growing increasingly despondent as he discarded paper after paper.

Then, in the *Sunday World*, he found a headline and a photo of interest.: Lurgan man signs on at cop shop he blew up.

The image had been taken from a distance, probably on a phone and presumably sold to the newspaper, but it was just about clear enough for Sam to make out the same beige coat of the man he had passed less than an hour before. He lifted the paper to stare closer, becoming increasingly convinced that the person in the image was the man in the estate.

The story, written in harsh but ballsy journalese, confirmed his suspicions and hurtled him forward by a thousand paces: Former Provo, Kevin "Grim" McGleenon, has been forced to sign his bail at the very police barracks he once helped blow up. The alleged leading dissident was caught on camera entering the heavily fortified Musgrave Police Station in Belfast on Monday. Police sources confirm that McGleenon must prove weekly that he has not done a runner following his arrest in connection with the New IRA bombing of Ballycastle last month. Another man wanted for questioning about the explosion, in which two children and two adults were killed, has absconded across the border. Our camera caught McGleenon entering the base following a meeting with his solicitor. It must have been an embarrassing trip for the former Provo, who, as a 21-year-old was convicted of bombing the same police station in 1988.

Sam looked up and fell into a thousand-yard stare. So he'd had Grim in his sight. But so did the DET. Removing him without getting caught would be a hell of a challenge.

"Who is this?"

The father was not amused at Sam's refusal to identify himself to his secretary.

"I need to take you up on that offer – if it still stands."

"Oh, hello. Yes, of course. What do you need?"

"There's a burner left at reception at the place we last met."

"A burner?"

"A phone. Not registered. Doesn't matter. When you get it, there's only one number programmed into it. Call the number and I'll fill you in then."

"Now?"

"Ideally," Sam said.

"Ok," said the father, and Sam hung up.

He left the call box and continued his run. The time had come to start training again and his muscle memory wasn't quite what he had hoped. Four miles into a painful climb, the burner in his own pocket started to chime. The screen confirmed that the father had done as he'd been asked.

"Bit cloak-and-dagger, is it not?" he began.

"Not without good reason," Sam panted.

"Are you otherwise engaged?" the father asked, a little perturbed.

"I'm running. It's not fun."

"I don't imagine it is. What can I do for you, Sam?"

"I'd be grateful if you could help me with a vehicle. Ideally a small tradesman's van with shelves and stuff in the back. It will have to have tools and kit in it – and a high-vis vest and a hard hat. It's an odd ask, I know, but what do you reckon? Can you help with that?"

"Absolutely, provided I can have it back."

"No guarantees, to be totally honest, but that would be my intention, for sure. The van can't be marked, though – no branding or names up the side or company logos."

"Ok. I have a small fleet. When do you want to collect it?"

"I don't, John. I want it left in the Quays Shopping Centre in Newry, north of the border. It won't look out of place if it's left there during the day – there's work going on at the moment, so it will fit right in with the southern reg and everything. The key can be left in the exhaust."

"Fine, Sam. I had thought you'd want something difficult."

"If I come to you in the future with a trickier ask, would you be receptive?"

"That rather depends on how tricky it is," the father said.

"Can you have the van left on Saturday?"

"Shouldn't be an issue."

"Grateful, John. Be good."

―――――――――

The clerk stared at the plastic boxes, each clipped shut with security bindings, and despaired at where to start. Replacement versions had arrived, mysteriously, in Amazon packaging at her home the night before, and she was worried that she might replace them incorrectly.

The timing of the delivery meant that "they" knew she'd say yes before they'd even approached her. Troubling, because it suggested they had something else up their sleeve if she had refused. As things stood, all they'd had to do was offer her promotion. "Acceleration", the woman had called it. "Never look back. You'll be on the fast track, and you'll be protecting valuable information".

The clerk drew the little clippers out of the Amazon box and began snipping the clasps, laying the exact numbered replacements beside each box to ensure there was no risk of being caught. "Only the boxes from England," she kept saying to herself, referring to the serial numbers of the paper manifest – all twenty-seven of them. She'd be there all night.

In the corner the photocopier was spitting out sheets by the hundred, reading from the tiny card that had arrived in the Amazon package. She didn't even have time to look at what the boxes contained, such was the demand to replace the bales of A4 with the warm, fresh pages from the photocopier. Then on with the clasps. Fiddly. And then a mountain of paper to be removed from the building when she got notification that the cameras in the hall and stairs were down.

She slowed as the night went on and began to wonder if she'd sold her soul for a rung on the ladder.

"Whatever happens, act with conviction and nobody'll know any different."

Not military advice – that of the priest at Sam and Shannon's wedding. It had worked as intended. Sam, drill on his belt and toolkit over his shoulder, limped with affect through the gate of one of the most secure police stations in Belfast. The shutters were at least forty feet high; the pedestrian entrance was similarly corrugated and led down a barriered walkway to a security hut twenty metres inside the compound.

The limp and beard were part of the distraction and a rein-

forced baseball cap pulled low gave him confidence that overhead cameras wouldn't be able to pick out his eyes or nose. The
van had freshly-pinched plates – liberated from Lisburn park-
and-ride, and by the time the southern registration was back on
the vehicle it would be safely in the Republic and unlikely to be
troubled again.

Sam reckoned he was about a minute ahead of his mark,
which was as much as he should need. Inside the guard hut he
waited to be called forward by a member of the unarmed
civilian staff.

"Eh, who are you here for?"

"Hoping you'd tell me," Sam grunted, looking around at the
screens to determine what the camera angles were like – any
lower than he'd anticipated and he'd have to abort. Not an
attractive option, especially as Isla was only with her grandparents for a night. He really had to get this done now.

"Have you no contact inside?" the guard asked.

"Just told that there's an issue with the lighting in one of the
offices," Sam said.

The guard moved to lift the phone, Sam moved with him,
clasping his wrist and spinning him so that his legs crossed and
the imbalance made him fall backwards allowing the noose of
a cable tie to slip easily onto one wrist and then the other.
Shouting started and was calmed with a split tennis ball forced
into his mouth and a tear of duct tape ripped and bound to
hold it in place. Sam bear hugged the man and pulled his arms
and chest over the counter, imagining there was an emergency
buzzer lurking somewhere out of sight. The man lay on the
ground and looked up at Sam, terror in his eyes. Sam didn't like
that and prodded him with the toe of his steel toecap boot,
rolling the bloke over. He was young, not fit. The wrong person
in the wrong job.

Sam peered up again at the cameras looking for Grim,
looking for the DET op who would be following him and

looking at the main police station building in case another civilian guard might emerge. Nothing. He leaned down to the man on the floor.

"Where's your jacks?"

The man's head jerked forward awkwardly.

"I'm gonna help you up, then you're gonna shuffle in there. Make a noise, whatever you might hear, and you'll meet your maker this day. Understood?"

The man snorted his agreement like a horse through his nostrils.

Sam bundled the bloke to his feet and walked him like an upright mermaid through a tiny dark hall. He turned at Sam's insistence and plonked onto the toilet seat. The door was closed. Six steps back he watched as Grim approached the gate and Sam heard the buzzer sound. He leaned over the counter and reached his gloved hand out to press a green knob, which infuriatingly and worryingly triggered the car barrier to lift behind a closed gate. He hoped nobody noticed and tried an orange button instead, dreading what might elevate next, but the gate pushed open and Grim sauntered towards him. Sam scanned the external cameras and saw a car move slowly on the one-way street, a passenger get out and make her way to a joke shop across the way. The passenger was a fit-looking woman, low, burly – she moved fast and with strength.

Grim came into the guardroom like he'd done it a million times before. He didn't even look up at Sam but reached across the counter to lift the sign-in book. He scribbled on it and turned to wait for one of the security staff to emerge. Home from home.

"Grim," Sam said, at which the man froze for an instant before looking up at the workman. "Yes or no?" Sam said.

"No," Grim said, but Sam didn't have time for fucking about.

"Yes, I think." He was as sure as he could be that he was

looking at the right man – he even had the same coat on, but nonetheless Sam glanced at the sign-in book and caught "McGleenon" scrawled on the page. He reached for the hammer on his belt.

"What the fuck!" Grim started to lift his hands to his face as the clawed curl of the hammer came in an arc towards him, but he'd not been prepared for any such attack – particularly in a police station, and from a person who wasn't a police officer.

His eyeball vanished into his skull and Sam left the hammer hanging out of his face as he moved in for information despite the screaming.

"Who do you report to?"

The yelling was deafening in the small room, and then the guard in the bogs added to the cacophony by kicking and trying to howl. Grim slumped back against the counter, panting and heaving out noise.

Sam gave the hammer handle a jiggle. "You've still got one eye. Want to lose it too?"

"Naw, naw!"

"Who else? Names!" Sam shouted above the noise. He looked up at the cameras to see a car approach the gate. "Names!" he screamed in Grim's ear.

But Grim couldn't articulate anything.

Sam knew he was out of time, so he had one last go. "Who made the bomb? Who was the organiser?"

The single eye in Grim's head rotated to his assailant in shock, and Sam realised he hadn't been clear enough in his questioning.

"Who made the bomb?" he shouted, sucking the claw from Grim's face and brandishing the hammer over his shoulder, readying for another blow.

"Manager!" Grim shouted.

"Who's that?"

"Organiser," Grim panted.

"Where's he?"

"Republic." Grim's hands were above his head now, fingers outstretched.

"Where?" Sam screamed.

The car outside started blowing its horn and a buzzer went off on the counter and a phone started ringing.

"Fuck you!" Grim gargled, which was a regrettable mistake, and the last words he ever uttered.

Sam was out of time. The hammer did its work and was wiped on Grim's shirt. He slipped the surgical gloves into his tool belt, replaced the hammer on its loop and did as a priest had once advised.

There is only so much flicking a woman can do. The op peeled through catalogue after catalogue pretending to peer at cowgirl and pirate outfits while gazing between wisps of plastic hair dangling from wigs at the window of the fancy dress shop. The view was good – straight at the front gate of the police barracks.

"Need a hand?" A teenager behind the counter wasn't impressed at the op's indecisiveness.

"No, thanks." She kept her reply brief, keen to not adopt an accent for longer than was necessary.

A car approached the station gates but wasn't permitted access. A horn sounded, and again. Eventually an angry-looking suit climbed out and pressed a buzzer, staring, livid, up at a security camera.

A burst came over the net. "What's happening?"

"Hard to decide," the op replied slowly, conscious she was within earshot. Libby, at the other end, was wise to the steer and stayed silent. The op continued to stare at the station, turning plastic-coated pages absently.

The suit then marched to the smaller pedestrian gate and hit a different buzzer. Still, no response.

"He's been in there for twenty minutes," Libby said. "Would like you to move on?"

The op moved outside and walked ten feet past a boarded up hardware shop and got on the net.

"Left the premises."

Libby was particularly nervous because she'd overruled the opso, who she respected, and while he hadn't lost his temper, he'd been angry. She could see he felt let down. She was using his team to operate outside their designated area – Belfast fell into a different DET jurisdiction – and any of the Belfast teams could easily pick up on their comms. Her superior had insisted they keep the operation to those who already knew about it, that there was too much to lose by widening the knowledge pool further. She had done as she was told. Then, to make matters worse, the opso arrived into the room and watched her playing with his train set.

"Are you picking anything up inside the barracks?" the op on the ground inquired.

Libby, painfully aware of the opso's presence, nodded at one of his team, directing him to take a look into comms from within the police station.

"He normally just walks in and signs on. I wonder if they've arrested him again?" came over the net.

The opso watched with curiosity and a sliver of satisfaction that this unauthorised observation was going to hell in a handbasket.

"If they've arrested the mark, then at least we know where he is," said Libby.

"I'm pretty exposed here. I can't really go back into the shop," came the op over the net.

The man at the computer bank turned to Libby, conscious of the opso's presence, and sheepishly addressed the spook rather than his own boss. "There's nothing to suggest that the mark has been arrested. In fact ..."

"What?" said Libby, increasingly alarmed.

"I've looked at the camera footage inside the compound and I can't see the mark entering the police station itself."

"What?" Libby almost shouted.

The man just shrugged and Libby got back on the net. "The mark definitely entered the barracks, yes?"

"Affirmative. Standby." There was a pause of static. "Pedestrian gate opening, workman emerging. Suit approaching the gate, car still stationary at vehicle entrance."

"Libby, get her out of there." The opso's affection for the young woman eventually overrode his irritation. "Something's not right, extract her."

Libby bristled at the suggestion from an older man in front of others, yet she appreciated the concern in his voice. She pressed the transmitter. "Extract, extract."

The man at the screen bank turned with alarm to Libby. "There's an emergency call for two ambulances."

"What?"

"Someone in the station has requested two ambulances."

"Is the call live?"

The man started tapping a touchscreen, trying to select the right line, then two voices came through a small speaker.

"Is the casualty breathing?" a woman was asking.

"No," came a panicked response. "He's dead."

"Are you sure, sir?"

"I'm a police officer twenty years," barked the man on the other end of the line. "He's fucking dead. He's missing an eye and there's a hole in the back of his head!"

"Ok, sir," said the calm despatcher. "Can you describe the other casualty for me?"

"He's fine. He's just shocked – he'd been tied up. You know what, just make it one ambulance. This body won't be fit to be taken away until the SOCO team has been. What a fucking mess."

"SOCO, sir?"

"Scene of crime officers," the man said. "This body won't be going anywhere soon."

Libby stared at the opso. "What the hell's going on?"

"Whatever it is, you need to get my team as far from there as possible and make damn sure nobody knows we were near it," he growled.

Only one person in the room looked at the workman who had strolled nonchalantly from the station, apparently without a care in the world.

How long would it take them to work out what had happened?

No matter how much planning went into a thing, there was never an occasion when actions hit every beat. Today was no different. Sam's frustration nearly caused him to eject the hammer out the open window into the River Lagan as he crossed the bridge, but he checked himself and his temper in time to hold on and dispose of it as planned.

The back roads to the border took him away from most cameras, but his refusal to use any electronic navigation meant constant reference to old maps. The van had served its purpose and would now be returned to the father of the heiress. The hammer would end up in the Boyne River and Sam would catch the airport bus and be back at the boat by teatime.

He imagined they'd be searching for the strange workman by now. The guard on the gate would have given his statement, they'd have tracked his entrance and exit from the station. They may even have pieced together his transformation in the subway from workman to suited lawyer-type with gym bag. He ticked off the CCTV points on the way through the city centre:

into Victoria Square, his second change of look in the jacks of a Costa Coffee that had no cameras and his avoidance of tracking that eventually led to the basement car park. He'd changed again in the van, put a mask on and driven up the ramp and out. In a lay-by forty miles from Belfast he'd burned the lot in undergrowth.

They would piece it all together – he was sure of that. It was just a question of how long it would take. So long as he got the van south of the border before they linked it to the killing, he should be ok. The wheels and plates would be changed, but beyond that there was nothing to distinguish the van from any other of its make and model. There would be nothing – no DNA, no identifiable face match or camera image, that would place him in the police station.

But he was disappointed with himself. He had been too preoccupied with getting in and out without being spotted by the DET. It suddenly felt ill-conceived, impulsive. He had spent too much time working out *how* to do it instead of focusing on *why* he was doing it. Killing a man in front of so many cameras had left insufficient time to extract information. Sam now realised that Grim's removal had been too emotional – too much of a venting of anger and not enough about establishing the next lead. Where had it got him? One man deservedly dead, but all he'd left with was confirmation that this 'manager' had run off to the Irish Republic. Not much to hang your hammer on.

Sam decided to take a step back. Maybe some time would help, some mulling over. He settled on a period of normalisation.

It didn't last long.

———

Every keystroke is recorded. That mantra rattled around the

opso's head as he tapped on regardless. He was in intelligence gathering – it made sense that he would look at the files. Whether anyone coming behind him would join the dots was questionable. They'd need to know what he knew, and he wasn't even sure whether he knew what he thought he knew.

He began with outliers – pretending he was looking for things he simply had no interest in: owner of the destroyed café, owner of the bomb vehicle, hostilities within dissident ranks. Blowing some around as he went, he eventually moved on to where he had really wanted to begin: victims. He began with the dead. The adults yielded no names of interest, no paramilitary or military connections. Then the children – again, nothing. Which, for a moment, came as a surprise. The opso thought he'd been onto something. He paused for a while, staring at the screen. Then another thought occurred to him: the injured.

It took a while to access the hospital manifests. They were reasonably well protected, and the encryption took a while to reverse. There were dozens of people, some lightly maimed, some burned, many with shrapnel wounds or glass lacerations from the windows. He hunted the adults in full knowledge that the women affected may not hint at a connection – so few women took their husband's names any more. Three hours later he rose and paced, stiffening and cranky, still suspicious.

He had a coffee and returned to the screen. The children had been taken to various hospitals – Belfast, Antrim and the least serious to Causeway. He scrolled though each before resting on one.

The opso had expected it, yet was still stunned to find it.

For the sake of completeness and muddying the waters for future investigations, he forged on immediately, searching each and every child. But he already had all the information he required and couldn't help wearing a small smile.

"This is getting out of hand, Libby."

"We were out-of-area. Belfast is not our patch," she said.

"It had to be you. We can't involve other detachments."

The superior's calmness was deeply unnerving.

"I don't know what to say to you. It's ... it's a disaster."

"Yes," he said, and allowed the silence to fester.

"I'm sure the police are livid."

"They can't be, can they? He was killed on their premises."

"But I'm sure they'll be demanding footage?"

"Of course, so what is there?"

"Again, honestly this time – there's nothing. We didn't pick up anyone following him beforehand. We're sure he had no tail – apart from us. We don't have any anomalies. All we've got is one of the best ops watching a workman emerge, but she was in a small shop and couldn't linger, and because she didn't think anything of the workman, when the alarm went off she was extracted. At that point we shut down in case the cops picked up on our interest again."

"Then the police should already have all the footage they could need. I mean, this happened on their area."

"Yeah, I mean, I don't know what we could provide."

"Ok, Libby, let the hounds chase. We have no fox in this hunt."

"You don't want us to find out who killed him?"

"Not if it means the police become aware of our extracurricular interest. We'll go back to what we do best – prior knowledge, intelligence. Investigation is for the police."

The superior ended the call leaving Libby more confused than ever.

The colours always amused him when the little bundles emerged wrecked and wrapped in coats of many colours, lunch boxes swinging, rucksacks like little bergens weighing down their knackered bones.

He loved collecting Isla from school; the smile he received, the chat about the day behind and the evening ahead. It was the sweet spot before the drudgery of home-work and the contrariness born of exhaustion immediately prior to bed.

"Hello, huggle-bug," he said to her, leading to minor alarm as she looked around to ensure nobody else had heard.

Content, she broke into a cheeky grin. "Hello, Daddy-o."

Sam had been noting, with no great enthusiasm, how grown up she was becoming. He was pleased to see her speech and understanding of things develop and mature, but he lamented the dilution of innocence he was witnessing as ques-tions and curiosity about the world and its workings gradually gave way to opinions. She seemed to devour current events and process them without him even managing to understand where she was gleaning the information.

"Daddy, did you know Donald Trump is building a wall to stop Mexicans coming to America?" she began.

"Yes, darlin'."

"Like, why would he want to stop them? Anyone should be allowed to go anywhere. It's not fair."

"Stop saying 'like'," was all Sam could manage, for the person he saw in the rear-view was becoming a mirror image of someone else; full of the same ambition for humanity, trying – as he often saw it - to polish the turd.

"Why does he not just let those Mexicans come in and get jobs?"

"Dunno. What did you learn today?"

"You're not answering the question, Daddy."

"You're exactly like your mam, you know." It just came out.

She stared at him; he stared back. Neither knew what to say for a moment.

"I love you."

"Luff you," she said.

They drove for a while in silence. Sam was concerned that a box may have been opened that he would struggle to close. He was tired and still irritable at his lack of progress on the issue at hand. He glanced sheepishly into the mirror but on each occasion found Isla in profile, watching the world slip by, and he worried about the thoughts crashing around behind her flickering eyes.

Beyond her head he caught sight of a blue saloon – nothing fancy, but not a car he'd seen before. His anxiety rose a little as he checked again before the entrance to the boatyard. It stayed with them, so he changed his mind at the last minute and swerved out of the turn.

"Where are we going?"

"Just testing the tyres," he said, keeping an eye on the vehicle to their rear.

"For what?"

"See if they grip ok on the corners."

"Cos it's a new van?"

"Yes."

"Why don't they check that at the hire shop?"

"It's not hired," he said. "It's hire purchase."

"What's that mean?"

"How do you even know what 'hire' is?" Her sponge-like consumption was genuinely baffling.

She just shrugged. "What is hire purchase?"

"The garage owns the van, but I pay it off bit by bit."

"Like a borrow?"

"It's called a loan."

The saloon stayed right where it was. The back window on the new van was too high for him to see the driver properly, and

the vehicle stuck too close for him to make effective use of the
wing mirrors.

"What's a loan?"

"I'll explain later, Isla."

"Trump, Mexicans, loans – you're not telling me stuff,
Daddy."

"What?" he gasped incredulously, but she was in a hump.

He pulled in and the saloon was forced to pass. He looked
down on it from his cab, noting the lack of personal additions –
no bits on the dash or in the rear, no child seat, no stickers.
Instinct curdled a mild concern but nothing more than that,
and so he turned the new van and tried to shake off his suspicions. They drove silently back to the boatyard. Sam dismissed
his thoughts and started gathering the bags and rubbish from
the cab. He slid the side door open and leaned in to help Isla
down from the pristine vehicle.

"Who's that?" she said over his shoulder.

"Friend of your dad's," was all he heard as he froze, trying to
place the Scouse voice.

"Are you from England?" Isla asked, as Sam pushed her
back into the van and slid the door in front of her. "Daddy!"

Sam's muscles contracted as his mind tried to catch up with
his body. There was absolutely nothing to hand that could act
as a weapon, so he turned and braced for impact.

"Wow, calm now. I know what you're capable of, fella."

His eyes may have crept back into his face and gravity
forced features south, but Sam's memory finally fired as he
recognised a man he had spent short bursts of over-approxi-
mate time with.

"Luke."

"Peter."

"His name's Sam," he heard Isla shout from inside the van.

"I know!" The man smiled.

"What are you doing here, Luke?" Sam spluttered.

"Real name's Rob."

"You seem to know mine," Sam said, and they shook hands and fell into a half embrace.

"Why are you here?" Sam was concerned and confused.

"To help," Rob said.

"With what?"

"If you're doing what I think you're doing, then I'm here to keep you out of trouble – and maybe give you a hand."

Sam struggled to conceal the horror that shot up his spine and into his neck. He was ticking through options immediately. Who had sent him? What did he know? Why now? "What do you mean?" was all he managed, trying to keep his face open and surprised.

"You know the business – eyes and ears and all that."

"You're not still on the job, are you?" Sam was still trying to make sense of the visit.

"Certainly am, mate."

"Bit old for digging into ditches."

Rob snorted a small, ironic laugh. "Worse than that, fella. I'm the opso these days."

20

"We should get out in front of this, no?" Libby was exhausted. She managed to maintain her deference but it was being sorely tested.

"And how do you propose we do that?"

She looked at the suede shoes on her superior's feet. She hadn't seen suede shoes on anyone else for twenty years. The soles were some sort of rubber, which might explain how he'd managed to creep up on her.

"Well, we could throw a ring around the bomb team, prevent another killing."

"You think the bomb team is being targeted here?"

"Well, don't you?"

"I don't know," he said, while giving the impression that he knew very well.

"Deirdre Rushe – she came out of the dust like republican woodworm, totally unexpected. She was involved. She's dead. Then Grim – killed under our noses. Grim is a close associate of the boss, so the boss's position is precarious, surely? And there's the manager—"

"Who is out of our jurisdiction, Libby."

"Maybe we don't care if they get taken out?" she suggested, eyes wide open, imploring an indication of what her boss desired.

"In that event who would we concentrate upon? Is it not better to keep certain leaders alive so that we might better monitor the foot soldiers?"

"Is it?" Libby's head began to shake like a forlorn puppy. The tiredness was drawing her close to admissions she would otherwise never make to a man who held her career in his clutches.

"Yes. Structure within an illegal organisation makes our job easier. When the enemy splits or fractures, it becomes hard to control. This is all useful learning, Libby."

"Not if you don't tell me what the objective is," she stammered. "Sorry. I just ... I could really do with a steer here. Please."

"Protect the senior figure. It is he who holds the cards. He will put in place a new team. Do what is within your reach and let go of that which is not."

"So ignore the manager?"

"He is across the border in the Republic of Ireland. What can you do?"

"I could get Laurel and Hardy to inform the Guards that there's a man at risk in their patch?"

"From whom – from whom is this man at risk?"

"We don't know, but shouldn't we be trying to find out?"

"I have told you before, Libby. We are in the futures business. Where events have already occurred, they are a matter for the police. Our remit is to gather intelligence that could prevent atrocities in the United Kingdom – of which the Republic of Ireland is not part."

"So do we involve Six?"

"Are you really suggesting we go to MI6? What would we

say? That there appears to be a person killing dissident republicans? What is new about that?"

"Well, we think it's linked to the Ballycastle bomb."

"Do we?"

"Don't we?"

"We don't know." The superior's hands opened wide with a shrug.

Libby felt like she'd just had her argument tied in knots. She began to doubt herself. "So protect the boss?"

"Clear enough as an objective, isn't it?"

"Yes," she said, as one suede shoe crossed another and the grey slacks fell into their careful creases and left her office as silently as they'd arrived.

"I know what you're thinking, fella."

"I doubt that." Sam stared at his old colleague. He still wasn't sure whether he was looking at a friend. If they'd been close mates, they'd have kept in touch, wouldn't they? Then again, Sam had fought and almost died for men he no longer saw or heard from. He and the man opposite hadn't even known one another's real names, but they'd shared some serious experiences – some pretty awful, some pretty binding.

"Where'd you go after the DET?"

"Back to my old gaff," Sam replied, still wary.

"Back to the brotherhood?"

"Some called it that."

"But not the Ruperts, eh?"

"I wasn't an officer back then."

"You became one, though, didn't you?"

Sam notched up the information. The opso had obviously been digging. "Wasn't like that so much in the SBS."

"What, you all ate and drank together, did you?"

"More so than your lot," Sam said, recalling that the opso had been a para. "Airborne officers were a breed apart."

"That's cos we were animals. Who would've drank with us? Can you see an officer drinking pints of piss?"

"I can't even see a marine doing that sort of nonsense."

The opso bristled a little, then looked away in defeat. "Was a bit pointless, all that."

"Different days."

Sam stared at the opso, shadow-boxing, allowing silence to force his visitor to explain his presence. The only sound was Isla's Kindle rattling away to *Horrible Histories*.

"You don't need to worry, Sam. I'm not here to annoy you."

"No?"

"No," said the opso, his Scouse accent suddenly persuasive. "I'm here to catch up."

"You said you were here to help me."

"I am, Sam. I am. If you'll let me."

"Help me do what?"

"Have you anything to drink on this fine vessel?" The opso scanned around.

"Tea?"

"That's not really what I was thinkin', Sam, to be honest, fella."

Sam leaned forward and lifted a lid from the centre of the table. The casing kept litre bottles upright during stormy weather.

"Ah, might have known," the opso said, as a golden bottle was drawn out. "Gunpowder-proof, eh?"

Sam reached round behind him and lifted two heavy tumblers over between his fingers.

"Careful there. It's a lubricant."

"Well, I'm here to talk, Sam."

The opso rasped on first glug, suppressing his surprise at the potency of the liquid. They sat in silence for a long while.

"So how did you end up here?" Sam began.

"Long story, fella. But once I knew to look for you, you wasn't that hard to find."

"So how did you find me?"

"Every school has a list of children in it."

"You looked for Isla?"

"I did."

"Why?"

The opso drained his class and cocked it. Sam did the dutiful thing and wet it.

"To find you."

Sam closed his eyes with impatience. "How did you know to look for Isla?"

The opso closed his eyes and recounted from memory: "Ireland. Isla. Child. Seven years. Unaccompanied. Conscious. Had been in the care of mother of a friend. On holiday. Parents uncontactable."

Sam looked hard at the man opposite, trying to contain his anger.

The opso saw his mistake and put up a hand in mitigation. "That's what the hospital file said, mate. That's all it said."

Sam knew staff like the opso were trained to recall what they had seen. It was all part of the job.

"And that brought you here? You came to – what, sympathise?"

"No. Well, yeah. What happened was a fucking disgrace, mate, but, I'm here to help, really."

"So you said. Help what?"

"You see, I recognised you."

"I don't follow."

"Yeah, but *I* do, Sam. You know that. It's what we do. And I saw you."

Sam's breath was shortening as he waited for a line that didn't come.

The two men hunted each other's eyes; one making a bad effort to persuade of good intent, the other debating whether to add to his body count for the week.

Eventually the opso tried again. "Look, Sam, I've been around the block, as you know. I'm tired of all the messin' and the games they play. You-know-who, they're still at it – pulling operations and stopping jobs with no explanation. Letting stuff through. It's wrong. It's just wrong. And when I saw you, I thought – well, at least someone's got the balls to do the right thing."

Sam looked at the opso and wanted to believe him but couldn't take the chance.

"Isla! Get into bed, darlin. I'll be in in a while. You can have pizza in bed and your iPad tonight."

"Ok, thank you, Daddy!" she called back, happy at the treat.

Sam turned to the opso. "You're hooked up?"

"No, mate, no. Honestly."

The opso lifted his shirt.

"Come on. Rips now aren't what they were. There's a million ways you could be rigged. You're a bloody specialist, for fuck's sake."

"Look, mate," the opso stood, "take it all."

Before Sam could object the opso had dropped his jeans, kicked off his shoes and sat back down in his shorts before removing his shirt and leaving the bundle on Sam's side of the table. Sam stooped to pick up the jeans and shoes and with the shirt took it above deck, leaving it under the spray hood. He retrieved a boiler suit from the cockpit locker and handed it to the opso.

"I'll get you a fleece."

"No need, mate, this rum is burning me from the insides." He smiled widely, attempting to find levity in the situation – which was just about balanced but could tilt without return at the smallest puff.

"I think you need to do the talking for a while," Sam said.

"Ok, fella," the opso said, falling into his old accent – content that he would be understood. "Well, I run the bloody show now, as I mentioned before. It's not as big a team as it was during the war, like, but the tech is better, so there's more covert cameras and the recording kit is amazin'. And we've got loads of other toys that means we don't have to deploy ops."

Sam splashed the glasses again, confident in his ability to sustain the assault on his sensibilities better than the man he was drinking with. "Carry on."

"So, anyways, we were watchin' some suspects for the police, like. You know, the people in the frame for the bombin'. And one of them ends up dead. Weird, like."

Sam's heart began to pound as his eyes bored into the opso.

"She and her old man were killed while we had a car right outside the house. So, like, whoever did it, knew what they were about. We still don't know how the killer got in or out or how they left the town. It's a proper mystery."

It was the opso's turn to stare at Sam. There was not so much as a flinch.

"Then we have this other mark, miles away. Out-of-area technically, but for whatever reason the job of tracking him fell to us. And lo and bloody behold, he ends up dead an' all."

Sam stayed silent, his face blank.

The heavy glass rotated in the paw of the opso as he peered out uncertainly from under his brow. "I saw you."

Sam's silence lasted a full minute and compelled the opso on.

"In Craigavon – you walked past him, the mark. Man known as Grim."

Sam saw no point in saying anything. There was no immediate benefit to a denial, and as interrogations went this was hardly the worst he'd endured.

"Then, few days later, like, we're tracking this Grim guy as he signs on for his bail in Belfast. We follow him from his solicitor's office to the police station and in he goes – but he doesn't come out. In fact, the only person who comes out is a lad with a limp and a tool belt and a drill – looks the part. We can't see his face but we can track him through the town, into the shopping centre and away. And we can place him over the border in a little white van and then we lose him altogether."

"Careless," said Sam, his first utterance in ages.

"Or not," the opso held up his finger, "or not, my friend."

"How d'you mean?"

"Well, it's up to me, isn't it – how far we track a vehicle in another jurisdiction. Least it was that night. We can stick by the rules and close down the surveillance in another sovereign country, like Ireland – or we can quietly watch whatever we like, can't we? We can track a van like that with a satellite or other kit. Whatever we like, really."

"So you're saying you stopped watching this van?"

"That's right, mate." The opso was getting a little cockier.

"Why would you do that?"

"Because I recognised him – Bob the builder."

"Who was it?"

"Come on, fella, this is getting silly now. I'm here to help."

"You want to help me because I apparently walked past a man in Craigavon who was later killed in Belfast?"

"A man who was in the frame for planting the bomb that injured your daughter and killed her little mate."

Sam stared again, hunting for any betrayal in the opso. Were they trying to get him through the back entrance?

"Let me get this straight. You saw me in Craigavon, walking past some bomber. Then you saw a workman leaving a police station in which the bomber went into but didn't come out. And as a result of that you think you need to help me?"

"The bomber was killed in the police station, Sam. You'll have heard that on the news."

Sam shrugged. He had no intention of offering anything.

"See, I reckon it's about time somebody just snuffed these bastards out. We sit every day and we watch them and we follow them, and we stop them doing what they're trying to do – but sometimes we don't."

"Don't what?"

"Stop them. Sometimes we're told to just watch."

Sam's interest piqued as he realised what he was being told.

"You were watching the bomb vehicle?"

The opso's hands went up in defence, realising what he'd implied. "Now, fella, I didn't say that. I didn't say anything about the bomb vehicle."

"Didn't need to. You lot had eyes on," Sam said with conviction.

"Right, you need to get that out y'er head, mate. That's not what I said."

"You were watching that fucking car." Sam leaned in, his voice hard but contained – barely. "And you knew there was a bomb in it."

The opso sat back, worried but resigned to the fact that he'd rumbled himself. "If we get into this, will you believe me that I'm here to help?"

"We're getting into this whatever you're here for."

The opso closed his eyes for a moment, then nodded. "We had the car," he conceded.

Sam looked at him, wondering whether his old colleague was here out of guilt or with the intention of closing Sam down. "Keep going, Rob. You're in it now."

"This can't go anywhere – this is incendiary, Sam. This is beyond career wrecking – this is shutdown stuff. If anyone finds out – they'll find a way to finish us both."

Sam just nodded.

"I don't know what the target was but it wasn't Ballycastle."

"Who was running this? Not the cops?"

"No, no," the opso said. "It was our friends."

"Box?"

"Yeah. They've a bright spark in our team – young lass. She's smart as a fox, but a long way off experienced. She was told to watch the vehicle, then some kid comes and spends the night in it after a row with a known head – the woman who was giving him lodgings – the one who was killed. But I think you know more about her than I do."

"Wrong," said Sam, and he meant it. "Keep going."

"So this kid, a known associate of Kevin McGleenon, Grim, also now dead, manages to detonate the bomb prematurely, we think."

"You knew there was a bomb in a car and you let it sit there. For how long?"

"Days, mate. Days we watched it."

"Why didn't you send in the alley cats?"

"It wasn't an ATO call, mate. This was an op run by the spooks – Box had control. I didn't know why they were watching it. I still don't know."

"But they've told the police they had eyes on it?"

"Have they fuck. It's closed doors, mate, wiped cards, records rewritten. We were not there, at least not that they can prove."

Sam thought about the photographer and what he had said about his material being ditched at the scene by a big bloke.

"Army technical officers could have defused it. You could have saved my kid going through all of that. Have you any fucking idea how much trauma that child has had? She's only seven years old," Sam growled.

"I don't know the details, Sam, but I know you were bereaved if that's what you mean."

"My wife was murdered, and Isla saw it."

"Fuck me, mate, I'm sorry. I didn't know. Honestly. What happened?"

"Not the point. Point is, you could have stopped Isla's friend being killed. You could have stopped those others being murdered."

"It wasn't my operation, Sam. I was providing the team, the logistics, but I keep telling you – it was Box. MI5 trump us, you know that better than anyone. They'll have had a good reason, like."

"There is a good reason to allow kids to be blown up?"

"Well, they didn't know that was gonna happen, fella, did they?" The opso found himself defending the very people he didn't agree with.

"So you know who the bomb team was?" Sam seized on a thought.

"I know who Box think it was."

"And you reckon this Grim person was one of them?"

"And Deirdre Rushe. The dead woman. But somehow you knew that too."

Sam shook his head. "What has she to do with it all?"

"She provided the safe house for the kid in the car. I assume he was to transport the vehicle to the target."

A veil of guilt lifted from Sam when he realised the old woman's despatch hadn't been entirely unjust.

The opso's head tilted a little in curiosity. "Did you really not kill her?"

Still suspicious of listening devices, Sam opted to simply shake his head.

"But you were at the police station?"

Sam shook his head again.

The opso stared, then smiled, as if he understood the game and could play as well as anyone.

"You still seem happy to drop your trousers," Sam said. "Once a para, always a para. Get what's left of your kit off. We're going for a swim."

"So when will I hear from you?"

Libby looked at the clerk quizzically. "How do you mean?"

"Well, what's next promotion-wise?"

"Promotion?"

"You said I'd be accelerated if I helped?"

Libby didn't enjoy this part of the job, but she knew it came with the territory. "You want us to accelerate someone who has just been instrumental in perverting the course of justice?"

The clerk wasn't stupid, nor was she soft. She'd grown up in the gnarly streets of west Belfast where a career in law was seen as a means of beating the Brits at their own game. "You made a deal. I did my bit."

"And we are grateful."

"You can't just walk away from what you promised. I know what you've done."

"But you don't know who we are, do you?" Libby tilted her head in an almost sympathetic way.

The clerk feigned indignance and went through the motions she'd half expected to be forced to adopt. "But you made a promise. I could go to the chairman of the inquiry and—"

"You'll do no such thing," Libby bared her teeth, "or your brother will be exposed."

The clerk pretended to be stunned. "How do you—"

"Same way you do," Libby said. "We found it on his computer."

The clerk clutched her forehead, feigning anguish, and Libby went in for the kill.

"You see – you are ours now. That's how this thing works. You do something illegal – very, very illegal, then you are compromised. We will require your assistance from time to time, and you will move up or down or stay in the same position according to what works best for us. Do you see?"

"You're going to control me?" the clerk asked. "Manipulate me, my career?"

"Yes," said Libby, then she turned on her heel with the last of the boxes and walked out the door.

The clerk walked slowly up the stairs and unstuck her phone from the globule of Blu-Tack she'd wedged onto the door frame. She checked the image and sound, compressed the conversation and emailed it to said brother. They'd have fun the next time they chose to hack into his hard drive.

Sam lowered the dinghy into the water and pushed it into the breeze. He stripped naked and slipped down off the scoop at the transom of the cutter, regulating his breathing as the cold water tried to rob him of air. He was well used to making his mind ignore the sensation – telling his body that it wasn't feeling pain and discomfort, rather it was simply a sensation to be dampened, but airbornes weren't so used to immersion – either that or the opso had long forgotten how to handle it. He opted for a macho drop straight in and surfaced like a thirsty hound.

Sam sidestroked to the dinghy and clambered in. It would have been warmer to stay in the water but he wanted the opso at a shivering disadvantage and craving comfort. His visitor followed panting and splashing and Sam hauled him out – glancing around in the dark to make sure there was nobody around, and that he was still well within sight of the boat on which his daughter slept.

"This is a bit extreme, mate," the opso managed, his glory shrivelled and cupped as he lay against the air tank. "Grown men, in the nuds, skinny-dipping. It's nearly winter!"

"Who else knows?" Sam shot back.

"No one, honestly. Just me."

"How do you know?"

"I recognised ye. We practically lived together for months, mate. I know ye. Then it was, like, confirmed when y'er kid was in the mess of the bomb, ye know. It made sense."

"Who was on the bomb team?"

"The kid, the bloke called Grim, another fella they talk about as the manager. And then they're all run by you-know-who."

"Who?"

"The boss – Sean Gillen."

"He's been around for a long time," Sam said, recalling the name. "He's still a player – even after all that stir?"

"Prison just made him harder."

"Still. That lot just sounds like the delivery team."

"How d'ye mean?"

"You were in Iraq – you know the score. Same in Afghan. Take out the delivery team – they're always replaced, but you need to take out the engineer."

"Y'er right, mate. I agree. But that's more difficult."

"Why?"

"Cos we don't know who that was. Look, mate, I'm fucking freezing. Can we not go back? You get the point, don't ye, that I'm not fucking wired for sound here?" The opso opened his hands exposing his tackle, his face contorted and rattling with the cold.

"Why don't you know who made the device? If you were following the bomb vehicle, you know where it came from."

"Yeah, we do, but it was over the border. It came out of a shed in Donegal."

"Well, then, who owns the shed?"

"Dunno."

"But you have the address?"

"I s'pose we do."

"So if you want to help, that would be helpful."

"Ok."

The opso had been ill-prepared for his late-night dip and in his discomfort would have agreed to just about anything. Sam was determined that if his old colleague had been sent to nail him, not one spoken, whispered word could be recorded while they drifted in their bollock-nakedness in a dinghy on a lough.

"And another thing."

"Hurry up, fella, we're gonna get fucking hypo here."

"This manager. I want him. And his boss."

"With pleasure, mate. 'Bout time they were shut down."

"So I'll take you back and get you warmed up, but I'll be making another request at some stage. In fact, I'll be insisting on it."

Funds were running low. The manager was too proud to ask for further discount from the landlady – she'd done a month-long deal as it was. He'd prepared for a cross-border excursion – a timeout in case things went pear-shaped, but five thousand euros wasn't much south of the border. He'd spent a grand on accommodation, half again on food. Then there was mobile phone credit for the burner he'd bought. He would have to stop using data – but then that was his only means of following his own case.

Plus, he was bored shitless. Three TV channels were all the bed and breakfast offered. The landlady didn't seem impressed that he stayed in the house so much. She'd suggested he go for a round of golf on the course he could just about see from his bedroom window. Golf. Hardly. The only thing he had ever swung was a baseball bat – and even that hadn't been to his liking.

So he went for long walks and drank tea in expensive Carlingford cafés, and gradually became a curiosity for the locals – the lonely bloke they saw on the road who didn't really speak to anyone. It was only a matter of time before someone realised who he was, and then he would need every cent that was left of his cash stash, and to move on.

———————

"This is only gonna work, mate, if you learn to trust me."

Sam walked the opso to his car. Both had the stirrings of hangovers but Sam was keen to get this blast from the past off the boat before Isla woke.

"It's not personal, Rob – it's just the way we're built. You know that."

"Well, whatever, mate. But I tell ye this, I admire what you're doing even if I can't quite work out how you've been doing it."

Sam said nothing. They got to the opso's Ford and stared at one another, before slapping shoulders and falling into another muscular embrace.

The opso took the chance to whisper into Sam's ear. "It's not rips you want to watch for, fella. It's mobile aerial platforms."

Sam gripped him a moment longer. "What?"

"Drones, mate, size of your hand. We've cut the staff in half cos of them. Amazing little things."

The men drew apart.

"Is there one watching us now?"

"No, mate," the opso said with a sigh. "I'm not here to screw you over. I'm here to help you finish these bastards. It's long overdue and I want them gone. I think deep down you know that."

Sam knew what had happened to the opso's father all those years ago.

"My little girl only has me left. I cannot go down. Do you understand that?"

The opso looked back towards the boat. "Yes, mate, I get it. And I promise you, I'll do what I can, but I'm not alone in that ops room. There are other DETS and other agencies. You need to be so fucking careful. These MAPs, they're incredible. They're not buzzing around like you'd expect. You can't even hear them."

"Good to know. So when do you start – helping?"

"Greenore."

"What?"

"The manager. He's in a guest house in Greenore. It's in—"

"I know where Greenore is."

"He walks every day. Round the village in the morning, then down by the lough at night."

"What time?"

"Nine, never later than ten. By the ferry port. Every night. He's there – just staring, taking the air."

"At what?"

"Across the lough."

"To the north?"

"Seems so."

"Same place every night?"

"Yeah. Railings at the terminal."

"Exactly the same spot?"

"Yeah."

"Have you a photo?"

"Have you lost your mind? Never heard of collusion? The days of the military passing images to mercenaries are long gone. You don't even get to take a phone out of the unit these days, mate."

"Have you got eyes on him?"

"Yeah, so be careful."

"What about the rest. The others."

"I'll be in touch, mate. Somehow."

Sam nodded. In his heart he believed the opso was genuine, but he had too much to lose to allow himself to be sure.

The boss was prepared for prison. He'd spent half his adult life in one, but not for nothing. He resented the prospect of being sent down for someone else's disaster. There was no return for Ballycastle, no message; nothing that would keep the fight alive. In fact – the event had been utterly counterproductive. There was no propaganda in killing children. All that did was secure a backlash. He had imagined a spectacular that would secure admiration within his own ranks. The higher the pedestal upon which his people placed him the less likely they were to question his motivations and decisions. Every now and then someone in his position had to pull off a major coup – a high-profile killing, one that would make the national and international news. Such events kept the dream alive, it allowed fresh recruitment and gave his role in this struggle purpose.

Without such events there was nothing. There was the dole or a life of ordinary decent crime. He'd gone down the dissident route, so there was no cushy job in government or Sinn Féin or community work for him. All ties had been severed, not that he wanted back into the fold.

He was just the same as the recruits he was grooming but he was in harder, in deeper, with no choice.

Except now he was stitched in from all sides.

The opso stared at Libby and decided to feign anger. "You lot want to make your minds up."

"I know."

"Why would we pull the plug? We have this guy in Bally-castle the day before the bomb exploded. We know he's an associate of Grim. We know he's a close friend of the unit's leader. Bloody hell, we watch lesser people more closely, Libby."

"But he's out of our jurisdiction."

"We are always watching people out-of-area!"

"I don't mean out of this DET's area, I mean he's outside the state – outside the UK! He's in the Republic of Ireland. This could cause diplomatic ructions."

"They'll never know we're there – they don't have the tech. You know that, Libby."

"It's too dangerous. Too risky."

"This is an order?"

"If you want to make it that. Just pull the team out."

"They're not on land, they're at sea – and they're using the best of kit. This doesn't make sense."

"You make a point," Libby relented, "but that's what has come down from above, so we have to do it. I'm sorry, but that's just the way it is."

"So you agree with me – we should be keeping eyes on him?"

"Doesn't matter what I think," she said. "It matters what our superiors think. And they say get out of Dodge."

The opso was delighted but managed to appear incensed.

"Let's go for a spin in the new van."

"Where to?"

"Wanna go see Sinead?"

"No, Daddy."

"Why? I thought you liked Sinead."

"I do, but Dublin's a long way."

"No, it's not."

"It's five hundred miles, Daddy."

"It's about one hundred miles – an hour and a half. That's, like, the length of a movie on your iPad."

"Is it?"

"You can sit up front and choose the music."

"Can I?"

"Yeah, but if you're watching your iPad, you have to wear headphones."

"Ok."

What was the point in earning that money in Venice, thought Sam, if he couldn't treat his kid to a night in a hotel every now and again.

Áine answered the intercom, which was good news and bad.

"You're like a bad penny."

Sam looked around in vain for the camera through which the twin was evidently eyeing him.

"You'll never find it. It's either small or very far away."

The door buzzed and Sam led Isla into a plush marble atrium with a curving staircase; stainless and spotless on account of never being used. The lift to the right stood open but Sam didn't know what floor he was going to. A door opened well above them.

"Seven!" echoed, to which Isla answered with excitement.

"On the way, Sinead!"

"That's not Sinead," Sam said.

"Sounds like her."

"It's her sister, Áine."

"Her twin sister?" Isla said. "That's why she sounds just the same."

"That's about as far as the similarity goes," he muttered.

The door to the flat was ajar when they got out of the lift, so they tapped and walked in nervously to see Áine filling a kettle.

"Hello, there," came from behind, and Sam turned to find Sinead drying her hair with a towel, fresh from the shower.

"Sorry. Bad timing."

"'Tis not," she said. "Hello, me little flower." Sinead bent down to give Isla a hug, watched intently by Áine.

"You live in a posh house."

"I know," said Sinead. "Áine bought it for me." She winked at Sam. "This, Isla, is my twin sister."

"Hiya," Áine said. "Heard a lot about you. D'ye want a bar?" Áine brandished a packet of Kit Kats.

Isla bashfully shook her head.

"I'd say you do, you're just shy cos I'm new to ye. We'll be fine in a while, you and me. Now come on and get a bar."

Curiously, Isla took the familiarity as it had been intended and walked forward and took a Kit Kat from Áine.

"What d'ye say?" said Sam.

"Never mind y'er oul fella, Isla. You and me will be fine without thank yous, thank you very much. Now come on, let's see what's on the telly."

She held out her hand and to Sam's surprise, Isla took it. They walked off and Sinead and Sam had barely hugged hello when he heard the pair laughing from the other room.

"You should have told me you were coming."

"Sorry. It's great to see you, but it's not just a social visit, so I didn't want to phone."

Sinead stiffened just a little. Then her eyes fell and her poise relaxed. "At least you're honest about it. Are you here to see me or her?" She nodded to the living room.

"Both of you."

"Do you need Isla minded again?"

"No, no, I'm not offloading, I just need someone I can trust."

"Right so. Are you staying long?"

"Well, depends. I wondered if you'd like to come for dinner

with us tonight? Maybe like the night in Gigha – some seafood somewhere? Bring herself if you want to."

"I'm sure she'd love a night with you, Sam."

They smiled at each other.

"So maybe business first, pleasure later?"

"I'll need to plead with your other half for that."

"Áine!"

The sister appeared at the doorway, brows raised in scornful inquiry.

"Sam needs your help."

"No shit."

"Kids present," Sinead said.

"More than one." She looked at Sam but pulled the door behind her.

"I hear you've got a spaceship of tech here," Sam said. "Was hoping for some guidance."

"Is this guidance going to end up with someone dead?"

"Course not," Sinead said and looked at Sam, who said nothing.

Áine shook her head, unconvinced. Sinead's eyes creased, the left side of her lips stretching.

"All I want to do is look something up without anyone ever knowing I looked it up. That's all."

Which was true.

"Well, you can help with that, can't you?" Sinead said.

"Monkeys can help with that," Áine replied. "It's what other animals do with such information that concerns me." She looked straight at Sam.

"Make the world a safer place?" he said.

"Listen to Kofi Annan." Áine nodded her head in Sam's direction.

"Just give him a hand," Sinead said sighing, "then we'll all go out for tea."

Sinead disappeared and Sam heard a hairdryer blow before Áine stopped staring and started speaking.

"C'mon so, the boss has spoken."

She led him through an incredible river-view lounge. Isla had almost disappeared into a golden shagpile rug as deep as a field of rapeseed. A short hallway led to a door with *Mission Control* etched into it. There were no windows inside, and the room was lit by blinking LEDs and server stacks. Áine pulled a cord that cast a soft light over three keyboards and tapped a screen, bringing it to life. She hammered away on the keyboard for a few minutes and eventually an input bar appeared.

"Ok. This is a search engine. It's not Google, but it'll find anything you need to find. Whatever you're doing, you'll be dark – which means I'll be protected from whatever the hell you're up to. So fill your boots. Let me know when you're done, and we'll swab the place and get rid of your smell."

"Thank you. I think."

Áine left the room without another word.

Sam started with the easy stuff. He began with "mobile aerial platform" and spent ten minutes scrolling past cherry pickers and diggers on the backs of lorries. He added "drone" to the mix, then "military" and eventually "reconnaissance". Then he got lost in cyberspace for almost an hour investigating the present capabilities of the military packaged into the size of a Snickers bar. Sam shook his head at the imagery that could be relayed by tiny silent devices that returned to their pods at the touch of a button using GPS. His mind reeled through the possibilities until he got an indication of the cost – tens of thousands of euro per unit.

"We have a hungry young woman out here!" Sinead called at the door.

He looked up at the clock. He'd become immersed in the drone stuff and hadn't even looked at what he needed to find. He closed down the browser and reopened it, hammering in "dissident republican" then "manager". It didn't take long to find what he was looking for. There, in glorious colour, courtesy of a dozen newspapers, UTV and Sky News, were images of the next man on the list.

Sam closed everything he could see to close and readied himself for a nice night in good company, but he remained distracted by the drones. He opened the door, with one more glance behind, and walked into bright, startling daylight. The sisters had given Isla a coat of make-up, the type of girly treat he had no capacity to provide. She radiated excitement as she anticipated his reaction – she was almost shivering.

"Ah, Isla, you look so beautiful," he said. "So grown-up, what age are you – twenty-five?"

"No! That's so old. I'm nineteen, Daddy!"

"Wow, you look it darlin'."

Her smile was as wide as the Liffey itself.

"We are at your disposal," said Sinead, who for the first time that Sam could remember was wearing a dress. Áine appeared to have wilted and accepted the invitation too.

Sam nodded appreciatively. "Why don't we ask John along? It would be good to catch up with him."

"What do you want me to do with this?" The clerk's brother stared at the screen. The video had ended. "You pair make me sound like some sort of weirdo who's downloaded child porn."

"S'pose we do," his sister said. "Never thought of that."

"Who's the blade?"

"When are you going to stop talking about women like that?"

"What does she know about me?"

"I'd say she knows everything." Her brother's face was blank. She wondered if he was capable of reaction.

"Who is she?"

"Someone who wanted me to do something illegal for them, and they used you as leverage to get me to do it."

Which was not entirely true, but it was close.

"I got you in trouble?"

"It's done. Now you've got to help me limit the damage."

"What did they get you to do?"

"There's no benefit in you knowing. But they have me, and they have you by the balls, and unless we build in an insurance policy they will always have us."

"Have they got evidence on me?"

"They've been rummaging around. I imagine it's enough for you to go to jail for years. Oh, wait – I'm a lawyer, I know it's enough for you to go to jail for years." He stiffened at the prospect.

"So what do you need me to do?"

"Find her." The clerk pointed at the screen.

"How? If she's some sort of—"

"Agent? Spook?"

"Yeah."

"That's your problem, little brother. I'm sure you'll work out a way cos if you don't – you're going to prison. And so am I."

John seemed to relish the company – particularly that of Isla, who coaxed a dormant or unrealised grandfather in him. He joked and played and made things with napkins, and he received sufficient reward for his efforts too. Isla responded with giggles and drawings and questions. All in all, it was a very easy evening in a typically expensive Dublin restaurant.

Eventually John rose to excuse himself. Sam gave him five minutes and took the opportunity to follow. The jacks were down two flights of stairs and were comparatively dingy. He found the father drying his blue-veined paws beneath an incredibly noisy blower.

"She's a credit to you, Sam," he shouted.

"She's taken a shine to you, anyway," Sam shouted back.

"That child is a breath of fresh air. Brings it all home a bit – what could have happened." John gave up on the dryer and shook his hands before rubbing them, looking around himself conspiratorially. "How's it all going?"

"Well. Everything is going well. I wanted to say thank you for your help before."

"You have done more for me that I for you, Sam," said the father.

"I was paid for that. You were helping for better reasons."

"Perhaps not better, Sam, but for good reasons."

"Well, I appreciate it. So, just to be clear, dinner this evening is on me."

"Thank you." The father nodded. Monetary gestures were of no impact beyond the regard they conveyed. "Now, you let me know if there is anything else I can do."

"Are you sure?" Sam asked warily.

"I'm sitting in a house in Ballsbridge with a wife who does not like me and a daughter who barely grunts in my direction. I have money coming out my ears and few friends. If there is a purpose that can serve, then I am sure. Absolutely."

Sam shrugged a little – what the hell? Perhaps he'd been thinking about this all along.

"Do you fancy flying, John, without getting in an aircraft?"

"What?"

"Let's buy a Black Hornet. It's expensive, but it might be fun."

21

"What's happening?" the opso asked one of his team at the computer bank.

"Just pulling out the observation team on Carlingford Lough," she said.

"Good hiking up round there," he muttered.

"Dissident hotbed," came the reply. "More arms in Omeath than a crate of starfish."

The opso grunted. It was true. They believed there were weapons dumps all over the Cooley Peninsula courtesy of an old IRA quartermaster who had settled in the area.

"Good views, though. Any pictures?"

She leaned forward into her mic. "Any images available?"

"Standby," came the reply, the thrum of a diesel engine clear over the net.

A monitor flickered to the right of the bank and the opso watched as it panned and pulled focus. The dim foredeck of a fishing boat was revealed as dawn tried to break through the gloom. Three of his team had been living aboard the vessel for a week. The specialists he had chosen had been delighted at the prospect of some time at sea – their natural habitat. One was a Royal Marine, another a specialist on secondment from the Norwegian Special Forces, while the sergeant leading them had been a member of the opso's Special Reconnaissance Regiment. The opso was still in the habit of referring to it as "the DET" because it was still the same sort of people doing the same sort of work.

The opso triggered the lever on his deep chair, allowing it to keel back while he put his feet up – wishing he was aboard the boat on the screen. He pulled over the day's reports and began flicking, glancing up every so often at the feed, enjoying the unusual scenery being fed into his own windowless, dimly lit room.

His operatives got on with their tasks – drawing up manifests for the week ahead, requirements from the techs and spanners, plotting routes and deployments. The opso poured through the intel. None of their watch list appeared to be doing anything out of the ordinary.

He didn't know what made him look up when he did – two seconds later he would have missed it. The prow of the fishing boat rose a few feet to capture a sailing yacht headed the opposite direction. Even at a glance he knew her; he'd had a drink aboard and stayed the night. He even fancied he recognised the lonely figure at the wheel, and smiled.

"Ok, cut the feed and wipe the cards. We're not supposed to operate down there, so let's make sure there's nothing that could come back to bite us."

The image went black and the tapping of his team began as all memory of the deployment was erased.

With any single-handed sail comes thinking time.

Ordinarily, if Sam made it through a week without speaking to anyone other than Isla, that suited him just fine. But he had a nagging guilt, and on the long solo run to Carlingford he admitted to himself that he'd have to address the Sinead situation. He knew he was being unfair. He owed her so much. But to unravel his emotions would open up a new front in the battle to clear his mind. To allow Sinead in, was to push Shannon out. Yet he knew make-or-break time was nearing. And until he worked it out, he couldn't keep asking her to mind Isla – who was, instead, spending the weekend with her grandparents.

He slipped through the entrance to the dilapidated marina before six o'clock – too early for anyone to approach him for a mooring fee. There were several empty berths and he took one that was almost masked by a forgotten catamaran nail deep in limescale and green weed. Sam made up the warps and prepared a bundle of cash in the hope that an attendant might accept the money, pocket it and leave the ledger empty. Then he got his head down – he'd been sailing all night and he had a longer night ahead.

———

"I often wondered where you went on your downtime."

The opso looked at Libby as she struggled up to the flat rock. "Clears the head, the fresh air. I like the altitude."

"I forgot you were in the Parachute Regiment. You must miss the wind whistling through your ears when you're cooped up in the ops room." Libby was breathing hard. She'd obviously not spent her own days off wisely.

"That was a lifetime ago. I've been in the 14th for twenty-five years."

The older hands never took it well when people referred to the modern name for their unit – as if it somehow offended the memory of those who had gone before.

"Why did you bring me here?" she asked. "Bit out-of-area for us, isn't it? This place is full of unfriendlies."

The opso looked down over the valley below. The Mourne Mountains were tiny compared to where he had trained, and Libby was right – there was no end of hostility to the British military in the villages beneath them, but there was support too in the mixed-up communities and between the unmarked boundaries that separated United Kingdom unionists from Irish nationalists.

"Don't you ever wonder about your enemy – what motivates them to do the things you try to stop them doing?"

Libby thought for a minute. "Not really, to be honest. I thought it was pretty straightforward. They want a united Ireland with no British in it. The majority of people who live here don't want to be Irish. So that's democracy, and democracy needs protected."

"But did you never wonder why they want it so much? Why they're prepared to go to jail for a reunified Ireland – to be killed for it, even?" the opso pressed.

"I know the history," said Libby with determination. "But that's not the point. The point is to stop them killing each other."

"And that's why you're here?"

"Well, yeah."

"Not because a stint in Northern Ireland is good for the CV?"

"That too," she said unabashed. "What I don't understand is why you've spent so long here. It's pretty irregular."

The opso went quiet for a moment and looked down into the scenery. "See that stretch of the lough?" He nodded beneath them.

"Yeah?"

"That's Narrow Water."

The name rang a bell but Libby hadn't even been born when the place name had morphed into a byword for an atrocity. Like Omagh. Or Loughinisland. Or Greysteel. Or Kingsmill.

She stared and waited.

"That's where my dad was killed."

Libby closed her eyes for a moment, the significance dawning. "He was a para too," she said softly, the detail still hazy in her mind.

"That's why I joined. I was nine years old when he died. They triggered the bomb from over there." The opso pointed to the mountain range opposite their own, across a narrow sea, in a different country.

"How many were killed that day?"

"Depends how you count them. But eighteen."

"How often do you come here?"

"Not often."

"That's why you're so committed to the place?"

"It was – before, initially."

"How do you mean?"

"When I first came here I was a para on patrol – I wanted to kill everyone, but then I got older, and as the peace process settled and we were able to get out of the camps more I started walking in the hills. Then I began to understand more about what we were doing here."

"You're not going to tell me you went native, are you?"

"You can understand another point of view, Libby, without agreeing with it. You'll understand that as you get older."

The condescension grated on Libby, but she allowed him his seasoning. "So what did you understand?" Libby couldn't completely conceal her scepticism.

"See this stone we're standing on?"

Libby looked down. It was broad and flat, like it had been placed there by an army of Egyptian slaves. "Yeah?"

"It's a Mass rock."

"A what?"

"During Penal times – when Catholicism was banned, the

faithful used to sneak up here and a priest would appear, say Mass, then sneak away again before he got strung up."

"That was like, what, four hundred years ago?" she said dismissively.

"Something like that."

"So it's a bit of a stretch – no disrespect – to say that that's why the IRA does what it does."

"Maybe," said the opso, staring across at the mountains from where his father's fate was decided. "But they still talk about it in Mass now. They remember the sacrifices they made to practice their faith. The priests tell their congregations about their forebears and how they risked Cromwell's wrath to preach."

"Priests were banned then?"

"Funny enough, so were some Presbyterians."

"Protestants?"

"Yeah, there was a time when the Prods wanted shot of us as well."

"So this lot have more in common than they think."

"I'd say so. But that is one thing they *have* forgotten."

"Long memories here," Libby mused. "Selective."

"There was a reason for what happened here. No matter how wrong it all was, it didn't come from nothing."

"What are you trying to tell me?"

"I'm saying that then – back then – they could rationalise what they were doing just the same as we could justify what we did. It was a war. We were never able to call it that, but that's what it was. A grubby, indecent war. And with every person that died there was more bitterness. And with the families of the folks killed in Ballycastle, there will be more of that. More kids like me who will grow up without their parents, who will want to kill dead things. More parents who will die long after their kids. It's just so wrong."

"Well, that's what we're here for, isn't it? To stop that," Libby said with certainty.

"Except we could have and we didn't."

She stiffened. "It went off prematurely. You know that."

"You and I both know we weren't going to disarm that device. We were going to let it get to its destination and explode."

"I do not know that!" Libby rounded.

The opso held her stare and lowered his voice. "You know that," he said. "I'm not saying you had the information or understood what the game was at the time – for the record, and for what it's worth, I think you're a good person – but you know now that we were going to let that bomb detonate."

"I don't know, and how you can be so sure?" Libby attempted, but she knew he was right.

"We had Deirdre Rushe, we had the manager, we had the kid. That was all we was ever gonna get, Libby. There was no grand plan to catch anyone else cos there was nobody else to get. No senior IRA man was going to approach an armed device – especially when it got to its destination."

"So what's your grand theory, then?" she asked. "Why would we be asked to let the bomb vehicle proceed?"

The opso noted the tacit admission but chose not to seize upon it. "Maybe to quash the remnants of support for the dissidents? Bomb goes off, kills a few innocent people, the public's disgusted. You tell me, Libby. That's your end of the business."

"We wouldn't allow that."

"No?"

"No," Libby said firmly.

"I've been around your organisation longer than you've been in it, Libby. I'm not so sure."

"Olden days," she said, and it was the opso's turn to bristle.

"We had a chance to analyse the device and maybe let the plods get the DNA of the bomb maker. Instead we were babysitting the fucking thing so it could travel. There was no advantage in letting it get to its destination and then deciding to dismantle it. None that I can see anyway. There was no advantage in taking the risk of letting it drive through traffic and towns either. That thing was gonna go off no matter what. And we allowed that. It just means probably less people died in Ballycastle than where it was supposed to go."

"Fewer," Libby muttered.

"What?"

"Fewer people."

"So you're better educated than me, Libby.

"This country is full of horrible brutality."

"Can't argue with that. But it's no different to any other place – except here it's done in the name of a cause that sticks all that hatred into one big spittoon. In England it's just the same but it looks like something else – gang murders or modern slavery."

Libby sighed. They were alone in the hills, and as a fog rolled in from the sea they could both feel the creep of history, the importance of the distant past and the uselessness of what they had done.

"You're right," said Libby softly.

"Which bit?"

"All of it," she conceded. "I don't know what we were doing. Those people shouldn't have died. I can't ..." She stared away from him.

"It's not your fault, Libby."

"It's certainly not *your* fault."

The opso said nothing but placed his hand on her shoulder and patted it.

"Why did you bring me here?" she asked again as she turned, her eyes pooling with tears.

"If you're going to work here, it's useful to get a feel for the place outside the barracks. Turned out for me that the people

here are actually quite nice. They deserve not to have to deal
with shit like what happened in Ballycastle. They'd give you
the everything they have, some of them. It's like home, really –
in Liverpool. Them that has nothing will give you everything."

"That's nice and all, but what are you trying to tell me?"

"It's time this war – or what's left of it – was finished. Over.
Done. No more dead children splattered over walls. That's all."

Isla's playlist made Sam smile. He could always rely on it to get
the blood pumping when he woke. Dolly reminded him that
the tide was going to turn, so he reached for his wetsuit.

No heavy food – he wouldn't have the luxury of turning
back if he got cramp. He ate a protein and energy bar and drank
some water instead. His neoprene balaclava sealed off almost
all noise and his goggles were heavy-duty – designed to protect
from tear gas as well as water. He rolled down, clicking each
vertebra, then lay on his front arching his back loosening up for
the cold, hard job ahead. Shoulders warmed and stretched, he
quickly climbed the stairs, paced across the cockpit and slid
immediately and almost silently over the side. He resurfaced,
calming his breathing as his wetsuit did its job and turned the
icy water into warmth. He checked his goggles for steam or
ingress, then swam a conventional breaststroke in case anyone
noticed him. When safely outside the harbour, he reverted to
an energy-saving sidestroke that he had been taught many
years before and settled into the two-kilometre crawl.

When his wife wrapped a scarf around her face, the boss knew
it was time to take a walk. She was just home from work, so it

was unlikely she was volunteering to go out of her own volition. Something was up.

He climbed the stairs and swapped his slippers for shoes, pulled on a jacket and got his face buff from the drawer. Then they slipped without a word through the back door and made for the lough-shore walk.

"Ye get a call?" he asked from behind the fleece on his face.

"Early on. Lucky there was nobody in the office."

"What did they say?"

His wife fidgeted for a moment and then thought better of it. "There's an increase, so there is, cos of some incidents."

The boss turned and fixed her with a cold stare. "What did I tell you?"

"To remember every word."

He raised an eyebrow, waiting for more, like a brutal teacher with a cane in hand.

"Word for word," she stammered.

"So. Word for word. What did they say?"

"I ... I ..." she choked, now deeply afraid.

"You only have one job to do. What did they say? Be careful – be very careful."

"That's what they said."

The boss lowered his voice further. "No, it's not. You know it's not. Think, woman, what did they say?"

She was close to tears knowing what was coming. She had a choice to make: get the message right and get a beating when they got home, or get it wrong and get a bigger beating when they got home. Her fidgeting morphed into action and she drew a piece of paper from her pocket and read: "Surveillance is increased. There have been a number of unfortunate incidents. Do not deviate from routine. Do not become concerned about headlines."

The boss looked at his wife holding the scrap of paper torn

from some civil servant's notebook. He pitied her. "What have you done?" he asked softly with utter menace.

"I ... I took the message."

"You wrote it down."

"I was going to memorise it and burn the paper."

"What about the pad you wrote it on?"

"What?"

"You tore that piece of paper from a notepad."

She looked forlornly at the scrap in her hand but said nothing.

"Wouldn't take much for someone to see what you had written, would it?" The boss placed his hand gently on her shoulder. "You know what's next."

His wife nodded her head, tears now soaking into her scarf.

"Give me the page."

She handed over the piece of paper.

The boss placed it in his pocket and looked up to the sky in a display of frustrated disappointment. He could hear the gentle buzz of insects, out of season – but the seasons were all over the place these days. And then he took his wife's hand and led her home for her punishment.

The manager laid down his gnarled paperback. The pages were the colour of unmilked tea. He hadn't taken in a word for almost a full chapter; he had read but was unable to remember what the story was about. Nor was he able to admit to himself what was wrong.

He rolled upright on his creaky bed, pulled on his shoes and headed out for his evening walk. Without the fresh air there would be no hope of sleep. He went the long way, down the shore road, past the beach café – now shuttered with its "minerals" and "confectionery" signs painted out. He paced past the steels in the holding pens of the port, gazing at the cranes and the old lighthouse, no longer blinking. Then he made his way through to the point, the tarmac of the terminal.

In truth, it wasn't much of a landing – a wide slipway with pillars to allow the small car ferry to buffer against in the tide. The free movement of people, he thought, and took up his customary lean by the orange life ring, gazing across the lough at a state he hated, where he had been reared, and which he missed terribly.

"Paul!"

The manager flinched. Had he imagined it?

"Paul!"

He looked down into the gloom, searching in panic at the water's surface.

"You're ok, Paul, we're friendlies."

The manager's head told him to run but his body was frozen in panic.

"Paul, listen."

The manager hunted the darkness beneath his feet but could see nothing. The voice wasn't shouting, but rasping, over the lap of the sea on the rocks.

"We've got a boat here. Your wife has already accepted help. She's on her way to a new life in a new country. We'll take you to her."

The manager had always half expected an approach, but not like this. They usually turned up in suits at the barracks after an arrest.

"Not interested," he called at the sea, still unsure where the voice was coming from and utterly confused.

"Up to you, Paul, but you've no wife to go home to. Kids are away too, and their families. They chose to leave ... after what you did."

"I did fuck all," he barked at the reflection of the moon.

"Police were looking for you. They arrested your wife. The whole estate saw it."

"Why would they lift her?"

"To find you. She's gone now. She took the soup."

"She wouldn't have done that," the manager said, trying to persuade himself.

"That bomb killed kids. Your family's dirt in your town. None of them were interested in hanging around."

"They wouldn't leave."

"All gone. You've nothing to go back to."

There was silence for a solid minute.

"Where?" he said, eventually.

"Nicer place than you came from anyway."

"The grandkids?"

"All of them. So make-your-mind-up time. You can join her and have a new life, or stay here and eventually get extradited."

"I'm not a tout."

"Up to you. But they can place you in the town with Deirdre Rushe. You're either coming with us or you're going to jail. No doubt about it."

The manager's head was reeling. Would his son have left with the grandchildren?

"There's a boat down here."

The manager turned to look at the dilapidated ferry port, then at the lights of the occupied north. "No," he said.

"Alright, last chance. You'll not see them grow up. We're leaving now."

The manager's muscles flexed then relaxed. This is a trick. This must be a trick. He stepped up onto the metal crossbar and swung his leg over the top railing, turning to lower himself onto the slippery rocks. "Where are you?" he called.

"Keep coming down to the tide," Sam said. His body was still immersed, his heart hammering. He knew the opso's team could well be watching and hoped his heat signature was concealed by the freezing water. He wanted the DET to think the manager was on the cusp of suicide. He heard a stumble and a slip. "Easy, Paul, just keep coming. Listen to my voice and keep coming towards me. Have you a phone in your pocket?"

"No."

"Where is it?"

"At the digs."

"Ok. Come on, just a few feet more."

"Where's this boat?" Panic crept into his voice. The manager's head loomed black against the floodlights behind.

"I'll bring it over now," Sam said. "You need to come down here to the water's edge."

"There's no fucking boat," the manager said, turning suddenly and slipping on the weed of a rock.

Sam struck like a crocodile, reaching out of the water and catching the manager's ankle, hauling him to a slip and a yell. He hoped for consciousness as he heard his head crack a stone. Sam hove hard and got a knee, then a belt, then a shoulder and pulled his mark into the water.

The manager struggled as Sam spoke in his ear. "Easy now, easy. This'll be handier if you just let it happen."

The manager struggled and kicked but Sam's arm was round his neck and his legs were kicking powerfully away from the shore.

"I'll take you to the boat, but I need to know where the bomb was made. D'ye understand, Paul? I need to know who made the bomb." Sam struggled to stay afloat and speak at the same time with the manager across his belly.

"There's no boat," the manager babbled.

"How d'ye think I got here?" Sam panted.

The manager settled a little. "Donegal," he said.

"Where in Donegal?"

"Where's the boat?" the manager said.

"Who made it?"

"Two brothers."

"Names?"

"Don't know."

"Last chance," Sam said. They were five hundred metres offshore and he could feel the current gripping them and drawing them out of the lough towards the open sea.

"I don't know." The manager's voice was calming, his body succumbing to the temperature of the tide.

"What do they do?"

"Make bombs."

"For work – what do they work at?"

"Smugglin'. Where's this boat?"

"Smuggling what?"

Sam could feel the manager's resignation as the carcass on top of him deflated and gave up.

"There's no boat," he said.

"No," said Sam. "There's no boat."

"I'm dead," said the manager.

"Yes," said Sam, and let him go.

Their bodies separated and in moments Sam had lost sight of the manager. He lay on his side and began the long crawl inshore to avoid the worst of the tide, before steering a course back to the marina.

Unless he'd been picked up from above, his old colleagues would have to believe the manager had done himself in.

22

"What the actual fuck, Libby?"

She had never heard her superior swear before.

"He's only missing. He's run, I guess. We'll pick him up quickly."

"You *hope* he has done a runner, you mean, but he could just as easily be dead."

"We'll find him," she said, but in her heart she feared she'd lost another one.

"The chatter is not good, Libby, not good at all."

"What chatter?"

"Social media, messages, calls – known dissidents. They know he's gone missing. His family said they haven't heard from him in two days. You can guess the rest."

"What?"

"They're saying we took him."

"Like, turned him?"

"No, that would suit us rather well. On the contrary, they are saying state forces are up to old tricks."

"What, like, killed him?"

"There was a time," he mused.

"The olden days." The words were out before she realised what she'd said, but she was tiring of war stories spun long before she'd even been born. Her superior chose to either ignore the comment or file it away as another example of her unsuitability for discreet work.

"Put yourself in their shoes, Libby. They are looking at two of their own dead in Ballycastle. An idiot with a smashed jaw who says he was attacked by a professional. Then we have a dead man in – of all places – a police station, one of the most heavily fortified in the United fucking Kingdom and some hard-hatted assassin walks in and beats him to death with a hammer."

Libby saw his point but stayed quiet.

"Now the manager's wife and children are preparing to hold white-line pickets claiming state collusion in murder. So, I repeat, Libby – what the actual fuck is going on?"

"I don't know."

"Well, what is this unit doing? What sort of fucking leadership are you giving these bloody people?" he suddenly shouted.

Something inside her cracked short of snapping. She was damned if she was going to take the blame for what he had ordered.

"*You* told me to divert all attention to the boss. *You* told me to take eyes off the manager."

"I did not tell you to stop doing your bloody job. Does that mean you bring a halt to gathering?"

"How can we gather if we take eyes off the main protagonists? I'm sorry, but that's what you told me to do."

"Think, Libby," he said, suddenly calmer.

"Think what?" She had her dander up and her mind could see nothing but the fire of indignation.

"This does *look* like something we have the capacity to do, does it not?"

Libby's mouth fell open in disbelief, her shoulders plunged towards the desk, hands flat on the surface, fingers spread. "What?"

"If we decided to remove certain people without leaving any sort of traceable lead—"

"I don't under ..."

"Think, Libby. *Think*. How has someone killed four people right under our noses? We are the best in the world at this caper, are we not? We have the best tech, the best-trained people, and yet, *and yet*, someone has killed four suspects without us having so much as a sliver of an idea who it is."

Libby was reeling. "You're saying it's one of us?" Her mind took her immediately to the Mass rock and a recent conversation.

"Where would an assassin get such information? Who the bomb team was, where they were living or hiding?"

"The police?" Libby ventured.

"For that chap Grim, perhaps. For Deirdre Rushe, possibly. But that does not explain how they were taken out while we had them under surveillance, does it? And there is another glaring flaw in that argument."

Libby knew it. "The manager."

"Quite. Nobody was supposed to know where the manager was. Nobody other than us. And we can tell from interrogation of the police database that they had no clue as to where he was either. So who knew?"

"The dissies themselves? He had a phone."

"And we have every word they utter monitored, recorded and transcribed. They're not eating themselves, Libby, not yet. This is not some feud like they used to get into in the '80s."

"You really think it's one of our own?"

"No, much worse than that."

"What's worse?"

"I think it is one of yours," he said.

The clerk's brother left it four days before linking back into the chat room he used with like-minded people in faraway bedrooms. It took two years to be approved for membership and the tiniest slip-up was guaranteed to result in expulsion.

His latest post had returned sixteen suggestions. Fourteen pointed him in the same direction: China. Not that anyone said China; that would be stupid. He and his friends had developed their own language that couldn't be explained or taught. It required careful learning over a long time in a black corner of an unsearchable space on the dark web. It wasn't like leetspeak, used in the fledgling days of the internet. Their speak was refined, constantly shifting. He had no doubt that the NSA and similar organisations were constantly cracking it, so they kept moving and modifying, trying to stay a step ahead. Not that they were in the business of bringing down of governments. They were simply curious, hunting for gaps in the digits that would reveal openings. It was coding for the love of code. Nobody in their group was naïve – there could be spooks lurking, posing as one of them, but it wasn't an issue so long as they didn't try to bring down a superpower.

So from his bedroom in a Belfast council flat that he shared with his ageing mother and her crippling arthritis, he whiled away his nights looking at the weaknesses in the defences of businesses. Where those vulnerabilities proved serious, he'd drop them a line and occasionally earn himself the price of a highly specced car by offering advice on how to close the chinks. He had built quite a reputation among lead developers and product managers in big corporations. It was lucrative, yet he neither declared a penny of it nor spent it; he wouldn't know what to spend it on.

But now they knew his worth – the Brits, or whoever his sister had fallen foul of. They'd probably looked at his earnings, scattered around the globe, in crypto. He could stand to lose it all, not that that would bother him greatly, but he wouldn't function in a prison. If they found a way to take him from his screen and make him stare at the wall, that would be too much of a struggle. He wouldn't cope with talking to other men. The only people he verbally spoke to were his ailing mother and his sister. They had always looked out for him – protected his peculiarity and kept him from those who could potentially harass him. He knew that his mind functioned differently to others, but he was ok with that. He only wished his mum and his sister were.

So, the Orientals. He could see why the Chinese wanted that sort of tool, but dabbling with them was likely to land him in trouble. This was not a decision to take lightly. He heard his sister on the stairs – his mother couldn't manage the climb, and his door opened.

"Would you not turn on a light at least?"

"Go ahead."

"And open a window. It smells like fish in here."

"Go ahead."

"Mum says she hasn't seen you today?"

"Been working."

"On what?"

"This thing for you."

"Is that what you want to ask me?"

"I can do what you want, probably. But it's dangerous."

"It's already dangerous."

"For you."

"Well, thanks, little brother, for your concern."

"You don't understand."

"Then tell me."

"You can't get caught doing this type of thing."

"Well, then, what's the problem?" she said.

"No, I mean if you get caught, you're in jail. Immediate."

"Immediately," she corrected him.

Water off a duck's back. "Maybe in America."

"Serious?" she said.

"Serious-ly," he replied. He might be odd but he was a million miles from stupid.

"Well, they already know about your extracurricular activities, so I suppose if they want to do you, they can anyway."

"Can they arrest you too?" he asked.

"Probably."

"What did you do?"

"Something stupid."

"What about Mum? If we both go to jail."

His sister just stared at him. She had no answer to that. "How can you stand being in this room all the time? It's just like prison."

"It's really not," he said, and he knew she understood.

"How big's the risk?"

"Using a Chinese platform, if I input the image, it will probably find her. But then someone somewhere will probably ask – why the interest in her?"

"And what will they do then?"

"Who knows? Depends who she is."

The sister thought for a while. They hadn't much to lose. They were already being blackmailed, and once you start it never stops.

"Do it."

"What about Mum?"

"Mum will be ok," she said, but she wasn't at all sure that was true.

The brother turned to the screen. He lifted a small pen-like tool to a pad and conjured the image of Libby taken from his sister's phone. He spliced the video into a series of screen grabs and deployed them into the dark fibre tunnels of cyberspace.

"What now?" his sister asked.

"We wait."

The opso tried to shake off the notion straight after it happened, but it niggled. Libby and her attitude towards him in the ops room.

He'd greeted her with a smile and she'd visibly shuddered. Ordinarily it would have been easy to dismiss as pressure or fatigue, but they'd spent what he thought was a good day together in the hills of south County Down. They'd talked and even laughed a little; there had been lunch in a gully and dinner in a seafood restaurant. It had all been very pleasant. And now she was stammering excuses to get away from him.

"The mark's not moved in a day. Just wondering if he's still breathing," was all she said in greeting.

The opso couldn't quite make out whether that was a jibe or a deflection. "We have the house covered front and back and we have audio inside. Is there any suggestion that things aren't right in there?"

"Well, he beat the shit out of his wife," she said.

"Is that what's wrong?" The opso settled on a diagnosis for Libby's fractiousness and prepared himself for the backlash – but none came.

"Just make sure this one doesn't follow the others," she snapped as she swept out of the room, ceding oversight.

The opso looked round at the staff at the monitor bank. "I take it she's been up all night?" he asked.

"She only just arrived – her coffee's still warm. Must be something you said." One of the old hands smiled.

"She's cranky today."

"She's full of questions too."

"Like what?"

"She wanted the manifests for the days Deirdre Rushe and

her old man were killed, and the names of everyone involved when Grim was bumped off."

"Did she say why?"

"Nope."

"Did you give them to her?"

"Yeah. Should I have waited?"

"No, no, that's ok. We're here to share with our intelligence colleagues."

"Is there some sort of investigation? Cos we wiped most of the stuff."

"But she knows that," the opso said. "It was she who requested it."

"Well, now they seem to want to look at it again."

The opso said nothing but thought of his own search history. Careful as he had been, if he was under scrutiny, and it felt like he might be, then he would have to find another tighter tunnel through which to communicate.

The message was, well, nondescript: *Be good to catch up.*

He'd used WhatsApp. Min. Sam's deceptively unthreatening-looking friend. Min, however, was still in the job – now a vintage marine, and was a ferocious leader with a nut as hard as a farrier's anvil. Sam didn't hear from him often but when he did it was normally related to an event – a sports result between Min's native Scotland and Ireland, or a reference to one of their old colleagues, a death invariably.

Be good to catch up was a new phrase. Subtly unusual.

Sam replied in kind: *Where? When?*

The hole. Forty clicks.

Now Sam knew something was up. "Forty clicks" was a phrase he would never forget. It was the distance they'd covered to get out of a messy situation in Tamil-controlled Sri

Lanka, by boat, on foot and in the end by swimming. They'd been sent on a covert op to extract someone who didn't deserve it and it had gone very badly wrong. Because of the secrecy of the debacle they'd come to refer to the incident only as "forty clicks" and it had become a byword for urgency. The hole. One of the most stunningly beautiful places Sam had ever been to.

He decided to mix business with pleasure and sent two more messages: *I'll get to it* to Min, and then he opened his end-to-end app installed by Áine, used mainly by Sinead. He had been assured to rest confident in its encryption capabilities. *Fancy a boat trip?*

"What's that?" the clerk asked.

"A response," her brother said.

"That's a response?" she said, staring at the wall of digits scrolling up the screen.

"There's probably a message in there."

"It's like a word search without any actual words."

"There are words. You just need to know how to read them."

"You're a weirdo."

"We think you lot are the weird ones," he said.

"*We*? Who is *we*?"

"My mates."

"You don't have any mates. You stare at this computer for twenty hours a day."

His special category status made it almost impossible for him to take offence. It was one of the benefits of his condition. "You only think that," he said, which rather stumped his normally un-stumpable sister.

"S'pose you do talk to the Tesco delivery driver," she tried.

"Mum does that," he said. "I just pay for it."

"How? With bitcoin?"

The brother had learned to ignore elements of what was said to him. He was good at filtering: he subsumed what he needed to understand and left what his sister called humour in the air.

"There are returns," he said, his eyes flickering and dancing over the code.

"Meaning what?"

"Probability matches."

"Translate, please," she said.

"The tool takes the images of the woman. Identifies key trigger points. In her face. Maps eye spacing, architecture. Head. Jaw. Cheekbones. Unique. Facial fingerprint."

"I'd assumed that kind of thing could already be done."

"Some off-the-shelf packages manage. Chinese tool maps the eye. Different. Retina recognition works but you need the actual eye. This does it with a photo or a video. Cranks probability to a match even if the pictures are crap."

"Are they crap? That's a good phone."

"They're crap."

"So what do the Chinese say?"

He hammered like a side drummer and within minutes had brought up two old profiles, a Bebo account and a MySpace.

"I remember those," she said.

"Social media's ancestors. Looks like her?"

"It's *definitely* her," the clerk said.

"Singer," the brother said. He tried to play one of a dozen videos of a young woman at microphones on a variety of stages but they wouldn't work. "Expired."

"What's her name?"

"Meadow."

"Must be a stage name – or she has hippy parents. Is there a surname?"

"Gaines. From Kent."

"Course she is."

"Is Meadow a real name?"

"It is in Kent."

"I can't see Ireland any more," Isla said excitedly.

The binoculars swung around her little neck, her arms were tucked into her life jacket and she was content to be back at sea. Sinead was partly the reason – Isla had company other than Sam. He was growing to appreciate her needs as she matured, to understand that he alone couldn't provide all the patter she required.

Sinead had her eyes closed – a good sign, Sam thought. She appeared at ease with the arrangement – incomplete as he knew she felt it to be. They ran before the wind, and Sam toyed with the idea of doing it in one – straight up the outside; the west coast of Jura. More open water, better sailing, less comfort.

"Will I make a brew?" Isla asked, eager.

"Since when did you call it a *brew*?"

"Sinead calls it a brew."

"Ok. Careful with the—"

"I know, I know," she sang. "Turn the gas off after and test it with a match."

She scuttled below. Sam pulled up a chart on the plotter. They'd been sailing for fourteen hours. They could either go to Gigha for a slap-up feed or gybe and head out into the North Channel at speed. He wondered whether the women could face it – another ten hours probably through an unnerving night.

"Isla?"

"Yeah?"

"Will we just keep going – straight to the monk's castle and the monastery?"

"Why?"

"Cos we'll get more time there, then."

"How long will it take to get there?"

"One sleep and two movies."

"Ok," she shouted.

"Fine by me," Sinead spoke without opening her eyes.

"You sure?"

"I was dreaming of a steak but if you two are happy, who am I to intervene? Especially if I get to watch two movies."

A smile crept across her face, and Sam pushed away the passing realisation that she was really very pretty.

Her eyelids lifted slowly – giving him time to glance away, yet for some reason he didn't seize the opportunity and she found him looking. She smiled contentedly. Then she drifted off again, but the curl on her lips remained. Sam held his gaze and tried to force himself to deal with the warmth he felt, to allow the guilt to pass, to imagine a state of happiness after such despair.

"Here you go, Daddy-o." Isla appeared with his aluminium cup. "And I used two teabags."

"You're the best tea-maker in Ireland."

"In Scotland," she corrected him.

Sinead's smile had spread. She was an acoustic voyeur to the patter of a pair who had for so long known no other yet were grateful for her intrusion.

"Giv'us a snuggle," Sam said, and Isla fell in under his wing on the rail of the boat. There they sat for a half hour, rolling with the sea and supping tea. Sam wondered if things could feel any better given their circumstances.

"What are you doing?" The opso didn't shout. He knew very well what they were doing. Enormous fingers curled around his armpit, ready to apply pain to his pressure point; a grip he was acutely familiar with. "There's no need to restrain me," he said.

"I'm sorry but we've been told not to take chances," said a small man, who the opso assumed was an MP.

He knew better than to fight back. The man was half his age, and if he was indeed military police, he would be exceptionally able – contrary to appearances. The man on his other shoulder was equally unimpressive looking – which only served to make the opso more wary.

They led him through the doorway as his team looked on in disbelief. He noted that not one of them raised an objection.

"Am I being arrested?"

"Not if you come easy," the smaller of the small people said.

He was paraded awkwardly down the hall, the little men wheeling him sideways to allow all three to navigate the turns, and then he saw her, crestfallen and confused. Libby lingered in a doorway. She hadn't been crying, but she wasn't far off it. Her head gave a barely perceptible shake as he was whisked past. The opso couldn't work out whether it was a gesture of apology or disgust.

"What's going on, Libby?" he tried, building the foundations of a façade of ignorance.

She remained silent – as he knew she must.

And then he was marched outside, across the yard and into the intelligence block. Two more corridors, two turns, and then a windowless room, two suits and no smiles.

23

S am threw out the anchor off Iona and felt the tide haul *Siân*'s hull against the breeze. He wasn't confident that the hook would hold beyond the turn, and so cajoled the women into action.

"Right, we've got three hours before the tide turns, then we go somewhere special for the night."

"Ok, Daddy-o," Isla chanted, the promise of shore and a new place bubbling.

On the quay Sam made a deal with a local fisherman to collect two lobsters on the way back.

"I like the scenery already," Sinead teased.

Even clad in his wellies and jumper, Sam recognised the man's aesthetic appeal, but if she was seeking a rise from him, she was disappointed. They walked up a gentle hill towards St Colmcille's Monastery where Sam hired headsets for Sinead and Isla and they set off listening to tales from the sixth century.

He took the opportunity to ping a message to Min: *Hole ten clicks.* He received no reply. It could be hours or days before his friend appeared. He caught up with the women and enjoyed watching them sync their eye movements to the stories they were being told through the headphones. Their brows rose and pupils widened at the brutal history of warriors and battles in the preservation of faith.

On the stroll back he waited outside every little shop while countless woollen articles were purchased – never to be worn again. On the quay Isla peered in terror at the lobsters and their arthritic movements, daring to touch an antenna before recoiling immediately. He doubted whether she would eat one later.

"What now, skipper?" Sinead asked.

"Now to one of my favourite places on earth," he said, and moved forward to wind the anchor up.

They slipped into the channel and headed south towards the Isle of Mull, the current heaving and skiting them sideways. Sam aimed the bow towards craggy pointed rocks and both Sinead and Isla turned quizzically towards him.

"Ehm ..." was all the elder could manage, reluctant to question him.

"You sure you know the way, Daddy?" Isla fretted.

"I need you to be very quiet for the next little while and let me work the chart," he said, lifting a little compass to his eye and taking a bearing, then another.

He reduced the revs and the boat slipped out of the main tidal flow as he consulted the chart. Both Sinead and Isla looked alarmed but remained largely silent as bid.

"I could touch that rock," Isla whispered to Sinead, whose nervousness bordered excitement.

Sam pressed the bow directly at a wall of rock – his crew now convinced that he'd gone mad and had settled upon scuppering them. In the last moment before the boat touched he threw the wheel over and hit the throttle, spinning the stern around. The boat nestled between two walls of rock cut like coral – its abrasive qualities threatening anyone daft enough to give them a rub and disturb their statuesque silence. Sam pushed on gently; the sun beating down on the wash, its noise amplified as the boat squeezed between the stones. Seagulls could barely be heard above the heave of the sea. And then, again, he threw the wheel – this time to port – to reveal their destination.

"Wow," Sinead breathed.

"This is so cool, Daddy!" Isla squealed, delighted by the echo of her voice off the atrium of stones.

They were surrounded by a wall of rock – a shelter built by God from ferocious winds and brutal seas, for those with the courage and faith to enter. The water beneath them looked bluer and the rock had a sandy warmth.

"Welcome to Tinker's Hole," Sam said to enormous smiles.

Within minutes the anchor was down and ten minutes later all three were jumping or diving off the transom.

"Who've you been talking to Rob?" the first suit began. They stood, he sat. Nobody moved very much. There were no cameras - a table and three chairs the only furniture in an otherwise bare room.

"'Scuse me?"

"We're not here to fuck around."

"Am I?"

"You've been passing information on known terrorists to an outside agent and those targets are being assassinated."

"So I'm a tout now, am I?"

"Yes."

"Don't hold back, mate."

"We aren't friends to informers."

"That's exactly what you are. Day in, day out, sneakin'

around recruitin' people. I've worked alongside you lot for years. I know how you operate."

"It's how you've been operating, *opso*, that's the issue here. Who are you passing information to?"

"No one."

"You must think we're remedial."

"How have you worked that out?"

"Do you think we're unable to read?"

"Everyone who goes to Oxford can read, can't they?"

"Are you intent on making this dreadful situation worse for yourself?"

"Do I need a rep here?"

"This isn't that sort of interview."

"What sort of interview is it?"

"The sort where we get answers to our questions and you end up in the glasshouse before you find yourself guilty of some serious civilian offence."

"Ah, a fit-up."

"Something commensurate to your actual crime, but not quite our problem."

"And what is my *actual crime*?"

"Passing information to a third party to enable people to be killed."

"What third party?"

"Exactly."

"Look, lads, I think we're talking in circles here."

One of the suits leaned forward and pushed a page towards him. The opso looked at columns of his database search terms, the relevant ones highlighted.

"It's my job to look into known heads."

"You do appear to have been taking your job more seriously of late."

The opso said nothing.

"Extracurricular searches around Deirdre Rushe, Paul

Hagan, Sean Gillen. Searches for known bomb makers in County Donegal. Very diligent."

"I've been decorated for this stuff," the opso said, unable to suppress his irritation.

"We've had the search pattern assessed by our very accomplished behavioural analysts. Every keystroke tells a tale – or so they tell me. They determined that your method of rummaging around in the records is symptomatic of someone trying to conceal their real intent."

"What a crock of shit, mate."

"Again, not mates. This is really quite an established method."

"Won't stand a chance in a court martial, though, will it?"

"There won't be a court martial, Rob. This is a straight demotion, isolation, humiliation. Two years in the glasshouse and then a long life among ordinary decent criminals."

"On the basis of me doing my job diligently? I don't think so."

"Who did you tell, Rob?"

"Tell what?"

"You gave away the manager. You gave away Deirdre Rushe. You gave away Grim. Four people are dead."

"Agreed, four people are dead, and we have no idea what's going on cos you lot are retracting surveillance to cover up that you knew there was a bomb in that car!"

"You're angry, Rob. You're so angry you've done immeasurable damage."

The suit's quiet companion fluttered a hand to silence his partner. A suppressed gesture not lost on the opso.

"What damage?" he clutched at the slip-up.

"You admit you did this?"

"I admit nothin'," he spat. "What damage has been done?"

The suit shifted uncomfortably. The silent one withdrew

the page of search terms and made to rise, and then the pieces fell into place for the opso.

"Ah, I see, I see."

The two interrogators scraped back their chairs, shuffled past him and left the opso to his isolation, and the realisation that a valuable informer was now dead, or was about to be.

The big dish was landed into the cockpit, claws hanging over the edge dripping in garlic butter.

"I don't like them," Isla said, unable to take her eyes off the black beads above the antennae.

"You didn't try it yet," Sam said.

"I don't want to, Daddy," she said, almost alarmed.

"Just as well I made you ham and cheese spaghetti then."

"Yesss," she hissed.

Sinead had just cracked the first claw when the sound of an engine bounced off the walls of their amphitheatre. Sam turned to watch as a huge black rigid inflatable boat came into the hole, drawing its wash behind.

"Ah, that's a shame," said Sinead. "Thought we were going to have the place to ourselves."

Sam stood up. "Someone I want you to meet," he said, and was rewarded with an intrigued smile on Sinead's face. *Introductions!*

The rigging slapped hard against the mast and Isla forked her spaghetti to keep it on the plate, while the large, sinister-looking boat circled around and came alongside. Sam caught a warp. A tall man held the gunwale, while a stocky little bloke sprang up and over the guard rail in one motion.

"What about ye, ye big lummox," he called before embracing Sam.

To Sinead the whole arrival had come as a shock and she stood straightening her hair and shirt.

"That's Danny." Min gestured over his shoulder as he turned to the cockpit. "Hallo, wee lassie," he said to Isla, who looked confused at first.

"Isla, you remember Min?" Sam said.

"Mini Marine." Isla nodded.

"C'mere and gimme knuckles, wee darlin'," he said, and Isla obliged.

"And this is Sinead," Sam announced.

"Sorry for y'er trouble, sweetheart," Min said, shaking her hand and holding her by the elbow, looking long into her eyes as he assessed the dynamic. "Lovely to meet ye."

"Min and I worked together for years," Sam said. "He's an old pal."

"You served together?" Sinead said. "You're a former marine?"

"No former, am still at it, darlin'. Somebody's got tae mind the young wans," he said, nodding at Danny.

"Well, you're just in time for dinner," she said.

"Smashin', darlin'." Min sat down. "Danny, y'ev an hower tae yersel', son, but dinnae crash that bloody boat!"

The coxswain nodded, took the bowline from Sam and puttered off round the corner.

"So, Sinead, Isla, tell me all about yersels – school, work, music, boys?" He winked at Isla.

"No way," she replied.

As rum was poured and tails were split, the chat came easy in the hole on the Isle of Mull.

***

"So we know who she is," the clerk said. "Now how do we find her?"

"Go to Kent?" her brother asked, devoid of sarcasm – of which he was incapable.

"She's not in Kent. She's here."

"Start where you last saw her."

"She'll not be there again."

"Car reg?"

"If I had one, I wouldn't know what to do with it."

"I would."

"What?"

"Rape the DVLA database. Get an address."

"You can get into the driver licensing database?"

"Yes," he said, not boasting – not able to. Just stating a fact.

"Have you done it before?"

"Yes."

"Why?"

"To prove old methods pointless."

"You don't elaborate much, do you?"

"I was chatting to mates about intelligence gathering in the olden days."

"Online?"

"Yeah."

"That's not chatting."

He ignored her.

"Well?"

"Someone said that's how the IRA used to target police and prison officers."

"How?"

"They had someone in the driver licensing office or the sorting office of the post."

"I'm sure it doesn't say on a driver's licence that a cop's a cop or a screw's a screw."

"They knew the names of the cops and warders from being in jail or from being arrested. All they wanted was the address."

"Oh."

"Old-fashioned."

"So what was your contribution to this *chat*?"

"Hacked the database while we were talking."

"To prove what?"

"Humans aren't necessary."

"In intelligence gathering?"

"Yes."

"Do you think you're smart?"

"No."

"Really?"

"I am smart. That's all." Not boasting. Not able. Just a fact.

"So how would *you* find that woman?"

"Meadow?"

"Yeah, like, duh?"

"Don't do that."

"Ok,sorry, but what would you do?"

"Parents."

"What?"

"She's young. Parents still probably alive. She maybe speaks to them."

"How do you find them?"

"Look for databases in Kent, get an address, hop on the IP, have a look at their email, maybe their hard drive."

"As easy as that?"

He sat silent.

"Then what?"

"Then, if she's there, follow it back the way."

"To wherever she is?"

"Yeah."

"Would you do that for me?"

"Who is Meadow?"

"Possibly intelligence."

"Police?"

"Maybe, maybe more."

"How much more?"

"A fair bit more."

"I've no interest in hacking a policewoman."

"Then you won't like what she might be."

"If she's higher up, that's interesting."

"What?"

"It's ..." he shrugged, "harder."

"You'd do this cos it's a challenge?"

The brother just nodded.

"You're seriously twisted, you know that?"

"Think I might hit the sack and let you two boys talk salty."

"We might have bin marines, darlin', but there was precious little water most a' the places we were sent tae."

"I'm too pissed to imagine what you pair got up to." She smiled, and to Sam's surprise she leaned forward and gave Min a kiss on the cheek – which was more than she offered him. "Lovely to meet you, Min."

"You too, sweetheart. I'll be away aff by the mornin'. Mebbe see ye again before long, aye."

"I'll try not to wake Isla," she said, holding her finger perpendicular to her lips, wobbly, but not quite messy.

"I might rob y'er man here for a wee burn in the speedboat whenever that long wet streak a' pish gets back here."

"You lads do whatever you want, I'll be dead to the world," she said as she pulled the hatch closed with a rattle and a grind. "Oh, sorry, shush." She giggled.

Min waited until Sinead had stopped bouncing around below before he turned to Sam. "Ye no – like ... bunkin' up, then?"

"She stays in with Isla."

"Oh?"

Sam stayed silent.

"She's a looker."

Sam remained inscrutable.

"Got tae get back on the bike sometime, Sammy boy."

"Let's not start talking about riding," Sam said.

"I was nae goin tae."

"Where's your mate?"

"If ye turn on the mast headlight, he'll scoot over. Told him to hang fire on Iona."

Sam reached in and flicked the toggle. "Where we going?"

"Ye not want a wee burn in the new boat? She's a beast of a thing."

"So long as we're not away for long. Neither of them can hold her off if the anchor drags."

"Safe as houses in here, but we'll no' be long, Sam."

The growl of the engines was absent this time and only the lights betrayed Danny's arrival.

"She's very quiet."

"He's showing aff. That's her on electric propulsion."

"No prop noise," Sam remarked.

"No prop."

"Oh?"

"Jet. For rivers. She can be dropped by heli, motored as far as ye want, then switched to this stealth-like mode. Ye canny hear the motor even when y'er sittin' on it. Danny's probably mindin' no' tae wake the wee un."

"You couldn't wake her with a hammer when she's been at sea all day."

"She's a lovely young lassie, Sam."

"She is."

Both men prepared to jump aboard as the menacing boat pulled up.

"Danny, sit y'ersel' in the cockpit here and keep an eye on

this fine vessel. I'm going tae remind this man what it's like tae have toys tae play wi'."

Danny stepped onto *Siân* as ordered while Min took the helm of the other boat and they slid silently out of the hole. Once beyond the echo, Min offered Sam the wheel, knocked a switch to disengage the electric jet and reverted to petrol.

"Where do ye want to go?" Sam asked.

"Let's listen to Mendelssohn."

Sam plotted a course from memory, turned north and opened up the engine. His neck strained at the acceleration, holding onto the wheel to stay upright. Min had anticipated the surge and smiled knowingly.

"Told ye! She's a bloody animal!"

Within ten minutes they could just make out the black circle of Fingal's Cave on Staffa. Sam had always thought of it as an island – many others argued it was a rock. Regardless, it had held an odd allure for the German composer; his overture – the Hebrides, inspired by its loneliness and isolation; a tribute to the natural sounds of the rise and fall of the sea.

"Long time since I was in there," he shouted as the boat was depowered.

Min leaned forward and touched a screen on the console. "C'mon, we'll just about fit."

"No way," Sam said. "She's too big to go in."

"Watch this," Min said, and tapped a few icons on the screen. "Take y'er paws off the wheel, pal."

Sam lifted his hands as if the helm was hot and watched in astonishment as the engine switched itself off and the boat navigated itself through the rock-strewn entrance and into the chiming cavity. Min fired on a few lights that bounced and rippled around the stunning ceiling. Sam looked up and round at the beautiful rocks – a mirror image of those on the Giant's Causeway on the Antrim Coast; a different country with a sister

geology. Min tapped and swiped and the boat held itself in
position.

"This is amazing."

"Aye. Well, so's what you've been doing." Min's tone had
changed dramatically.

Sam looked straight at him, worry creeping through his
shoulder blades and into his neck. "What?"

"I'm with ye, pal. Never worry about that. But Rob, the opso,
he's bin lifted."

"Shit." Sam closed his eyes.

"Dinnae panic. He wis a' the end of his rope wi' it all
anyway. He wis lookin' out a' the job. He'd had enough."

"But – arrested?"

"Kinda. From what I can gather – which is nae much, by the
way."

"How do you know?"

"Cos I've bin questioned mysel'. He'd bin in touch."

"How did that go?"

"They've nothin' – nothin' on him and nothin' on me. It'll
be fine. But I've tae tell ye somethin'."

"What?"

"They're on this, and in a big way. You make a wrang move,
y'er for the clink. No question."

"That it?"

"You know what Mendelssohn was on about when he wrote
thon choon?"

"I do."

"Aye, well, isolating y'ersel' and that kid's no gonna dae
much good."

"Min—"

"Naw, Sam, hear me oot. You and me's old pals and a've
earned the right to say ma piece. You should take that lassie
you've met and ye should enjoy a second chance. No tae many
gets wan."

"You've made your point."

"And Greencastle."

"What?"

"That's where the bomb came from."

"Fuck, Min, you know how to turn a corner. Greencastle, Donegal?"

"Aye."

"Anything else?"

"Dissidents involved in drug smuggling. Two brothers. Right up your street too."

"How do you mean?"

"By sea, sunshine. They bring the snort in by sea."

The opso stared at his Crocs. His room was as good as he could hope for given that he was confined. Quarters were better than holding cells, not that those had been used for nearly two decades now. They'd been rough then and were no better now. Perhaps the only reason he hadn't been sent there was because they were full of bits of kit held by the spanners and the techs, as well as old computers and monitors that were yet to be cleansed and destroyed.

The opso looked around. It was a far cry from what he'd been offered when he first joined. He had an en suite, for a start, he had a tiny kitchenette, a nice desk with a lamp. His mattress was his own – purchased from a real civilian shop and devoid of skin-piercing springs. Gone were the frisky pictures torn from mucky magazines. Instead, his own photography – panoramics, sunrises and sets over the local scenery reminded him of his love that had grown for this godforsaken landscape. He wondered whether he would ever walk the hills again as a free man. Unlikely. They'd find some way to bang him up.

Yet and all, he couldn't lament the loss of his freedom. The time had come. No one else need feel the grief he'd endured as a young man. If only they'd moved sooner to wipe out the leadership of the remains of the paramilitaries – the most bitter and manipulative of the dregs of the war. If only they'd ignored the deals done by the spooks and the civil servants perhaps there wouldn't have been a bomb in Ballycastle.

And then a notion occurred to him: cover up. That's what Libby's lot were best at. It made sense that the deeper the shit, the greater the need to have the real story concealed. The logic was convoluted but it was there. If he could find a way to let Sam finish the group, the spooks would have to conceal the truth – exposure would be too embarrassing. The opso needed to make sure nobody got to Sam before he was finished. That was his best hope.

24

Seventy-five nautical miles, six knots minimum cruising speed, thirteen hours max.

Sam was worried for the opso. Rob had done him a favour, but Sam couldn't help but feel that his old colleague had failed. He'd known about the bomb vehicle, so he should have forced its deactivation. No question. While Sam appreciated the opso's attempts at repentance, there was part of him that felt he deserved his place in military prison. Rob would survive in the glasshouse, and he'd keep his counsel.

Sam was beginning to feel the wind at his back. He now had the information he required and Min was adamant they hadn't yet identified him – in fact, Min said the questioning made it clear they had no idea who was removing the dissidents.

"John, it's Sinead."

Sam watched her make a call for him.

"I'm well, thanks, and you?"

She's so polite, Sam thought, this could last forever.

"And how's Kaitlin?"

Spoilt little bitch.

"Ah, I'm sorry. It's gonna take time."

It's gonna take a lobotomy.

"And Julianne?"

Out the back, digging for gold.

"Yes, they're fine – all grand. Happy out, actually."

Sam suddenly felt guilty for his ungenerous thoughts towards John's dreadful family.

"Grand, grand. So, John, your friend and mine was wondering if you'd had that delivery yet?"

Sam looked to sea and hoped hard.

"Ah, good, he'll be pleased. Then would it be possible to send it on for us?"

Jurisdictional advantage – no border to cross with odd military-grade equipment, no checks, less hassle.

"Ok, well, we'll let you know where. Apparently they're keen to get going, so they'll be in touch. And, John, thanks a million."

Sam smiled.

"Take care and God bless," she said, before looking up at Sam. "So how does he know where to send this stuff – whatever it is?"

"Put your phone down below, sure."

Sinead did as she was bid and returned to the cockpit.

"Coordinates," Sam said.

"And how does he get those?"

"They'll be with him already. He checks his old-fashioned pigeon hole every day."

"I see," she said. Her tone had changed.

"What?"

"You'd planned all this out."

"What?"

"When you asked me on holiday."

"No," he said.

"No?" she looked at him, almost accusingly.

"Really. No," he replied.

"Coincidence, then?"

Sam hadn't intended to explain everything – fewer people equalled lower risk, but now he felt he had to. "I didn't bring you as cover," he said.

"What did you bring me as?"

"A friend."

"A friend," she sighed as she repeated the response.

"Min said he wanted a chat. I've wanted you to meet him for a while. He's, like ..."

"Your bessie?"

"What?"

"Your best friend."

Sam thought for a moment. "He's a good mate, but ..."

"But what?"

"But, well, you might be my best friend."

"Oh," she said, shock on her face. Perhaps she wilted a little. She had got more than he was used to giving.

"I didn't know what Min wanted to talk about. I thought he maybe needed a hand with something. Instead, he was offering me help with something."

"I assume it's something you're not going to tell me about?"

"Not that I don't want to, just that it's best for you if that's the way it is."

"So Min's sending the coordinates."

"Aye."

"John's not technical. Will he know what they are?"

"I'm hoping he can work out what coordinates are for. Min's got access to internal and external postal systems and has a small army at his disposal. Literally. He'll manage to get a message out undetected."

"Smart."

"But not thought-through or contrived or pre-planned."

"Ok, so where next?"

"I'm going on a drug run."

"Well, Sam Ireland, life around you is never dull."

————————

Two days was all it took.

"You found a meadow in a field?" the clerk asked.

"What?"

"Never mind. What's she doing – living in a field?"

"It's not a field," her brother said.

"What is it then?"

"Google Maps has to blur out security installations on their satellite imagery."

"Oh?"

"Otherwise the MoD would shut it down."

"This is a Ministry of Defence field?"

"It's not a field."

"How can you tell? It looks like a field."

"It's got over a thousand separate cabled accesses. Fibre, and Cat 6 way before its time. All protected. It's a former army base. Certain."

"It could be a housing estate or internet points for squaddie accommodation."

"Squaddies were all gone before this sort of fibre was commercially available. This is high-end stuff. It's military."

"So she's in there."

"Well, that's where she sends her mum emails from."

"You're sure?"

Her brother just stared at the screen, as close to impatient as he could get.

"So how do I track her down?"

"They eat, don't they?"

"What?"

"They go out. Socialise. Now the war's over."

The clerk thought for a moment. It was true. The military wasn't as confined to barracks as it had been during the conflict. "Wonder where they go."

"Friendly towns," he said. "Hardly Derry."

"No, not Derry. Limavady, maybe?"

"Your problem," he said.

"Generous."

"I don't get it."

"What."

"Why you care. Why you want to find her."

"Because I don't make a living in front of a computer screen. I worked my fucking arse off to become a lawyer. I fully intend to get to the top of my game. I am not going to let some fucking Brit bitch blackmail me and keep me down."

"That's what she's doing – this blade singing karaoke?"

"That's what she will do unless I put an end to it before it starts."

"Glad I'm on your side. I need to clean behind me now. We're done?"

"We're done," she said.

No thanks offered. None required.

———

The women got off in Glenarm.

"You know what to do?" Sam checked.

"Bus to Larne. Train to Belfast. Train to Dublin. I think we'll manage."

"Not that," he said, exasperated.

"I know," she said. "And, yes, I know what to do. You know what not to do too?" she whispered, giving him a hug.

"Get caught," he said.

"Get hurt," she replied.

They fell apart and he hoisted Isla onto his shoulder. "You have fun with the girls, my darlin'."

"When are you coming to get me?"

"Few days."

"Yesss! Thank you, Daddy."

"You're getting so big," he said.

"You mean too heavy to lift."

"I'm getting old."

"No, you're not," she said indignantly.

"Thank you, wee love. Now take care and be good."

And they were off.

And he was on.

Thursday night. Friday night. Saturday night. The clerk spent over a hundred pounds on cover charges and soft drinks hunting for a Meadow in a haystack. The woman probably didn't even go out at night.

She realised how uncomfortable it remained to be a single woman going to pubs and clubs alone.

Eglinton, Ballykelly, Limavady, Coleraine. She'd even ventured as far as Portstewart where there was too much nightlife to be sure she hadn't missed a beat.

But there was no choice. Ms Meadow had her by the bits. If she wanted to be free, she needed to send a very clear message.

The opso heard footsteps on the polished corridor. He swung his legs around and prepared to be led away for a fresh round of questions, yet instead of a key in the lock he got a knock.

"That a joke?" he said.

"They've locked you in?"

"Libby? Sure, you know they have. I'm under arrest in 'ere."

He heard a sigh before the feet walked away and two sets of footsteps came back. The door rattled and was unlocked.

Libby peered in. "Bit smelly in here, mate," she said.

"Yeah, well, they've locked the bloody windows too. Four days is a long time, Libby."

"I didn't realise they'd slammed you up."

"Really?"

"Really."

"Where did you think I was?"

"Your team have been told you're on compassionate."

"Oh?"

"They think your mum's not well."

"They're right. She's dead."

"They don't appear to know that."

"How would they?"

"What have you done?"

"So you're the soft soap."

"No."

"C'mon, we'd all try it. Send a friendlie to crack the nut."

"No."

"Right, Libby. Right-o."

"What have you done?"

"Nothin'. Not that that'll change anythin'. They need someone for the leak and it might as well be me."

"Not if it's not you."

"I know you believe it's me, the way you were with us in the ops room."

"What are you talking about?"

"Don't, Libby. I know you've suspected me for a while. Did you flag me?"

"No!"

"Tell me this, honestly, Libby. Did you suspect before we went walkin'? In the hills, like. Is that why you came with me?"

"No, I bloody didn't," she said, and turned to make an indignant exit, but paused. "You tell *me* this, *honestly*. Why did you contact someone in Scotland?"

"Who?"

"A tactical officer from command. A Royal Marine."

"Min? He's an old mate. He served here years ago. I'm in touch with him regular, like."

"Not that regular."

"See, you do suspect me if you're checkin' me comms, Libby. You do think somethin's up."

"It's what they're pointing at to prove you're guilty. They're listing irregular activity."

"And what's irregular about me rubbin' up an old mate?"

"Whoever is doing this is good. They're very fucking good."

"You mean taking out the dissies? Well, more bloody power to 'em, Libby, whomever they are. But I didn't start it, I tell you that with my hand on my heart."

"So what did you talk to him about?"

"Who?"

"The marine."

"About gettin' out. Life after, like. Starting up our own thing. We'd always talked about it – a security company."

"You want out?"

"Looks like it's gonna happen whether I want it or not."

"With this officer?"

"Wait – you don't think it's him, do you? Ha! You think Min might be taking them out? He lives between Faslane and Arbroath, for fuck's sake."

"He's got the skills, he was DET, 14th Int. He knows how we work – how you work."

"A lifetime ago, maybe. He was good, too. Check him out, sure. See where he was on the dates of the killings. If it was him, I'd give him my full support, Libby. Every ounce of it. But you're on the wrong path there."

"We know," she said.

"Wha?"

"We checked. He was training at command in Scotland when all the murders happened."

"Then what are ye here for?"

"To look you in the eye and see if it was you."

"And what do you think?"

"Honestly, Rob? I don't know."

Sam experimented on dry land at first. The aroma of new plastic, hardware, wafting from the box reminded him of Christmas as a child. He clipped on the belt. The docking station amused him. He'd been out of the military long enough to be astonished at how much the tech had evolved.

Looking at his console, the instrument acquired a GPS signal and he began the launch procedure. Then the docking station flipped open and a barely discernible hum began. The tiny helicopter rose like a wasp from his hip, leaving a spare hibernating in his berth. The wasp rose to head height and turned automatically to stare at him, awaiting command. Sam suppressed a little snigger and directed the device to the distance – as Isla would call it, watching everything the wasp could see on a tiny monitor as it shot off into the dusk.

The image was incredible given the size of the drone, which could easily rest in Sam's hand. The relay of pictures was almost immediate – he tested it a few times by reducing speed to hover, and working out what the delay was. Less than a second, he reckoned. And all of that without a wireless bubble. Astonishing. Thank goodness for wealthy sponsors like the heiress's father. Two drones at twenty thousand per chopper. And each no bigger than a banana.

FINN ÓG

Which made him wonder – were they like ants? Could they carry more than their body weight?

Libby shook her head at how clichéd the meeting was. To her left the superior sat staring at the sea. She noticed a damp patch on his shirt. It had a hint of red. It distracted her until she realised that he must have treated himself to a ninety-nine before they met. How ordinary, she thought, that this man should behave like anyone else, even if he does dress like he's about to watch a polo match.

"Your unit is under investigation."

"I don't have a unit. I'm independent."

"Yes," he drawled. "The DET to which you are attached is being examined."

"By us?"

"Of course by us. But now also by themselves."

"Why?"

"Because four people are fucking dead, Libby," he snarled.

"Yes," she mimicked back in a similar drawl, which provoked a sideways stare from the superior, realising he was losing her.

"You're going native," he stated.

"I just don't see how it came from them. They're a good team – tight as a nun's chuff."

"The nun appears to be ageing."

"So what do you want me to do this time?"

"This time?"

"Last time I had to pull a move with some lawyer woman, which was pretty distasteful, by the way, and made absolutely no sense—"

"I'd advise you to never raise that again, Libby."

"Then you wanted me to spy on a friend."

"That's your job."

"Still. He's on our side."

"Or not. You sure he's not more than a friend? You sure he hasn't been to unauthorised areas?"

Libby worked hard to suppress a sudden swelling of hatred for her boss.

"Thought as much," he nodded, satisfied, smug.

"Incorrect," she said. "Absolutely incorrect, but I respect him. He's a good man."

"The implication there is that you do not respect me – but then I never professed to being a good man."

"I didn't say that."

"Well, he's for the glasshouse, in any case. What we need to do is extract you from this diabolical mess with all haste."

"It's that serious?"

"I'm not in the business of prediction, Libby, as you know, but I would be surprised if that detachment survives the week."

"Bloody hell. Who will watch the X-rays, then?"

"The days of human deployment are drawing to a close, Libby. Perhaps it's time to switch from manual to automatic, as it were."

Libby said nothing but stared out at the beautiful green sea.

"And a reminder," he said, as he shuffled his velvety shoes and made to rise. "That job in Belfast that you rather foolishly alluded to is to be kept discreet. Utterly. Do you understand that, Meadow?"

The use of her real name ran through her like a static shock. All she could do was nod.

By that morning the clerk was on the cusp of nursing a horrendous hangover but she was still sufficiently inebriated to get up ahead of the pain. Despondency at a lack of progress, at her long shot having failed, had led to a glass of wine, then another, a beer, a vodka, two vodkas, five, sambuca, bad company and then dancing – she thought. She needed to eat.

"Room number, please?"

"I didn't book breakfast," she told the Spaniard, or Portuguese, or Mexican. "How much?"

"Just sixteen pounds for full Irish and twelve for continental."

She handed over her card.

"Which?" the waiter asked, waiting for clarification.

"Full," was all she managed.

Her table sat by an enormous window but she was in no form to enjoy the view. She devoured her first coffee and held out the mug gesturing for more with such impatience that the waitress couldn't ignore her – much as she appeared to want to.

"Listen, I'm not feeling great," she said. "I'll leave you a massive tip if you just bring me a full breakfast, the whole works, everything and brown sauce, please."

"Ok," said the young woman, unsympathetic but not one to stare a gift horse in the mouth.

When it came, her arms worked like a fiddler's elbow before she sat back, exhausted and content – at least until she could beat some painkillers into her. She'd be fit to drive in an hour or so, she naively reckoned, if she could find her car.

She looked into the sun, closed her eyes and allowed it to warm her face. The rest for a few moments nearly sent her to a slumber. She looked down before opening her eyes to avoid the glare. Her vision settled on a pair of suedes as they padded down the road outside. *Prick*, she thought, imagining the sort that would buy such articles; a judge on a long weekend was her instinct – like every weekend for the judiciary.

Beyond the slacks was an expensive shirt complete with cufflinks. Her lazy hangover gaze fell back to the shoes and followed them across the road and into the passenger side of an unremarkable car. Before the door closed, the clerk looked up and caught sight of the driver. Her heart faltered. She grabbed for her bag and rummaged for her phone. A swipe up triggered her camera. A swipe right and she had the video. She tore out of the restaurant, ignoring the shouting waitress behind her.

"I'll be back in two minutes!"

She crossed the road and made sure the framing was correct, walking past the car in which the ponce and her target were facing one another in conversation. The clerk passed by unnoticed, went around the rear of the vehicle, opened WhatsApp and then changed her mind. She scrolled through the screens and found the encrypted app her brother had placed on her "crap" phone and forwarded him the video: *Meadow and a weirdo* she wrote as a title. That will do rightly, she thought. Her brother had the woman's email address and the clerk now had leverage.

At exactly the same time Sam was fewer than six miles away, sailing back and forth around the Greencastle coast. He'd been at it for thirty hours, tapping the chart-plotter screen every time he passed a buoy marking the presence of a lobster pot. In the old days they'd caught plenty of drug smugglers that way. Marines were ideal for such work – long hours on dark nights tracking boats and marking their drops.

As darkness fell Sam returned to as many buoys as he could, catching each with the boat hook and beginning a backbreaking haul to retrieve the cage at the bottom. No wonder, he thought, that even the smallest fishing boats have winches. After sixteen, he began to lag and wondered if the process was hopeless. He'd bagged about twenty good-sized crab, but none of the lines or creels concealed drugs.

He hauled out the small jib and arched himself backwards,

trying to loosen up and crack out a few vertebrae. The night was soft, the breeze inoffensive, but the search hopeless. There were hundreds of buoys, any one of which could be used to hide drugs – or none of them. To search like this was madness, despite the established process of bringing snuff and junk into an island like Ireland.

It was easy, really. Rather than human mules and their intestines, smarter smugglers exploited fishermen. A boat from Scandinavia, Spain or anywhere in Europe would meet an African or an American vessel and take on a load. That could happen anywhere from the Med to the Atlantic. Then they'd go about their usual catching and landing, steaming north and eventually head for an Irish port. Exchanges might happen along the way – between boats that shared a common owner – and then the wraps would be attached to a buoy, the GPS coordinates relayed and the buoy chucked over the side. Eventually, someone, somewhere, would lift the loot, bring it ashore and a car would arrive. The driver – often a foreigner with little more than a license, would ping the boot with strict instructions not to look in the mirror. He'd drive to wherever he'd been told to go and would again trigger the release on the boot. He'd be paid, and the drugs would make their way to a kitchen table to be cut with baking soda or talcum powder and then onto the street.

Big profits and low risk. For those actually making the mega-money, anyway.

Sam called it a day, fired up the engine and headed for shore.

"Mum?" Libby saw the number appear on her personal mobile phone and immediately thought something was wrong with her dad. Unscheduled calls from home were discouraged.

"Hello, dear. I know it's not our day to catch up but we've had this email—"

"Mu-um," Libby said impatiently, assuming it was some sort of scam her mother wanted advice on.

"It's a photo of you – that's all. I don't know why it's come to us. Who is he?"

"What?"

"There's no writing – just the picture."

"Can you send it to me?"

"How do I do that?"

"Can you see where it says *reply* and *reply all* and *forward*?"

"Hang on, I'll start up the computer."

Libby couldn't supress an exhale of frustration. She'd been in the middle of digging through the opso's files looking for a thread to pull. This photo probably came from an old school pal trying to get in touch.

"Ok, the email is open."

"Right. Look along the top and find the 'forward' button."

"Got it."

"Now type in my email address."

"M-e-a-d-o-w-dot-m-u-s-i-c—

"Yes, that one, Mum. It should come up automatically."

"Yes, dear, it has."

"Ok, just click 'send'."

"That's it away to you now. I'm sure it will be with you today."

Libby shook her head in annoyance. "It'll be here right now, Mum. Hang on."

She took her phone from her ear and opened up her mail app. Among the rubbish was a message from her mum. She opened it and stared at a picture of her and her superior sitting in a car. "Mum, sorry, I gotta go," she called into the handset without returning it to her ear.

Sam wasn't confident about the seabed. It seemed too sandy to definitely grip the anchor, so he was restless. He was reluctant to set the anchor alarm to alert him if the boat began to drag because that would require his position to be identified by GPS coordinates and place him where he didn't want to be placed.

He'd been determined not to sail into Greencastle – to do so would draw attention in a small Donegal fishing village. Fishermen and sailors seldom enjoyed a harmonious relationship; the former generally taking the view that sailors were pompous toffs who caused mayhem in working harbours. Sam had some sympathy with them.

Instead, he had headed north-west to Culdaff, just off a beach, for a bit of peace and thinking time. It was sufficiently isolated – the nearest neighbours being abandoned static caravans oxidising a mottled brown in the salt air.

Eventually he gave up on sleep and decided to bring a sleeping bag up to the cockpit. After two hours in the dark he became distracted by a sweeping headlight. He wrestled down into the bag and thought of other things until, five minutes later, he saw the light again. He rose, cocooned, and peered out to sea. Nothing. Sam turned and watched the headland, from where the light must have come. For ten minutes, nothing. His eyes began to water in the gentle breeze and then suddenly, the unmistakable flash of headlights aimed out to sea.

He dismissed it at first as likely to be teenage shaggers bumping the dimmer lever ith a bare arse. But caution crept in and he thought about what Min had said. They'd questioned the opso – they had a trail. They'd even pulled Min in for a going-over. When it came to hunting, he knew the DET were more than adept.

He kicked off the bag and in his socks went forward and

pressed the windlass button to raise the anchor. Then he shook out the small jib and quietly slipped away from shore.

But the scenarios kept coming at him. Here he was assuming the lights had something to do with him, which was paranoia, was it not? He was hauling ass away from a phantom surveillance vehicle that was signalling to someone at sea. Perhaps he was headed the wrong direction – straight into their hands? Surely, if someone was looking for him, they would get the police to make an arrest? Police don't do boats. His mind was leaping and diving, especially when he realised he had just unfurled a great white sail. Even on a moonless night a light sweep would pinpoint him. He rolled it away and started the engine, deciding to motor hard offshore and stay there until he worked out what to do next. He reminded himself that sleep deprivation made for dark imaginings – hallucination, even, so he tried to calm his mind and simply make out into the Atlantic. With sea, space and rest would surely come a plan.

And then the engine stopped with a bang.

Diving at night was no craic. Sam could well remember his first combat dive course after passing selection. One day he was a Royal Marine, the next he was part of a squadron, a troop, a member of the Special Boat Service, and far too buoyant for his own good.

"What the fuck is wrong with you?" the instructor had yelled. "You're like a cork out of a bottle."

Sam couldn't argue. He had to tuck more weight than anyone else into his kit to submerge properly. While others struggled with their eyes and ears and orientation, he couldn't even get beneath the surface without working hard to stay down.

Nonetheless, he curled and flipped under the boat to try

and see what was going on with the engine. The bang had been very loud and he assumed he'd hit a plank of driftwood or debris. Again and again he thrashed his feet to try to get a good look at the driveshaft, his waterproof torch about as useful as a candle. Three inspections later he determined that there was heavy plastic baling involved. He sawed along the propshaft in the hope of freeing something he couldn't see, before gasping to the surface for a few minutes to recover. The boat began to turn stern to the wind. He held still, trying to work out what was happening, and realised that whatever he had hit was securing *Siân* in the water.

Not a random piece of debris, then, he thought. But it was deep, really deep. Two hundred feet or more. That would be a lot of line for a lobster pot or mooring. Had he hit a navigation buoy? If so, how had he not seen it on the chart?

Then creaking began, like a tautening, a strain. Sam instinctively pushed himself away from the hull, now alarmed at what he didn't understand. Like a blast of a landmine, water exploded around him and a huge black something burst from the sea. At first Sam thought it was a basking shark, so violent had its arrival been – then it settled on the surface, static, inert, definitely non-biological.

Sam tapped it a few times and was satisfied that it was a container of some kind, bound heavily. New energy entered his lungs and legs and he used the davit lines for lifting the dinghy to haul the box aboard. In the cockpit he set about attacking the outer shell, his anticipation building. In his haste and excitement he forgot that the box was no longer anchoring him and *Siân* was now drifting aimlessly. Inside were tightly packed flare canisters – the type used by any commercial boat. His heart sank a little. Flares were hard to dispose of legally and some fisherman had likely dumped out-of-date stock over the side. He sat back in abject disappointment – and then he heard it.

He had barely turned towards the noise when his whole visibility was filled with the looming bow of a fishing boat, steaming fast towards him. Sam leapt to the console and pushed the starter. The exhaust coughed, the impeller span and three seconds later the turn over converted to combustion and he hammered the throttle forward as hard as he could. He reached for the wheel but even the spin he gave *Siân* wasn't enough to avoid a glancing blow. Sam cringed as he heard the tear of aluminium and the crunch of timber below. He looked behind to see the fishing boat wheel to starboard.

"What the fuck!" he yelled after her.

Computation takes time when cold, wet and distracted. It hadn't dawned on Sam that the fishing boat, ten times the mass of his own yacht, hadn't hit him by freak accident.

The bigger boat had nearly turned but its circle was too large. It wouldn't be able to hit *Siân* again without slowing, reversing and coming at him again. Sam realised that that the fishing boat could do nothing to him so long as he remained amidships. If she were to come at him from any significant angle, weight, height and power would finish him. So Sam hammered the bow thrust, gunned the throttle and spun the wheel to draw himself parallel to the fishing boat, which predictably began to buffer up against the hull side-on. The grubby bigger boat had a necklace of old tyres strung along its hull, suggesting it hadn't been long at sea. They took some of the impact as *Siân* and the brute came together again.

For ten minutes the fishing boat and *Siân* kept pace with one another. The fishing boat ought to have had more speed but Sam had *Siân* opened up more than he'd ever attempted before – 8.6 knots, and worked into the larger hull so that the fishing boat dragged him along at the same pace.

Where was the crew? he wondered. Why had nobody come on deck to throw stuff at him?

And then he realised – there was no crew.

If there had been any spare hands aboard, they'd have fired a flare or hit him with a grappling hook – a fish box, even. He was ten feet beneath them and a sitting duck. So it was clear: there were only two people in the tussle. And where there were two, Sam had an advantage.

He looked around, up at the imposing hull to his left. He grabbed one of the knives he'd been using but he wanted something that would give him leverage to swing from a distance. The dinghy had been dumped by the davits, so he grabbed an oar from its side tank, set the autohelm to keep *Siân* in towards the fishing boat and then used the old tyre dangling from its side to spring up and onto the deck of the trawler.

The boat was a mess. She plainly hadn't been used for fishing in a very long time. The winches were rusted and looked all but seized, there were no nets and the hold cover had been welded shut. Sam moved towards the wheelhouse and put his boot to the door, nearly defacing himself as it swung back in anger at the force of his own blow. Inside, the console was equally antiquated – there were no modern fish finders, radar or instruments. Nor was there anyone at the wheel.

What the fuck is going on? Sam thought, as he moved forward to see how the boat was being steered.

"Don't be touching anything, now," came a gruff country voice from behind.

He's calm, thought Sam. Confident. He must be better armed than me.

"Put the wee knife down."

Sam ignored the command and turned to find a fit-looking fifty-something in grubby jeans and a shoulder-patched jumper staring at him intently. Sure enough, he had an old Stirling rifle in his hand. Sam had never used a Stirling but it had been the weapon of choice of clandestine units that had preceded him. From the pictures on the walls of the ops room he knew the rifle loaded from a magazine at the side – which, in this case, was missing. His head was warmer now, and working better, so he hedged for a moment to see where this would take them. He dropped the knife but kept the oar.

"You tried to sink me."

"You lifted something that wasn't yours."

"Salvage," Sam said.

"Did you open it?"

"It's just flares."

"Aye."

"Hardly warrants a sinking."

"Who are you?"

"I'm sailing. Who are you, more like?"

"You Irish Navy?"

"In a sailing boat?"

"Are ye?"

"Don't think navy personnel travel alone."

The man grunted. He had been wedged in behind a cupboard, but as he pushed to full height Sam became aware of the scale of the challenge.

"You shouldn't have been so nosey."

"Your flares hit my prop and stopped my engine. What choice did I have?"

"You didn't need to go hoking in the box."

Sam began to realise that he might have hit the jackpot. The box was evidently more important to this man than a simple illegal dumping of flares. He thought about the manager's final words, and cut to the chase. "You a bomb maker?"

The man's brow crunched immediately, his left eye all but closing. "What d'ye say?"

He was clearly flustered but Sam already knew all he needed to know. Somewhere on this boat would be enough information to get to the next stage. He walked forward.

"I'll put a bucket of lead in ye," the hulk warned.

"There's no magazine in that gun," Sam said and whacked

the man as hard as he could in the temple with the oar. The man caught it as Sam retracted for a second blow and he lurched forward like a sprinter out of blocks, pushing the oar at Sam and keeping the pair apart.

Sam hit the console and his back pressed up against the window of the wheelhouse. Out of the corner of his eye he could see *Siân*'s mast. He grabbed the knife and raised it towards the man's head, but the older bloke was lightning fast. He snapped Sam's wrist in his massive clutch and began to twist. Sam had no option but to begin some groundwork – he needed to take the man's legs from beneath him. An ankle stamp and a knee kick freed him from the grip, but he'd lost the knife and was left only with the oar. The man was now on his knees in front of him, so Sam used his left hand to go for an eye and using the oar as a spear he aimed – not for the first time, at the now screaming and gaping hole of the throat. As he'd done once before, he gripped the oar at the point of thrust, as a pole-vaulter would, and rammed it into the airway.

The heaving began. The man, speared like a fish, flailing like catch, exhausting and expiring; the remaining eye bulging in disbelief.

Sam opened the few files in the wheelhouse while the hulk settled into death. There was no time and he hadn't been wearing gloves. The boat would need torched. He tore out a sheet from the middle of one folder – an insurance cover note with an address at the top. In another folder he found a fishing licence, laminated and ready for naval inspection. The address on both was the same. He then turned to the body on the floor and began a shakedown. He found a wallet and an old phone with actual buttons on the front.

Someone values his privacy, Sam thought.

He looked at *Siân*'s mast. She had slipped aft marginally – he had to move quickly. He skipped over the side, threw the papers and the phone below deck, and lifted the dinghy's petrol can. Back on the fishing boat he doused the wheelhouse, ripped out the VHF radio, rubbed the brown and blue wires together and then, for ease, used matches that were sitting by a small camping stove to accelerate the process. The whoosh of flame was gentle enough to allow him to get out easily, and he took his canister with him back onto his own boat. He turned the helm to starboard and the two vessels parted, the fishing trawler heading out into the Atlantic – a burning funeral pyre to a man who thoroughly deserved his cremation.

And them Sam turned to the dinghy and spotted his mistake.

25

L   ibby had debated at length whether to inform her superior. They'd been seriously compromised and to not tell him was to risk his life – but she was so cross with him that she reckoned she would manage to get over his death. That would have resulted in an investigation, during which the email from the anonymous contact would be discovered and she would be exposed for withholding vital information. Hence the bollocking she was getting.

"You let someone follow you?"

"Well, with respect," she began, although she meant no respect at all, "they may have been following *you*."

"Then why did they use your personal email address?"

"They actually emailed my mother."

"Your mother!"

"Yes," she conceded. It did indeed appear that she was the target.

"And now my face is in the hands of some, well – who knows? Could be a fucking foreign agency, Libby!"

"It appears so," she replied calmly. Her days in the service felt numbered, which was ushering in an odd sense of relief and detachment.

"Do you wish to keep your job, Libby?" he growled.

"Ideally," she replied, astonished at her own ambivalence.

"Are you goading me?"

"Yes, I want to keep my job."

"Then find out who compromised you. More importantly, find out why!"

The phone slammed down and she heard a commotion outside. She walked down the corridor, still slightly stunned and oddly nonchalant about what her superior had said, to find six military cars in the yard between her accommodation block and the operations unit. The doors were open and DET staff were being ushered into the back seats of the waiting vehicles. She hurried outside and asked one of the spanners what was happening.

"We're being shut down." He shook his head.

"What?"

"Seems there's been some internal investigation. The opso's been taken away and the staff are being driven to Belfast for debrief. Only me and the techs are staying."

"The opso's gone already?"

"He's in the front car – on his own."

"What's it about?" Libby asked, pretending to know nothing.

"You'd know more than I would but I'd say they reckon all the X-rays being bumped off was our fault."

"They didn't tell me they were doing this," she said.

"It's not your lot. This is our team – military. I asked if there would be a replacement staff but nobody answered. Some other detachment will likely take over our area. Probably Lisburn, or West Det."

"Bloody hell," Libby muttered as the first of the vehicles pulled away. "All the techs are still here?"

"Yeah."

"Tell them I want to speak to them in the ops room, 1600 hours."

Lough Swilly looked shallow, so Sam decided to cut his losses and limp into the marina. As such installations went, it was pretty isolated, not a human in sight, although the facilities were in good order. He examined the damage and was pleasantly surprised to find it all repairable without the need to bring in specialists.

He woke from a four-hour sleep, showered and set about the next bit of his plan. It needed to be finished before the burning fishing boat was found, towed and examined. His sleep began to feel like a luxury.

He looked at the map and reckoned on a fifteen-mile yomp across manageable terrain. When he was twenty-five he'd have allowed four hours max, complete with bergen, webbing and a rifle. Now he settled realistically on six hours, with half the kit. He gathered up his little helicopters, food, water, the dead man's mobile and set off.

On the climb he felt every month he'd been away from the Marines. His calves strained like the shore lines on a ship, his quads roared and he thanked God he didn't have to carry weight on his shoulders – at least his lower back was spared that pain. By mile four, though, his body and mind had settled into a familiar, if distant, routine; one commanding and calming the other, muscle memory easing the shock and generating a rhythm. As in years past, he ran downhill and walked the inclines, using a paper map to avoid dwellings and farmhouses. No electronic navigation.

Throughout he thought back to his escape exercises in the final throes of selection to become a member of the special forces. It had been horrific, the hours spent evading capture, but his mind back then had been fit for it. He had gained a reputation for deviousness, a canny ability to find his way out of tight situations.

After five hours he came to a hill and took a bearing. The address he'd found on the boat insurance document rested silently beneath him – a sprawling farm, as unkempt as any other. There were old vehicles of various kinds turning to rust in the overgrown yard. There was a silo, a pit, a massive shed wide and high enough to accommodate combines and balers, and then various outhouses, groaning and grunting to the shuffle of cattle. There was a dog on a chain, no doubt feral and fed with a pitchfork. It howled and strained on its leash, giving Sam comfort that its agitation was a default and not inspired by his arrival.

There was no immediate evidence of surveillance, but then there wouldn't be. His former colleagues would be well concealed and over the border there would be no error made.

In a hollow behind a ridge hedge he moved a few large rocks and allowed himself some depth. There he arranged his new toys, ran through a rough plan, pulled over the tarpaulin and settled into a doze to wait for moonlight.

He woke to find the lip of his covering revealing nothing but darkness and drew back the tarp to appraise the house beneath. Satisfied that all was quiet, he began the launch sequence, releasing the little bird from beneath his cover. The first helicopter shot off into the night and Sam quickly fought to orient himself to the surroundings from above. Everything looked a little different, smaller, insignificant. He buzzed the heli around his own hole and, satisfied he was undetectable, sent the device down to the farm.

He began with the shed that stood without doors. The heli peered in, sending Sam images of dark and brutal-looking farm machinery. Then he went to the cattle shed and the outhouses.

Sam noted that one had a steel door and two hefty padlocks. The door was large enough to allow a significant vehicle to enter – a car or a van, but probably not a tractor.

Then he sent the chopper to the house, looking for light beneath the curtains. There was none, even though the barking became ferocious. He hit hover mode, found the dead man's Nokia and slipped in the battery. It came to life and he brought up the only two numbers stored in the phone – both without names. He sent them both the same text: *There's someone outside.*

"We didn't do this," Libby began, "but we need to fix it."

The techs looked at her blankly, then two of them turned for guidance to a third, who sat forward in her seat.

"Didn't do what?"

"Whatever it is that your bosses are accusing this detachment of."

"Which is what?"

Libby sighed. They hadn't been properly briefed – nobody told anyone anything in this game. "It seems the military believe the opso, possibly some others, have been passing information to whoever killed the X-rays."

"The dissidents?" the tech asked.

"Yeah, but I, for one, don't believe that. Do you?"

They looked awkwardly at one another.

"We were asked to sift through the opso's search history and file requests."

"And?"

"And some of it did seem like it could be used to gather information on the X-rays."

"Really?"

"Yeah, kind of."

"Could he just have been doing his job?"

"Yeah, yeah, he could," said the lead tech, who looked at her colleagues, "but he'd have been doing it better than he used to do it."

"Do you think he was lazy?"

"No!" she protested.

"No, definitely not," said one of the two blokes.

"Then what?" asked Libby.

"It's just that ... his approach was generally more old school, in a way. He preferred operational, eyes-on type intelligence gathering. It wasn't his default to hunt through files or make links that way."

"So that was a change in behaviour?"

"Yeah."

"And that's what you passed on to ... to who?"

"To your team, Box, originally. Intelligence asked for it. Then our own detachment asked for another sift – and we passed that on too."

"And now he's in jail."

"Well, we were just doing what we were ordered to do."

"Yeah, well, now it's just you three, two spanners and me until further notice. So I suppose we try and get him out."

"Do we?" one of the blokes asked.

"Do you believe he's been setting people up to die?" Libby asked – and as she did so she wondered if she cared whether he was guilty.

"No," said the woman tech firmly. The two men eventually shook their heads in agreement.

"So let's get to work to see if we can help him. We need to agree to keep this to ourselves for obvious reasons. Are we all clear on that? Anyone not happy can leave now and nothing more will be said."

Each of the three nodded.

"Agreed," said the woman tech.

"First, I need to know how I got compromised."

"*You* have been compromised?" the woman asked.

"There's something going on. I don't know what it is but we need to root out what's happening. My mother was sent this email." She offered her phone around.

"Who's the man?"

"Can't get into that but he's important, senior and deeply unhappy. I need to know where this came from and what it's about. Let's get you to start there." She nodded at the woman. "And you two, let's see if there's any pattern to these X-ray murders, anything geographic or methodical that can link the way each dissident died. Then we might make progress to find out who is doing it."

As she finished laying out orders it occurred to her that if they did find out the opso had been managing the murders, it would make little difference to her. She'd stick by him. He'd looked after her and he was a good man.

Nothing happened. The dog did pirouettes in the yard, dragging his chain to a bind around him. Still, not a light came on, not a being emerged.

Sam waited for fifteen minutes and began to doubt his plan. His assumptions had been wrong. He'd calculated that dissident republicans would come out fighting, possibly armed and aggressive.

Twenty minutes after the text had left the handset, a car approached. It bumped and flickered towards the lane of the farm, then doused its headlights and crept down to the yard. Whomever that is, thought Sam, they know the place well enough to drive the lane in the dark.

He took the heli on a sweep of the perimeter, looking not for dissidents but for military – detachment staff. He wanted a heads-up in any roused interest. He dove the heli towards clumps of grass, mounds of rock, he even ran it along hedges, which he knew to be futile; any covert camera would be brilliantly concealed.

The car sat motionless in the yard. The dog, curiously, had calmed. Then the handset lit up in Sam's paw.

No sign of anyone. Max was going mad. You inside?

Sam realised that the bomb makers lived separately. Stupid. They were brothers, not lovers. No doubt one had been left the farm, the other probably took land nearby. He considered what to write back and whether to send it to both numbers stored in the phone.

Just checking the outbuildings. Unlock the shed.

It was a risk tonally and descriptively. Who knew what they called the steel-fronted outbuilding. Who knew if the brothers used "please" and "thank you". Who knew if they were smart enough to consider such things at in the early hours.

Nonetheless, a light came on as the car door opened and a man of similar size to the dead trawlerman climbed out. His bulk was evident from his need to place a hand on the roof of the car just to lever himself free of the vehicle. He mooched over to the outbuilding and Sam sent the heli as close as he dared, wary of the buzz it emitted. The man picked a key from a bunch and freed the higher of two padlocks. Another key was used for the lower lock and from Sam's vantage point he could hear the door creak open. The phone lit again. This time the second number in the phone glowed.

You both ok?

Sam ignored it. He was sure in himself that the man he was watching was the brother of the bloke he'd despatched at sea. He sent the helicopter on one final sweep, then recalled it, quietly shaking off the cover that concealed him and allowing an appreciative snort as the heli flew back to its cradle. The lid closed, Sam pulled on his balaclava and left his entire kit under the wrap with a few rocks to keep it down. He allowed his bones and muscles a quick stretch ahead of the exertion he was about to put them through before wandering down to finish the job.

"Ma'am?"

"You don't need to call me Ma'am," Libby said for the fourth time.

"Sorry."

The new team was clustered in a circle in the ops room. The data speeds were faster there, according to the techs.

"What have you found?"

"Early days but the lifeboat's towing a fishing vessel to Greencastle."

"Not really the brief," Libby said. "Greencastle, Donegal?"

"Yeah, and I know but two X-rays have a fishing boat licensed to them in Greencastle, Donegal."

"Oh-kay ..." said Libby, still suspecting the tech was stretching.

"We had them under surveillance until recently."

"Wait – the farmers? Two brothers?"

"Yes. We tracked stolen fertiliser equipment from Fermanagh to their farm a few months back. We believe they manufactured the Ballycastle device for one of the dissie IRA factions."

Libby stared in silence at the tech for a moment, then posed the obvious question.

"What are farmers doing with a fishing boat?"

"According to the intelligence log they're known smugglers. Fishing boat is a cover to land their drugs by sea."

"Ok, so their fishing boat has broken down. So what?"

"Seems it went on fire. Body reported aboard."

"I see," said Libby. But she didn't see at all.

"You better come," said the brother.
"Is it Mum?" the clerk asked.
"No."
"What then?"
"You better come round."
"Why?"
But he'd hung up.

Sam kept to the deeper gloom as he made along the grey concrete outhouses, slipping into a doorway at one point when the dog heard him and went into orbit. His gloved hand reached out to steady himself in the complete darkness and rested on a bench. His finger brushed an object, light and grip-like – not a million miles from the feel of a handgun. Sam lifted it towards his face and used what reflective light he could to examine the object. It had two prongs and a switch at the thumb. He flicked the switch and heard a tiny whir as if it were preparing itself.

Happy days, Sam thought.

The man at the shed door was expecting his brother to appear. Instead he got a black-clad apparition with a cattle prod. The dog went ballistic as Sam rounded the corner of the outhouse and immediately lit the man up with a sustained jab to the neck. Sparky did its job admirably and the man juddered at the voltage. Sam let him quiver in his shock for longer than was absolutely necessary, and only released him from the current to save battery power for another jab later on. The man shook out on the ground for a few moments, before Sam gave him a kick and told him to crawl inside.

"Where's the light?"

The man couldn't speak. It would probably take a while. Sam had never used such a weapon before, but if it could motivate a cow to behave navigationally, he imagined a human would take its flow of electricity rather badly.

Sam located the light himself, pulled the cord and illuminated a terrorist's jewellery shop. He immediately closed the steel door, before turning to look again at the bomb factory before him. Benches of about twenty feet in length were racked one in front of the other, a production line of lethal intent.

The first was covered with dismantled alarm clocks, soldering irons, wire, strippers and mercury tilt switches. The second had more sophisticated circuit boards, more soldering equipment, bales of electrical wire and tubs of Vaseline. There were plastic surgical gloves at each station, small saws and knives and plastic takeaway boxes. The third table had the detonators, small tubes filled with some sort of explosive material and a wire protruding from each end. Sam quickly worked out that the current would explode the detonator, which would fire a larger explosive thereby blowing the contents of table four through limb, life, family and futures. The last table was, perhaps, the most horrifying. Metal shavings, rusted bolts, nuts, old bearings from cars or vehicle hubs and washers – hundreds of old washers.

Is that what ripped Molly apart? Sam wondered. Is that why her mother will never walk again? His thoughts led him an inevitable conclusion.

"This is what you were going to do to my daughter," he said to the mess on the floor.

The man looked up at Sam's balaclava. "Wha?" was all he managed. The man was younger but there was no doubt that he and the trawlerman shared a bloodline.

"You're going to die today," Sam said. "No point in pretending. Up to you how painful it is."

The man tried to make sense of what was happening.

"Answer my questions quickly, you'll die quickly. Fuck about, and you'll roar till the cock crows."

The man said nothing.

Sam lifted the Nokia and read out the other number stored in the memory. "Who is that?"

The man said nothing.

Sam leaned over and lit him up again, then undid his belt and hauled down his jeans. Nothing more frightening to a male human, he thought. Sam waited a moment and raised the prod again.

"Sister, me sister!"

"Where is she?"

The man took amperage to his tender quarters and began screaming his answers. "Inside! She's inside."

"Where's your brother?"

"At sea! At sea!"

"Your brother's dead."

"Wha'?"

"He choked on something yesterday. Who makes the bombs?"

"We do."

"Who?"

"Us. Me."

"Who else?"

Silence. Sparky roasted some nuts.

"Ma sister," he choked. Me brother."

"Why?"

The man stared incredulously at Sam, but Sam didn't really care what the answer was. The "why" was now irrelevant. It became beside the point the moment one of their devices eviscerated Isla's little friend.

"Gimme your phone."

The man was incapable. Sam shook his pockets and out fell another Nokia. He lifted the handset.

"Code?"

"2-9-1-hash," the man said.

There was the text from the sister. Sam began a reply: *Come out to the ...* Sam paused. "What do you call this place?"

"Feed shed," said the man.

Feed shed, Sam finished. He looked down at the man.

"Who is the CO?"

"What?"

"Of your little army. Who's in charge? Who makes the calls?"

The man shook his head in defiance. Perhaps he didn't want his sister to realise he had imparted information.

Sam didn't want any screaming to deter her arrival, so he walked to the table, lifted a soldering iron and drove it through the man's eye. There was no reaction, just a horrible mess as the ooze pooled by his skull, the lead straggling to a plug nearby.

Sam flicked off the light and waited by the door. Eventually he heard a shuffle. She's in her slippers, he thought.

"Hugh?" a woman said. She sounded older than both men. "Hugh, you in there?"

Sam waited. It took a full minute of silence – the dog had calmed at her presence, before she came forward and pulled on the light. The sight before her was utterly confusing – her brother lay with a wire and a plug sticking out of his face, his head in a halo of gunge.

"Hugh!" she screamed.

Sam stepped in behind her and put the woman to silence. "Don't turn round," he said.

She froze. Her flowery dressing gown looking utterly ridiculous and domesticated in a shed full of death.

"Your brother failed to tell me who the CO is. I need to know who orders the attacks. You give me that, you won't finish the night like either of your brothers."

"Either of them?" she stammered.

"Both dead. One at sea, and you can see the rest. Tell me now."

"Gillen," she whimpered.

"Gillen what?"

"Sean Gillen."

"Where can I find him?"

"Lurgan."

"Craigavon?"

"Lurgan," she said firmly.

"He ordered Ballycastle?"

The woman shook her head – whether in desperation, grief or otherwise he couldn't tell.

"He ordered a device," she said. "Doubt it was meant for Ballycastle."

"Where was it meant for?"

"Belfast, I think. Didn't ask."

"Didn't care."

"No. Who are you?"

Sam had a worry there was a listening device in the shed. Someone could well be catching every word. They had form for that – even in the seventies and eighties they'd been able to listen to bad stuff happening. He'd probably said far too much as it was.

"Anyone else?"

"What?"

"In the leadership."

"Hagan. Few others. But Gillen's the commanding officer," she said.

Sam took two steps, snapped her neck and moved to take a closer look at some of the lunch boxes stacked on the last table.

"Somebody's following the trail."

"You really need to open a window," the clerk said.

"You need to listen. They're knocking down walls quick."

"What are you talking about?"

"Whoever is trying to identify you is joining the dots around the globe and they're good."

"But not good enough to identify me, are they?"

"They might be good enough to identify *me*," he replied.

"Thought you were the dog's balls?"

The brother said nothing.

The point had been to send a message to the woman. Perhaps the message hadn't been clear enough. "Send Meadow's mother another email. Tell her to tell her daughter to back off or she and the old geezer go viral."

"Will she know what you mean?"

The clerk hadn't thought of that. Perhaps this Meadow woman blackmailed a new person every day.

"Sign the email 'from the photocopier'."

"What can you get from the Garda?" Libby asked. She had gone from nonchalant to quietly terrified. One more death and the superior might find a way to do more than sack her.

"Not a lot. It's normally the detachment staff who monitor southern security force comms – I don't have access. I can see what they're logging on their computer systems but I can't rip their phone calls."

"Who's at Greencastle?"

"Coastguard, lifeboat, ambulance, Guards, pathologist en route."

The opso would have had a Garda contact – Libby just didn't have the experience. "Who can we try?"

"For what?"

"To find out whose the body is – to find out if it's an accident."

"It's not an accident," chirped one of the male techs.

"How d'you know?"

"Local newspaper woman is tweeting about it. Says she's got a source that says the man had an oar rammed down his gullet."

"What?"

"An oar. I assume like a rowing boat has?"

"Would an oar fit down a throat?"

Nobody replied for a moment but the tapping intensified.

"Yes," said the other male tech.

"Yes, what?" Libby snapped.

"An oar can fit down a throat."

"How do you know?"

"Europol has a case in Italy where a man was killed by an oar forced into his airway."

"Well, there you go," said Libby, who all but slapped her thigh in amazement.

"Funny," said the tech.

"How's that funny?" asked Libby.

"Dead man was Irish."

"Oh?"

"He'd been on trial for murder shortly before his death."

"When did this happen?"

"Just a few months ago, actually."

"Really?"

"The end of a paddle, or oar, from a Plastimo rubber dinghy was found lodged in the man's airway. That's all it says."

"And he was Irish?"

"Yes. Let me look him up here—"

The woman tech was way ahead. "His name was Delaney. He'd been cleared of rape and murder in Dublin earlier in the year."

"How weird is all this?" Libby said. "How far have the Italians got with it?"

"No arrests," the tech said. "There was some sort of manhunt on the island of Lido, Venice, about a month before the body was found, but there's no detail and no confirmed link. Europol is completely stumped, it seems."

"Sounds like a rabbit hole for us." Libby began to dismiss the coincidence.

"They had prints."

"Fingerprints?"

"Yeah, but no match."

"Can you get a copy?"

"Probably. Take a while, though."

"Not sure it's worth it," said Libby.

"This reporter's tweeting again. Claims a known dissident republican is believed to have died in a boat fire in Donegal."

Libby stared, stunned.

"She's not directly saying it's the man with the oar down his throat, but it seems to add up that they're the same."

"Get the prints," Libby said.

The boss stared at the radio.

Three dead. Greencastle.

"Jeannine!" he shouted.

His wife scuttled into the kitchen and waited. He pulled out a notepad and pencil and tore the first page off the pad and scrawled: *Go next door and get on Facebook. Find out what's going on in Greencastle.*

Familiar with the need to keep their search history clear, the Gillens had an arrangement with the neighbours.

The boss made a cup of tea and sat down at the kitchen table, waiting. He rolled the dial on the wireless, seeking out other stations and more information. There was very little, but he knew what was happening. He gulped down the tea and went upstairs to pull on some clothes.

"Sean," he heard his wife say from the hall below.

"We're going for a dander," he said.

Down by the lough she muffled her mouth and began to talk. "Two men and a woman are dead – one man on a fishing boat, he was burned, then a man and a woman at a farm, both found in a shed, both murdered."

"Any names?"

"No, but the *Independent* says they're known republicans."

"It said *dissidents*, didn't it?"

The wife nodded nervously, knowing how much he hated the phrase.

"I'm going to have to get offside for a while," he said.

"Where will you go?"

"Sure, if I told you that, I wouldn't be offside, would I?"

"Want me to get you a pack?"

"Aye. Plenty of cash and a burner. Tell one of the young fellas to get me a car."

She went one way, he the other.

Sam watched the boss return to his house. Sam had left Donegal with one last job to do, then he would give it a rest.

The boss hadn't been away long – a short stroll down by the water's edge. His wife, Sam presumed, had a scarf around her face. They'd paused for a few moments under a copse of trees.

The location was well chosen – the foliage protected them from watching eyes behind or at the sides. The only view was from the water. They parted and went separate ways – as if they had orders and were setting to it. Sam knew instinctively that they'd regroup.

Libby sighed with agitation at the third email in the space of a day. Her mother was proving to be a real distraction, and she was tiring of having to assure her that everything was ok and that, no, she wasn't dating a much older man.

Meadow, this arrived for you just now. Not sure what it means, love.

Libby scrolled down the forwarded email, taking note of the delivery time and date: *Tell your daughter to back off or the old geezer goes viral. The photocopier.*

Libby crawled with realisation. The clerk. Clever – little – bitch. She's used her brother, thought Libby. Fuck.

"Concentrate on the Greencastle thing," she barked at the techs. "The photograph issue is solved, so you can drop that."

The techs didn't even turn around. They just stared at their banks of monitors and hammered away on their keyboards.

The clerk would need cauterised, and so would her brother.

Sam placed his head on the steering wheel and forced himself to think. He was tired – it had been a log sail to get the boat back to the yard and he hadn't stopped since. Now that he had located the boss – on the shore of a land locked Lough Neagh, Sam was sure the man would run. Too many of his team had been wiped out, he would be worried for his own safety. Time was short and Sam had to act quickly.

He began to drive, unsure of what to do, staying off major

routes with their cameras and sticking instead to winding country lanes.

That's how he saw it. In the garden of a run-down cottage was a long lake boat. Perched on the thwart was a car dealer's sign: For Sale £350.

Sam turned, pulled in and looked at it from a distance. It was a timber clinker-built boat, traditional on inland waters. The trailer looked fine and there was a small outboard, 2-horse-power, old but presumably functional – there would be no point in having it on the boat otherwise.

He walked to the door of the house and knocked with his foot.

No answer. No car in the driveway.

In the van he lifted the passenger bench seat and retrieved the envelope of cash he kept wedged behind the leisure battery. He counted out three hundred and fifty pounds, rolled the money tight and bound it with tape. Did he need to worry about prints? Not if the boat wasn't linked to anything, he thought.

The bundle went through the letter box, and Sam hooked the boat to the back of the van and drove off.

"I can't officially obtain the prints without making a formal request," said the woman tech.

"Can you get them unofficially?" Libby asked, tiring.

"Of course," said the tech.

"Let's do that, then," Libby said sarcastically.

"Do you want them directly or shall I run them?"

Libby sighed in exasperation, then heard the rumble of a convoy outside. She stood and walked to the window. Three large unmarked vans had pulled up outside. She turned to the lead tech.

"Send the prints to me right now then delete everything you've been doing. Everything!" Panic filled her. She gave the tech a small card drive. "Put the prints on that. This is between us," she said. "Understood? This is a murderer we're looking for."

"Ok," said the tech, clearly not giving one fuck.

The door burst open as the card slipped into the coin pocket on Libby's Levi's.

"Step away from your workstations," barked a butch woman in military-police uniform. "Now!"

The techs rolled back in their seats.

"Done?" Libby whispered to the woman tech.

She nodded.

Four men began unplugging the computers and carrying them outside. To Libby's surprise, they appeared to be taking machines at random – no screens, just drives and keyboards. More men arrived and led the techs out. Libby turned to see them being escorted to one of the vans.

"What's going on?" Libby asked the woman.

"Shut down. All military staff are being withdrawn to Palace Barracks."

"Why?" Libby asked.

"Not at liberty."

"Come on," Libby growled. "I've worked with this team for two years."

"Investigation. Civil authorities want to know what's been going on, so we've been drafted to do a first comb through."

"And what about me?" she asked.

"You aren't military staff. I have no jurisdiction."

"I see," said Libby.

"But you will have to vacate your quarters and leave the base."

"Ok," said Libby, relieved to be relieved.

Sam drove as far as he could bear to given the time constraints. North-east of Lurgan he came off a minor road and rattled onto a track with grass sprouting through the middle of the tarmac. The only eyes on him belonged to cows. Two miles in, he took a chance and drove the van across a field, turning by the shore before unhitching the boat. He pushed her hard over ruck and mud, eventually getting the transom to lift as she slipped into Lough Neagh.

From the back of the van he retrieved a spinnaker and an old tarpaulin, a spare petrol can and the only oil he possessed – for the diesel van's engine. Not ideal, but still a lubricant. He gently set a little lunch box onto the soft spinnaker, then drove the van and trailer under a thicket of hedge and trees in the hope that any farmer would mind his own business. Back at the boat he settled his toys, shoved off and drifted for a while. The breeze was taking him gently west, so he took the oars and began to pull, correcting his track south. Round a headland he shipped the oars and lowered the small engine.

There is no way this will work, he told himself. He took off the petrol cap and was happy to find the tank empty – nothing worse than old fuel. He had no idea what mix was required, so he bet on a ratio of fifty to one and deposited very rough estimates of oil and fuel. Choke and air open, he tentatively pulled the cord. Nothing. Again. Nothing, not a croak. He tried to warm her with a frenzy of pulls, then resigned himself to a series of checks: spark plugs, carb, fuel filter. He worked fast and convinced himself that nothing would bring the motor to life – the plug was dirty, the carb was grimy, the filter full of crap. Fifteen minutes later and all reassembled, he gave it another stroke and the little engine coughed, growled and almost turned over. Two more hauls on the cord and she began to hum. Sam put the wind at his back and headed for the southern shore.

"They were hot, now they're not," said the brother.

"Translate," the clerk scolded.

"They were looking, and close – they're good. Then they just stopped."

"Who?"

"The people you upset. Threatening intelligence people isn't smart."

"How would you know?"

"My friends. If you get close to intelligence agencies, you vanish."

"Your *friends* have vanished?"

"Yes."

"How do you know? Just because they're not online any more, doesn't necessarily mean they're in jail."

"I don't think they're in jail. If they were in jail, we'd be able to find them."

"Online?" said the clerk sceptically.

"Yes."

"By hacking?"

"Yes."

"So where are they?"

"Yes."

"Yes, what?"

"Yes, where are they."

"It's like talking to a rubber duck."

Ignored.

"So you think it was a mistake sending the message to Meadow?"

"Yes."

"And you're only telling me that now."

"You're the client. I do what you ask."

"I'm your sister."

"I'm just a rubber duck."

"What does it mean that they've stopped looking."

"Either they stopped caring or they've finished."

"Finished what?"

"Finished looking."

"Why would they do that?"

"Maybe they lost interest."

"Or?"

"Maybe they found you."

Libby stood in the holding cells and stared at the computers. She had no idea where to start and she had little time.

This was the hardware graveyard where machines were sent to be wiped then destroyed. What she needed was a very old machine, pre-networking. One with information on the drive itself rather than a remote server. One that wouldn't betray her interest or tell someone somewhere that she was still on post in a base she was supposed to have vacated.

They were heavy, huge, stacked in tens and unmarked. There was no way to begin with logic, so she pulled in a desk, got a power cable, a monitor, a keyboard and a mouse. Then she took the first from the top and fired it up.

The engine's drone was soothing. Sam dozed on the pleasant putter south, the autumn sun on his face. What he was doing on Lough Neagh didn't stand out. He was involved in the same pastime as thousands of others – fishing in a lake boat. Except he didn't have a fishing rod.

The whiff of unleaded petrol was pleasant as the wind whipped it across his upturned face. The bow rose with his weight aft, and he looked at the tarpaulin under which his tools lay. He didn't give the next steps a great amount of thought – so much depended on the unpredictable. He put his trust in the breeze and relaxed for the first time in days.

The clerk reckoned she'd got lucky once, so she was incredibly unlikely to get lucky again. But she had no idea what else to do. She drove to the only place she thought might provide an opening.

Most of the former army base had been turned into an affordable housing site. Old billets had been replaced by semis, each with a strip of garden. But the telltale was Google – that spot on the satellite shot that was mandatorily blurred. An edict from the Ministry of Defence, the clerk wagered. The place where all that fibre was pointing. The place from where emails were sent from a Meadow to her mother.

Libby's superior read the briefing note and wondered what to do with his wayward protégé.

Gillen was on the cusp of fleeing but was surrounded by special reconnaissance operatives. The superior had insisted they be drawn from the Lisburn headquarters rather than north DET. His plan was to discredit all that happened there to make it the military's problem: their fuck-up, their tidy-up.

But that left Libby. A problem. The one woman who knew the truth.

The opso would be discredited, jailed and when eventually released would wither in a council house. By that time nobody would care about events in Ballycastle. No journalist or statutory agency would put stock in the word of a convicted criminal.

Libby, though, what to do, what to do? Not only did she know about the bomb, he'd chosen her to manage the clerk's destruction of the files. She may not have known the reasons behind that operation, but she was smart enough to join the dots. Libby also now knew that Deirdre Rushe had been an asset, which was surmountable but unhelpful. Worst of all, she appeared to have been compromised.

The simplest solution, as ever, was not the easiest solution.

He made a call for unofficial close-quarter surveillance. This time the X-ray was one of his own.

Libby restacked the first few computers as meticulously as they had been stored, but her patience was quickly wearing thin. By the twelfth hard drive, she began to wonder whether any of the disk memories held the information she was seeking.

She knew it was only be a matter of time before someone came looking for her. She'd cleared her quarters and forced everything she owned into two waterproof roll-top bags. To anyone taking a cursory look, she was gone, but her tally at the gate wasn't through and if they checked, they'd discover she was still on-base.

Computer thirteen was sure to bring bad luck. She was no software developer, but she knew how to crack a frame built on the old Windows 95. She got in quickly and started hunting the drive. Nothing. Well, nothing of use.

And then a zip file, without a name.

She clicked it and opened a series of file names. They were

listed under familiar themes: spanners, techs, ops. She looked at the dates, well old. What she really wanted was a hard copy of a fingerprint database. She was about to zip up and unplug when a thought entered her head. If this was a staff manifest from times gone by, perhaps the opso was there as a younger man. Curiosity compelled her to look for a photo. Had he been handsome back in the day?

She was surprised to find a file for a young recruit seconded from the Parachute Regiment. He'd been quite good-looking in a gnarly sort of way. Detailed in it was a breakdown of his past: son of a soldier killed at Warrenpoint, mother with mental health issues. He'd had two spells in prison for group-related violence, one at a football match. Libby read how he'd witnessed a hooligan attack on a fan who had become isolated from his own crowd. The opso had apparently stepped in and viciously wounded three of the attackers. She wouldn't hold that against him.

She scrolled knowing she didn't have time to pry, and, there, at the bottom, his stats were listed: height, weight, blood group, medical conditions – he was allergic to penicillin as a child. She hadn't been looking for it, but, interestingly, his DNA record and fingerprints were logged and on file too. She imagined the ops had all been fingerprinted to exclude them from any crime scene investigation. Libby was fearful that the opso might match the print on the memory card in her pocket. If he was somehow involved in taking out the dissidents, frankly she'd prefer not to know.

Which made her wonder how she really felt about him. Why was her instinct to protect him if he did, in fact, prove to be a killer?

She inserted the card into the computer, convinced that the systems were so far removed by date that they wouldn't be compatible enough to read one another. Yet up popped her file branches and she opened what the tech had given her. As she did so, an application was offered – some form of matching software. Even back then the systems had been advanced, she realised. She opened the software. It was before drag and drop days, so she uploaded the prints from the oar discovered in the man's throat in Venice. Then she opened the file with the opso's prints.

A bar appeared, darkening from left to right at a painful pace. Libby watched it, increasingly convinced that the opso couldn't be involved because he was in jail when the dissident was burned at sea – wasn't he? Her trepidation rose as the bar neared the end of its slow journey: 3% match.

She exhaled with relief. The violent attack in Liverpool would put many a person off, yet somehow to her it was a brave act, worthy of admiration.

The screen opened a new window. In the box was an offer – did she want to run the prints against other files?

Yeah, like there was time.

She looked at the pile of computers she'd dumped and thought it best to put them back the way they were so nobody knew what she'd done. She turned to the screen and was about to click 'no' when she thought – what the hell? This stacking is going to take me fifteen minutes, why not let it run?

Her back was to the monitor when the results finished churning. She stretched her spine at the lugging of weight and moseyed round to switch off the last of the machines. She raised her eyes to the screen and there, in black and white, was the results: ninety-eight per cent match, and an image of a man she'd never seen before: Sam.

26

There were three prongs to the little anchor Sam found under the thwart, along with an old extendable fishing rod. The prongs folded out but he had serious doubts as to whether it would hold him and the boat in place. Still, he rowed until he was about a mile from the copse of trees where Gillen and his wife had last met. Too far for the human eye to identify him – but also too far for him to identify anyone ashore. But then Sam had his own means of seeing things up close.

The boat yanked to a stop as the anchor bit the bottom. Sam smiled at its unexpected ability to grip. He unpacked the spinnaker – knowing that the light sail material when bunched up would give all the heat of a sleeping bag. He threw the tarp over it to conceal the bright colours and lay across the seat. The boat lay perpendicular to the shore, giving him a near perfect view of the copse. The green tarpaulin all but concealed him as he dozed. Just another fisherman at anchor, wasting the day, waiting for a nibble.

Libby stared at the man who might have done so much damage to her team, to the opso's operation – and, arguably, to security in the north-west. But, then again, she thought, looking at his photo, maybe he'd tidied it up.

Sam Ireland, she read. He'd been in his early twenties when the file was downloaded onto the computer she'd found. Seconded to 14th Intelligence from the Royal Marines. There had been some debate about whether to deploy him to Northern Ireland given that he was from the place, but they had settled on the notion that his local accent and knowledge could prove useful at a crucial time in the fledgling peace process.

Then came the personal stuff – the psych analysis: Apolitical. A keen understanding of the politics of the region, but a lack of unionist sentiment should not be read as a risk. This recruit is equally ambivalent to nationalist politics and is motivated by a curious moral code, unusual in a solider of his age. The most worrying aspect of his personality is his liberal attitude.

Libby snorted. Nobody in the military liked a liberal. The navy wouldn't have liked her hippy upbringing, for sure. Yet Sam Ireland's commanding officer had offered a positive reference of sorts: From unstable beginnings this man has all the makings of an officer, but having been identified as such, he declined the opportunity to take up a place in YO batch. So far, despite promotion and encouragement, he has declined to enrol for AIB. Ireland was promoted rapidly and is particularly adept when waterborne. I nonetheless have reservations about his internal processing; unclear as to whether he would, in the heat of things, follow orders that conflict with his sensibilities. Regardless, a natural leader by example and strength of character. Almost silent at times, occasionally unnervingly so. A conundrum. Perhaps time and further action will iron out the questions, but his ability is among the finest I have ever seen.

Libby looked at the image. Sam Ireland appeared average in every way, yet there was something about his stare that suggested a layer of intelligence, perhaps danger. She wondered whether he was capable of smiling.

His history was equally vague. There was reference to an incident prior to his arrival at the commando training centre in Devon, but it was listed simply under motivation: following an incident in Belfast, Northern Ireland, he was offered and accepted a place at Lympstone. Excelled in the recruitment test and throughout but was given to periods of introspection that worried training staff. Had the air of combustibility without ever having lost control.

Weird, thought Libby. His academic scoring was through the roof for a rating, but she couldn't see from the file whether he'd done A levels or been to college. The last entry was perhaps the most telling: Assume nothing with this soldier. He will protect his team and work until he drops, but he is much too freethinking on occasion.

Which said everything and nothing.

"Did you kill all these people?" Libby asked aloud to the screen.

All she knew for sure was that he'd touched an oar that had ended up down a throat, and that a similar method of murder had been discovered one thousand miles west on a boat. Particularly adept when waterborne, she read again. It worried her that he'd served with the opso. She was certain that if anyone else came to know what she knew, the opso was finished. Any investigator would conclude that this Sam Ireland had been fed information about dissident republicans. Specifically, dissidents who were connected in some way to the Ballycastle bomb. The detachment that had been following that bomb was under the opso's command. The opso and this man Ireland were, at the very least, acquaintances. He could easily have been passing the intel. Everything rang of collusion, the filthiest word in Northern Ireland. It looked like setting people up to die. The opso would never see the sky again unless she ...

Libby ran it around her mind quickly. The details would come, but if she could sever the link between the opso and this man Sam, that should have a favourable impact. If they couldn't get the opso for collusion, she certainly wouldn't let them get him for her own agency's security failures. She needed to see him.

The clerk knew that to park outside the gate of the base was to hoist a flag with "Arrest me" written on it; though she felt no less comfortable sitting at the edge of the civilian road, about half a mile from the entrance to the barracks, for seven hours. If it even was a barracks. It certainly had a big enough gate.

Night came and she considered giving up. There was no way she could spot anyone in a car at night. Several groups of vehicles had passed her, vans and cars – all of them seemed to be travelling together – and she had struggled to see into any of them. The whole thing was probably pointless, but she had no alternative, so she pulled her coat round her, reclined the car seat and tried to sleep.

Sam had been sure that the Gillens would return for a regroup, a chat away from the house. He wondered why he'd allowed himself to be so certain. And if they returned in the dark, how would he know?

He admonished himself for a few minutes, staring at his kit and becoming increasingly forlorn. And then a thought occurred. He switched on the helicopter command console and began to scroll through the menu. At "heat signature" he clicked into the options.

Attaching the belt to his waist, he began the launch sequence and sent the small heli into the air as he stared down into the bilge to conceal the light from the screen that relayed the helicopter's vision. The heli covered the mile in less than two minutes. As gently as he could, Sam brought the device down to rest among the foliage – facing the area where Gillen and his wife had last stood.

Then he rearranged his little boat, bunching the sail into the V shape of the hull, and pulling the tarp clean over the top. He needed to be able to watch the screen all night, and he needed to remain unseen from the shore or above.

Libby unscrewed the casing of the computer and used a screwdriver to lever out the hard drive. She put the outer shell back on and stacked the unit exactly as it had been before she'd found it. Then she went upstairs, grabbed her bags and walked out in search of a staff car. The storeroom was empty – it was 3 a.m. after all. Then she realised that the staff had all been taken back to Belfast. Stupid. How was she supposed to get off base?

She wanted to get away before anyone came looking for her. She desperately wanted to destroy and dispose of the hard drive so that nobody could map the prints against a friend of the opso's, whom she needed to talk to, so she did the only thing she had the power to do – she shouldered her bags, signed out at the gate and started walking.

Sam was dozing when the screen lit up, but his eyes pulled focus immediately and he stared intently at what the heli onshore was relaying.

It took him a moment to understand what was happening. At first he thought it was two men getting on it in the bushes – the heat signatures showed two bodies moving in unison. Then he realised they weren't quite touching but were definitely working hard – the glow from the human shapes was red, so there was a lot of heat in what they were doing.

Gillen and his wife? Sam wondered. No. Both appeared to be male – or at least large.

Then the penny dropped. DET. Ops. They're digging in.

Fuck.

It was hard for Sam to estimate distances. How far from where the Gillens had stood had the operatives chosen to make their hide? It did tell him one thing for sure – the DET expected the Gillens back. And that, at least, was something.

The clerk was freezing. Too cold to sleep and too afraid of attracting attention to start the car engine. She lay as far back as the passenger seat allowed and waited for sunrise – as much for the heat it might bring as for the light to watch faces.

She was debating whether to turn on the radio for company, wary of the glow it would emit, when an odd apparition appeared at the edge of her focal length. From the gloom ahead the clerk could make out some sort of bulbous shape meandering towards her. She tried to suppress her panic – the dark figure had rounded edges like misshapen wings.

What the fuck is that? she thought, staring at it all the while pushing her neck lower into her shoulders. The figure lumbered on, gradually becoming larger. Then it paused, turned to the side and seemed to peer down, losing one of its wings in the process. Then the other wing fell off and the clerk could make out a person rummaging in one of the spherical wing things.

Bags, the clerk thought. Someone carrying bags.

The figure stood upright, still at right angles to her car, and began a stamping motion. There followed a curious ritual in which the figure crouched down and began swinging something at the ground as if hammering a nail into the floor. The clerk could just make out a quiet crunching at the end of each swing. She became convinced that this was preparation for an approach to her car and made up her mind to swing her leg over the handbrake and manoeuvre awkwardly onto the driver's side, scrabble for her keys and start the engine. With the turn of the key came the lights, which gave the clerk and the apparition the shock of their lives.

There, in the beam, was Meadow with a baton in her hand.

The clerk automatically started to pull out, forgetting her purpose entirely. Meadow returned to her previous endeavours and kicked something down what appeared to be a grating. The clerk flashed by, headlights on full beam and drove at speed down the road, breathing hard and stunned at what she had just seen. Only when she was two miles away did she realise that fate had presented her with an opportunity she couldn't have manufactured if she'd tried.

Why had she not flattened the bloody spook?

She turned the car and stuck her boot to the board, hunting the hedges for the woman who had threatened her, slowing a little as the glow of red lights came into view. That was the spot, or close to it. She had no choice but to indicate out, and as she rounded a saloon vehicle she saw Meadow throwing her bags into the back seat. In the nearside rear-view mirror she watched her opportunity vanish into the passenger seat.

Sam watched the glow of red turn to amber and then blue as the ops in the dugout cooled from their exertions.

Why did they need to get so close?

Perhaps they'd lost audio on Gillen, he reasoned. Maybe he'd changed his clothes to flee. Maybe the DET had a device in a jacket he'd discarded? He couldn't quite work out what was wrong with the scenario but it wasn't right.

Then it came with a jolt: they think he's next. They think Gillen's the outstanding link to the Ballycastle bomb. They know he's about to be killed.

Sam suddenly understood what the DET were thinking. He cast his mind back to operations in the late nineties, when he was a young op being briefed on movements and tasked to do certain things in certain scenarios. Where there was an Article Two, right to life consideration, they identified the target, carried out appreciations and modelled likely scenarios the attackers could adopt. The DET would then build counter-insurgency tactics around those, sometimes deploying multiple teams well in advance. Some might dig in, just as the two men had done this evening.

That meant they were anticipating an attack on foot. Placing two ops so close suggested they had no air support, otherwise they would simply watch for anyone approaching and take them out at a distance from the Gillens. There was a distinct advantage to that – the Gillens would be unaware of the imminent threat.

If there had been air support available, Sam would already have been arrested. His heat signature would have shown up on any helicopter, Gazelle or drone flying over the area. Which told him they hadn't anticipated an attack from the sea. Which was good.

But Sam had no intention of taking out two operatives to get Gillen. The two men dug in by the copse of trees were younger versions of him – skilled and seasoned probably and working to protect life. Even the lives of terrorists. Which made him wonder about the effort the DET was going to to protect Gillen.

Perhaps they couldn't take the heat in the press about the other killings – dissident groups shouting about a return of the British government's shoot-to-kill policy; state forces complicit in murder, they were saying; collusion, collusion, collusion. Maybe that's why the DET couldn't afford one final assassination – the highest profile of them all: Gillen, the leader. Maybe that's why they wanted to keep him alive.

Sam's jaw tightened as he stumbled upon the alternative. Maybe they needed Gillen. Maybe his endurance was central to some policy. Maybe, maybe, he was a brussel – a sprout. How the locals and the press described a tout – an informer – an agent of the state.

That would make sense too – that they actually had the boss in their pockets. Which made Sam think that someone much higher than the opso had known about the Ballycastle bomb and had done nothing to prevent it.

Sam descended into a state of deep calm. His mind landed softly on an area of extreme focus. He shut all else out and mapped his next steps meticulously.

Libby's hitch-hiking got her dropped off right outside Belfast City Airport, where she hired a car for the short journey to Palace Barracks on the edge of Holywood. MI5's local head-quarters rested by Belfast's lough shore, not far inside the perimeter of the base. Her pass was examined, her car checked and she was waved through the gate. Instead of rolling down the hill towards her own service's building, she turned right towards the military police offices.

She swept into a visitor's space and marched straight through the doors, past reception and towards the custody sergeant's desk. She held up her pass, noting the lance corporal's stripes, and was mildly pleased there was no three stripe present.

"You've got north DET operations officer in custody." A statement, not a question.

"Ma'am," the Scarlet clipped.

"Bring him to an interview room, please."

"Yes, Ma'am," he snapped, then turned and made off towards the cells.

Two minutes later she saw the opso being led up a corridor, no cuffs, and turned into a room on the right.

The lance corporal emerged, held the door and looked at Libby. "Ma'am," he said.

She walked towards him, convinced there would be an intervention at any moment. "Thank you," she said. "I won't be long."

"Do require additional presence?" he asked.

"No, thank you," she said. "If you could make sure I'm not disturbed, though," she said.

"Yes, Ma'am," he said, and closed the door behind her.

The appearance of DET operators meant Sam would have to tinker. Tinkering left uncertainties, gaps, openings, lines of investigation.

The plan had been to leave a forensic trail that suggested to journalists that the killings had been part of some internal feud. He wanted to draw attention away from some rogue operative on the loose, and Sam calculated that the spooks, for convenience, would seize such a narrative and allow it to run. A feud as an explanation suited everyone. Paramilitaries were notorious for shooting their way out of arguments. How much better to make that case than to blow up a dissie with a dissie bomb like the one he held carefully in his hand?

Sam sighed. He lamented the looming need to use it for purposes other than he'd intended.

———

The superior stared at the red light flashing on his silent phone. Military. Not a particularly welcome interruption. He ignored it. Within a minute the light began flashing again. It was distracting. He ignored it and it stopped. The pause this time was shorter. When the red light began again he was half expecting it and whipped up the receiver.

"What is it?" he barked.

"Libby Green entered Palace Barracks twenty minutes ago."

"Oh?"

"She was in a hire car from Belfast City Airport."

"She's at Loughside?"

"No, actually, she went to RMP. She's in the custody suite."

"What?"

"She is interviewing the operations officer from north DET, sir."

"What!" he yelled.

"We have no jurisdiction to prevent—"

"Why did you not tell me sooner?" he shouted.

"We have been calling—"

"Can we hear what they are saying?"

"Well, yes, if you think that's proper. We would need a—"

"Don't you dare tell me I need a warrant. Just get that conversation patched through to me right now!"

There was a crash as the handset was dropped. The superior could hear orders being issued at the other end before the handset was scooped up again.

"We think we may have to hold the phone up to a speaker."

"Fine. Just hurry up."

Eventually a faint conversation could be heard, in which a man and woman were talking in muted voices.

"You need to warn him," the opso said.

"How?"

"Well, now you know where he is, you need to go there and tell him to get offside for a long time, this time."

"Ok," Libby could be heard. "Anything else?"

"That drive needs destroyed."

"Already done."

"Is there anything else linking him?"

"I'm the only one with the full picture. Without the drive, nobody's gonna make the link easily."

The superior's ear pressed hard into the receiver of his handset.

"Ok, well, now you need to take care. They might be looking at you."

"What if he goes again? What if there are others?"

"Inevitable."

"Really? Why is he so determined?"

"I can't tell you that, but his reasoning is good, Libby. I promise you that. One day I'll explain everything, but not here, not in this place."

"Ok. Are you ... are you going to be ok?"

The superior could just make out a distant commotion. The conversation became more urgent and more hushed.

"Libby, I didn't set this up – I found out about it after it started. That's the truth."

"I know. I believe you."

"Libby, you need to take care of yourself."

"So do you. You can't take the fall for this – for any of it."

"Well, if you can get to him and ..."

The superior's jaw muscles bulged as he ground his teeth in anger when he heard the door burst open. There were chairs grating backwards, shouts of unauthorised entry and the line rattled and banged.

"What's going on?" the superior yelled into the phone.

"I thought you wanted the meeting to end?" said the man at the other end.

"Not while they were fucking talking!" yelled the superior. "Morons!" He slammed down the phone.

———

The screen on the heli remote-control panel came to life. Heat signatures – someone was moving.

Sam strained to see what was happening but the heli in the copse was at ground level and aimed at where he guessed the Gillens might stand. He couldn't see the dugout hiding the DET operatives, yet their movement was registering. He strained to understand what was going on.

The glow on the left of his screen was green – warm but not hot. Sam gave the heli blades a little buzz to lift it a few inches and reframe its shot, touching the joystick gently and watching the image lift. The other joystick controlled the tail. He nudged it with his frozen forefinger, clumsily, and the screen began to spin. Panicking slightly to correct it, he attempted to bring the heli down to start again. His heart fell as he watched the screen tumble upside down. With his thumbs he tried both levers both ways but was rewarded only with a shake of the screen. The blades were evidently stuck in the ground, the heli upside down and useless.

Not good, he thought, until it got worse. Inverted, he watched as a massive hand reached down and wrapped around the helicopter. The imagery became blurry as the device lifted and Sam was treated to a full facial of a man in a night mask, night-vision goggles and a thin balaclava.

Libby knew she was in a convoy, even though she couldn't see any vehicles behind or in front of her. They could well be overhead. She suspected that the military police had been ordered to place a lump on her hire car, but she didn't care. For her it was all about genuine justice. To hell with her superior. To hell with allowing kids to be killed. To hell with the big picture, and to hell with letting an innocent, decent man take the fall for murders carried out by someone else.

Libby's main anger was directed at her boss – there was no way she wanted him to get his way. Screwing him over and getting the opso released went hand in glove. She had no intention of sacrificing the opso for his friend, this killing machine, this Sam Ireland. If anyone was to go down for the murders, it would be Ireland himself. And so Libby headed to the coast, to the place the opso said she was likely to find him. And then, when the right man went down, she reckoned the opso would be released, and her superior put out to pasture. For that reason she cared not one jot for the Gazelle she assumed was overhead. Bring it on, she thought. The more people present when I confront this dangerous fucker, the merrier.

"Alpha team to control."

"Send, Alpha."

"Alpha to control. Can you confirm we have aerial eyes on, over?"

"Control to Alpha, send again please, over."

"Control, do you have an aerial platform on location, over?"

"Negative, Alpha. What is the nature of the inquiry?"

The central operations officer was stirred from his slumber in the Lisburn DET control room. He pulled on his headset and listened.

"Control, Alpha. I am holding a military-grade drone."

"Alpha, Control. Please confirm that you have discovered a drone on location?"

"Affirmative. Believe it to be a Black Hornet or similar."

The operations officer pressed his transmission button.

"Alpha, this is command. Confirm please where the device was discovered."

"Command, Alpha. Approximately ten feet from location. Believe it fell from the sky in last three minutes. Over."

"Alpha, is the drone transmitting?"

"Command, Alpha. Hard to say, but I'm familiar with these. They're capable of sending medium-res imagery."

"Alpha, command. Disable immediately. Repeat, disable immediately."

"Understood."

Sam sat in his boat and watched the screen flicker and die.

Well, that's fucked that, he thought.

The superior took a call he'd been expecting.

"We have eyes on your staff as requested."

The superior bristled a little at the implication that *his* staff had gone rogue. Still, it was no time for point-scoring – he needed the DET to perform for him. It was time to tidy-up the whole disastrous mess.

"Where is she?"

"Driving along the coast of County Antrim curiously."

"I want to know who she's going to meet."

"Well, it does seem there is someone with her."

"With her?"

"In a car behind. Headed the same direction. She could be being followed."

"By you," the superior said.

"Well, yes, but remotely. We have her tracked and vis from above, but we wouldn't put a car in an area as remote as that."

"Who's in the car behind? Could it be the man we're looking for?"

"Negative," said the DET commander.

"How do you know?"

"The person behind is a woman."

"You can tell in the dark?"

"We can."

"Well, have you checked the plates of the car?"

"Of course."

"Who owns it?"

"I have a question for you first."

The superior stiffened. He wasn't accustomed to being interrogated by the military – even senior officers.

"Go on?" he allowed.

"Are you double jobbing us?"

"What?"

"Are you watching us watching them?"

"You're asking if my agency is keeping tabs on you following my intelligence officer? Well, the answer to that is no," he barked sarcastically.

"That's not what I'm asking. I'm wondering whether you have eyes on any other operation."

"I'm quite sure I have no idea what you are talking about."

"You are the senior political advisor in Northern Ireland. Correct?"

"Correct," said the superior, proud of his status as the head of MI5 in the region.

"So could anyone else be monitoring us while we carry out your orders?"

"Where is all of this coming from, colonel?"

"It's a yes or no, really."

"No," snapped the superior. "Nobody is watching you – nobody from my end anyway. Why? Have you got a situation?"

"We all have a situation, it seems," said the colonel. "Lots of people on edge trying to blame one another for this series of events."

"You have the advantage on me, colonel. I don't know what you're talking about."

"Mmm ..." mumbled the colonel, clearly unconvinced.

"Who is in the car behind?" ventured the superior.

"Just some lawyer lady. Probably unconnected."

The superior decided not to show any interest.

The central operations officer had expected a call to say everything was ok. Instead, he got a visit from the brass. Everyone in room leapt to their feet.

"Withdraw your men."

"Sir?" he asked the colonel, who was dressed in civvies, befitting the dreadful hour.

"Immediately. Withdraw the team."

"All of them? We have five posts—"

"Every last one. And make a record of it – we don't want any questions here. If M-I-fucking-5 want us on the hook for this trouble, they've another thing coming."

The opso turned to his team and pressed transmit. "All call signs, all call signs, this is command. Extract, extract, extract."

One by one the teams acknowledged the order. Alpha came back on the net.

"Confirm we leave rogue device at location?"

The opso turned to the colonel who nodded his head.

"Affirmative," relayed the opso.

"We can't have them denying anything," said the colonel. "Those slippery fuckers will not hang this on the military. Let them watch us leave. This is their problem now."

"Alpha, command. Turn the device back on, replace it and extract."

"Carry on," clipped the colonel, who turned and left the room.

Libby pulled in tight to a hedge and hunted to her right for signs of a boatyard. There was little moon and no reflection from house lighting. She tapped the GPS on the hire car. It had taken her to the correct postcode, yet there was no sign of a yard of any sort on the map. She readied to get out and take a look along the shore with a flashlight.

The clerk rounded a corner and saw the glow of the GPS, followed by a car light as the driver's door opened. She slowed to a crawl.

Libby saw the car light behind her and smiled in the sure knowledge that the DET was on her tail. Come with me, she thought. You'll come in handy when it comes to an arrest.

The clerk caught Libby in her headlights for the second time in a matter of hours She knew not to miss her chance again.

Libby flashed the light in a "come on" gesture.

The clerk came on, slow at first, but with Libby now in the middle of the tight country road, she dropped the gear back into second and hit the pedal. Libby took a moment to register, then leapt towards her own car, the door still open. The clerk hit her on the hip as Libby dived for the driver's seat. Libby span with the impact, hitting her own door and falling behind the accelerating vehicle. She watched it stop, almost helpless to move, expecting someone to come and help her. Instead she got the white reverse lights, the accelerator got a hammering and the clerk rolled back over Libby's torso, only stopping to change gear and take a run at her head.

The central operations officer called the colonel.

"Sir, it seems you were right. We have a rogue team operating."

"In Craigavon? After the Gillens?"

"No, sir. Well, perhaps. Not sure. I'm talking about the other active op following the intelligence agent. The car I mentioned has just run over and very likely killed the mark."

"What?" said the colonel, astonished and suddenly afraid of the inevitable rebound. "The intelligence agent is dead?"

"Rural location, sir. The intelligence agent left the vehicle and the following car hit her hard."

"Accident?"

"Negative, sir. Returned to finish the job."

"Where is the car now?"

"Driving at speed from the scene, sir."

"This is the car driven by the lawyer?"

"Yes, sir."

"Did she get out at all?"

"Negative, sir. Just reversed over the intelligence officer and ran back over her again."

"Stop the follow," the colonel said. "Whatever this is, it's not our fucking problem."

Sam watched the camera on the helicopter reboot. He was

again treated to the image of an operative in night-vision goggles and a balaclava. This time the op placed the helicopter gently on the ground. Sam saw his boots, then a re-angling of the image. Then, bafflingly, the two men gathered their equipment and made off into the night. He watched their glow blur and fade. There was no question – the men had extracted.

Shit, thought Sam, they must know the Gillens aren't coming back. Worse still, maybe they know I'm floating offshore.

"Colonel, if this is another round-the-houses on who is watching who, then frankly I could do without it," said the superior.

"Are you going to tell me what's going on and why we're being drawn into it?"

"No more riddles, colonel. What on earth are you talking about now?"

"Why get us to follow your staff, only to watch them get killed? You did not detail us with a protection remit."

The superior stopped for a moment. "Killed? Who is killed? Which operation are we talking about here?"

"Don't bullshit a bullshitter," said the colonel. "I have documented our withdrawal from both observation operations. The DET is out of this, whatever this is!"

"Colonel, be very clear here. Who is dead?"

"Your intelligence officer – the woman formally seconded to north DET. Elizabeth, Libby."

"Dead," said the superior. "Dead how?"

"Road traffic collision, I imagine you'll call it. Why you did it is your business, why you drew us into it is beyond me, but be clear on this – we weren't tasked with protection here and we have extracted. We no longer have eyes on in County Antrim or

Craigavon. We are out. I have made a referral to the GOC. We are done here."

The line went dead. The superior pursed his lips and swayed his head. A familiar feeling crept up his spine, one of possibility. Provided he could ensure there were no loose ends – and he could work out where Libby had been going and why, maybe this could sort itself out nicely.

Sam debated whether to extract. They'd found the military-grade helicopter and they knew it wasn't theirs – so who did they think owned it? The person they were there to stop – the killer? Are they searching for me?

They'll assume I'm on land at first, so they haven't extracted – they're hunting on foot or in the air. They'll look for a heat signature within the operational radius of the helicopter. I'm cold, I'm in the hull of a boat in the water. How easily will they see me?

One way to find out, he thought. He lifted the control and flew the heli a mile into the air – careful to keep it over the copse. He could see two bodies making fast through the over-growth but they didn't appear to be searching. He caught another pairing moving at speed towards a road. He watched them stand for a moment, change direction slightly and a car arrive. The pair got into the vehicle and it drove off.

To the extreme left another twosome was running red hot headed for a large, warm vehicle.

If he strained, he could just about make out the tiniest heat signature on the water about a mile from shore. There I am, he reckoned, huddling deeper into the hull, hoping to chill himself further.

All the hotspots were now in vehicles, gone. What the hell is going on, he wondered?

The first the opso knew something was wrong was when two unidentified men in polo shirts and chinos came to take him away.

He wanted to ask where they were going but he knew "Not far," was the only likely response, so he stayed silent and appraised the men: no firearms, no weapons of any kind, fit, mature, confident.

He was invited to take a back seat in a black Mercedes Vito van with electric sliding doors. One of the polo shirts climbed in beside him and they journeyed for two full minutes to the Loughside compound. MI5 Headquarters – why?

The opso was brought into a pleasant enough holding room not far from the door. The tables were the same as in any office but there were no screens and no phones. He sat for a long while until a man in red trousers and an expensive shirt padded in. He was early sixties, the opso reckoned, overconfident and immediately loathsome.

"We need to share some information," he began.

"Do we now?" said the opso, every chip of his Birkenhead accent spitting sarcasm.

"I have information about Libby and you have information I require."

"Oh?" said the opso, suppressing his alarm.

"We need to know who Libby went to meet."

"When?"

"After you and she met, against regulation, I might add, at the military police holding centre."

"Who she went to meet?" The opso attempted to find out how much this man knew.

"Don't fucking fuck with me, you Scouse scumbag!" the man suddenly exploded. He drove back his chair and stood roaring at the opso. "Answer every question I ask and I shall tell you what has happened Libby!"

The opso had been through it many times with condescending seniors. It no longer riled him as it once had.

"I suggest you sit your flabby arsehole down," said the opso, "or you will leave with nuthin', and I will be in exactly the same position I was in when I arrived."

The superior leaned over the opso and with gritted teeth said, "Who was Libby on her way to meet, and why?"

"Well, if you don't know that, you need a better operations officer. Did you not place her under surveillance? You look like you've been sittin' at a desk too long pushin' pencils, podge mate."

The superior couldn't contain his anger. "Of course we monitored her!"

"Then what are you askin' me—?" the opso began but stopped. The man was asking because she hadn't arrived.

"She worked for me. I need to know what she was working on."

But the two men were now on different tracks.

"What's happened?" the opso's calm had deserted him. "Where is she?"

"Tell me where she was going and why. Then I shall give you the information we have."

"The information *we have*? The information *we have*? Has she disappeared or wha'?"

"Who was she going to meet?"

"No."

"What do you mean *no*?"

"You tell me what happened, then we might talk. But, no, I'm not talking till then."

"You are in a very precarious position. You are looking at a serious stretch – a prison term, loss of career, loss of status. I can help."

"You'll never help the likes of me – I'm too convenient for you. You'll blame me for letting that bloody bomb sit when it was probably you who wanted it that way. If you're Libby's boss, then you're to blame, so you're not going to help me in any way at all." The opso was stubborn in his resignation. He had no doubt of his fate, he had nothing to lose, nothing to win.

The superior stared hard at him. "Did Libby know who was taking out the X-rays?"

The opso simply smiled back at the superior, who took the smirk as it was intended.

"Was she going to meet their killer?"

The opso said nothing.

"What agency did the killer work for?"

The opso actually snorted at that. "You know absolutely nuthin', do ye? And you're meant to be the intelligence wing."

"Why was he killing the dissidents?" The superior sounded more and more desperate.

The opso leaned forward at his desk and whispered at his soft-shoed interrogator. "You think I just came up the Mersey in a bubble? Fuck you. Fuck the games you play. Fuck the agency you work for. And fuck your pompous bloody attitude."

The superior stood up. This line of inquiry was closed. "Libby's dead," he said, and left the room.

Sam debated whether to bring the heli back to the boat. Would that tell the DET where he was operating from? Were the DET still monitoring the copse at all? He couldn't work out what was going on. They appeared to have left – but why? Had the heli's presence spooked them? Had they decided to put their own drone into action instead?

His time was up and he triggered the Hornet's return to its cradle. If the DET was deploying an aerial platform, he had a

tight window to get out of there. He glanced at the monitor to
make sure there was enough juice in the battery to make the
flight when he noticed two more heat signatures on the edge of
the forest. Sam tapped the device back into manual and slipped
under the tarpaulin again, willing his body temperature down
and huddling into the hull once more. Had the ops returned?

The two bodies muddled slowly as if in conversation as they
walked. Sam looked at the monitor – 5 a.m., no time for a
morning stroll. Could it be?

His hopes rose a little when the pair reached the copse,
stopped and began gesticulating towards one another. Sam
could just make out the first daylight through a crack in the
tarpaulin, so he sent the heli a little closer to take a look. The
bodies were handing things between themselves, not fighting –
more of an exchange.

Sam went as close as he dared, turning the heli's tail to the
rising sun. There was no doubting it, Sam was looking at Mr
and Mrs Gillen in the dawn.

He hit the repatriate button, urging the little bird back to its
perch as fast as possible.

———

The superior hadn't got what he wanted from the opso, but he
wasn't sure it mattered. He looked at the internal base CCTV
from north DET and noted Libby's interaction with three technical staff. He could interrogate them, for sure, but with Libby
now dead was there any need for further personal exposure?
He did, after all, still have his most important asset in the dissident group.

He couldn't afford anyone else finding whatever Libby had
found. If she had discovered information that could exonerate
the opso, that wouldn't do at all. The superior had chosen his
fall guy and that was that.

The CCTV footage showed Libby spending four hours in one wing of the building. Whatever she'd found in there had to be destroyed. The superior decided to follow old tracks. He lifted his phone and placed an order for an extremely hot accidental fire in the old building at north DET.

Sam struggled to rub heat into his hands to get the lunch box secured. The deliberately tied granny knots, careful that no forensics could suggest the involvement of a sailor.

The device looked simple enough in its rudimentary circuitry. It came with its own phone, its own battery and even appeared watertight. The trick was to get it lifted into place.

Sam switched helicopters for the one with the fuller battery life and attached the thin rope from it to the food takeaway box. Then he sat back and thumbed the joystick to engage the blades, pushing it further and further, but all the little device could manage was a low hover. He swore. One gust of wind between the boat and the copse ashore could land the whole thing in the lough. He would have to deploy both helicopters, one of which was short on power. The other danger was that they could easily be drawn together by the weight of the weapon, their blades meshing and plucking the whole device out of the sky.

He lashed a second fixing to the device, praying that a dead man in Donegal had known what he was doing with explosives and electronics. Then he switched the remote panel to dual control and tried to fly the helis separately but simultaneously, about two feet apart. Up the device went, dangling precariously between two machines that hadn't been designed to carry anything. Still, they flew, drawing horribly close together on occasion, until Sam could see them no more except through the display on his remote.

They covered the mile stretch of water in less than a minute and Sam opted to let them down as soon as he saw grass. He knew he couldn't be far from the Gillens, but he had no idea what the range of the device was – assuming it worked at all.

Then he watched as a boot appeared and for the second time the heli was lifted and stared at. Gillen, straight down the barrel, with his wife in the background.

Sam fumbled for the phone as the heli was dropped and the boot flashed into frame before it crushed the expensive little article. He dialled the only number on the Nokia, held it to his ear but didn't hear it ring. Instead he heard an explosion – a beautiful and satisfying detonation – like a bale of bricks being dropped from a crane on a construction site.

He flipped the tarpaulin and stared at the shore. There were no flames; there was no movement.

Loud bangs before 6 a.m. were unusual and Sam couldn't afford an inspection. He ripped the cord of the outboard, hauled in his anchor and headed for where he'd abandoned his van. As he motored, he smashed the Nokia and the heli remote to pieces with the anchor and bit by bit deposited them into the lough at intervals.

The Donegal man had known what he was doing, Sam thought, taking a certain pleasure from the fact that the bomb makers' own phones had been the ones used to target the man who had commissioned the devices. The wiring had been straightforward in the end – the tables in the feed shed had provided a tutorial of sorts. Sam settled on a job hopefully complete, and an unconfirmed kill.

It wasn't the colonel who called the superior, it was the director of special forces. He wasn't amused.

"So, to be clear," he began, "you have embroiled my staff in a series of incomparable fuck-ups, you have requested the deployment of various special reconnaissance units – for which you really ought to have accounted to the chief constable, by the way, you have then, for reasons unknown, chosen to monitor those units while deployed, only to have your own staff and assets neutralised. Does that about sum it up?"

The superior sighed. "That is indeed how it may look, major general, but I am honestly as baffled as you are as to what, or who, was watching the whole thing. The drone in question was not mine."

"Six? Are we to believe that MI6 is watching MI5?"

"Maybe the Irish—" floundered the superior.

"Let's not turn a debacle into a pantomime. The Irish would have no interest, let alone capacity, to conduct such activity. I think you ought to put your house in order."

"Understood," was all the superior could think to say.

"Gillen," said the general, "I assume he was of value and that his death in some twisted way contributed to you burning down a military building?"

The superior grunted. He would never acknowledge such a statement.

"Well, so long as the wife survives – clinging on, I understand – you will have your work cut out for you. I trust, given what we now know, that you shall not endeavour to implicate us in this sordid affair?"

"No, major general."

"Oh-kay, then," he said, chipper and assured. "I very much hope never to speak to you again."

The phone was cradled. The superior reached for a bottle and a glass.

Sam drove sensibly; speed could draw unwanted attention.

Nonetheless, he was desperate to see Isla now that the job was done. He surfed the radio stations as he went, but all he could get was a headline on a bulletin that may or may not relate to him.

"A man has died and a woman's been injured in an incident in the Craigavon area. The woman was transferred to Belfast's Royal Victoria Hospital where she is believed to be in a critical condition. There are no further details."

If that's them, I'll settle for that, thought Sam, until a different commotion grabbed his attention. On the road ahead, normally a narrow passageway to the boatyard and a few coastal walks, was a stream of police incident tape. He drew into the side of the road and walked to the cordon. A uniformed policewoman complete with flak jacket approached him.

"Road's closed, I'm afraid, sir. You'll have to turn around."

"But I live down there," he said. "What's happened?"

He could see blood on the road in front, a forensic tent and two scenes-of-crime bods crouching in white telly-tubby suits with blue feet and hands.

"We weren't aware of any dwellings on this road, sir?"

"I live on a boat, just down there. At a pontoon."

"Do you have any other means of approaching it?" The young officer looked a little confused.

"Not unless I swim."

"Wait there, please," she said, thumbing the transmitter on the mic at her lapel. As she turned a black people carrier pulled up and a close-cropped suit emerged from the passenger seat.

Not good, thought Sam, as he noted the circular pin on his lapel, which told those in the know that he was armed. He was light on his feet and acted like he owned the place. He marched past Sam and lifted the tape, flipping open a wallet and showing it to the cop whose eyes opened in surprise. The suit turned quickly to glance at Sam, giving him a curious coating. Looking at the cop, he nodded his head towards Sam.

"Local resident," she explained.

The suit carried on and paused to peer at the blood on the road, then he walked over to have a chat with the SOCOs.

The cop returned. "You'll have to make the rest of the way on foot, sir, I'm afraid."

"What happened?"

"Road traffic accident," she said.

"Then why is it being treated like a crime scene, and why are there intelligence personnel here?"

"I can't give you any information, I'm sorry, sir."

Sam knew by the man's mannerisms that this was a background bloke, a fixer, a tidier-upper. He was accustomed to obedience and had probably seen messy situations before. His self-assuredness brought with it the air of command.

Sam turned to robocop. "Look, I'm a local. Has someone from this area been killed?"

"I really can't—"

"You can tell me if local people are involved, surely?"

"Ok, sir, if you leave now and reverse your van to a convenient place off the road, I can confirm that nobody local has been injured or involved in any way."

Which, for Sam, was more worrying. He immediately prepared for the worst, running through the possibilities. If the spooks are here, it's likely because whoever is dead was coming to meet me. If someone not local is dead, and the spooks are interested, it's most likely to be the opso because he's the only one who knows I'm here. Why would someone kill the opso? Would he not have seen someone following him? Maybe they were here to whack me and needed the opso to identify me – to lead them to me?

Maybe, maybe, maybe. But it felt plausible. Maybe they were waiting for him on the boat, but unlikely. They'd have assumed the opso was en route to a discreet meet, in a remote location, wouldn't they? Maybe they don't even know about the boat. Unless …

"There wasn't a child here, was there?" he spurted in panic.

"Sir, you need to turn back."

"I have a daughter. Was there a child involved?"

"No, sir."

"How about a woman from Dublin – Sinead?"

"Sinead what?"

Sam's heart sank. Why would Sinead have come back without Isla? He'd been out of touch for a few days. Was everything ok with Isla? "Is it a woman with black hair, tall?"

"I can't confirm the gender of anyone involved, sir."

"Can you tell me if a woman was involved?"

"If there was a woman involved, what would be your relationship to her?" the cop inquired, inscrutable.

Sam's head reeled. "She's … my girlfriend."

The cop held up a palm and turned away again to speak into the radio. Sam strained to hear what she was saying but it was muffled and the response was delivered directly into the cop's ear.

She turned back. "What colour of hair and eyes does your girlfriend have?"

"Black, and greeny-brown."

The cop walked to the scenes-of-crime officers but addressed the spook, who turned to appraise Sam once more before looking away. It took too long for her to return to the cordon.

"Sir, I can tell you that nobody involved here had that eye colour or black hair."

"And nobody from Dublin?"

"Sir, I am not able to—"

"Do you know if there was anyone from Dublin?"

"No, sir, we don't believe there was anyone from Dublin. Now you really must—"

"I'm away. Thank you. Thanks."

Sam left as directed, then parked up in an old farm laneway and waited. He gave it a while then walked to the shore and swam to the boat, listening by the hull for any movement inside. After fifteen minutes of freezing his nuts off, he was satisfied there was nobody aboard and climbed the bathing ladder.

Inside, he found his phone and called Sinead, but Sinead knew who he'd want to hear.

"Hallo, Daddy," Isla's little voice answered, always sounding younger on the phone.

"Hello, wee lamb, how are you doing?"

"Good."

"Whatcha doing?"

"I'm making a cake with Sinead."

"Go way," he said. "And how have you been?"

"Good. When are you coming to get me?"

"Well, can I talk to Sinead quickly to make arrangements?"

"Ok."

The phone rattled as it was handed over.

"Well, sailor, how are things?"

"Not just quite what I'd want them to be. Listen, haven't a whole lot of time but can you guys meet me in ..." he looked at the clock on the bulkhead, then the list of times for high water Dover. He grabbed the tidal atlas, estimating the flow south, "ten hours in Dún Laoghaire?"

"Everything ok, Sam?" Concern crept into her voice.

"If you can both come, it will be. Both of you – ok, Sinead?"

"Eh ... ok," she said.

"Also, can you tell our friend I lost the present he sent me. If he could just make sure there's no receipt, please, that would be great."

"I thought you'd want a receipt?"

"Not for this yoke, no. He'll understand it all."

"Oh-kay," she said, as if talking to a madman.

"Bring plenty of stuff, Sinead."

"What stuff?" she was saying as he hung up and readied to depart.

27

The superior came off the phone to Libby's mother having gushed about how sorry he was to have lost Meadow, an incredible member of the team, in such unfortunate circumstances. A London staffer had been sent to do the door knock; his call was just a follow-up, which had the unfortunate effect of increasing the number of questions: had she really died in a car crash? No, she was knocked down by a hit-and-run driver. Was there anything they weren't telling her? Had she died doing something important? No, the silly bitch was ignoring orders, the superior thought, taking flights of fancy – but, no, I'm deeply sorry, Meadow did indeed die in a freak accident. We will, of course, do all we can to find the driver, et cetera, et cetera. And it was in the countryside? And you have no idea what she was doing there? Yes, indeed, Mrs Meadow or whatever your name is, we haven't a clue what she was doing as she was off duty and on her own time and what have you.

Which then made him wonder, again, about where this had all happened. Google became his friend after the call finished and he zoomed in to reappraise the area.

Libby had made deliberate turns; she didn't appear to have been hunting in the dark.

The superior lifted the phone and made a call. "Well?" he asked.

"I'm just back from the scene."

"Did you see if there was a GPS in her car?"

"Plods have the car. It's been towed."

"Get me that GPS quickly. It probably has her destination in it."

"But—" came the suit's voice.

"But what?" the superior barked.

"There's nothing there. It's a road to nowhere – literally. Isn't it more likely she was on her way to a meet a CHIS?"

"She wasn't running any sources – she was a DET liaison. Now get me that GPS."

The superior noodled around Google Maps a little more, zooming and squeezing. Whatever way he looked at it the road led to a walk by the sea and a small boatyard-cum-car park. Street view gave a clear picture of the place: dilapidated, forlorn, forgotten, full of potholes and puddles, but there was a jetty thing. He lifted the phone again.

"I'm on the way now."

"Where to?" the superior snapped.

"To get the GPS."

"Were there any boats in the boatyard?"

"Eh ... well, yes, I think so. Yeah, old ones. Why?"

"Were there any boats floating?"

"Eh ... I don't know. I didn't really look. Sorry."

"Get down there now and see if there are any boats there."

"What about the GPS?"

"Forget the bloody GPS. Just see if there are any boats there."

The clerk stared at her brother as he tried to compute what she'd just told him.

"Over how?"

"All you need to know is that it's over."

"How can it be over?"

"There are ways to do things without a computer."

He looked at her as if to say, *Are there*?

"The person who was, kind of, blackmailing me ... she's gone."

"Gone where?"

"Gone, gone, not-coming-back gone."

He just looked at his sister blankly.

"It's over, I'm telling you."

"So nobody's looking at what I'm doing any more?"

"Far as I can tell."

"If you say so."

"I say so."

She'd done her best, and her best had been brutal.

Sam looked at two weather apps before he turned everything off. They both told him the same thing: fog.

In normal circumstances, with modern technology, fog was nothing to worry about. He had GPS and a chart plotter that told him where he was. He had AIS, which told him where every tanker, ship, container vessel and fishing boat was – plus, it told them where *he* was. Even in the blind density of Irish fog vessels could move around one another without too much concern. He had a radar and he had a radio. Easy-peasy. In normal circumstances.

But the spook's presence at the road traffic collision galvanised Sam's suspicion that he'd been rumbled, which meant he had to go dark – all navigational toys had to be switched off. He didn't want anyone using the automatic identification system to follow his progress, he didn't want his VHF radio pinpointed with any sort of radio direction finder. He was suspicious even of the ability to monitor radar sweeps. He ripped the radar reflector off the mast and threw it to the waves. Everything had to be powered down, which meant old-school navigation with no visibility and no lighthouse beams; just the log to give him the speed of the boat, the echo sounder for depth, a swinging compass and his ears fine-tuned for foghorns – across one of the busiest ports in Europe.

Once the phone was off he regretted not sending Sinead to Howth, north of most of the shipping lanes and separation areas. But it was too late. Sinead would know where to go. The three of them had enjoyed ice cream at a kiosk on one of the most-walked piers in the world. If he could find it. In the fog.

"Two things," the spook said.

The superior found himself leaning forward onto his toes. "Go on?"

"There are no boats floating here now. The owner of the yard says he lets some bloke who lives on a yacht with his daughter berth there. Says the bloke goes off for spells but this is their main dock."

"A bloke with a kid doesn't sound like who we are looking for."

"I saw him, actually. He was at the police tape earlier. The cop on duty confirmed he told her he lived on a boat. No boat there now, though."

"When did it leave?"

"Couldn't be more than six or seven hours ago."

"How far can you get in a boat in five hours?"

"I, eh, I have no idea."

"What did you make of him?"

"The yard owner?"

"No, the man who lives on his boat."

"Sorry. Unwashed, half a beard. Looked like a vagrant, to be honest."

"Young? Old? Fit? Fat?"

The spook closed his eyes and regretted not appraising the local bloke more closely.

"Forty-ish, gnarly – like a fisherman, strong, for sure. Grizzled, I would say. Anxious that his girlfriend and kid hadn't been in the smash."

"Name?"

"Sam. The fella here couldn't remember his surname."

"Really? Was he giving you the runaround?"

"No, I think he genuinely never knew."

"Kid must go to school?"

"Yeah, I'll check."

"What's her name?"

"Isla, apparently. Like the Scottish island, he said."

"Spelt I-s-l-a-y?" asked the superior, composing an urgent GCHQ request.

"Don't know, sorry. I didn't think so. I didn't know that was how the island was spelt."

"Do you not drink whisky?"

"Sorry?"

"Islay – it's home to Lagavulin, Laphroaig, many others."

"I don't drink at all."

"What about the boat? Motorboat? Big, small?"

"That, the yard owner *was* able to help with. Fifty-seven-foot cutter, aluminium, beautiful, he said. Well equipped. He could sail around the world on her, apparently."

"What do you think?" asked the superior. "Could he be our man?"

"I honestly thought he was a fisherman."

"Fishermen have a certain resilience, they're tough."

"This fella had definitely spent too much time in the sun – his face was creased and cracked and probably made him look older."

"What was he wearing?"

The spook closed his eyes again and thought. "Heavy jacket, waterproof, no brand. Heavy denims. He had wraparound-sunglasses tan lines. Soft climbing boots, I think."

"Military issue?"

"Don't think so – they would have registered."

"Anything else before I get this off for analysis?"

"Well, this guy's wife was killed a few years back."

"Oh? Killed how?"

"She was murdered by some Lithuanian. That's all anyone here knows."

Sam suddenly realised how long it had been since he'd properly used parallel rulers and dividers. He plotted his variation and deviation, magnetic and true compass bearing, his allowances for push and pull by wind and tide, and marked the spots on his course where he ought to see differences in depth. It was the only way he could possibly tell for sure where he was, given the extremity of the fog he was anticipating.

For all he knew, it might have set in already. The darkness was like a blanket around him and he hadn't seen a navigation light in over an hour. All he could see beyond the boat was the phosphorescence of the trail behind, his speed steady at nine knots, his anxiety through the roof. How many people were looking for him was anybody's guess. How he would find the entrance to Dún Laoghaire Harbour was a mystery. He set about doing what most sailors do in extreme situations: he said a prayer.

To get his request into the priority queue, the superior had to provide justification. He mulled that, unsure as to whether to commit to it: murder of a valuable asset. murders of multiple watch-list suspects following a bombing, murder of an agent.

It didn't read well. He was the senior man in Northern Ireland. To tell another agency, this time the listening and data-gathering station, GCHQ, that they had overseen such a series of disasters, wasn't appealing. It was akin to hoisting a flag that said "I've made a balls of it".

He'd always hated GCHQ anyway, since he'd been over-looked for a director's post there. His reward for that failure was to be sent to Northern Ireland – a "development opportunity" in a tough area. He'd wanted in on the fight against the Islamic extremists, instead he'd been lumbered with the old war against the Irish.

He had no idea how many approvals his request would have to go through to come out top of the pile; how much embarrassment and sniggering his name would be subjected to in his absence. Still, if this sun-baked suspect was their man, he might save some face. It was unlikely, but time was short. He hit send.

With the dawn came disorientation. At least when it had been dark Sam couldn't see what he couldn't see. Now, though, he was surrounded by a white blankness complete with bone-chilling groans from foghorns on passenger ferries and ships. The temptation was to close his eyes and hope for the best, but the moment he looked away from the compass the boat veered off course and he found it impossible to know which way he was pointing.

He lifted the chart for the hundredth time, estimating the point at which he would reach the shipping traffic separation area, banking on the ferries using the mid-channel and acutely aware that there were small fast boats whizzing up and down, delivering pilots onto tankers to ensure their safe delivery into Dublin Port. If one of those hit him, it would be over.

Instead of rounding Howth Head and heading straight for Dún Laoghaire Harbour, he opted to navigate between two rocks. His thinking was twofold: he'd been stupid to tell the cop that his "girlfriend" was from Dublin – it gave the authorities a likely destination if anyone was looking for him, although they wouldn't anticipate him going rock-hopping in the fog. Secondly, ships don't like rocks – they're hard to manoeuvre around and most vessels avoid them like the plague. But Sam was set, variations in depth would help him decide where he was and rocks have markers. Provided he was on the correct side of them, they would orient him and provide a good bearing to the harbour.

He aimed to keep the Burford Bank close to starboard and the Kish Lighthouse well to port, hoping to get a glimpse of a light through the murk to help him decide where he was.

Every ten seconds he lifted the binoculars hanging from his neck, scanning and willing the north Burford marker into view. According to time and speed, he reckoned it must be less than fifty metres away from him, but he knew that a small mistake an hour previous could place him on the stones. He was about to move and check his workings again when right in front of him, less than ten feet away, the enormous yellow-and-black cardinal loomed, flashing a quick white light. It shocked him utterly, despite the fact he'd been expecting it. It was the first thing he'd seen for hours and in panic he threw the wheel, losing sight of his guide, before slowing the engine and returning to course, creeping along the edge of what he now knew to be the sandbank. He kissed into starboard until the depth began to shallow, easing in and out. The danger was to go aground – only to be revealed at right angles, high and dry, when the fog lifted.

Gently he guided the boat along the edge of the shallow, hunting for his next confirmation, SAM 4, flashing yellow. Yet it never came, and Sam began again to doubt himself and his calculations. Where he thought it was time, he nudged the helm to starboard, still kissing the shallower water, conscious that the marker he should have seen was now likely behind him. He had one last chance for confirmation before he hit the shipping separation zone, the south cardinal marker, telling him that the rock was now to his rear.

His mind began to play tricks in the fog. He rounded startled on a teeth-rattling burst from a gaseous horn. The ship it belonged to sounded like it was immediately behind him. He leaned over to increase speed to try and outrun the unseen menace, then forced himself to calm down. He could just as easily drive his home straight up a rock. He scanned all around him with the binoculars, veering dangerously off course in the process, his ears hunting for any indication of a thrum of an engine. None came.

He slowed to one knot of speed, and again began to pray, and with that came the next blast of the tanker's horn, definitely further away and to his right – meaning that the vessel had passed in front of him, which suggested he might be past the rock.

And then came the cardinal, two triangles pointed down, it's light still barely perceptible but he didn't care. He just knew he had to increase speed to skip across the shipping zone as fast as he was able. He took the new course direct for the harbour entrance and threw his fate to God.

The last thing the superior wanted or needed was the visit that had been demanded of him, yet he had no option – politically – to avoid it.

"Chief constable, please come in. We are rather in the middle of it here, so I am grateful for you making the trip."

"I'd have cycled here if I thought it would help get any answers to what the hell is going on."

"I'm now in a better position to brief you, chief."

She sat down, unbidden, and nodded.

"Tea, coffee?"

"Just get on with it."

"Sean Gillen's death marks what we believe could be the conclusion to all this. His wife is, as I understand it, critically ill?"

"She's not going to make it," confirmed the chief.

Excellent, thought the superior. "Here is what we believe has happened."

"Well, you damn well ought to *know* what's happening given that you deployed the Special Reconnaissance Regiment *without* my authorisation."

"I did, but for good reason, chief."

"Which is?"

"Let me get to that. First, we believe there has been a monumental falling out among the dissident groupings over access to arms dumps."

"I know that."

"That has led to internal criticisms over how the Ballycastle bomb was actually detonated. We believe, in fact, that the bomb maker was misinformed about the type of detonator he was handling, the mix of fertiliser and indeed the strength of the plastic explosive."

"Well, you should know. I believe you were watching the bloody bomb all the way from Donegal!"

The superior held his hands to try to calm the chief but left the accusation without reply as he continued twirling and spinning on his mop-up journey. "As you know, the Donegal bomb factory was not previously known about, and was tricky to penetrate for political reasons – being as it is, in the Irish Republic."

"Never stopped you before."

"No, well. The killings in Ballycastle, in your own police station and indeed in Greenore in County Louth are, we believe, a result of the internal dispute."

"They're feuding. That's your story?"

"They are plainly feuding, chief. This is a fallout among thieves."

"You think they have the capacity to kill a man in a police station and get away? You really believe that? More importantly, do you think *I* should believe that?"

"Few are better versed on the workings of the front security hut than dissidents on bail, chief."

She sighed in exasperation. "And Gillen?"

"We believe he was handling a device intended for another target on his list, and that in his carelessness he detonated it and killed himself and potentially his wife."

"So you had eyes on all this?"

"No! Not at all. In fact, if you check with the military, you will see that we did not have eyes on any of this at the time of the explosion. I am quite sure that the military will corroborate that the DET. The Special Reconnaissance Regiment were not deployed at the time of any of this deeply unfortunate sequence."

The chief constable stared at the superior for a long while.

"Next to nothing you have just told me is true."

"It is a plausible explanation, chief. It is an explanation for the newspapers, and for the security correspondents and for the public. This dissident faction is an organisation intent on murder. It is, in effect, eating itself. The power of that among would-be joiners is substantial."

"So we are all to be happy about this trail of murder – this bloodbath?"

"These are ruthless killers, I don't need to tell a police officer that. So I would respectfully suggest that we need not be overly upset at the passing of such a group of ne'er-do-wells. This feud has taken out the leadership of a very dangerous and unpredictable organisation."

"I don't know what you wanted that bomb in Ballycastle to achieve. I don't know if you tampered with it or got the DET to tamper with it or if you brought in the bloody SAS. I don't know if you manufactured this feud – I doubt that there was even a feud. What I do know is that the remains of a military-grade drone were discovered plastered with Gillen's entrails up a tree in Craigavon. So I *do know* you were there in some form or another. What I *do know* is that you have made that *my* problem, because I now have to mop up and close down any wagging tongues that might convey that sort of information from forensics, to investigating officers and, God forbid, an inquest."

"Yes, we couldn't have that sort of information surfacing at an inquest."

"So let me be clear on this. I will do my best, but if you ever deploy special forces in my country again without proper consultation, I shall publicly demand that you are removed from post."

"Your message is clearly understood, chief constable. I'm sure it is of no benefit to remind you of the assistance we were able to render regarding that precarious position you found yourself in a few years ago. Thank you for your time."

The chief went white then red.

"If people knew what really went on, stunts like this would persuade even our local politicians that the police are the best lead for terrorism in this country." With that she opened the door and couldn't help but smash it shut behind her.

Sam could hear someone whistling. He heard a reel spin and the plop of a weight hit the water, and knew that anglers must be standing on the pier.

"Hello!" he called.

"Who's that?" he heard a Dublin accent, as close as if it were within touching distance.

"I'm on a boat but I can't see the breakwater. Which side are you on?"

"You really in a boat? I can't see ye."

"Please, before I end up on the rocks – tell me what side of the harbour you're on."

"The side with the lighthouse."

"So you walked down the pier?" From the Sandymount side?"

"Yeah."

"Do me a favour, stamp your feet."

"Wha?"

"Stamp your feet!"

"I'm wearing trainers, mister."

"The echo of your voice is hard to follow. Can you hit something metal? I'll move on the first sound."

"A'rioight."

Sam heard a clank. "Thank you. Are you close to the edge of the pier?"

"Right on it."

"Thanks a million. You might just have saved my ass."

"No bother."

Sam turned the boat from memory, sixty degrees into a harbour he knew well in daylight and with good visibility. He travelled what he estimated was fifty feet, then took a ninety-degree turn to starboard.

"Excuse me!" he called again.

"Yeah?" he heard the Dub again.

"I'll give you a hundred euros if you walk down the pier talking to me so I can estimate how close I am to you."

"Ah, you don't need to pay me, brother. I'll give ye a hand, like."

"Thanks a million."

"Ok. What's your name, brother?"

Sam followed the guide conscious that there could be boats moored in his path. "Gillen," was the only name that popped into his head. "And you?"

"People calls me Outspan."

"Like from The Commitments?"

"Yeah. If ye can't see the head on me, it must be misty."

"A redhead?"

"On foire, my friend."

"What's your real name?"

"Niall."

"Thanks for this, Niall."

"No bother."

"Can you walk me to the ice cream kiosk, Niall?"

"I don't think it's open, brother. If ye want a ninety-nine, you might have to go up to the Forty Foot."

"Very funny, Niall."

"There's an Italian place there. Old Ginelli own'd it but he died a few weeks back."

Sam needed to keep him talking. "What did he die of?"

"He died of a Tuesday."

"Very good, Niall."

"Buried on a Friday. There was plenty at it, like, to see him off. Hundreds and thousands, actually."

"You should be on the telly."

"You should be in the nuthouse for messin' about in the pea soup, Gillen."

Sam steered around a racing yacht and continued prompting. "What do you work at, Niall?"

"Nuttin'," came the reply. "I'm only fifteen, like."

"You sound older."

"You sound ancient, Gillen, but, like, I wouldn't be commenting cos that would be ageist."

"Do you do stand-up?"

"I'm standing up right now, Gillen."

"You should give it a crack."

"You're tiring me out here, Gillen. This is a long bloody pier."

"Sorry, Niall."

"Maybe I will take a few euros at the end if that's a'rioight. Might need a cone me'sel, like."

"You'd be welcome to it, Niall."

"What are ye doin' now?"

"Putting fenders out to stop the boat bouncing off the quay."

"I thought that's what I was doin'?"

"When I tie up, I mean."

"Oh, rioight. Are ye too hungry to pay the marina fees?"

"Something like that."

"So ye'll give me a hundred euros to walk the pier, but you won't give the marina a clutch of cash to get a good night's sleep."

"I'm not stopping."

"Are ye tellin' me that ye want me to walk ye all the way back to the end again?"

"Are you telling me that'll be two hundred euros?"

"I'm tellin' ye that you're as cracked as a bottle if you're going back out in that."

"How far do you reckon now?"

"Length of a football field, maybe."

"D'ye play a bit of football?" Sam ventured, keeping the conversation alive.

"I do, in me bollocks, Gillen. Can't stand those GAA types."

"Fair enough." Sam laughed.

"There ye go, brother. What'll it be – a screwball, a slider?"

"Is it open, right enough?"

"No, Gillen, it's not open, but there's a queue outside anyway. How are ye, luv? Bit of a bad day for the young 'un."

"Yeah, we're meeting someone here," Sam heard Sinead say.

"Is his name Gillen?"

"No, it's—"

"Sinead!" Sam called.

"Sam! Where are you?"

"I thought your name was Gillen?" said Niall.

"Daddy!" Isla called.

"This is gas," said Niall.

"Hang on, I'll be up in a minute to bring you down to the boat."

"The three of you were working with one of my intelligence team – Libby – now dead."

"Yes, sir, briefly," said the woman tech.

"Why?"

"Because she asked us to," said one of the blokes.

"Have you got Tourette's?" the superior snapped round.

"No, sir."

"I find talking to you computer types difficult enough without smart-arse comments from those on the spectrum! I'll talk to the organ grinder, understood?"

The young man sat bemused and silent.

"Libby knew we were among the last people on-base and requested our help," the lead tech said.

"Help with what?" the superior snarled.

"Well, initially an email that had come to her mother, but then she quickly told us to drop that and—"

"Did you see this email to her mother?"

The tech suddenly sensed danger. She had been summoned to speak to the intelligence chief who, it turned out, was the man whose photograph had been in the email. Resting on her confidence in her team's ability to wipe drives, she lied.

"No, sir. As I say, Libby told us to drop it pretty much immediately."

"Why?"

"Because we got word of another X-ray killing."

"Which one?"

"The fishing boat murder, Donegal. The bomb maker – the smuggler – the dissident."

"So what happened next?"

"She got us to monitor it to try to find information."

"And?"

"There was a tweet from a local reporter that said the X-ray had an oar rammed down his throat."

"Oh?"

"Then there was a fire on the boat."

"So what did Libby ask you to do then?"

"Well, one of us," the tech nodded to the berated bloke, "found another murder in Venice that was similar."

"Similar how?"

"Suffocation by, well, oar."

"You were all rather clutching at straws, were you not?"

"Yes," said the tech, increasingly pissed off at the superior's attitude.

"So what then?"

"Can I ask a question, sir?"

"What?"

"How did Libby die?"

"That's nothing to do with you!"

The tech's shutters began to rise. There was nothing in this for her or her team. There was nothing but danger in telling this arrogant bastard that they had got any further. "Sorry, sir."

"So what of this Venice thing?"

"Nothing, sir. Libby also thought it was a red herring, and then the MPs arrived and took us to Palace Barracks."

"That's all? There was nothing else?"

"No, sir. Nothing. We just ... got debriefed."

"And you didn't see the email that had been sent to Libby's mother?"

"No, sir."

"Why did you wipe the computers?"

"Sir?"

"There was nothing on your computers when they were seized."

"Standard practice, sir. We couldn't be sure who had arrived in the black vans – they were unmarked, so we set about a full erasure."

The superior stared at the woman tech, wondering whether he had got the full story, wondering whether it mattered.

"Dismissed!" he spat.

The techs got up and left the superior to his thoughts of an oar, a foreign murder, a fisherman and a missing yacht.

"Ridiculous," he said aloud.

And yet, there was a certain symmetry to the whole affair.

"Sam ..."

His head was buried in Isla's hair and she hugged him.

"Sam."

Sam looked beyond Isla to Sinead who was holding out her phone to him. "Our friend is on the phone."

"Your phone?"

"No, one he gave me."

"Ok."

He lowered Isla. "Two minutes, wee darlin'," he said.

He took the phone from Sinead with a smile of thanks. "John, how are you?"

"Good, Sam. Good. There are some things I'd like to know."

"Ok?"

"I've been keeping a close eye on things in the north, in the news. I'm wondering if you might know if the men in the headlines of late were connected to what happened to that poor child and her mother?"

Sam closed his eyes, conflicted between the insecurity of the line and his desire to help the old man.

"I believe they were, John."

"That's good. That's good. Just, by the way, these phones are off the shelf, as it were. Best I could manage. I hope that's—"

"That's grand, John. Don't worry."

"I'll let you go now, Sam. Oh, something else, there is no receipt for that thing, no way to prove purchase. I'm sorry."

"That's good to know, John. Again, I'm—"

"I know, Sam. I know. And thank you. Thank you. Godspeed."

The superior was just about to chase up his GCHQ request and summon an all-points alert on a fifty-seven-foot vessel, possibly headed south down the Irish Sea, when his door opened.

His door never opened without a knock first or an introduction from his personal assistant.

The superior's superior walked in. Tight trouser suit, pitch-black hair, dark skin, enormous glasses – a bombshell in every imaginable way.

"Oh, shit," said the superior.

"Correct," she said, closing the door.

"They obviously showed you my request for analysis."

"Yes."

"Can you at least tell me if we got the right man?"

"Your authorisation to make such requests is revoked. Your position is no longer tenable. You know that, don't you?"

"Of course," he said, attempting to summon some dignity.

"We will need you to be debriefed and then you will leave the service."

"Pension?"

"As is at time of leaving. Usual caveats – any issues or indiscretions, the payments stop. We've looked into your finances and know you have first-family payments to maintain, and that consequently you have no savings. So, buttoned lips, eh?"

"Of course."

"Chop-chop, time to get going."

"Just like that?"

"Unless you want me to arrest you?"

"For what?"

"Running undisclosed agents, allowing one of your team to be exposed – now dead, attempting to remove evidence from a public inquiry that implicated you in nefarious affairs of the past – how's that for a start?"

"That was to everyone's benefit!"

"This way is best. You whimper out the door with an income or you go to prison. Up to you."

"Was it him?"

"Who?"

"The man in the boat? The man who lived with his daughter?"

She just stared at him.

"Please. Tell me that at least. Was I right?"

"It was a feud," she said. "Nobody has anything to gain from a cannon on the loose, and if there was a cannon, it is aboard ship and on the run. Unlikely to return. Regardless, a dangerous little cell is no more."

"That's it? Really, we're going to do it this way?"

"You're on the easyJet to Luton in two hours. I suggest you hop to it."

"EasyJet?"

"Efficiencies. You're out. Now, get on the phone, get yourself a taxi and we will get you as far as the gate."

"Will I, like, eh, batter on, Gillen?" Niall asked, shuffling in the fog at their rear.

"Sorry, Niall. Sinead, have you any cash? Sorry to ask but—"

"I've about eighty euros," she muttered, lifting her bag and rooting immediately.

"You're a'rioight, Gillen. You're grand, honestly. Happy to lend y'is a hand."

"No, no, here, Niall, here, thanks a million. I might not have got in without you."

"No sweat. Thanks, Gillen."

"His name's Sam," Isla scolded.

"Whatever," said Niall. "I might get back to me rod and tackle, like?"

"Yes, yes, of course, and thanks," said Sam.

The three of them watched the teenager lope off counting the cash and pushing it into his back pocket.

"So what now?" Sinead asked.

"Did you bring stuff?"

"I brought an overnight bag and some clothes, but I wasn't sure if—"

"Ok."

"Are we going home, Daddy?"

"No, darlin', we're going on an adventure."

"Not a long one?" Isla asked, wary of a long sail.

"Yes, wee lamb, a long one."

"Daddy," her shoulders fell in disappointment, "I thought we were going home?"

Sam half turned to Sinead and rushed it out as fast as he was able. "I wondered if we could start a new home. Maybe somewhere else. Maybe somewhere warm. Maybe, like, where *Pirates of the Caribbean* is? Maybe, like, away, far away?"

Sinead looked at him, unsure as to whether she was understanding him correctly. Her hands disappeared into the cuffs of her jumper. "Who are we talking about here?" she asked nervously.

"I'm talking about Isla, me and you," he whispered.

"As, like, what?"

"As, like, a family."

"Are you asking me something here, Sam?"

"Yes, Sinead, I'm asking if you'll come with us."

"As a family?"

Sam turned desperately towards Isla. "You'd like that, wouldn't you, Isla?"

Please say yes, he thought, please say no. Just say what you think. Shit, this was so badly thought-out.

"I think you should come with us," Isla said, totally matter of fact.

"Either way, we really, really need to go now."

"What have you done?"

"Later, I promise, but we need to go. And, well, we can go together, the three of us. We can take it slow—"

"We've been taking it slow," Sinead shot back. "Any slower we'll all be dead before—"

"If you change your mind, you can get off on the other side."

"All this time, all this – whatever this is, and now it's, like – we gotta go right now, in the fog, in a rush, like – right now!"

"Go for it, girl." Niall suddenly appeared out of the gloom, fishing rod and tackle box in hand. "Sure, he'll probably crash into the pier without his trusty mouth in the mist. You'll be able to get off in fifty metres, like."

"Thanks, Niall." Sam shook his head.

"If ye hurry up, girl, I'll talk y'is out again."

Sam looked at Sinead, willing her to decide.

"What about Áine?"

"You've got a clear phone – call her, tell her."

"The charity?"

"Trickier. Take leave, take time off. It'll manage without you for a wee while."

"My car?"

"Áine will get it."

"This is really it?"

"We won't be back, not for a long time."

"Whatever you've done—"

"Not now, Sinead," he said, nodding at Niall's back.

Then she made a gesture that let Sam know one way or the other, and he shouted into the fog. "Niall, I need a hand!"

AFTERWORD

I set out to write a trilogy, and a trilogy has been written. Whether there are any more Sam and Isla stories is, frankly, up to you, the reader.

All feedback and reviews are welcome - indeed essential - they are the lifeblood of any writer in the digital age.

These links take you directly to the relevant pages, the 'customer reviews' button in a little down the page on the left hand side. I'd be hugely grateful.

Amazon UK
Amazon.com
Amazon Australia

ACKNOWLEDGMENTS

This book is a little different from the previous two. Northern Ireland is a place apart. People took all sorts of personal risks here. All sorts of people. There was cowardice, certainly, but there was undoubtedly bravery in buckets. There was sacrifice and, tragically and enduringly, there were people taken from their families with no reason, no explanation, no rationale and no sense. There were also attempts to justify the taking of life.

So my first thanks is to those who for years did their absolute best to follow a decent and honest path through the desperate years of the Troubles and who struggle, still and will always, with the aftermath. There are such people on all sides. Those who I have known, a little or a lot, have their stories in this book.

Closer to home, I want to thank the ladies, as always, although they may never read this text. My pal in Stroke City for first eyes, as ever, and Victoria for catching all that I drop. She's an accomplished juggler. To Mark Dawson for his encouragement, and to my family for humouring this caper, ill-advised as it may prove to be.

Get in touch, share your thoughts, or explore some of the inspiration for the story at:

www.finnog.com

or on

www.facebook.com/finnbarog

Printed in Great Britain
by Amazon

MARIE VON

Krambambuli

UND ANDERE ERZÄHLUNGEN

MIT ERINNERUNGEN
AN DIE DICHTERIN VON
FRANZ DUBSKY

PHILIPP RECLAM JUN. STUTTGART

Universal-Bibliothek Nr. 7887
Alle Rechte vorbehalten. Lizenzausgabe des Winkler-Verlags in München.
Gesetzt in Petit Garamond-Antiqua. Printed in Germany 1979.
Satz: Walter Rost, Stuttgart. Druck: Reclam Stuttgart
ISBN 3-15-007887-3

Krambambuli

Vorliebe empfindet der Mensch für allerlei Gegenstände.
Liebe, die echte, unvergängliche, die lernt er – wenn überhaupt – nur einmal kennen. So wenigstens meint der Herr
Revierjäger Hopp. Wie viele Hunde hat er schon gehabt,
und auch gern gehabt, aber lieb, was man sagt lieb und un-
vergeßlich, ist ihm nur einer gewesen – der Krambambuli.
Er hatte ihn im Wirtshause Zum Löwen in Wischau von
einem vazierenden Forstgehilfen gekauft oder eigentlich
eingetauscht. Gleich beim ersten Anblick des Hundes war er
von der Zuneigung ergriffen worden, die dauern sollte bis
zu seinem letzten Atemzuge. Dem Herrn des schönen Tieres, der am Tische vor einem geleerten Branntweingläschen
saß und über den Wirt schimpfte, weil dieser kein zweites
umsonst hergeben wollte, sah der Lump aus den Augen.
Ein kleiner Kerl, noch jung und doch so fahl wie ein abge-
storbener Baum, mit gelbem Haar und gelbem spärlichem
Barte. Der Jägerrock, vermutlich ein Überrest aus der vergangenen Herrlichkeit des letzten Dienstes, trug die Spuren
einer im nassen Straßengraben zugebrachten Nacht. Obwohl sich Hopp ungern in schlechte Gesellschaft begab,
nahm er trotzdem Platz neben dem Burschen und begann
sogleich ein Gespräch mit ihm. Da bekam er es denn bald
heraus, daß der Nichtsnutz den Stutzen und die Jagdtasche
dem Wirt bereits als Pfänder ausgeliefert hatte und daß er
jetzt auch den Hund als solches hergeben möchte; der Wirt
jedoch, der schmutzige Leuteschinder, wollte von einem
Pfand, das gefüttert werden muß, nichts hören.
Herr Hopp sagte vorerst kein Wort von dem Wohlgefallen,
das er an dem Hunde gefunden hatte, ließ aber eine Flasche
von dem guten Danziger Kirschbranntwein bringen, den
der Löwenwirt damals führte, und schenkte dem Vazierenden fleißig ein. – Nun, in einer Stunde war alles in Ord-

nung. Der Jäger gab zwölf Flaschen von demselben Getränke, bei dem der Handel geschlossen worden – der Vagabund gab den Hund. Zu seiner Ehre muß man gestehen: nicht leicht. Die Hände zitterten ihm so sehr, als er dem Tiere die Leine um den Hals legte, daß es schien, er werde mit dieser Manipulation nimmermehr zurechtkommen. Hopp wartete geduldig und bewunderte im stillen den trotz der schlechten Kondition, in welcher er sich befand, wundervollen Hund. Höchstens zwei Jahre mochte er alt sein, und in der Farbe glich er dem Lumpen, der ihn hergab, doch war die seine um ein paar Schattierungen dunkler. Auf der Stirn hatte er ein Abzeichen, einen weißen Strich, der rechts und links in kleine Linien auslief, in der Art wie die Nadeln an einem Tannenreis. Die Augen waren groß, schwarz, leuchtend, von tauklaren, lichtgelben Reiflein umsäumt, die Ohren hoch angesetzt, lang, makellos. Und makellos war alles an dem ganzen Hunde von der Klaue bis zu der feinen Witternase; die kräftige, geschmeidige Gestalt, das über jedes Lob erhabene Piedestal. Vier lebende Säulen, die auch den Körper eines Hirsches getragen hätten und nicht viel dicker waren als die Läufe eines Hasen. Beim heiligen Hubertus! dieses Geschöpf mußte einen Stammbaum haben, so alt und rein wie der eines deutschen Ordensritters.

Dem Jäger lachte das Herz im Leibe über den prächtigen Handel, den er gemacht. Er stand nun auf, ergriff die Leine, die zu verknoten dem Vazierenden endlich gelungen war, und fragte: »Wie heißt er denn?« – »Er heißt wie das, wofür Ihr ihn kriegt: Krambambuli«, lautete die Antwort. – »Gut, gut, Krambambuli! So komm! Wirst gehen? Vorwärts!« – Ja, er konnte lange rufen, pfeifen, zerren – der Hund gehorchte ihm nicht, wandte den Kopf demjenigen zu, den er noch für seinen Herrn hielt, heulte, als dieser ihm zuschrie: »Marsch!« und den Befehl mit einem tüchtigen Fußtritt begleitete, suchte sich aber immer wieder an ihn heranzudrängen. Erst nach einem heißen Kampfe gelang es Herrn Hopp, die Besitzergreifung des Hundes zu vollziehen. Gebunden und geknebelt mußte er zuletzt in einem

Sacke auf die Schulter geladen und so bis in das mehrere Wegstunden entfernte Jägerhaus getragen werden.

Zwei volle Monate brauchte es, bevor der Krambambuli, halb totgeprügelt, nach jedem Fluchtversuche mit dem Stachelhalsband an die Kette gelegt, endlich begriff, wohin er jetzt gehöre. Dann aber, als seine Unterwerfung vollständig geworden war, was für ein Hund wurde er da! Keine Zunge schildert, kein Wort ermißt die Höhe der Vollendung, die er erreichte, nicht nur in der Ausübung seines Berufes, sondern auch im täglichen Leben als eifriger Diener, guter Kamerad und treuer Freund und Hüter. »Dem fehlt nur die Sprache«, heißt es von anderen intelligenten Hunden – dem Krambambuli fehlte sie nicht; sein Herr zum mindesten pflog lange Unterredungen mit ihm. Die Frau des Revierjägers wurde ordentlich eifersüchtig auf den »Buli«, wie sie ihn geringschätzig nannte. Manchmal machte sie ihrem Manne Vorwürfe. Sie hatte den ganzen Tag, in jeder Stunde, in der sie nicht aufräumte, wusch oder kochte, schweigend gestrickt. Am Abend, nach dem Essen, wenn sie wieder zu stricken begann, hätte sie gern eins dazu geplaudert.

»Weißt denn immer nur dem Buli was zu erzählen, Hopp, und mir nie? Du verlernst vor lauter Sprechen mit dem Vieh das Sprechen mit den Menschen.«

Der Revierjäger gestand sich, daß etwas Wahres an der Sache sei, aber zu helfen wußte er nicht. Wovon hätte er mit seiner Alten reden sollen? Kinder hatten sie nie gehabt, eine Kuh durften sie nicht halten, und das zahme Geflügel interessiert einen Jäger im lebendigen Zustande gar nicht und im gebratenen nicht sehr. Für Kulturen aber und für Jagdgeschichten hatte wieder die Frau keinen Sinn. Hopp fand zuletzt einen Ausweg aus diesem Dilemma; statt mit dem Krambambuli sprach er von dem Krambambuli, von den Triumphen, die er allenthalben mit ihm feierte, von dem Neide, den sein Besitz erregte, von den lächerlich hohen Summen, die ihm für den Hund geboten wurden und die er verächtlich von der Hand wies.

Zwei Jahre waren so vergangen, da erschien eines Tages die Gräfin, die Frau seines Brotherrn, im Hause des Jägers. Er wußte gleich, was der Besuch zu bedeuten hatte, und als die gute, schöne Dame begann: »Morgen, lieber Hopp, ist der Geburtstag des Grafen...«, setzte er ruhig und schmunzelnd fort: »Und da möchten Hochgräfliche Gnaden dem Herrn Grafen ein Geschenk machen und sind überzeugt, mit nichts anderem soviel Ehre einlegen zu können als mit dem Krambambuli.« – »Ja, ja, lieber Hopp...« Die Gräfin errötete vor Vergnügen über dieses freundliche Entgegenkommen und sprach gleich von Dankbarkeit und bat, den Preis nur zu nennen, der für den Hund zu entrichten wäre. Der alte Fuchs von einem Revierjäger kicherte, tat sehr demütig und rückte auf einmal mit der Erklärung heraus: »Hochgräfliche Gnaden! Wenn der Hund im Schlosse bleibt, nicht jede Leine zerbeißt, nicht jede Kette zerreißt, oder wenn er sie nicht zerreißen kann, sich bei den Versuchen, es zu tun, erwürgt, dann behalten ihn Hochgräfliche Gnaden umsonst – dann ist er mir nichts mehr wert.«

Die Probe wurde gemacht, aber zum Erwürgen kam es nicht, denn der Graf verlor früher die Freude an dem eigensinnigen Tiere. Vergeblich hatte man es durch Liebe zu gewinnen, mit Strenge zu bändigen gesucht. Es biß jeden, der sich ihm näherte, versagte das Futter und – viel hat der Hund eines Jägers ohnehin nicht zuzusetzen – kam ganz herunter. Nach einigen Wochen erhielt Hopp die Botschaft, er könne sich seinen Köter abholen. Als er eilends von der Erlaubnis Gebrauch machte und den Hund in seinem Zwinger aufsuchte, da gab's ein Wiedersehen, unermeßlichen Jubels voll. Krambambuli erhob ein wahnsinniges Geheul, sprang an seinem Herrn empor, stemmte die Vorderpfoten auf dessen Brust und leckte die Freudentränen ab, die dem Alten über die Wangen liefen.

Am Abend dieses glücklichen Tages wanderten sie zusammen ins Wirtshaus. Der Jäger spielte Tarock mit dem Doktor und mit dem Verwalter. Krambambuli lag in der Ecke hinter seinem Herrn. Manchmal sah dieser sich nach ihm um, und der Hund, so tief er auch zu schlafen schien, begann augenblicklich mit dem Schwanze auf den Boden zu klopfen, als wollt er melden: Präsent! Und wenn Hopp, sich vergessend, recht wie einen Triumphgesang das Liedchen anstimmte: »Was macht denn mein Krambambuli?« richtete der Hund sich würde- und respektvoll auf, und seine hellen Augen antworteten: Es geht ihm gut!

Um dieselbe Zeit trieb, nicht nur in den gräflichen Forsten, sondern in der ganzen Umgebung eine Bande Wildschützen auf wahrhaft tolldreiste Art ihr Wesen. Der Anführer sollte ein verlottertes Subjekt sein. Den »Gelben« nannten ihn die Holzknechte, die ihn in irgendeiner übel berüchtigten Spelunke beim Branntwein trafen, die Heger, die ihm hie und da schon auf der Spur gewesen, ihm aber nie hatten beikommen können, und endlich die Kundschafter, deren er unter dem schlechten Gesindel in jedem Dorfe mehrere besaß.

Er war wohl der frechste Gesell, der jemals ehrlichen Jägersmännern etwas aufzulösen gab, mußte auch selbst vom Handwerk gewesen sein, sonst hätte er das Wild nicht mit solcher Sicherheit aufspüren und nicht so geschickt jeder Falle, die ihm gestellt wurde, ausweichen können.

Die Wild- und Waldschäden erreichten eine unerhörte Höhe, das Forstpersonal befand sich in grimmigster Aufregung. Da begab es sich nur zu oft, daß die kleinen Leute, die bei irgendeinem unbedeutenden Waldfrevel ertappt wurden, eine härtere Behandlung erlitten, als zu anderer Zeit geschehen wäre und als gerade zu rechtfertigen war. Große Erbitterung herrschte darüber in allen Ortschaften. Dem Oberförster, gegen den der Haß sich zunächst wandte, kamen gutgemeinte Warnungen in Menge zu. Die Raubschützen, hieß es, hätten einen Eid darauf geschworen, bei der ersten Gelegenheit exemplarische Rache an ihm zu nehmen. Er, ein rascher, kühner Mann, schlug das Gerede in den Wind und sorgte mehr denn je dafür, daß weit und breit kund werde, wie er seinen Untergebenen die rücksichtsloseste Strenge anbefohlen und für etwaige schlimme

Folgen die Verantwortung selbst übernommen habe. Am häufigsten rief der Oberförster dem Revierjäger Hopp die scharfe Handhabung seiner Amtspflicht ins Gedächtnis und warf ihm zuweilen Mangel an »Schneid« vor; wozu freilich der Alte nur lächelte. Der Krambambuli aber, den er bei solcher Gelegenheit von oben herunter anblinzelte, gähnte laut und wegwerfend. Übel nahmen er und sein Herr dem Oberförster nichts. Der Oberförster war ja der Sohn des Unvergeßlichen, bei dem Hopp das edle Weidwerk erlernt, und Hopp hatte wieder ihn als kleinen Jungen in die Rudimente des Berufs eingeweiht. Die Plage, die er einst mit ihm gehabt, hielt er heute noch für eine Freude, war stolz auf den ehemaligen Zögling und liebte ihn trotz der rauhen Behandlung, die er so gut wie jeder andere von ihm erfuhr.

Eines Junimorgens traf er ihn eben wieder bei einer Exekution.

Es war im Lindenrondell, am Ende des herrschaftlichen Parks, der an den »Grafenwald« grenzte, und in der Nähe der Kulturen, die der Oberförster am liebsten mit Pulverminen umgeben hätte. Die Linden standen just in schönster Blüte, und über diese hatte ein Dutzend kleiner Jungen sich hergemacht. Wie Eichkätzchen krochen sie auf den Ästen der herrlichen Bäume herum, brachen alle Zweige, die sie erwischen konnten, ab und warfen sie zur Erde. Zwei Weiber lasen die Zweige hastig auf und stopften sie in Körbe, die bereits mehr als zur Hälfte mit dem duftenden Raube gefüllt waren. Der Oberförster raste in unermeßlicher Wut. Er ließ durch seine Heger die Buben nur so von den Bäumen schütteln, unbekümmert um die Höhe, aus der sie fielen. Während sie wimmernd und schreiend um seine Füße krochen, der eine mit zerschlagenem Gesicht, der andere mit ausgerenktem Arm, ein dritter mit gebrochenem Bein, zerbleute er eigenhändig die beiden Weiber. In dem einen derselben erkannte Hopp die leichtfertige Dirne, die das Gerücht als die Geliebte des »Gelben« bezeichnete. Und als die Körbe und Tücher der Weiber und die Hüte der

Buben in Pfand genommen wurden und Hopp den Auftrag bekam, sie aufs Gericht zu bringen, konnte er sich eines schlimmen Vorgefühls nicht erwehren.

Der Befehl, den ihm damals der Oberförster zurief, wild wie ein Teufel in der Hölle und wie ein solcher umringt von jammernden und gepeinigten Sündern, ist der letzte gewesen, den der Revierjäger im Leben von ihm erhalten hat. Eine Woche später traf er ihn wieder im Lindenrondell – tot. Aus dem Zustande, in dem die Leiche sich befand, war zu ersehen, daß sie hierher, und zwar durch Sumpf und Gerölle, geschleppt worden war, um an dieser Stelle aufgebahrt zu werden. Der Oberförster lag auf abgehauenen Zweigen, die Stirn mit einem dichten Kranz aus Lindenblüten umflochten, einen ebensolchen als Bandelier um die Brust gewunden. Sein Hut stand neben ihm, mit Lindenblüten gefüllt. Auch die Jagdtasche hatte der Mörder ihm gelassen, nur die Patronen herausgenommen und statt ihrer Lindenblüten hineingetan. Der schöne Hinterlader des Oberförsters fehlte und war durch einen elenden Schießprügel ersetzt. Als man später die Kugel, die seinen Tod verursacht hatte, in der Brust des Ermordeten fand, zeigte es sich, daß sie genau in den Lauf dieses Schießprügels paßte, der dem Förster gleichsam zum Hohne über die Schulter gelegt worden war. Hopp stand beim Anblick der entstellten Leiche regungslos vor Entsetzen. Er hätte keinen Finger heben können, und auch das Gehirn war ihm wie gelähmt; er starrte nur und starrte und dachte anfangs gar nichts, und erst nach einer Weile brachte er es zu einer Beobachtung, einer stummen Frage: – Was hat denn der Hund?

Der Krambambuli beschnüffelt den toten Mann, läuft wie nicht gescheit um ihn herum, die Nase immer am Boden. Einmal winselt er, einmal stößt er einen schrillen Freudenschrei aus, macht ein paar Sätze, bellt, und es ist geradeso, als erwache in ihm eine längst erstorbene Erinnerung ...

»Herein«, ruft Hopp, »da herein!« Und Krambambuli gehorcht, sieht aber seinen Herrn in allerhöchster Aufregung

9

an und – wie der Jäger sich auszudrücken pflegte – sagt ihm: »Ich bitte dich um alles in der Welt, siehst du denn nichts? Riechst du denn nichts? ... O lieber Herr, schau doch! riech doch! O Herr, komm! Daher komm!...« Und tupft mit der Schnauze an des Jägers Knie und schleicht, sich oft umsehend, als frage er: Folgst du mir? zu der Leiche zurück und fängt an, das schwere Gewehr zu heben und zu schieben und ins Maul zu fassen, in der offenbaren Absicht, es zu apportieren.

Dem Jäger läuft ein Schauer über den Rücken, und allerlei Vermutungen dämmern in ihm auf. Weil das Spintisieren aber nicht seine Sache ist, es ihm auch nicht zukommt, der Obrigkeit Lichter aufzustecken, sondern vielmehr den gräßlichen Fund, den er getan hat, unberührt liegenzulassen und seiner Wege – das heißt in dem Fall recte zu Gericht – zu gehen, so tut er denn einfach, was ihm zukommt.

Nachdem es geschehen und alle Förmlichkeiten, die das Gesetz bei solchen Katastrophen vorschreibt, erfüllt, der ganze Tag und auch ein Stück der Nacht darüber hingegangen sind, nimmt Hopp, eh er schlafen geht, noch seinen Hund vor.

»Mein Hund«, spricht er, »jetzt ist die Gendarmerie auf den Beinen, jetzt gibt's Streifereien ohne Ende. Wollen wir es andern überlassen, den Schuft, der unsern Oberförster erschossen hat, wegzuputzen aus der Welt? – Mein Hund kennt den niederträchtigen Strolch, kennt ihn, ja, ja! Aber das braucht niemand zu wissen, das habe ich nicht ausgesagt ... Ich, hoho! ... Ich werd meinen Hund hineinbringen in die Geschichte ... Das könnt mir einfallen!« Er beugte sich über Krambambuli, der zwischen seinen ausgespreizten Knien saß, drückte die Wange an den Kopf des Tieres und nahm seine dankbaren Liebkosungen in Empfang. Dabei summte er: »Was macht denn mein Krambambuli?«, bis der Schlaf ihn übermannte.

Seelenkundige haben den geheimnisvollen Drang zu erklären gesucht, der manchen Verbrecher stets wieder an den Schauplatz seiner Untat zurückjagt. Hopp wußte von diesen gelehrten Ausführungen nichts, strich aber dennoch

ruh- und rastlos mit seinem Hunde in der Nähe des Linden-
rondells herum.

Am zehnten Tage nach dem Tode des Oberförsters hatte er
zum ersten Mal ein paar Stunden lang an etwas anderes
gedacht als an seine Rache und sich im »Grafenwald« mit
dem Bezeichnen der Bäume beschäftigt, die beim nächsten
Schlag ausgenommen werden sollten.

Wie er nun mit seiner Arbeit fertig ist, hängt er die Flinte
wieder um und schlägt den kürzesten Weg ein, quer durch
den Wald gegen die Kulturen in der Nähe des Lindenron-
dells. Im Augenblick, in dem er auf den Fußsteig treten
will, der längs des Buchenzaunes läuft, ist ihm, als höre er
etwas im Laube rascheln. Gleich darauf herrscht jedoch tiefe
Stille, tiefe, anhaltende Stille. Fast hätte er gemeint, es sei
nichts Bemerkenswertes gewesen, wenn nicht der Hund so
merkwürdig dreingeschaut hätte. Der stand mit gesträub-
tem Haar, den Hals vorgestreckt, den Schwanz aufrecht,
und glotzte eine Stelle des Zaunes an. Oho! dachte Hopp,
wart, Kerl, wenn du's bist; trat hinter einen Baum und
spannte den Hahn seiner Flinte. Wie rasend pochte ihm das
Herz, und der ohnehin kurze Atem wollte ihm völlig ver-
sagen, als jetzt plötzlich, Gottes Wunder! – durch den Zaun
der »Gelbe« auf den Fußsteig trat. Zwei junge Hasen hän-
gen an seiner Weidtasche, und auf seiner Schulter, am wohl-
bekannten Juchtenriemen, der Hinterlader des Oberförsters. Nun wär's eine Passion, den Racker niederzubrennen
aus sicherem Hinterhalt.

Aber nicht einmal auf den schlechtesten Kerl schießt der
Jäger Hopp, ohne ihn angerufen zu haben. Mit einem Satze
springt er hinter dem Baum hervor und auf den Fußsteig
und schreit: »Gib dich, Vermaledeiter!« Und als der Wildschütz zur Antwort den Hinterlader von der Schulter reißt,
gibt der Jäger Feuer ... All ihr Heiligen – ein sauberes
Feuer! Die Flinte knackst, anstatt zu knallen. Sie hat zu
lange mit aufgesetzter Kapsel im feuchten Wald am Baum
gelehnt – sie versagt.

Gute Nacht, so sieht das Sterben aus, denkt der Alte ...

Doch nein – er ist heil, sein Hut nur fliegt, von Schroten durchlöchert, ins Gras ...

Der andere hat auch kein Glück; das war der letzte Schuß in seinem Gewehr, und zum nächsten zieht er eben erst die Patrone aus der Tasche ...

»Pack an!« ruft Hopp seinem Hunde heiser zu: »Pack an!« Und: »Herein, zu mir! Herein, Krambambuli!« lockt es drüben mit zärtlicher, liebevoller – ach, mit altbekannter Stimme ...

Der Hund aber – –

Was sich nun begab, begab sich viel rascher, als man es erzählen kann.

Krambambuli hatte seinen ersten Herrn erkannt und rannte auf ihn zu, bis – in die Mitte des Weges. Da pfeift Hopp, und der Hund macht kehrt, »der Gelbe« pfeift, und der Hund macht wieder kehrt und windet sich in Verzweiflung auf einem Fleck, in gleicher Distanz von dem Jäger wie von dem Wildschützen, zugleich hingerissen und gebannt ...

Zuletzt hat das arme Tier den trostlos unnötigen Kampf aufgegeben und seinen Zweifeln ein Ende gemacht, aber nicht seiner Qual. Bellend, heulend, den Bauch am Boden, den Körper gespannt wie eine Sehne, den Kopf emporgehoben, als riefe es den Himmel zum Zeugen seines Seelenschmerzes an, kriecht es – seinem ersten Herrn zu.

Bei dem Anblick wird Hopp von Blutdurst gepackt. Mit zitternden Fingern hat er die neue Kapsel aufgesetzt – mit ruhiger Sicherheit legt er an. Auch »der Gelbe« hat den Lauf wieder auf ihn gerichtet. Diesmal gilt's! Das wissen die beiden, die einander auf dem Korn haben, und was auch in ihnen vorgehen möge, sie zielen so ruhig wie ein paar gemalte Schützen.

Zwei Schüsse fallen. Der Jäger trifft, der Wildschütz fehlt.

Warum? Weil er – vom Hunde mit stürmischer Liebkosung angesprungen – gezuckt hat im Augenblick des Losdrückens. »Bestie!« zischt er noch, stürzt rücklings hin und rührt sich nicht mehr.

12

Der ihn gerichtet, kommt langsam herangeschritten. Du hast genug, denkt er, um jedes Schrotkorn wär's schad bei dir. Trotzdem stellt er die Flinte auf den Boden und lädt von neuem. Der Hund sitzt aufrecht vor ihm, läßt die Zunge heraushängen, keucht kurz und laut und sieht ihm zu. Und als der Jäger fertig ist und die Flinte wieder zur Hand nimmt, halten sie ein Gespräch, von dem kein Zeuge ein Wort vernommen hätte, wenn es auch statt eines toten ein lebendiger gewesen wäre.

»Weißt du, für wen das Blei gehört?«

»Ich kann es mir denken.«

»Deserteur, Kalfakter, pflicht- und treuvergessene Kanaille!«

»Ja, Herr, jawohl.«

»Du warst meine Freude. Jetzt ist's vorbei. Ich habe keine Freude mehr an dir.«

»Begreiflich, Herr«, und Krambambuli legte sich hin, drückte den Kopf auf die ausgestreckten Vorderpfoten und sah den Jäger an.

Ja, hätte das verdammte Vieh ihn nur nicht angesehen! Da würde er ein rasches Ende gemacht und sich und dem Hunde viel Pein erspart haben. Aber so geht's nicht! Wer könnte ein Geschöpf niederknallen, das einen so ansieht? Herr Hopp murmelt ein halbes Dutzend Flüche zwischen den Zähnen, einer gotteslästerlicher als der andere, hängt die Flinte wieder um, nimmt dem Raubschützen noch die jungen Hasen ab und geht.

Der Hund folgte ihm mit den Augen, bis er zwischen den Bäumen verschwunden war, stand dann auf, und sein mark- und beinerschütterndes Wehgeheul durchdrang den Wald. Ein paarmal drehte er sich im Kreise und setzte sich wieder aufrecht neben den Toten hin. So fand ihn die gerichtliche Kommission, die, von Hopp geleitet, bei sinkender Nacht erschien, um die Leiche des Raubschützen in Augenschein zu nehmen und fortschaffen zu lassen. Krambambuli wich einige Schritte zurück, als die Herren herantraten. Einer von ihnen sagte zu dem Jäger: »Das ist ja Ihr Hund.« –

13

»Ich habe ihn hier als Schildwache zurückgelassen«, antwortete Hopp, der sich schämte, die Wahrheit zu gestehen. – Was half's? Sie kam doch heraus, denn als die Leiche auf den Wagen geladen war und fortgeführt wurde, trottete Krambambuli gesenkten Kopfes und mit eingezogenem Schwanze hinterher. Unweit der Totenkammer, in der »der Gelbe« lag, sah ihn der Gerichtsdiener noch am folgenden Tage herumstreichen. Er gab ihm einen Tritt und rief ihm zu: »Geh nach Hause!« – Krambambuli fletschte die Zähne gegen ihn und lief davon; wie der Mann meinte, in der Richtung des Jägerhauses. Aber dorthin kam er nicht, sondern führte ein elendes Vagabundenleben.

Verwildert, zum Skelett abgemagert, umschlich er einmal die armen Wohnungen der Häusler am Ende des Dorfes. Plötzlich stürzte er auf ein Kind los, das vor der letzten Hütte stand, und entriß ihm gierig das Stück Brot, von dem es aß. Das Kind blieb starr vor Schrecken, aber ein kleiner Spitz sprang aus dem Hause und bellte den Räuber an. Dieser ließ sogleich seine Beute fahren und entfloh.

Am selben Abend stand Hopp vor dem Schlafengehen am Fenster und blickte in die schimmernde Sommernacht hinaus. Da war ihm, als sähe er jenseits der Wiese am Waldessaum den Hund sitzen, die Stätte seines ehemaligen Glükkes unverwandt und sehnsüchtig betrachtend – der Treueste der Treuen, herrenlos!

Der Jäger schlug den Laden zu und ging zu Bette. Aber nach einer Weile stand er auf, trat wieder ans Fenster – der Hund war nicht mehr da. Und wieder wollte er sich zur Ruhe begeben und wieder fand er sie nicht.

Er hielt es nicht mehr aus. Sei es, wie es sei! ... Er hielt es nicht mehr aus ohne den Hund. – Ich hol ihn heim, dachte er, und fühlte sich wie neugeboren nach diesem Entschluß.

Beim ersten Morgengrauen war er angekleidet, befahl seiner Alten, mit dem Mittagessen nicht auf ihn zu warten, und sputete sich hinweg. Wie er aber aus dem Hause trat, stieß sein Fuß an denjenigen, den er in der Ferne zu suchen ausging. Krambambuli lag verendet vor ihm, den Kopf an

14

die Schwelle gepreßt, die zu überschreiten er nicht mehr gewagt hatte.

Der Jäger verschmerzte ihn nie. Die Augenblicke waren seine besten, in denen er vergaß, daß er ihn verloren hatte. In freundliche Gedanken versunken, intonierte er dann sein berühmtes: »Was macht denn mein Krambam...« Aber mitten in dem Worte hielt er bestürzt inne, schüttelte das Haupt und sprach mit einem tiefen Seufzer: »Schad um den Hund!«

Die Spitzin

Zigeuner waren gekommen und hatten ihr Lager beim Kirchhof außerhalb des Dorfes aufgeschlagen. Die Weiber und Kinder trieben sich bettelnd in der Umgebung herum, die Männer verrichteten allerlei Flickarbeiten an Ketten und Kesseln und bekamen die Erlaubnis, so lange dazubleiben, als sie Beschäftigung finden konnten und einen kleinen Verdienst.

Diese Frist war noch nicht um, eines Sommermorgens aber fand man die Stätte, an der die Zigeuner gehaust hatten, leer. Sie waren fortgezogen in ihren mit zerfetzten Plachen überdeckten, von jämmerlichen Mähren geschleppten Leiterwagen. Von dem Aufbruch der Leute hatte niemand etwas gehört noch gesehen; er mußte des Nachts in aller Stille stattgefunden haben.

Die Bäuerinnen zählten ihr Geflügel, die Bauern hielten Umschau in den Scheunen und Ställen. Jeder meinte, die Landstreicher hätten sich etwas von seinem Gute angeeignet und dann die Flucht ergriffen. Bald aber zeigte sich, daß die Verdächtigen nicht nur nichts entwendet, sondern sogar etwas dagelassen hatten. Im hohen Grase neben der Kirchhofmauer lag ein splitternacktes Knäblein und schlief. Es konnte kaum zwei Jahre alt sein und hatte eine sehr weiße Haut und spärliche hellblonde Haare. Die Witwe Wagner, die es entdeckte, als sie auf ihren Rübenacker ging, sagte gleich, das sei ein Kind, das die Zigeuner, Gott weiß wann, Gott weiß wo, gestohlen und jetzt weggelegt hätten, weil es elend und erbärmlich war und ihnen niemals nützlich werden konnte.

Sie hob das Bübchen vom Boden auf, drehte und wendete es und erklärte, es müsse gewiß irgendwo ein Merkmal haben, an dem seine Eltern, die ohne Zweifel in Qual und Herzensangst nach ihm suchten, es erkennen würden, »wenn

16

man das Merkmal in die Zeitung setze«. Doch ließ sich kein besonderes Merkmal entdecken und auch später trotz aller Nachforschungen, Anzeigen und Kundmachungen weder von den Zigeunern noch von der Herkunft des Kindes eine Spur finden.

Die alte Wagnerin hatte es zu sich genommen und ihre Armut mit ihm geteilt, nicht nur aus Gutmütigkeit, sondern auch in der stillen Hoffnung, daß seine Eltern einmal kommen würden in Glanz und Herrlichkeit, es abzuholen und ihr hundertfach zu ersetzen, was sie für das Kindlein getan hatte. Aber sie starb nach mehreren Jahren, ohne den erwarteten Lohn eingeheimst zu haben, und jetzt wußte niemand, wohin mit ihrer Hinterlassenschaft – dem Findling. Ein Armenhaus gab es im Dorfe nicht, und die Barmherzigkeit war dort auch nicht zu Hause. Wen um Gottes willen ging das halbverhungerte Geschöpf etwas an, von dem man nicht einmal wußte, ob es getauft war? »Einen christlichen Namen darf man ihm durchaus nicht geben«, hatte der Küster von Anfang an unter allgemeiner Zustimmung erklärt, aber auf die Frage der Wagnerin: »Was denn für einen?« keine Antwort gewußt. »Geben S' ihm halt einen provisorischen«, war die Entscheidung gewesen, die endlich der Herr Lehrer getroffen, und die halb taube Alte hatte nur die zwei ersten Silben verstanden und den Jungen Provi und nach seinem Fundort Kirchhof genannt. Nach ihrem Tode waren alle darüber einig, daß dem Provi Kirchhof nichts Besseres zu wünschen sei als eine recht baldige Erlösung von seinem jämmerlichen Dasein. Der Armselige lebte vom Abhub, kleidete sich in Fetzen – abgelegtes Zeug, ob von kleinen Jungen, ob von kleinen Mädchen galt gleich –, ging barhäuptig und barfüßig, wurde geprügelt, beschimpft, verachtet und gehaßt und prügelte, beschimpfte, verachtete und haßte wieder. Als für ihn die Zeit kam, die Schule zu besuchen, erhielt er dort zu den zwei schönen Namen, die er schon hatte, einen dritten: »der Abschaum«, und tat, was in seinen Kräften lag, um ihn zu rechtfertigen.

Da war im Orte die brave Schoberwirtin. Im vergangenen Herbst hatte Provi in einem Winkel ihrer Scheuer eine Todeskrankheit durchgemacht, ohne Arzt und ohne Pflege. Nur die Schoberin war täglich nachsehen gekommen, ob es nicht schon vorbei sei mit ihm, und hatte ihm jeden Morgen ein Krüglein voll Milch hingestellt. Die Gewohnheit, ihm ein Frühstück zu spenden, behielt sie bei, auch nachdem er gesund geworden war. Pünktlich um fünf fand er sich ein, blieb auf der Schwelle der Wirtsstube stehen und rief: »Mei Müalch!« Er bekam das Verlangte und ging seiner Wege. Einmal aber ereignete sich etwas ganz Ungewöhnliches. Der Wirt, der sonst seinen Abendrausch regelmäßig im Bette ausschlief, hatte ihn diese Nacht auf der Bank in der Wirtsstube ausgeschlafen und erwachte in dem Augenblick, als Provi auf die Schwelle trat und rief: »Mei Müalch!«

Was sagte der Lackel? Was wollte er? Schober dehnte und reckte sich. Ein verflucht kantiges Lager hatte er gehabt, seine Glieder schmerzten ihn, und seine Laune war schlecht. Der grobe Klotz Provi fand heute an ihm einen groben Keil. »Nicht zu verlangen, zu bitten hast, du Lump! Kannst nicht bitten?«

Der Junge riß die farblosen Augen auf, sein schmales Gesicht wurde noch länger als sonst, der große, blasse Mund verzog sich und sprach: »Na!«

Die Früchte, die ihm dieses Wort eintragen sollte, reiften sogleich. Schober sprang auf ihn zu, verabreichte ihm sein Frühstück in Gestalt einer tüchtigen Tracht Prügel und warf ihn zur Tür hinaus. Solche kleine Zwischenfälle machten aber keinen Eindruck auf den Jungen. Wie alltäglich fand er sich am nächsten Morgen wieder ein und forderte in gewohnter Weise »seine« Milch. Die Wirtin gab sie ihm, aber eine gute Lehre dazu: »Du mußt bitten lernen, Bub, weißt? – bitten. Bist schon alt genug, bist g'wiß – ja, wenn man bei dir nur was g'wiß wüßt'! –, g'wiß schon vierzehn. Also merk dir, von morgen an: Wenn's kein Bitten gibt, gibt's keine Milch.« Sie blieb dabei, ob es ihr auch schwer wurde. Wie schwer, sah Provi wohl, und es war ihm ein Genuß, eine Befriedigung seiner Lumpeneitelkeit. Ihm, dem Ausgestoßenen, dem Namenlosen, war Macht gegeben, der reichsten Frau im ganzen Orte Stunden zu trüben und die Laune zu verderben. Sie blickte ihm mit Bekümmernis nach, wenn er ohne Gruß an ihrer Tür vorüberging, zur Arbeit in den Steinbruch.

Dort taglöhnerte er jetzt beim Wegemacher, der ihn in Kost genommen und ihm ein Obdach im Ziegenstall gegeben hatte. Der Wegemacher brauchte nicht wie die andern Leute den Umgang mit Provi für seine Kinder zu fürchten. Die fünf Wegemacherbuben konnte der Auswürfling nichts Böses lehren, sie wußten ohnehin schon alles und waren besonders Meister in der Tierquälerei. Die Ziegen, Kaninchen, die Hühner, die ihnen untertan waren, und der Haushund, die unglückliche Spitzin, gaben Zeugnis davon, ihre Narben erzählten davon und ihre beschädigten Beine und ihre gebrochenen Flügel. Provi fand sein Ergötzen an dem Anblick der Roheit, den er jetzt stündlich genießen konnte. Er fing für die kleineren der Buben Vögel ein und gab sie ihnen »zum Spielen«, und diese Opfer konnten von Glück sagen, wenn sie kein allzu zähes Leben hatten.

Das ärmste von den armen Tieren der Wegemacherfamilie war aber die alte Spitzin. Sie lief nur noch auf drei Beinen und hatte nur noch ein Auge. Ein Fußtritt des Erstgeborenen unter ihren Peinigern hatte sie krumm, ein Steinwurf sie halb blind gemacht. Trotz dieser Defekte trug sie ihr impertinentes Näschen hoch und ihr Schwänzchen aufrecht, bellte jeden fremden Hund, der sich blicken ließ, wütend an, und ihre Beschimpfungen gellten ihm auf seinem Rückzuge nach. Die Söhne des Wegemachers fürchtete, ihn selbst haßte sie, weil er ihr ihre kaum geborenen Jungen immer wegnahm und, bis auf ein einziges, in den See warf.

Zur Zeit, in der Provi beim Wegemacher Steine klopfte und Sand siebte, bekam die Spitzin noch im Greisenalter abermals Junge, ihrer vier, von denen drei gleich ins Wasser mußten. Sie konnte kaum eines mehr ernähren, sie war zu alt und zu schwach, und es sah ganz danach aus, als ob sie nicht mehr lange leben sollte. Das Geschäft des Ersäufens übertrug der Vater an jenem Tage seinem Ältesten, dem Anton, und dem machte etwas, das einem anderen Geschöpfe weh tat, dieses Mal kein Vergnügen. Die Spitzin war bissig wie ein Wolf, wenn sie Junge hatte.

»Der Vater fürcht si vor ihr«, sagte Anton zu Provi, »drum schickt er mi. Komm mit, halt sie, wenn ich ihr die Jungen nimm, halt ihrs Maul zu, daß s' mi nit beißen kann.«

Im Holzverschlag neben dem Ziegenstalle, auf einer Handvoll Stroh, lag zusammengeringelt die schwarze Spitzin, und unter ihr und um sie herum krabbelten ihre Kleinen und winselten und suchten mit blinden Augen und tasteten mit weichen, hilflosen Pfötchen.

Die Spitzin hob den Kopf, als die Knaben sich ihr näherten, ließ ein feindseliges Knurren vernehmen, fletschte die Zähne.

»Dummes Viech, grausliches!« schrie Anton und streckte halb zornig, halb ängstlich die Hand nach einem der Hündchen aus. »Halt sie! halt sie! daß s' mi nit beißt!«

Schon recht, wenn s' di beißt, dachte Provi. Es fiel ihm nicht ein, sich um Antons willen in einen gefährlichen Kampf mit der Hündin einzulassen; nur um die eigene Sicherheit war ihm zu tun, und so nahm er seine Zuflucht zu einer Kriegslist, kauerte auf den Boden nieder und hob mit kläglicher Stimme an: »O die orme Spitzin, no jo, no jo! Ruhig, orme Spitzin, so, so ... ma tut ihr jo nix, ma nimmt ihr jo nur ihre Jungen, no jo, no jo!«

Die Spitzin zauderte, knurrte noch ein wenig, doch mehr behaglich jetzt als bösartig. Die Worte, die Provi zu ihr sprach, verstand sie nicht, aber ihren sanften, beschwichtigenden Ton verstand sie, und dem glaubte sie. Was wußte die Spitzin von Arglist und Heuchelei? Ein Mensch sprach einmal gütig zu ihr, so war auch seine Meinung gütig. Sie legte sich wieder hin, ließ sich streicheln, schloß bei der ungewohnt wohltuenden Berührung wie zu wonnigem Schlafe ihr Auge. Die Schnauze steckte sie in Provis hohle Hand und leckte sie ihm dankbar und zärtlich.

»No – also no!« rief er den Kameraden an: »Pack s' z'amm. Mach g'schwind!«

Anton griff zu, und im nächsten Augenblicke sprang er auch schon mit drei Hündchen in den Armen aus dem Verschlag, in großen, fröhlichen Sätzen über die Straße, die Uferböschung zum See hinab. Provi folgte ihm eiligst nach; den Hauptspaß, mit anzusehen, wie die Hündchen ertränkt wurden, konnte er sich nicht entgehen lassen.

Es war merkwürdig, daß von nun an die Nachbarschaft der Spitzin dem Provi völlig widerwärtig zu werden begann. Nur schlecht gefügte Bretter trennten seine Schlafstätte von der ihren, und jede Nacht störte sie ihn mit ihrem Gewinsel. Im Kopfe der Alten war ein »Radel laufet« worden, sonst hätte sie doch nach einiger Zeit begriffen: Die Jungen sind fort und nie, nie mehr zu finden, und man muß endlich aufhören, nach ihnen zu suchen. Dieses Mal hörte sie nicht auf. Sie mußte von einem Tag zum andern immer wieder vergessen, daß sie gestern schon alle Winkel umsonst durchsucht hatte. Sie schnüffelte, sie kratzte an der Tür, scharrte ihr bißchen Stroh auseinander und wieder zusammen, kroch hinter den Holzstoß, drängte sich in die Ecke, in der die Werkzeuge lehnten, warf einmal ein paar Schaufeln um und flüchtete voll Entsetzen. Eine Zeitlang war Ruhe, dann trippelte sie wieder herum und suchte und suchte! Und ihr Trippeln weckte ihn, an dem früher die brüllenden Rinderherden vorübergezogen waren, ohne ihn im Schlafe zu stören. Wenn er schlief, schlief er, verschlief Hunger und Müdigkeit; dazu vor allem brauchte er den bombenfesten Schlaf, um den er plötzlich gekommen war, denn jetzt schrak er auf beim Herumgehen und Schnüffeln der Alten. Und kalte Schweißtropfen liefen ihm über die Stirn in der »Baracken«, der den ganzen Tag die Sonne aufs Dach schien und in der es so heiß war, daß es in der Hölle nicht heißer sein kann ... Ob das auch mit rechten Dingen zuging, ob nicht etwas Übernatürliches dahintersteckte? Freilich, der Anton sagt, es gibt nix Übernatürliches. Aber der Allergescheiteste ist der Anton am Ende doch nicht, und

dem Provi ist manchmal sogar vorgekommen, daß er ein
großer Esel ist; was man allerdings nicht sagen darf, ohne
furchtbar gedroschen zu werden von ihm und von seinem
Vater; Provi weiß das aus Erfahrung.

An den Wegemacherleuten hatte er seine Meister gefunden,
die bändigten ihn mit Schlägen und mit Hunger. »Sticht
dich der Hafer?« hieß es bei der geringsten Widersetzlich-
keit, und von der elenden und ungenügenden Ration zog
ihm sein Herr die Hälfte ab.

Jeder andere wäre schon draufgegangen, sagte er sich selbst;
er jedoch wollte nicht draufgehen, er wollte noch viel Zeit
haben, um den Menschen alles Böse, das sie ihm getan hatten, mit Bösem zu vergelten. Daß es auch einige gab, die
ihm Gutes getan hatten, war längst vergessen; und was die
Schoberwirtin betraf, die alte Hex, gegen die hegte er einen
unversöhnlichen Groll. Warum schenkte sie ihm nichts mehr,
sie, die so vieles Geld hatte und so viele Sachen? Sie wußte
gewiß nicht, wohin mit ihrem Reichtum, und gab doch
nichts umsonst, wollte gebeten werden um ein paar armselige Tropfen Milch. Wie sie ihn ansah, wenn er vorüberging ... Förmlich herausfordernd: So bitt doch! – Die Krot,
die! die konnte warten. Einmal hatte sie ihn gar angespro-
chen: »Du schaust aus! Wie der leibhaftige Hunger schaust
aus! Hast noch nicht bitten glernt?« Er rief ihr ein freches
Schimpfwort zu und schritt weiter.

Eine Woche verging. Immer noch hatte die Spitzin sich
nicht ganz beruhigt, suchte und schnüffelte immer noch,
besonders bei Nacht, in ihrem Verschlage herum. So geschah es, daß sie den Provi einst zu besonders unglücklicher
Stunde weckte. Er hatte sich so spät erst auf seiner Lagerstätte aus Hobelspänen und schmutzigem Heu hinstrecken
können, weil er noch, nach beendetem Arbeitstage, die Ziegen, die der Wegemacher ins nächste Dorf verkauft, dorthin hatte treiben müssen. Und auch jetzt kein Ende der
verfluchten Plackerei, nicht wenigstens ein paar Stunden
ungestörten Schlafes? Die Spitzin scharrte und suchte und
suchte, und Provi drohte und polterte mit den Füßen gegen

22

die Bretterwand. Sie gab nach, ein Stück von ihr fiel krachend hinüber ins Bereich der Spitzin. Sie stieß ein erschrockenes Gebell hervor, das Kleine winselte, dann war alles still. »Teixel überanander, wirst jetzt an Fried geben, Rabenviech?« murmelte Provi und legte sich zurecht und zog die Knie bis zum Kinn herauf, denn so »schlief es sich ihm am besten«. Aber just jetzt wollte es mit dem Einschlafen nicht gehen, trotz der Stille und trotz seiner Erschöpfung und trotz seiner Schlaftrunkenheit! Allerlei Gedanken kamen einhergeschlichen, ganz neue Gedanken, nie von ihm gedachte. Ja, die Spitzin war ein Rabenviech mit ihrer Sucherei; wenn aber seine Mutter auch so gewesen wäre wie sie und so rastlos nach ihm gesucht hätte, sie hätte ihn gewiß gefunden; er hatte ja in der Zeitung gestanden, er war angeschlagen gewesen auf dem Bezirksamt. Am End hat sie sich's gar nicht verlangt, ihn zu finden. Die Zigeuner haben ihn am End gar nicht gestohlen, seine Mutter – »die miserabliche!« hat ihn ihnen am End geschenkt, noch draufgezahlt vielleicht, daß sie ihn nehmen … No jo! vielleicht wird sie sich seiner geschämt haben, war vielleicht was Hohes, eine Bauerstochter oder eine Wirtstochter … Verfluchter Kuckuck! wenn sie so eine Wirtstochter gewesen wäre und ihn behalten hätte … Alle Sonntag würde er sich seinen Rausch angetrunken haben, und den Montag hätte er immer blaugemacht und im Wirtshaus und auf der Kegelbahn geraucht, getrunken, gerauft. Ein Götterleben malte er sich aus, als – verfluchtes Rabenviech! die Spitzin nebenan wieder anfing zu stöhnen und zu kratzen und ihn aus seinen Träumen riß, die so wonnig gewesen waren. Voll Zorn richtete er sich auf, nahm ein Scheit Holz, trat über die niedergeworfenen Bretter in den Verschlag des Hundes und führte knirschend wuchtige Schläge gegen den Boden, auf dem die Spitzin im Dunkeln ängstlich umherschoß. Er sah nicht, wohin er traf, er drosch zu nach rechts und nach links, vorwärts und rückwärts, und endlich – da hatte er sie erwischt, da zuckte etwas Weiches, Lebendiges unter seinem wütend geführten Hieb. Ein kurzes, klägliches – ein anklagendes Geheul ertönte, gellte grell und förmlich schmerzhaft an Provis Ohr. Es überrieselte ihn. Was für ein seltsames Geheul das gewesen war ... No jo – das »Rabenvieh« hat jetzt genug, wird Ruh' geben, eine Weile wenigstens.

Er kehrte zu seiner Lagerstätte zurück, kauerte sich zusammen und schlief gleich ein.

Nach ein paar Stunden erwachte er plötzlich. Die aufgehende Sonne sandte einen feurigen Strahl aus, der ihm durch eine Luke in der Tür des Verschlages und durch die Bresche in der Wand leuchtend rot ins Gesicht blitzte. Er öffnete die Augen und stand auf. Die Spitzin kam ihm plötzlich und recht unbehaglich ins Gedächtnis. Wenn er sie »so« totgeschlagen haben sollte heute nachts, würde der Wegemacher, der keinen Eingriff in sein Eigentum duldete, schwerlich versäumen, ihn selbst halb totzuschlagen. No jo! dachte er und fuhr mit den zehn Fingern durch seine staubigen Haare, um die Heustengel zu entfernen, die sich in ihnen verfangen hatten.

Da rührte sich etwas zwischen den Brettern, da kroch es langsam heran. Die Spitzin kroch heran und schleppte ihr Junges im Maul herbei. Sie hatte es an der Nackenhaut gefaßt und benetzte es mit ihrem Blute; denn es floß Blut aus ihrem Maule, ein dünner Faden, die Brust entlang. Zu Provi schleppte sie ihr Junges, legte es vor ihn nieder, drückte es mit ihrer Schnauze an seine nackten Füße und sah zu ihm hinauf.

Und ihr Auge hatte eine Sprache, beredter als jede Sprache, die die schönsten Worte bilden kann. Sie äußerte ein grenzenloses Vertrauen, eine flehentliche Bitte, und man mußte sie verstehen. Wie das Sonnenlicht durch die geschlossenen Lider Provis gedrungen war, so drang der Ausdruck dieses Auges durch den Panzer, der bisher jede gute Regung von der Seele des Buben ferngehalten hatte.

– »Jo! jo!« stahl es sich von seinen Lippen. Er antwortete ihr, die nun hinfiel, zuckte, sich streckte ... die er erschlagen hatte und die gekommen war, ihm sterbend ihr Kleines anzuvertrauen.

24

Provi zitterte. Eine fremde, unwiderstehliche Macht ergriff ihn, umwirbelte ihn wie ein Sturm. Sie warf ihn nieder, sie zwang ihn, sein Gesicht auf das Gesicht des toten Hundes zu pressen und ihn zu küssen und zu liebkosen. Sie war's, die aus ihm schrie: Jo du! Jo du! – du bist a Muatta g'west! Sein Herz wollte ihm zerspringen, ein Strom von wildem Leid, von quälender Pein durchtobte es und erschütterte es bis auf den Grund. Ein vom himmlischen Schmerze des Mitleids erfülltes Kind wand sich schluchzend auf dem Boden und weinte um die alte Spitzin und weinte über ihr Kleines, das sich an seine Mutter drängte und sie anwinselte und Nahrung suchte an dem früher schon so spärlich fließenden und jetzt gänzlich versiegten Quell.

»'s is aus, da kriegst nix mehr«, sagte Provi, nahm das Hündchen in seine Hände, legte es an seine Wange und hauchte es an; es zitterte und winselte gar so kläglich. »Hunger hast, Hunger hast, no jo! no jo!« – Was anfangen mit dem anvertrauten Gut? »Verfluchter Kuckuck«, wenn doch noch die Ziegen da wären! Er würde eine melken, er tät's, trotz der schrecklichen Strafe, die drauf steht. Aber die Ziegen sind fort, und bis ihm jemand im Wegemacherhaus einen Tropfen Milch für einen Hund schenkt, da kann er lang warten. Ins Wasser dermit! wird's heißen, sobald sie hören, daß die Spitzin tot ist.

»Ins Wasser kummst«, sagte er zum Hündchen, das etwas von dem guten Glauben der Mutter an ihn geerbt haben mußte; es schmiegte sich an seinen Hals, saugte an seinem Ohrläppchen und klagte ihm seinen Hunger mit Stöhnen und Wimmern.

No jo! – er wußte schon; nur wie zu helfen wäre, wußte er nicht. Was soll er ihm zu essen geben? Um zu vertragen, was er hinunterschlingt, dazu gehört ein anderer Magen, als so ein Kleines hat ... Aber – verfluchte Krot! – jetzt kam ihm eine Eingebung, jetzt wußte er auf einmal doch, wie zu helfen wäre. Aber – verfluchte Krot! Dieses Mittel konnte er nicht ergreifen – lieber verhungern. Der Entschluß saß eisenfest in seinem oberösterreichischen Dickschädel ... Freilich dämmerte ihm eine Erkenntnis auf, von der er gestern keine Ahnung gehabt hatte — verhungern lassen ist noch etwas ganz anderes als verhungern. Das Kleine gab das Saugen am Ohrläppchen auf; davon wurde es ja doch nicht satt. In stiller Verzweiflung schlossen sich seine kaum dem Lichte geöffneten Augen, und Provi fühlte es nur noch ganz leise zittern.

Gequält und scheu blickte er zur toten Spitzin nieder. Ja, wenn das Junge leben soll, darf man ihm die Mutter nicht erschlagen.

»No, so kumm!« stieß er plötzlich hervor und sprang aus dem Stall in den Verschlag und schritt resolut vorwärts und dem Dorfe zu, biß die Zähne zusammen, daß sie knirschten, sah nicht rechts noch links und ging unaufhaltsam weiter.

Noch rührte sich nichts auf den Feldern, erst in der Nähe der Häuser fing es an, ein wenig lebendig zu werden. Ein schlaftrunkener Bäckerjunge schritt über die Straße zum Brunnen, der Knecht des Lohbauers spannte einen dicken Rotschimmel vor den Streifwagen. Aus dem Tor des Wirtshauses kam die alte Magd, von jeher Provis erklärte Feindin. Voll Mißtrauen beobachtete sie sein Herannahen, erhob die Faust und befahl ihm, sich zu packen. Ihn störte das nicht, er ging an ihr vorbei wie einer, der mit dem Kopfe durch die Wand will. Finster und entschlossen, das Kinn auf die Brust gepreßt, trat er durch die offene Küchentür. Die Wirtin, die am Herde stand, wandte sich ... »Grad zum Fürchten« sah der Bub aus, und seine Stimme klang so rauh und hatte etwas so Schmerzhaftes, als ob ihr Ton die Kehle zerrisse, durch die er gepreßt wurde: »Schoberwirtin, Frau Schoberwirtin, i bitt um a Müalch.«

Das war die Wendung in einem Menschenherzen und in einem Menschenschicksal.

Er laßt die Hand küssen

»So reden Sie denn in Gottes Namen!« sprach die Gräfin, »ich werde Ihnen zuhören; glauben aber – nicht ein Wort.« Der Graf lehnte sich behaglich zurück in seinem großen Lehnsessel: »Und warum nicht?« fragte er.

Sie zuckte leise mit den Achseln: »Vermutlich erfinden Sie nicht überzeugend genug.«

»Ich erfinde gar nicht, ich erinnere mich. Das Gedächtnis ist meine Muse.«

»Eine einseitige, wohldienerische Muse! Sie erinnert sich nur der Dinge, die Ihnen in den Kram passen. Und doch gibt es auf Erden noch manches Interessante und Schöne außer dem – Nihilismus.« Sie hatte ihre Häkelnadel erhoben und das letzte Wort wie einen Schuß gegen ihren alten Verehrer abgefeuert.

Er vernahm es ohne Zucken, strich behaglich seinen weißen Bart und sah die Gräfin beinahe dankbar aus seinen klugen Augen an. »Ich wollte Ihnen etwas von meiner Großmutter erzählen«, sprach er. »Auf dem Wege hierher, mitten im Walde, ist es mir eingefallen.«

Die Gräfin beugte den Kopf über ihre Arbeit und murmelte: »Wird eine Räubergeschichte sein.«

»O nichts weniger! So friedlich wie das Wesen, durch dessen Anblick jene Erinnerung in mir wachgerufen wurde, Mischka IV. nämlich, ein Urenkel des ersten Mischka, der meiner Großmutter Anlaß zu einer kleinen Übereilung gab, die ihr später leid getan haben soll«, sagte der Graf mit etwas affektierter Nachlässigkeit und fuhr dann wieder eifrig fort: »Ein sauberer Heger, mein Mischka, das muß man ihm lassen! Er kriegte aber auch keinen geringen Schrecken, als ich ihm unvermutet in den Weg trat – hatte ihn vorher schon eine Weile beobachtet ... Wie ein Käfersammler schlich er herum, die Augen auf den Boden geheftet, und

was hatte er im Laufe seines Gewehres stecken? Denken Sie:
– ein Büschel Erdbeeren!«

»Sehr hübsch!« versetzte die Gräfin. »Machen Sie sich darauf gefaßt – in Bälde wandern Sie zu mir herüber durch die
Steppe, weil man Ihnen den Wald fortgetragen haben wird.«

»Der Mischka wenigstens verhindert's nicht.«

»Und Sie sehen zu?«

»Und ich sehe zu. Ja, ja, es ist schrecklich. Die Schwäche
liegt mir im Blut – von meinen Vorfahren her.« Er seufzte
ironisch und sah die Gräfin mit einer gewissen Tücke von
der Seite an.

Sie verschluckte ihre Ungeduld, zwang sich zu lächeln und
suchte ihrer Stimme einen möglichst gleichgültigen Ton zu
geben, indem sie sprach: »Wie wär's, wenn Sie noch eine
Tasse Tee trinken und die Schatten Ihrer Ahnen heute einmal unbeschworen lassen würden? Ich hätte mit Ihnen vor
meiner Abreise noch etwas zu besprechen.«

»Ihren Prozeß mit der Gemeinde? – Sie werden ihn gewinnen.«

»Weil ich recht habe.«

»Weil Sie vollkommen recht haben.«

»Machen Sie das den Bauern begreiflich. Raten Sie ihnen,
die Klage zurückzuziehen.«

»Das tun sie nicht.«

»Verbluten sich lieber, tragen lieber den letzten Gulden
zum Advokaten. Und zu welchem Advokaten, guter Gott!
. . . ein ruchloser Rabulist. Dem glauben sie, mir nicht, und
wie mir scheint, Ihnen auch nicht, trotz all Ihrer Populari-
tätshascherei.«

Die Gräfin richtete die hohe Gestalt empor und holte tief
Atem. »Gestehen Sie, daß es für diese Leute, die so töricht
vertrauen und mißtrauen, besser wäre, wenn ihnen die
Wahl ihrer Ratgeber nicht freistände.«

»Besser wär's natürlich! Ein bestellter Ratgeber, und – auch
bestellt – der Glaube an ihn.«

»Torheit!« zürnte die Gräfin.

»Wieso? Sie meinen vielleicht, der Glaube lasse sich nicht

28

bestellen? ... Ich sage Ihnen, wenn ich vor vierzig Jahren meinem Diener eine Anweisung auf ein Dutzend Stockprügel gab und dann den Rat, aufs Amt zu gehen, um sie einzukassieren, nicht einmal im Rausch wäre es ihm eingefallen, daß er etwas Besseres tun könnte als diesen meinen Rat befolgen.«

»Ach, Ihre alten Schnurren! – Und ich, die gehofft hatte, Sie heute ausnahmsweise zu einem vernünftigen Gespräch zu bringen!«

Der alte Herr ergötzte sich eine Weile an ihrem Ärger und sprach dann: »Verzeihen Sie, liebe Freundin. Ich bekenne, Unsinn geschwatzt zu haben. Nein, der Glaube läßt sich nicht bestellen, aber leider der Gehorsam ohne Glauben. Das eben war das Unglück des armen Mischka und so mancher anderer, und deshalb bestehen heutzutage die Leute darauf, wenigstens auf ihre eigene Fasson ins Elend zu kommen.«

Die Gräfin erhob ihre nachtschwarzen, noch immer schönen Augen gegen den Himmel, bevor sie dieselben wieder auf ihre Arbeit senkte und mit einem Seufzer der Resignation sagte: »Die Geschichte Mischkas also!«

»Ich will sie so kurz machen als möglich«, versetzte der Graf, »und mit dem Augenblick beginnen, in dem meine Großmutter zum erstenmal auf ihn aufmerksam wurde. Ein hübscher Bursche muß er gewesen sein; ich besinne mich eines Bildes von ihm, das ein Künstler, der sich einst im Schlosse aufhielt, gezeichnet hatte. Zu meinem Bedauern fand ich es nicht im Nachlaß meines Vaters und weiß doch, daß er es lange aufbewahrt hat, zum Andenken an die Zeiten, in welchen wir noch das jus gladii ausübten.«

»O Gott!« unterbrach ihn die Gräfin, »spielt das jus gladii eine Rolle in Ihrer Geschichte?«

Der Erzähler machte eine Bewegung der höflichen Abwehr und fuhr fort: »Es war bei einem Erntefest und Mischka einer der Kranzträger, und er überreichte den seinen schweigend, aber nicht mit gesenkten Augen, sah vielmehr die hohe Gebieterin ernsthaft und unbefangen an, während ein

Aufseher im Namen der Feldarbeiter die übliche Ansprache
herunterleierte.

Meine Großmutter erkundigte sich nach dem Jungen und
hörte, er sei ein Häuslerssohn, zwanzig Jahre alt, ziemlich
brav, ziemlich fleißig und so still, daß er als Kind für stumm
gegolten hatte, für dummlich galt er noch jetzt. – Warum?
wollte die Herrin wissen; warum galt er für dummlich? ...
Die befragten Dorfweisen senkten die Köpfe, blinzelten einander verstohlen zu und mehr als: ›So – ja eben so‹, und:
›Je nun, wie's schon ist‹, war aus ihnen nicht herauszubrin-
gen.

Nun hatte meine Großmutter einen Kammerdiener, eine
wahre Perle von einem Menschen. Wenn er mit einem Vor-
nehmen sprach, verklärte sich sein Gesicht dergestalt vor
Freude, daß es beinahe leuchtete. Den schickte meine Großmutter anderen Tages zu den Eltern Mischkas mit der Botschaft, ihr Sohn sei vom Feldarbeiter zum Gartenarbeiter
avanciert und habe morgen den neuen Dienst anzutreten.

Der eifrigste von allen Dienern flog hin und her und stand
bald wieder vor seiner Gebieterin. ›Nun‹, fragte diese, ›was
sagen die Alten?‹ Der Kammerdiener schob das rechte, auswärts gedrehte Bein weit vor ...«

»Waren Sie dabei?« fiel die Gräfin ihrem Gaste ins Wort.

»Bei dieser Referenz gerade nicht, aber bei späteren des
edlen Fritz«, erwiderte der Graf, ohne sich irremachen zu
lassen. »Er schob das Bein vor, sank aus Ehrfurcht völlig in
sich zusammen und meldete, die Alten schwämmen in Tränen der Dankbarkeit.

›Und der Mischka?‹

›Oh, der‹ – lautete die devote Antwort, und nun rutschte
das linke Bein mit anmutigem Schwunge vor – ›oh, der –
der laßt die Hand küssen.‹

Daß es einer Tracht väterlicher Prügel bedurft hatte, um
den Burschen zu diesem Handkuß in Gedanken zu bewegen,
verschwieg Fritz. Die Darlegung der Gründe, die Mischka
hatte, die Arbeit im freien Felde der im Garten vorzuzie-
hen, würde sich für Damenohren nicht geschickt haben. –

Genug, Mischka trat die neue Beschäftigung an und versah sie schlecht und recht. ›Wenn er fleißiger wäre, könnt's nicht schaden‹, sagte der Gärtner. Dieselbe Bemerkung machte meine Großmutter, als sie einmal vom Balkon aus zusah, wie die Wiese vor dem Schlosse gemäht wurde. Was ihr noch auffiel, war, daß alle anderen Mäher von Zeit zu Zeit einen Schluck aus einem Fläschchen taten, das sie unter einem Haufen abgelegter Kleider hervorzogen und wieder darin verbargen. Mischka war der einzige, der, diesen Quell der Labung verschmähend, sich aus einem irdenen, im Schatten des Gebüsches aufgestellten Krüglein erquickte. Meine Großmutter rief den Kammerdiener. ›Was haben die Mäher in der Flasche?‹ fragte sie. – ›Branntwein, hochgräfliche Gnaden.‹ – ›Und was hat Mischka in dem Krug?‹

Fritz verdrehte die runden Augen, neigte den Kopf auf die Seite, ganz wie unser alter Papagei, dem er ähnlich sah wie ein Bruder dem anderen, und antwortete schmelzenden Tones: ›Mein Gott, hochgräfliche Gnaden – Wasser!‹

Meine Großmutter wurde sogleich von einer mitleidigen Regung ergriffen und befahl, allen Gartenarbeitern nach vollbrachtem Tagewerk Branntwein zu reichen. ›Dem Mischka auch‹, setzte sie noch eigens hinzu.

Diese Anordnung erregte Jubel. Daß Mischka keinen Branntwein trinken wollte, war einer der Gründe, warum man ihn für dummlich hielt. Jetzt freilich, nachdem die Einladung der Frau Gräfin an ihn ergangen, war's aus mit Wollen und Nichtwollen. Als er in seiner Einfalt sich zu wehren versuchte, ward er Mores gelehrt, zur höchsten Belustigung der Alten und der Jungen. Einige rissen ihn auf den Boden nieder, ein handfester Bursche schob ihm einen Keil zwischen die vor Grimm zusammengebissenen Zähne, ein zweiter setzte ihm das Knie auf die Brust und goß ihm so lange Branntwein ein, bis sein Gesicht so rot und der Ausdruck desselben so furchtbar wurde, daß die übermütigen Quäler sich selbst davor entsetzten. Sie gaben ihm etwas Luft, und gleich hatte er sie mit einer wütenden Anstrengung abgeschüttelt, sprang auf und ballte die Fäuste ... aber plötzlich sanken seine Arme, er taumelte und fiel zu Boden. Da fluchte, stöhnte er, suchte mehrmals vergeblich sich aufzuraffen und schlief endlich auf dem Fleck ein, auf den er hingestürzt war, im Hofe, vor der Scheune, schlief bis zum nächsten Morgen, und als er erwachte, weil ihm die aufgehende Sonne auf die Nase schien, kam just der Knecht vorbei, welcher ihm gestern den Branntwein eingeschüttet hatte. Der wollte schon die Flucht ergreifen, nichts anderes erwartend, als daß Mischka für die gestrige Mißhandlung Rache üben werde. Statt dessen reckt sich der Bursche, sieht den anderen traumselig an und lallt: ›Noch einen Schluck!‹

Sein Abscheu vor dem Branntwein war überwunden.

Bald darauf, an einem Sonntagnachmittag, begab es sich, daß meine Großmutter auf ihrer Spazierfahrt, von einem hübschen Feldweg gelockt, ausstieg und bei Gelegenheit dieser Wanderung eine idyllische Szene belauschte. Sie sah Mischka unter einem Apfelbaum am Feldrain sitzen, ein Kindlein in seinen Armen. Wie er selbst, hatte auch das Kind den Kopf voll dunkelbrauner Löckchen, der wohlgebildete kleine Körper hingegen war von lichtbrauner Farbe, und das armselige Hemdchen, das denselben notdürftig bedeckte, hielt die Mitte zwischen den beiden Schattierungen. Der kleine Balg krähte förmlich vor Vergnügen, sooft ihn Mischka in die Höhe schnellte, stieß mit den Füßchen gegen dessen Brust und suchte ihm mit dem ausgestreckten Zeigefinger in die Augen zu fahren. Und Mischka lachte und schien sich mindestens ebensogut zu unterhalten wie das Bübchen. Dem Treiben der beiden sah ein junges Mädchen zu, auch ein braunes Ding und so zart und zierlich, als ob ihre Wiege am Ganges gestanden hätte. Sie trug über dem geflickten kurzen Rocke eine ebenfalls geflickte Schürze und darin einen kleinen Vorrat aufgelesener Ähren. Nun brach sie eine derselben vom Stiele, schlich sich an Mischka heran und ließ ihm die Ähre zwischen der Haut und dem Hemd ins Genick gleiten. Er schüttelte sich, setzte das Kind auf den Boden und sprang dem Mädchen nach, das leicht und hurtig und ordentlich wie im Tanze vor ihm floh; einmal pfeilgerade, dann wieder einen Garbenschober umkreisend, voll Ängstlichkeit und dabei doch neckend und immer höchst anmutig. Allerdings ist bei unseren Landleuten eine gewisse angeborene Grazie nichts Seltenes, aber diese beiden jungen Geschöpfe gewährten in ihrer harmlosen Lustigkeit ein so angenehmes Schauspiel, daß meine Großmutter es mit wahrem Wohlgefallen genoß. Einen anderen Eindruck brachte hingegen ihr Erscheinen auf Mischka und das Mädchen hervor. Wie versteinert standen beide beim Anblick der Gutsherrin. Er, zuerst gefaßt, neigte sich beinahe bis zur Erde, sie ließ die Schürze samt den Ähren sinken und verbarg das Gesicht in den Händen.

Beim Souper, an welchem, wie an jeder Mahlzeit, der Hofstaat, bestehend aus einigen armen Verwandten und aus den Spitzen der gräflichen Behörden, teilnahm, sagte meine Großmutter zum Herrn Direktor, der neben ihr saß: ›Die Schwester des Mischka, des neuen Gartenarbeiters, scheint mir ein nettes, flinkes Mädchen zu sein, und ich wünsche, es möge für die Kleine ein Posten ausgemittelt werden, an dem sie sich etwas verdienen kann.‹ Der Direktor erwiderte: ›Zu Befehl, hochgräfliche Gnaden, sogleich ... obwohl der Mischka meines Wissens eine Schwester eigentlich gar nicht hat.‹

›Ihres Wissens‹, versetzte meine Großmutter, ›das ist auch etwas, Ihr Wissen! ... Eine Schwester hat Mischka und ein Brüderchen. Ich habe heute alle drei auf dem Felde gesehen.‹

›Hm, hm‹, lautete die ehrerbietige Entgegnung, und der Direktor hielt die Serviette vor den Mund, um den Ton seiner Stimme zu dämpfen, ›es wird wohl – ich bitte um Verzeihung des obszönen Ausdrucks – die Geliebte Mischkas und, mit Respekt zu sagen, ihr Kind gewesen sein.‹«

Der unwilligen Zuhörerin dieser Erzählung wurde es immer schwerer, an sich zu halten, und sie rief nun: »Sie behaupten, daß Sie nicht dabei waren, als diese denkwürdigen Reden gewechselt wurden? Woher wissen Sie denn nicht nur über jedes Wort, sondern auch über jede Miene und Gebärde zu berichten?«

»Ich habe die meisten der Beteiligten gekannt und weiß – ein bißchen Maler, ein bißchen Dichter, wie ich nun einmal bin –, weiß aufs Haar genau, wie sie sich in einer bestimmten Lage benommen und ausgedrückt haben müssen. Glauben Sie Ihrem treuen Berichterstatter, daß meine Großmutter nach der Mitteilung, welche der Direktor ihr gemacht, eine Wallung des Zornes und der Menschenverachtung hatte. Wie gut und fürsorglich für ihre Untertanen sie war, darüber können Sie nach dem bisher Gehörten nicht im Zweifel sein. Im Punkte der Moral jedoch verstand sie nur äußerste Strenge, gegen sich selbst nicht minder als gegen andere. Sie hatte oft erfahren, daß sie bei Männern und Frauen der Sittenverderbnis nicht zu steuern vermöge, der Sittenverderbnis bei halbreifen Geschöpfen jedoch, der mußte ein Zügel angelegt werden können. – Meine Großmutter schickte ihren Kammerdiener wieder zu den Eltern Mischkas. Mit der Liebschaft des Burschen habe es aus zu sein. Das sei eine Schande für so einen Buben, ließ sie sagen, ein solcher Bub habe an andere Dinge zu denken.

Der Mischka, der zu Hause war, als die Botschaft kam, schämte sich in seine Haut hinein . . .«

»Es ist doch stark, daß Sie jetzt gar in der Haut Mischkas stecken wollen!« fuhr die Gräfin höhnisch auf.

»Bis über die Ohren!« entgegnete der Graf, »bis über die Ohren steck ich darin! Ich fühle, als wäre ich es selbst, die Bestürzung und Beschämung, die ihn ergriff. Ich sehe ihn, wie er sich windet in Angst und Verlegenheit, einen scheuen Blick auf Vater und Mutter wirft, die auch nicht wissen, wo ein und aus vor Schrecken, ich höre sein jammervoll klingendes Lachen bei den Worten des Vaters: ›Erbarmen Sie sich, Herr Kammerdiener! Er wird ein Ende machen, das versteht sich, gleich wird er ein Ende machen!‹

Diese Versicherung genügte dem edlen Fritz, er kehrte ins Schloß zurück und berichtete, glücklich über die treffliche Erfüllung seiner Mission, mit den gewohnten Kniebeugungen und dem gewohnten demütigen und freudestrahlenden Ausdruck in seiner Vogelphysiognomie: ›Er laßt die Hand küssen, er wird ein Ende machen.‹«

»Lächerlich!« sagte die Gräfin.

»Höchst lächerlich«, bestätigte der Graf. »Meine gute, vertrauensselige Großmutter hielt die Sache damit für abgetan, dachte auch nicht weiter darüber nach. Sie war sehr in Anspruch genommen durch die Vorbereitungen zu den großen Festen, die alljährlich am zehnten September, ihrem Geburtstage, im Schlosse gefeiert wurden und einen Vor- und Nachtrab von kleinen Festen hatten. Da kam die ganze Nachbarschaft zusammen, und Dejeuners auf dem grünen Teppich der Wiesen, Jagden, Pirutschaden, Soupers bei schönster Waldbeleuchtung, Bälle – und so weiter folgten einander in fröhlicher Reihe ... Man muß gestehen, unsere Alten verstanden Platz einzunehmen und Lärm zu machen in der Welt. Gott weiß, wie langweilig und öde unser heutiges Leben auf dem Schlosse ihnen erscheinen müßte.«

»Sie waren eben große Herren«, entgegnete die Gräfin bitter, »wir sind auf das Land zurückgezogene Armenväter.«

»Und – Armenmütter«, versetzte der Graf mit einer galanten Verneigung, die von derjenigen, der sie galt, nicht eben gnädig aufgenommen wurde. Der Graf aber nahm sich das Mißfallen, das er erregt hatte, keineswegs zu Herzen, sondern spann mit hellem Erzählerbehagen den Faden seiner Geschichte fort: »So groß der Dienertroß im Schlosse auch war, während der Dauer der Festlichkeiten genügte er doch nicht, und es mußten da immer Leute aus dem Dorfe zur Aushilfe requiriert werden. Wie es kam, daß sich gerade dieses Mal auch Mischkas Geliebte unter ihnen befand, weiß ich nicht; genug, es war der Fall, und die beiden Menschen, die einander hätten meiden sollen, wurden im Dienste der Gebieterin noch öfter zusammengeführt, als dies in früheren Tagen bei der gemeinsamen Feldarbeit geschehen war. Er, mit einem Botengang betraut, lief vom Garten in die Küche, sie von der Küche in den Garten – manchmal trafen sie sich auch unterwegs und verweilten plaudernd ein Viertelstündchen . . .«

»Äußerst interessant!« spottete die Gräfin – »wenn man doch nur wüßte, was sie einander gesagt haben.«

»Oh, wie Sie schon neugierig geworden sind! – aber ich verrate Ihnen nur, was unumgänglich zu meiner Geschichte gehört. – Eines Morgens lustwandelte die Schloßfrau mit ihren Gästen im Garten. Zufällig lenkte die Gesellschaft ihre Schritte nach einem selten betretenen Laubgang und gewahrte am Ende desselben ein junges Pärchen, das, aus verschiedenen Richtungen kommend, wie freudig überrascht stehenblieb. Der Bursche, kein anderer als Mischka, nahm das Mädchen rasch in die Arme und küßte es, was es sich ruhig gefallen ließ. Ein schallendes Gelächter brach los – von den Herren und, ich fürchte, auch von einigen der Damen ausgestoßen, die der Zufall zu Zeugen dieses kleinen Auftritts gemacht hatte. Nur meine Großmutter nahm nicht teil an der allgemeinen Heiterkeit. Mischka und seine Geliebte stoben natürlich davon. Der Bursche – man hat es mir erzählt«, kam der Graf scherzend einer voraussichtlichen Einwendung der Gräfin entgegen –, »glaubte in dem Augenblick sein armes Mädchen zu hassen. Am selben Abend jedoch überzeugte er sich des Gegenteils, als er nämlich erfuhr, die Kleine werde mit ihrem Kinde nach einer anderen Herrschaft der Frau Gräfin geschickt; zwei Tagereisen weit für einen Mann, für eine Frau, die noch dazu ein anderthalb Jahre altes Kind mitschleppen mußte, wohl noch einmal soviel. – Mehr als: ›Herrgott! Herrgott! o du lieber Herrgott!‹ sprach Mischka nicht, gebärdete sich wie ein Träumender, begriff nicht, was man von ihm wolle, als es hieß, an die Arbeit gehen – warf plötzlich den Rechen, den ein Gehilfe ihm samt einem erweckenden Rippenstoß verabfolgte, auf den Boden und rannte ins Dorf, nach dem Hüttchen, in dem seine Geliebte bei ihrer kranken Mutter wohnte, das heißt gewohnt hatte, denn nun war es damit vorbei. Die Kleine stand reisefertig am Lager der völlig gelähmten Alten, die ihr nicht einmal zum Abschiedsegen die Hand aufs

Haupt legen konnte und die bitterlich weinte. ›Hört jetzt auf zu weinen‹, sprach die Tochter, ›hört auf, liebe Mutter. Wer soll Euch denn die Tränen abwischen, wenn ich einmal fort bin?‹

Sie trocknete die Wangen ihrer Mutter und dann auch ihre eigenen mit der Schürze, nahm ihr Kind an die Hand und das Bündel mit ihren wenigen Habseligkeiten auf den Rücken und ging ihres Weges an Mischka vorbei und wagte nicht einmal, ihn anzusehen. Er aber folgte ihr von weitem, und als der Knecht, der dafür zu sorgen hatte, daß sie ihre Wanderung auch richtig antrete, sie auf der Straße hinter dem Dorfe verließ, war Mischka bald an ihrer Seite, nahm ihr das Bündel ab, hob das Kind auf den Arm und schritt so neben ihr her.

Die Feldarbeiter, die in der Nähe waren, wunderten sich: ›Was tut er denn, der Tropf? ... Geht er mit? Glaubt er, weil er so dumm ist, daß er nur so mitgehen kann?‹

Bald nachher kam keuchend und schreiend der Vater Mischkas gerannt: ›Oh, ihr lieben Heiligen! Heilige Mutter Gottes! Hab ich mir's doch gedacht – seiner Dirne läuft er nach, bringt uns noch alle ins Unglück ... Mischka! Sohn – mein Junge! ... Nichtsnutz! Teufelsbrut!‹ jammerte und fluchte er abwechselnd.

Als Mischka die Stimme seines Vaters hörte und ihn mit drohend geschwungenem Stocke immer näher herankommen sah, ergriff er die Flucht, zur größten Freude des Knäbleins, das ›Hott! hott!‹ jauchzte. Bald jedoch besann er sich, daß er seine Gefährtin, die ihm nicht so rasch folgen konnte, im Stich gelassen, wandte sich und lief zu ihr zurück. Sie war bereits von seinem Vater erreicht und zu Boden geschlagen worden. Wie wahnsinnig raste der Zornige, schlug drein mit den Füßen und mit dem Stocke und ließ seinen ganzen Grimm über den Sohn an dem wehrlosen Geschöpfe aus.

Mischka warf sich dem Vater entgegen, und ein furchtbares Ringen zwischen den beiden begann, das mit der völligen Niederlage des Schwächeren, des Jüngeren, endete. Windelweich geprügelt, aus einer Stirnwunde blutend, gab er den

Kampf und den Widerstand auf. Der Häusler faßte ihn am Hemdkragen und zerrte ihn mit sich; der armen kleinen Frau aber, die sich inzwischen mühsam aufgerafft hatte, rief er zu: ›Mach fort!‹

Sie gehorchte lautlos, und selbst die Arbeiter auf dem Felde, stumpfes, gleichgültiges Volk, fühlten Mitleid und sahen ihr lange nach, wie sie so dahinwankte mit ihrem Kinde, so hilfsbedürftig und so völlig verlassen.

In der Nähe des Schlosses trafen Mischka und sein Vater den Gärtner, den der Häusler sogleich als ›gnädiger Herr‹ ansprach und flehentlichst ersuchte, nur eine Stunde Geduld zu haben mit seinem Sohne. In einer Stunde werde Mischka gewiß bei der Arbeit sein; jetzt müsse er nur geschwind heimgehen und sich waschen und sein Hemd auch. Der Gärtner fragte: ›Was ist ihm denn? Er ist ja ganz blutig.‹ – ›Nichts ist ihm‹, lautete die Antwort, ›er ist nur von der Leiter gefallen.‹

Mischka hielt das Wort, das sein Vater für ihn gegeben, und war eine Stunde später richtig wieder bei der Arbeit. Am Abend aber ging er ins Wirtshaus und trank sich einen Rausch an, den ersten freiwilligen, war überhaupt seit dem Tage wie verwandelt. Mit dem Vater, der ihn gern versöhnt hätte, denn Mischka war, seitdem er im Schloßgarten Beschäftigung gefunden, ein Kapital geworden, das Zinsen trug, sprach er kein Wort, und von dem Gelde, das er verdiente, brachte er keinen Kreuzer nach Hause. Es wurde teils für Branntwein verausgabt, teils für Unterstützungen, die Mischka der Mutter seiner Geliebten angedeihen ließ; und diese zweite Verwendung des von dem Burschen Erworbenen erschien dem Häusler als der ärgste Frevel, den sein Sohn an ihm begehen konnte. Daß der arme Teufel, der arme Eltern hatte, etwas wegschenkte, an eine Fremde wegschenkte, der Gedanke wurde der Alp des Alten, sein nagender Wurm. – Je wütender der Vater sich gebärdete, desto verstockter zeigte sich der Sohn. Er kam zuletzt gar nicht mehr nach Hause, oder höchstens einmal im geheimen, wenn er den Vater auswärts wußte, um die Mutter zu sehen,

an der ihm das Herz hing. Diese Mutter ...« der Graf
machte eine Pause – »Sie, liebe Freundin, kennen sie, wie
ich sie kenne.«

»Ich soll sie kennen? ... Sie lebt noch?« fragte die Gräfin
ungläubig.

»Sie lebt; nicht im Urbilde zwar, aber in vielfachen Abbil-
dern. Das kleine schwächliche, immer bebende Weiblein mit
dem sanften, vor der Zeit gealterten Gesicht, mit den Be-
wegungen des verprügelten Hundes, das untertänigst in sich
zusammensinkt und zu lächeln versucht, wenn eine so hohe
Dame, wie Sie sind, oder ein so guter Herr, wie ich bin, ihm
einmal zuruft: ›Wie geht's?‹ und in demütigster Freundlich-
keit antwortet: ›Vergelt's Gott – wie's eben kann.‹ – Gut
genug für unsereins, ist seine Meinung, für ein Lasttier in
Menschengestalt. Was dürfte man anders verlangen, und
wenn man's verlangte, wer gäbe es einem? – Du nicht, hohe
Frau, und du nicht, guter Herr ...«

»Weiter, weiter!« sprach die Gräfin. »Sind Sie bald zu
Ende?«

»Bald. – Der Vater Mischkas kam einst zu ungewohnter
Stunde nach der Hütte und fand da seinen Jungen. ›Zur
Mutter also kann er kommen, zu mir nicht‹, schrie er,
schimpfte beide Verräter und Verschwörer und begann
Mischka zu mißhandeln, was sich der gefallen ließ. Als der
Häusler sich jedoch anschickte, auch sein Weib zu züchtigen,
fiel der Bursche ihm in den Arm. Merkwürdig genug, warum just damals? Wenn man ihn gefragt hätte, wie oft er
den Vater die Mutter schlagen sah, hätte er antworten müssen: ›Soviel Jahre, als ich ihrer denke, mit dreihundertfünf-
undsechzig multipliziert, das gibt die Zahl.‹ – Und die ganze
Zeit hindurch hatte er dazu geschwiegen, und heute loderte
beim längst gewohnten Anblick plötzlich ein unbezwing-
licher Zorn in ihm empor. Zum zweiten Male nahm er gegen
den Vater Partei für das schwächere Geschlecht, und dieses
Mal blieb er Sieger. Er scheint aber mehr Entsetzen als
Freude über seinen Triumph empfunden zu haben. Mit
einem heftigen Aufschluchzen rief er dem Vater, der nun

klein beigeben wollte, rief er der weinenden Mutter zu: ›Lebt wohl, mich seht ihr nie wieder!‹ und stürmte davon. Vierzehn Tage lang hofften die Eltern umsonst auf seine Rückkehr, er war und blieb verschwunden. Bis ins Schloß gelangte die Kunde seiner Flucht; meiner Großmutter wurde angezeigt, Mischka habe seinen Vater halbtot geschlagen und sich dann davongemacht. Nun aber war es nach der Verletzung des sechsten Gebotes diejenige des vierten, die von meiner Großmutter am schärfsten verdammt wurde; gegen schlechte und undankbare Kinder kannte sie keine Nachsicht ... Sie befahl, auf den Mischka zu fahnden, sie befahl, seiner habhaft zu werden, um ihn heimzubringen zu exemplarischer Bestrafung.

Ein paarmal war die Sonne auf- und untergegangen, da stand eines Morgens Herr Fritz an der Gartenpforte und blickte auf die Landstraße hinaus. Lau und leise wehte der Wind über die Stoppelfelder, die Atmosphäre war voll feinen Staubes, den die Allverklärerin Sonne durchleuchtete und goldig schimmern ließ. Ihre Strahlen bildeten in dem beweglichen Element reizende kleine Milchstraßen, in denen Milliarden von winzigen Sternchen aufblitzten. Und nun kam durch das flunkernde, tanzende Atomengewimmel eine schwere, graue Wolkensäule, bewegte sich immer näher und rollte endlich so nahe an der Pforte vorbei, daß Fritz deutlich unterscheiden konnte, wen sie umhüllte. Zwei Heidukken waren es und Mischka. Er sah aus, blaß und hohläugig wie der Tod, und wankte beim Gehen. In den Armen trug er sein Kind, das die Händchen um seinen Hals geschlungen, den Kopf auf seine Schulter gelegt hatte und schlief. Fritz öffnete das Tor, schloß sich der kleinen Karawane an, holte rasch einige Erkundigungen ein und schwebte dann, ein Papagei im Taubenfluge, ins Haus, über die Treppe, in den Saal hinein, in welchem meine Großmutter eben die sonnabendliche Ratsversammlung hielt. Der Kammerdiener, von dem Glücksgefühl getragen, das Bedientenseelen beim Überbringen einer neuesten Nachricht zu empfinden pflegen, rundete ausdrucksvoll seine Arme und sprach, vor Wonne fast platzend: ›Der Mischka laßt die Hand küssen. Er ist wieder da.‹

›Wo war er?‹ fragte meine Großmutter.

›Mein Gott, hochgräfliche Gnaden‹ – lispelte Fritz, schlug mehrmals schnell nacheinander mit der Zunge an den Gaumen und blickte die Gebieterin so zärtlich an, als die tiefste, unterwürfigste Knechtschaft es ihm nur irgend erlaubte. ›Wo wird er gewesen sein ... Bei seiner Geliebten. Ja‹, bestätigte er, während die Herrin, empört über diesen frechen Ungehorsam, die Stirn runzelte, ›ja, und gewehrt hat er sich gegen die Heiducken, und dem Janko hat er, ja, beinahe ein Auge ausgeschlagen.‹

Meine Großmutter fuhr auf: ›Ich hätte wirklich Lust, ihn henken zu lassen.‹

Alle Beamten verneigten sich stumm; nur der Oberförster warf nach einigem Zagen die Behauptung hin: ›Hochgräfliche Gnaden werden es aber nicht tun.‹

›Woher weiß Er das?‹ fragte meine Großmutter mit der strengen Herrschermiene, die so vortrefflich wiedergegeben ist auf ihrem Bilde und die mich gruseln macht, wenn ich im Ahnensaal an ihm vorübergehe. ›Daß ich mein Recht über Leben und Tod noch nie ausgeübt habe, bürgt nicht dafür, daß ich es nie ausüben werde.‹

Wieder verneigten sich alle Beamten, wieder trat Schweigen ein, das der Inspektor unterbrach, indem er die Entscheidung der Gebieterin in einer wichtigen Angelegenheit erbat. Erst nach beendigter Konferenz erkundigte er sich gleichsam privatim nach der hohen Verfügung betreffs Mischkas.

Und nun beging meine Großmutter jene Übereilung, von der ich im Anfang sprach.

›Fünfzig Stockprügel‹, lautete ihr rasch gefällter Urteilsspruch; ›gleich heute, es ist ohnehin Samstag.‹

Der Samstag war nämlich zu jener Zeit, deren Sie«, diesem Worte gab der Graf eine besondere, sehr schalkhafte Betonung, »sich unmöglich besinnen können, der Tag der Exekutionen. Da wurde die Bank vor das Amtshaus gestellt ...«

»Weiter, weiter!« sagte die Gräfin, »halten Sie sich nicht auf mit unnötigen Details.«

»Zur Sache denn! – An demselben Samstag sollten die letzten Gäste abreisen, es herrschte große Bewegung im Schlosse, meine Großmutter, mit den Vorbereitungen zu einer Abschiedsüberraschung, die sie den Scheidenden bereiten ließ, beschäftigt, kam spät dazu, Toilette zum Diner zu machen, und trieb ihre Kammerzofen zur Eile an. In diesem allerungünstigsten Momente ließ der Doktor sich anmelden. Er war unter allen Dignitären der Herrin derjenige, der am wenigsten in Gnaden bei ihr stand, verdiente es auch nicht besser, denn einen langweiligeren, schwerfälligeren Pedanten hat es nie gegeben.

Meine Großmutter befahl, ihn abzuweisen, er aber kehrte sich nicht daran, sondern schickte ein zweitesmal und ließ die hochgeborene Frau Gräfin untertänigst um Gehör bitten, er hätte nur ein paar Worte über den Mischka zu sprechen.

›Was will man denn noch mit dem?‹ rief die Gebieterin; ›gebt mir Ruhe, ich habe andere Sorgen.‹

Der zudringliche Arzt entfernte sich murrend.

Die Sorgen aber, von denen meine Großmutter gesprochen hatte, waren nicht etwa frivole, sondern solche, die zu den peinvollsten gehören – Sorgen, für welche Ihnen, liebe Freundin, allerdings das Verständnis und infolgedessen auch das Mitleid fehlt – Poetensorgen.«

»O mein Gott!« sagte die Gräfin unbeschreiblich wegwerfend, und der Erzähler entgegnete: »Verachten Sie's, soviel Sie wollen, meine Großmutter besaß poetisches Talent, und es manifestierte sich deutlich in dem Schäferspiel *Les adieux de Chloë*, das sie gedichtet und den Darstellern selbst einstudiert hatte. Das Stückchen sollte nach der Tafel, die man im Freien abhielt, aufgeführt werden, und der Dichterin, obwohl sie ihres Erfolges ziemlich sicher war, bemächtigte sich, je näher der entscheidende Augenblick kam, eine desto weniger angenehme Unruhe. Beim Dessert, nach einem feierlichen, auf die Frau des Hauses ausgebrachten Toast, gab jene ein Zeichen. Die mit Laub überflochtenen Wände, welche den Einblick in ein aus beschnittenen Buchenhecken gebildetes Halbrund verdeckt hatten, rollten auseinander, und eine improvisierte Bühne wurde sichtbar. Man erblickte die Wohnung der Hirtin Chloë, die mit Rosenblättern bestreute Moosbank, auf der sie schlief, den mit Tragant überzogenen Hausaltar, an dem sie betete, und den mit einem rosafarbigen Band umwundenen Rocken, an dem sie die schneeig weiße Wolle ihrer Lämmchen spann. Als idyllische Schäferin besaß Chloë das Geheimnis dieser Kunst. Nun trat sie selbst aus einem Taxusgange, und hinter ihr schritt im Gefolge, darunter ihr Liebling, der Schäfer Myrtill. Alle trugen Blumen, und in vortrefflichen Alexandrinern teilte nun die zarte Chloë dem aufmerksam lauschenden Publikum mit, dies seien die Blumen der Erinnerung, gepflückt auf dem Felde der Treue und bestimmt, dargebracht zu werden auf dem Altar der Freundschaft. Gleich nach dieser Eröffnung brach ungemessener Jubel im Auditorium los und steigerte sich von Vers zu Vers. Einige Damen, die Racine kannten, erklärten, er könne sich vor meiner Großmutter verstecken, und einige Herren, die ihn nicht kannten, bestätigten es. Sie aber konnte über die Echtheit des Enthusiasmus, den ihre Dichtung erweckte, nicht im Zweifel sein. Die Ovationen dauerten noch fort, als die Herrschaften schon ihre Wagen oder ihre Pferde bestiegen hatten und teils in stattlichen Equipagen, teils in leichten Fuhrwerken, teils auf flinken Rossen aus dem Hoftor rollten oder sprengten.

Die Herrin stand unter dem Portal des Schlosses und winkte den Scheidenden grüßend und für ihre Hochrufe dankend zu. Sie war so friedlich und fröhlich gestimmt, wie dies einem Selbstherrscher, auch des kleinsten Reiches, selten zuteil wird. Da — eben im Begriff, sich ins Haus zurückzuwenden — gewahrte sie ein altes Weiblein, das in respektvoller Entfernung vor den Stufen des Portals kniete. Es hatte den günstigsten Augenblick wahrgenommen und sich durch das offenstehende Tor, im Gewirr und Gedränge unbemerkt, hereingeschlichen. Jetzt erst wurde es von einigen Lakaien erblickt. Sogleich rannten sie, Herrn Fritz an der

Spitze, auf das Weiblein zu, um es gröblich hinwegzuschaffen. Zum allgemeinen Erstaunen jedoch winkte meine Großmutter die dienstfertige Meute ab und befahl zu fragen, wer die Alte sei und was sie wolle. Im nämlichen Moment räusperte sich's hinter der Gebieterin und nieste, und den breitkrempigen Hut in der einen Hand und mit der anderen die Tabaksdose im Busen verbergend, trat der Herr Doktor bedächtig heran: ›Es ist, hm, hm, hochgräfliche Gnaden werden entschuldigen‹, sprach er, ›es ist die Mutter des Mischka.‹

›Schon wieder Mischka, hat das noch immer kein Ende mit dem Mischka? ... Und was will die Alte?‹

›Was wird sie wollen, hochgräfliche Gnaden? Bitten wird sie für ihn wollen, nichts anderes.‹

›Was denn bitten? Da gibt's nichts zu bitten.‹

›Freilich nicht, ich habe es ihr ohnehin gesagt, aber was nutzt's? Sie will doch bitten, hm, hm.‹

›Ganz umsonst, sagen Sie ihr das. Soll ich nicht mehr aus dem Hause treten können, ohne zu sehen, wie die Gartenarbeiter ihre Geliebten embrassieren?‹

Der Doktor räusperte sich, und meine Großmutter fuhr fort: ›Auch hat er seinen Vater halbtot geschlagen.‹

›Hm, hm, er hat ihm eigentlich nichts getan, auch nichts tun wollen, nur abhalten, die Mutter nicht ganz totzuschlagen.‹

›So?‹

›Ja, hochgräfliche Gnaden. Der Vater, hochgräfliche Gnaden, ist ein Mistvieh, hat einen Zahn auf den Mischka, weil der der Mutter seiner Geliebten manchmal ein paar Kreuzer zukommen läßt.‹

›Wem?‹

›Der Mutter seiner Geliebten, hochgräfliche Gnaden, ein erwerbsunfähiges Weib, dem sozusagen die Quellen der Subsistenzmittel abgeschnitten worden sind ... dadurch, daß man die Tochter fortgeschickt hat.‹

›Schon gut, schon gut! ... Mit den häuslichen Angelegenheiten der Leute verschonen Sie mich, Doktor, da mische ich mich nicht hinein.‹

Der Doktor schob mit einer breiten Gebärde den Hut unter den Arm, zog das Taschentuch und schneuzte sich diskret. ›So werde ich also der Alten sagen, daß es nichts ist.‹ Er machte, was die Franzosen une fausse sortie nennen, und setzte hinzu: ›Freilich, hochgräfliche Gnaden, wenn es nur wegen des Vaters wäre ...‹

›Nicht bloß wegen des Vaters, er hat auch dem Janko ein Auge ausgeschlagen.‹

Der Doktor nahm eine wichtige Miene an, zog die Augenbrauen so hoch in die Höhe, daß seine dicke Stirnhaut förmliche Wülste bildete, und sprach: ›Was dieses Auge betrifft, das sitzt fest und wird dem Janko noch gute Dienste leisten, sobald die Sugillation, die sich durch den erhaltenen Faustschlag gebildet hat, aufgesaugt sein wird. Hätte mich auch gewundert, wenn der Mischka imstande gewesen wäre, einen kräftigen Hieb zu führen nach der Behandlung, die er von den Heiducken erfahren hat. Die Heiducken, hochgräfliche Gnaden, haben ihn übel zugerichtet.‹

›Seine Schuld; warum wollte er ihnen nicht gutwillig folgen.‹

›Freilich, freilich, warum wollte er nicht? Vermutlich, weil sie ihn vom Sterbebette seiner Geliebten abgeholt haben – da hat er sich schwer getrennt ... Das Mädchen, hm, hm, war in anderen Umständen, soll vom Vater des Mischka sehr geprügelt worden sein, bevor sie die Wanderung angetreten hat. Und dann – die Wanderung, die weit ist, und die Person, hm, hm, die immer schwach gewesen ist ... kein Wunder, wenn sie am Ziele zusammengebrochen ist.‹

Meine Großmutter vernahm jedes Wort dieser abgebrochenen Sätze, wenn sie sich auch den Anschein zu geben suchte, daß sie ihnen nur eine oberflächliche Aufmerksamkeit schenkte. ›Eine merkwürdige Verkettung von Fatalitäten‹, sprach sie, ›vielleicht eine Strafe des Himmels.‹

›Wohl, wohl‹, nickte der Doktor, dessen Gesicht zwar immer seinen gleichmütigen Ausdruck behielt, sich aber allmählich purpurrot gefärbt hatte. ›Wohl, wohl, des Himmels, und wenn der Himmel sich bereits dreingelegt hat, dürfen hochgräfliche Gnaden ihm vielleicht auch das weitere in der

Sache überlassen ... ich meine nur so!‹ schaltete er, seine vorlaute Schlußfolgerung entschuldigend, ein – ›und dieser Bettlerin‹, er deutete nachlässig auf die Mutter Mischkas, ›huldvollst ihre flehentliche Bitte erfüllen.‹

Die kniende Alte hatte dem Gespräch zu folgen gesucht, sich aber mit keinem Laut daran beteiligt. Ihre Zähne schlugen vor Angst aneinander, und sie sank immer tiefer in sich zusammen.

›Was will sie denn eigentlich?‹ fragte meine Großmutter.

›Um acht Tage Aufschub, hochgräfliche Gnaden, der ihrem Sohne diktierten Strafe untersteht sie sich zu bitten, und ich, hochgräfliche Gnaden, unterstütze das Gesuch, durch dessen Genehmigung der Gerechtigkeit besser Genüge geschähe, als heute der Fall sein kann.‹

›Warum?‹

›Weil der Delinquent in seinem gegenwärtigen Zustande den Vollzug der ganzen Strafe schwerlich aushalten würde.‹

Meine Großmutter machte eine unwillige Bewegung und begann langsam die Stufen des Portals niederzusteigen. Fritz sprang hinzu und wollte sie dabei unterstützen. Sie aber winkte ihn hinweg: ›Geh aufs Amt‹, befahl sie, ›Mischka ist begnadigt.‹

›Ah!‹ stieß der treue Knecht bewundernd hervor und enteilte, während der Doktor bedächtig die Uhr aus der Tasche zog und leise vor sich hin brummte: ›Hm, hm, es wird noch Zeit sein, die Exekution dürfte eben begonnen haben.‹

Das Wort ›begnadigt‹ war von der Alten verstanden worden; ein Gewinsel der Rührung, des Entzückens drang von ihren Lippen, sie fiel nieder und drückte, als die Herrin näher trat, das Gesicht auf die Erde, als ob sie sich vor soviel Größe und Hoheit dem Boden förmlich gleichzumachen suche.

Der Blick meiner Großmutter glitt mit einer gewissen Scheu über dieses Bild verkörperter Demut: ›Steh auf‹, sagte sie und zuckte zusammen und horchte ... und alle Anwesenden horchten erschaudernd, die einen starr, die andern mit dem albernen Lachen des Entsetzens. Aus der Gegend des Amts-

hauses hatten die Lüfte einen gräßlichen Schrei herüber-
getragen. Er schien ein Echo geweckt zu haben in der Brust
des alten Weibleins, denn es erhob stöhnend den Kopf und
murmelte ein Gebet.

›Nun?‹ fragte einige Minuten später meine Großmutter den
atemlos herbeistürzenden Fritz: ›Hast du's bestellt?‹

›Zu dienen‹, antwortete Fritz mit seinem süßesten Lächeln:
›Er läßt die Hand küssen, er ist schon tot.‹« –

»Fürchterlich!« rief die Gräfin aus, »und das nennen Sie
eine friedliche Geschichte?«

»Verzeihen Sie die Kriegslist, Sie hätten mich ja sonst nicht
angehört«, erwiderte der Graf. »Aber vielleicht begreifen
Sie jetzt, warum ich den sanftmütigen Nachkommen Mischkas nicht aus dem Dienst jage, obwohl er meine Interessen
eigentlich recht nachlässig vertritt.«

Erinnerungen an Marie von Ebner-Eschenbach

Zdißlawitz ist ein kleines mährisches Dorf, an dessen Rande ein altes Schloß inmitten eines schattigen, verträumten Parkes liegt. Hier hat Marie von Ebner-Eschenbach am 13. September 1830 das Licht der Welt erblickt, und mir, als dem Sohn ihres ältesten Bruders, wurde, an dem gleichen Tag, allerdings um 53 Jahre später, dasselbe Los zuteil. So kam es, daß ich zwar unter ihren Augen aufwuchs, sie aber bereits eine ziemlich bejahrte Frau war, als sie schärfer in mein Bewußtsein trat. Und zwar geschah dies folgendermaßen:

Wenn ich an meine Kindheit zurückdenke, sehe ich mich als etwa sechsjährigen Jungen auf meinen Fußspitzen stehen, um irgend etwas zu Gesicht zu bekommen, das mich nichts anging. Zumal Tante Maries Zimmer erregten meine Neugierde. Sobald man sie zum Gutenmorgen- oder Gutenachtsagen betrat, war nichts Außergewöhnliches an ihnen zu bemerken. Was aber ging dort in der Zwischenzeit vor, da es strenge verboten war, ihnen unaufgefordert einen Besuch abzustatten? – »Tante Marie arbeitet«, hieß es dann, »und darf nicht gestört werden!« Worin bestand es wohl, dieses geheimnisvolle Arbeiten, das keine Störung vertrug und sich immer hinter verschlossenen Türen abspielte? Etwas sehr Wichtiges mußte es sein. Denn Papa selbst, der große, strenge Papa, blieb horchend davor stehen, bevor er eintrat, und tat es nie, ohne vorher angeklopft zu haben. Alles dies veranlaßte mich schließlich, einen gewaltsamen Versuch zu unternehmen, um der Wahrheit auf die Spur zu kommen.

Einmal, ziemlich früh am Morgen, schlich ich aus meinem Zimmer und gelangte unbemerkt zu den Wohnräumen Tante Maries. Einige Augenblicke hindurch zögerte ich noch. Dann aber besann ich mich nicht mehr lange, sondern riß die Türe auf und trat ein.

Tante Marie hatte an ihrem Schreibtische gesessen. Doch

mußte ich sie erschreckt haben, denn sie frug mich recht un-
wirsch, was ich denn wolle. Ich aber sah mich enttäuscht im
Zimmer um und frug selbst, anstatt zu antworten: »Wann
tut Sie denn etwas?« – Da glitt ein Lächeln über ihr Gesicht,
und sie begann es mir zu erklären. Ich aber verstand nicht,
oder vielmehr, ich wollte nicht verstehen, weil ich alles, was
sie da vorbrachte, für bloße Ausflüchte hielt, die den Zweck
verfolgten, mir das eigentlich Wissenswerte zu verbergen.
Doch sollte es nicht mehr lange dauern, bis ich in dieser Hinsicht eines Besseren belehrt wurde. –

Eines Tages verreisten meine Eltern, und ich setzte es mir in
den Kopf, daß ich während ihrer Abwesenheit der Haus-
herr sei. Da man mich durch gütliches Zureden von dieser
Ansicht abzubringen suchte, beschloß ich, einen sinnfälligen
Beweis dafür zu liefern. – Bei uns wurde immer um 1 Uhr
zu Mittag gegessen. Nun hatte ich die Beobachtung gemacht,
daß auf meinen Vater und auf meine Mutter gewartet
wurde, wenn sie sich zufällig verspäteten, und daß niemand
bei Tische Platz nahm, bevor sie kamen. Einmal also, als es
1 Uhr schlug, verbarg ich mich, um nicht zum Speisen ge-
führt zu werden, und begab mich in ein Fremdenzimmer,
das gerade unbewohnt war. Dort setzte ich mich in einen
Lehnstuhl und wartete. Bald merkte ich denn auch, daß ich
gesucht wurde. Ich hörte Schritte und Stimmen, die meinen
Namen riefen, rührte mich aber nicht. – Endlich wurde mir
die Zeit doch zu lang, und als jemand an der Türe meines
Versteckes vorüberging, blieb ich zwar sitzen wie bisher,
aber ich hustete. – Zufällig war es gerade Tante Marie, die
nun eintrat und mich frug, was ich denn hier treibe. – Da
gab ich ihr, im Bewußtsein meines Sieges, so nachlässig ich
nur konnte, zur Antwort: »Nichts! Ich lasse warten!«

Da aber habe ich sie, zum ersten Male in meinem Leben,
ernstlich böse gesehen. Mit einer Strenge, deren ich sie nicht
für fähig gehalten hätte, rief sie mir zu: »Wer bist du
denn, daß du alte Leute auf dich warten lassen willst? Ein
Knirps, der von der Liebe seiner Eltern lebt und nichts
wäre ohne diese Liebe.« – Für diesmal war ich kleinlaut ge-

worden und schlich davon. Im Innern aber war mein Trotz erwacht. Ich wollte schon zeigen, wer ich sei, und gerade Tante Marie sollte mich kennenlernen. Fühlen sollte sie's! Deshalb benahm ich mich von nun an ihr gegenüber sehr zurückhaltend und kühl. Wenn sie mit mir sprach, dachte ich mir meinen Teil, und gar, wenn sie etwas an mir rügte. Anlaß dazu gab ich ihr mehr als genug. Weil sie selbst überaus bescheiden war und sich immer im Hintergrunde hielt, suchte ich mich, ihr zum Trotz, vorzudrängen, wo es nur anging. Sooft es mir gelang, nahm ich bei Tisch das Beste für mich und fand es ganz natürlich, daß die andern, die nach mir kamen, sich bescheiden mußten. So trieb ich vielerlei Unarten, und je mehr Tante Marie sie mißbilligte, je mehr sie, im Verein mit meinen Eltern, mit wahrer Engelsgeduld mich davon abzubringen suchte, um so fester und stütziger hielt ich daran fest. Außerdem hatte ich oft genug Gelegenheit gehabt, ihre Nächstenliebe wahrzunehmen. Mit allen Armen im Dorf lebte sie, kannte jeden von ihnen, seine Wünsche, seine Hoffnungen, seine Sorgen, und half, sooft es nur anging. Deshalb begann ich, neuerdings ihr zum Trotz, ein hochfahrendes Benehmen zur Schau zu tragen und mir einzubilden, daß ich etwas viel Besseres sei als diese Leute, mit denen sich Tante Marie zwar auf eine Stufe stellte, die aber doch nur einfache Bauern waren und in ärmlichen Hütten wohnten, während ich in einem Schlosse aufwuchs. Infolgedessen sah ich, so geringschätzig als ich es nur vermochte, auf sie herab und blieb auch in dieser Hinsicht unverbesserlich. – So war ich sieben Jahre alt geworden, als ich mich einmal in meiner ganzen Herrlichkeit zu zeigen beschloß.

Unsere damalige Köchin war eine Frau, die Kindern gegenüber ein weiches Herz gehabt haben muß. Denn sie ließ sich tausenderlei Ungezogenheiten von mir gefallen, was ich mit meinem Selbstbewußtsein in Verbindung brachte und für den mir ihrerseits schuldigen Respekt hielt. Infolgedessen erwählte ich ihr Bereich, um die Sache auf die Spitze zu treiben und mir einen augenfälligen Beweis meiner Macht zu verschaffen, drang eines Tages in die Küche ein und begann, dort alles in Unordnung zu bringen, was mir gerade unter die Hände kam.

Die Arme hat es lange ertragen. Endlich riß aber auch ihr die Geduld. Mit einem Ruck, der ihre schmächtige Gestalt erzittern ließ, trat sie vom Herd zurück und wies mir, mit einer geradezu majestätischen Gebärde, die Tür. – Da muß ich wohl einige Augenblicke hindurch starr vor Staunen gewesen sein. Dann aber streckte ich mich, so hoch ich nur konnte, und rief in voller Entrüstung: »Sie ist ja eine gemeine Person!«

Die Wirkung dieser Worte war überraschend. Ohne sich weiter um mich zu kümmern, band sie sich eine reine Schürze um, rückte ihr Häubchen zurecht und sprach, als sie damit zu Ende war: »So! Jetzt gehe ich zur Mama!«

Da habe ich einen Fall getan, der um so tiefer war, je höher ich vorhin gestanden hatte. Die Angst vor dem nun herannahenden Strafgericht blies meinen Stolz hinweg wie Spreu. Ich vergaß mein Vorhaben, den Beweis, den ich mir schuldig zu sein glaubte, sowie die ganze Würde meiner Person und rannte der guten Alten nach, die mir bereits ein Stück Weges voran war, klammerte mich an sie, hielt mich mit beiden Händen an ihren Röcken fest und suchte sie mit aller Kraft zum Stehen zu bringen. Doch vergebens! Sie war unerbittlich geworden und schleppte mich, da ich nicht losließ, wie einen Ball hinter sich her.

So trafen wir Mama, die zufällig gerade in Tante Maries Begleitung war. Nun erhielt ich meine Strafe, sah aber mein Unrecht ganz und gar nicht ein, sondern blieb genau derselbe, der ich war – bis ich eines Tages erfuhr, Tante Marie habe aus Anlaß dieser Begebenheit etwas geschrieben, das sie mir demnächst selbst vorlesen wolle – weil es mir meine Fehler vor Augen führen und mich bessern würde. Hoffentlich! – Bald wurde ich denn auch zu ihr gerufen, mußte zuhören, und sie las. –

Anfangs interessierte es mich gar nicht, was ich da vorgesetzt bekam. Es war das *Hirzepinzchen*. Die Geschichte eines kleinen Jungen, der sehr keck und selbstbewußt war und die Liebe seiner Umgebung als etwas Selbstverständliches hinnahm, sie schlecht vergalt und in seinem Übermut schließlich sogar eine leibhaftige Fee als »gemeine Person« bezeichnete. Da merkte ich auf einmal, das war ja doch ich ... ich selbst ... und so lebendig geschildert, daß ich mich vor mir sah wie in einem Spiegel. Und nun lauschte ich ... lauschte gespannt und immer gespannter. Und als das Hirzepinzchen verzaubert war und die Fee die Liebe zu ihm aus allen Herzen getilgt hatte, da verstand ich auf einmal, daß es wirklich nur die Liebe der andern gewesen war, die meinem Leben Gehalt verliehen hatte. Und als das Hirzepinzchen das Gut, das es sich verscherzt hatte, durch Arbeit zurückgewinnen mußte und tatsächlich auch zurückgewann, beschloß ich, mich den Weg führen zu lassen, den Tante Marie mir da wies. Ich hatte zum erstenmal eine Kraft und eine Überlegenheit verspürt, der ich mich unterwarf. Als ich demnach, an dem nächsten darauffolgenden Weihnachtsabend, schöne vergoldete Äpfel und Nüsse zum Geschenk bekam, habe ich zwar einen schweren inneren Kampf gekämpft, jedoch diese Äpfel und Nüsse Tante Marie, deren Leben Nächstenliebe war, in der Absicht, es ihr gleichzutun, mit den Worten überbracht: »Da! Nimm Sie! Damit Sie auch etwas hat!« Allerdings muß ich meine Großmut bedauert haben. Denn ich fügte unmittelbar hinzu: »Essen kann Sie sie auch. Aber schad wär's halt!« Doch schloß mich Tante Marie dafür in ihre Arme. Und diesmal war ich stolz darauf, ihr Gefallen erregt zu haben. Ich wurde es aber noch weit mehr, als ich erfuhr, sie hätte diese meine Äußerung in einer Novelle verwertet und mich darin so brav geschildert, wie ich nun werden müsse: in *Fräulein Susannes Weihnachtsabend*.

Etwa um diese Zeit war es, daß ich einen mir bald sehr lieben Spielkameraden erhielt: einen Hund. Und zwar denjenigen, aus dem nicht lange danach der »Krambambuli« werden sollte.

In Zdißlawitz erschienen ab und zu in größeren oder klei-

neren Gruppen umherziehende Zigeuner. Sie blieben dann
während einiger Tage an Ort und Stelle, schlugen irgendwo
in der Nähe des Dorfes ihr Lager auf, zogen bettelnd von
Haus zu Haus und kochten sich des Abends an einem Feuer,
das sie zwischen aufgeschichteten Steinen unterhielten, ihre
Mahlzeit. Da geschah es einmal, daß ein junger, verhunger-
ter, bis auf die Knochen abgemagerter Hund, den eine solche
Gruppe mit sich führte, seinem Besitzer ein Stück Fleisch
buchstäblich vom Munde wegstahl, worüber jener in eine so
maßlose Wut geriet, daß er mit einem faustdicken Knüppel,
den er gerade zur Hand hatte, wie wahnsinnig auf das Tier
losschlug. Wahrscheinlich hätte er es zu Tode geprügelt,
wäre nicht zufällig mein Vater dazugekommen. Eine solche
Tierquälerei sehen und ihr ein Ende bereiten war für ihn
eine Selbstverständlichkeit. Der Zigeuner wollte zuerst auf-
fahren, besann sich aber bald eines Besseren, wurde unter-
würfig, ja kriecherisch, stieß jedoch weiterhin einen ganzen
Schwall von Verwünschungen gegen den Hund aus, so daß
mein Vater beschloß, ihn dem Machtbereich seines Peinigers
zu entziehen, und diesem eine nicht unbeträchtliche Summe
für ihn anbot. Der Zigeuner ging sofort auf den Vorschlag
ein, holte diensteifrig einen Strick, den er dem noch immer
leise wimmernden Tier um den Hals band. Doch traf es
nicht nur keine Anstalten, meinem Vater, der nun den Weg
heimwärts einschlagen wollte, zu folgen, sondern setzte
allen derartigen Absichten, obwohl der Zigeuner mit wohl-
gezielten Fußtritten kräftigst nachhalf, einen so verzweifel-
ten Widerstand entgegen, daß nichts übrigblieb, als es durch
jenen persönlich an seinen neuen Bestimmungsort führen zu
lassen. Dort wurde es in einen leerstehenden Verschlag ge-
sperrt, nachdem man es mit Wasser und Nahrung hinläng-
lich versorgt hatte, hoffend, daß sein Widerstand am nächsten Morgen gebrochen sein würde. Doch auch diese Berech-
nung erwies sich als falsch. Volle 24 Stunden hindurch lief
es wie gejagt, ohne auch nur für eine Sekunde darin inne-
zuhalten, die Nase dicht am Boden, im Kreise umher. Nur
wenn jemand in seine Nähe kam, zog es sich in die äußerste

Ecke des Raumes zurück. Dann sträubte sich sein Fell, seine Augen bekamen einen rötlichen, blutunterlaufenen Glanz und es ließ mit gefletschten Zähnen ein so wütendes Knurren hören, daß jeder Versuch, sich ihm zu nähern, aufgegeben werden mußte.

Alles dies hatte Tante Marie beobachtet und daraufhin ihren *Krambambuli* verfaßt. Aber noch während sie daran schrieb, vollzog sich mit dessen Urbild die große Wandlung. Zwar dauerte es mehr als volle drei Wochen, ehe sich »Treff« – diesen Namen erhielt er nun – mit seinem neuen Los abgefunden hatte. Doch was wurde er dann für ein Hund! Schön? Das waren andere auch. Was ihn auszeichnete, war eine fast beispiellose Liebe zu meinem Vater. Als hätte er begriffen, daß er diesem seine Rettung verdankte, ließ er sich, sobald er dessen Stimme nur hörte, nicht mehr halten. Ich konnte dann rufen und schreien, soviel ich wollte. Von dem Augenblicke an war ich für ihn überhaupt nicht mehr vorhanden.

So war etwa ein Jahr vergangen und der *Krambambuli* längst erschienen, als, wie inzwischen schon mehrmals, neuerdings Zigeuner ins Dorf kamen. Während ihnen Treff aber sonst nicht die geringste Beachtung geschenkt hatte, geriet er diesmal, sobald er das Rasseln ihrer Gefährte von der am Gartenzaun vorbeiführenden Landstraße her vernahm, in die lebhafteste Unruhe. Ab und zu dumpf aufheulend und unausgesetzt Witterung einziehend, begann er wie suchend hin und her zu laufen, so daß ihn mein Vater, dem der Zusammenhang erst nachträglich, leider viel zu spät, klarwurde, für erkrankt hielt und ihn zu seinem gewohnten Zimmerplatz führte, wo er sich auch sofort zusammenrollte und zitternd, wie von Fieber geschüttelt, liegen blieb.

So verging der Tag, und es dunkelte bereits, als mein Vater den gewohnten abendlichen Rundgang durch den Garten unternahm, bei dem ihn Treff regelmäßig zu begleiten pflegte. Diesmal schien das Tier aber noch nicht zu wissen, was es nun beginnen sollte, denn es blieb unbeweglich an seinem Platz, und erst als mein Vater die Türe fast schon hinter sich geschlossen hatte, folgte es ihm nach. Aber nicht freudig wie sonst, sondern nur ganz langsam und mit eingezogenem Schweif. Ins Freie gelangt, sprang es plötzlich und unvermittelt, wie von Liebe und Anhänglichkeit überwältigt, aufheulend an ihm empor. Dann stutzte es, horchte irgendwohin in die Ferne, heulte noch einmal dumpf auf und verschwand im Dunkeln.

Damit war Treffs Schicksal besiegelt, denn er ist nicht mehr zurückgekommen. Was sich mit ihm zugetragen hat, ist unaufgeklärt geblieben. Fest steht nur, daß sich unter den diesmal erschienenen Zigeunern tatsächlich sein früherer Besitzer befand, der es aber rundweg ableugnete, ihn wieder zu Gesicht bekommen zu haben. Beweisen ließ es sich demnach nicht. Doch ist es so gut wie sicher, daß er jenem als willkommene Speise gedient hatte, womit seine Treue in einer erschütternden Weise belohnt wurde. Gleichzeitig wird damit auch die Lebenswahrheit *Krambambulis* offenbar ...

Wie Tante Marie es in dieser Erzählung verstanden hatte, sich in eine Tierseele hineinzudenken, das beeindruckte mich schon damals. Aber freilich, als ich fähig wurde, ihren Wert ganz zu begreifen, war sie alt geworden, sehr alt, blieb aber geistig frisch und regsam wie nur je. Immer gleich schaffensfreudig führte sie ihr gewohntes Leben, stand nach wie vor lange vor Morgengrauen auf, um den Tag über zu arbeiten. Nur des Abends gönnte sie sich Ruhe und freute sich, wenn man zu ihr kam und sie zerstreute. — Im Gespräch wußte sie den geringfügigsten Dingen Bedeutung zu geben, so daß der Umgang mit ihr zu einem nie versiegenden Quell der Anregung wurde. Ihr Urteil war immer treffend und immer gerecht und doch verklärt von einer Milde, die alles entschuldigte und alles verzieh. Nur eines nicht: den Eigennutz! — Von sich selbst sprach sie fast nie, oder, wenn sie es doch tat, ungern und mit einer derartigen Bescheidenheit, daß sie sich buchstäblich verkleinerte. Ab und zu erzählte sie dann, wie schwer es ihr geworden war, sich durchzusetzen, wie lange ihre Arbeiten von Verleger zu

Verleger wandern mußten, bevor einer sich ihrer erbarmte, und wie spät sie, ungefähr schon sechzigjährig, ihre ersten Erfolge errungen hatte. Dann aber vergaß sie niemals hinzuzufügen, daß sie die Anerkennung, die sie jetzt genieße, in dem Umfange, wie sie ihr zuteil geworden sei, nicht verdiene. Dabei blieb sie, sosehr man auch widersprach, und nahm alle Ehrungen mit einer Dankbarkeit hin, als sei sie ihrer nicht wert. Doch fiel ihr das Schreiben selbst keineswegs leicht. Sie gehörte zu jenen Schriftstellern, die nie zufrieden mit sich sind und immer meinen, eine noch unfertige Arbeit aus der Hand gegeben zu haben. In diesem Zusammenhange erinnere ich mich an eine Begebenheit, die eine davon so grundverschiedene Geistesrichtung verrät, daß sich die entsprechenden Rückschlüsse zwangsläufig ergeben.

»On a ses ennuyeux comme on a ses pauvres«, hat irgendein Franzose gesagt. Für Tante Marie verkörperten sich diese »ennuyeux«, so etwa um die Jahrhundertwende, in der Person einer ›Kollegin‹, deren Name hier verschwiegen sein soll, weil sie es verstand, alles, was ihr an Talent fehlte, durch Selbstbewußtsein und Zudringlichkeit zu ersetzen, so daß es ihr schließlich gelungen war, sich einen, wenn auch nicht allzu weit reichenden kleinen Ruhm zu verschaffen. Natürlich hatte sie sich auch an Tante Marie herangemacht, die sich ihrer nicht zu erwehren vermochte, so daß sie jener schließlich sogar ziemlich regelmäßig Besuche abstattete. Anläßlich eines solchen Besuches frug sie einmal: »Wie lange haben Sie eigentlich zu Ihren *Aphorismen* gebraucht?« Und als Tante Marie nach kurzem Nachdenken erklärte: »Annähernd 35 Jahre«, entgegnete sie stolz und von oben herab, mit einem Klang von Geringschätzung in der Stimme: »Merkwürdig! Wenn ich mich zu etwas Derartigem hinsetzen würde« – hinsetzen! dieses Wort gebrauchte sie, »wäre ich in 8 Tagen damit fertig.«

Nun, sie hat sich nicht dazu »hingesetzt«. Hätte sie es aber auch getan, dürfte die Wirkung keine allzu nachhaltige gewesen sein, wogegen ich heute noch so manchen kenne, dem Tante Maries *Aphorismen* zu wahren Lebensführern ge-

worden sind, und während des Ersten Weltkrieges traf ich
sogar draußen, im Feld, Soldaten, die das Büchlein mit sich
führten. Ein beredteres Zeugnis für dessen Wert läßt sich
wohl kaum mehr ausstellen.

In unverminderter geistiger und körperlicher Frische hatte
Tante Marie ihr 86. Lebensjahr erreicht, als sie im März
1916 plötzlich erkrankte. Kurz vorher hatte sie ihr letztes
Werk, das sie selbst als ihr letztes bezeichnete, *Meine Erinnerungen an Grillparzer. Aus einem zeitlosen Tagebuch,*
dem Druck übergeben und dabei den Wunsch ausgespro-
chen, sein Erscheinen noch zu erleben. Die Erfüllung dieses
Wunsches wurde ihr zuteil, so daß es ihr vergönnt war,
Anfang und Ende ihrer Bahn zu überschauen. Am 12. des
genannten Monats starb sie, bei vollem Bewußtsein, nachdem sie von allen, die ihr nahestanden, Abschied genommen hatte, aufrecht in ihren Kissen, mit einem klaren, in
die Ewigkeit gerichteten Blick. –

Was aber Zdißlawitz betrifft, an dem sie mit allen Fasern
ihres Herzens hing und dessen Bewohner sie zu vielen ihrer
Erzählungen angeregt haben, so daß es sich aus ihrem
künstlerischen Gesamtbild nicht wegdenken läßt, so ist die
Zeit darüber hinweggegangen.

Der verträumte Park, mit seinen zum Teil uralten Bäumen,
umgibt das Schloß zwar immer noch, und vor dessen Ein-
gang plätschert nach wie vor leise ein Springbrunnen. Dennoch ist das Schloß kein Schloß mehr. Im Jahre 1945 wurde
es, im Zuge der Beschlagnahme des gesamten deutschen
Besitzes in der Tschechoslowakei, zum »Kulturhaus der Gemeinde« erklärt und dient seither der Abhaltung von Vor-
trägen und politischen Schulungen. Die gesamte Innenein-
richtung ist im Wege einer Versteigerung an die Meistbie-
tenden vergeben worden. Mit Ausnahme der Bibliothek!
Denn da diese größtenteils nur deutsche Bücher enthielt,
wurden sie auf offene Lastwagen geladen und kurzerhand
einer Papiermühle als Makulatur zugeführt, was sehr zu
bedauern ist. Denn diese Bibliothek war nicht nur an und
für sich stattlich. Tante Marie hatte es sich zur Gewohnheit

gemacht, alle ihr von auswärts zugesandten Bücher in ihr zu hinterlegen. Und da sie mit allen Dichtern und Schriftstellern ihrer Zeit zum mindesten in brieflichem Verkehr stand – darunter mit keinen Geringeren als Grillparzer, Gottfried Keller, Gerhart Hauptmann –, war hier eine Sammlung von Widmungsexemplaren vorhanden, die sich sehen lassen durfte. Nun aber gibt es im Bereiche des Zdißlawitzer Schlosses nichts mehr, das heute noch an Tante Marie erinnern könnte, außer einer Lindenallee, die quer durch den Park führt und der sie sowohl in ihren *Kinderjahren* wie in ihrem *Zeitlosen Tagebuch* ein wahrhaft zeitloses Denkmal gesetzt hat.

Franz Dubsky

Anmerkungen

3,9   *vazieren*, oberd., veraltet für (dienst)frei haben, unbesetzt sein, leer stehen; von lat. vacare, vgl. auch ›vakant‹, ›Vakanz‹ u. ä.

3,24 *Stutzen*, Stutzbüchse, Stutzer, seit dem 18. Jh. oberd. für kurzes Gewehr; wörtliche Bedeutung: Stumpf, verkürztes Ding.

4,8   *Kondition*, hier: körperliche Verfassung, Leistungsfähigkeit, Zustand, Beschaffenheit; von lat. conditio.

4,19 *Piedestal*, lat., germ., it.-frz., Fußgestell, Sockel für Figuren und Vasen; frz. pied, it. piede: Fuß, lat.-it. stare: stehen.

5,32 *Dilemma*, griech.-lat., Wahl zwischen zwei (unangenehmen) Dingen, Zwangslage; lat. dilaminare: entzweispalten.

6,35 *Tarock*, Siebenkönigsspiel mit 78 Karten für drei Spieler, im Deutschen seit dem 18. Jh., aus it. tarocco übernommen.

7,3   *präsent*, lat.-frz., anwesend, gegenwärtig.

7,13 *Heger*, Hüter eines Geheges, Waldaufseher; mhd., nhd. hegen: bewahren, pflegen.

8,11 *Rudimente*, Anfangsgründe, auch Bruchstücke, Reste; lat. rudimentum: der erste Unterricht, erste Versuch.

8,18 *Lindenrondell*, Rondell, Rundell: Rundteil, Rundbeet; frz. rond,-e: rund.

9,18 f. *Hinterlader*, Feuerwaffe, die durch die hintere Öffnung des Laufs geladen wird.

10,11 *spintisieren*, neulat., umgangssprachlich für grübeln, ausklügeln, Unsinniges denken oder reden; Anfang des 16. Jh.s, vermutlich Weiterbildung zu spinnen.

10,15 *recte*, lat., richtig, recht, wohl.

10,21 *Gendarmerie*, frz., seit dem 19. Jh. Bezeichnung für Polizei in Landbezirken, Landjägerei; ursprünglich schwergepanzerte Reiter, dann Reiterregiment (besonders in Preußen).

11,25 *Juchtenriemen*, Juchten aus poln. jucht oder russ. juht', gegerbtes Rind- oder Kalbleder, mit Birkenteeröl getränkt.

11,26 *Passion*, mhd. passie, passiōn, Leiden(sgeschichte) Christi; aus spätlat. passiō: Leiden, Erdulden, Krankheit. Seit dem 17. Jh. auch jüngere Bedeutung über frz. passion: Leidenschaft, Vorliebe, Liebhaberei. Hier in diesem Sinne gebraucht.

13,12 *Deserteur*, frz., Fahnenflüchtiger, Überläufer; lat. deserere: verlassen, aufgeben, im Stich lassen.

13,12 *Kalfakter*, um 1500 aus lat. calefactor: Warmmacher, Einheizer, später allgemein Aufwärter, durch Bedeutungsverschlechterung auch: Streber, der sich zu niederen Diensten drängt; Schmeichler, Zwischenträger.

13,12 f. *Kanaille*, frz., Schuft, Schurke; lat. canis: Hund, it. canaglia: Hundepack.

16,11 *Plache*, Plahe, Blahe, Blache: grobes Leinentuch, Wagenplane.

17,22 *provisorisch*, vorläufig, behelfsmäßig, probeweise; gelehrte Neubildung des 18. Jh.s aus lat. providere: vorhersehen, Vorsorge tragen.

17,29 *Abhub*, Speiserest, der von der Tafel abgetragen wird; Abfall.

21,13 *Im Kopfe der Alten war ein »Radel laufet« worden,* ein Rädchen locker, etwas verrückt.

22,6 f. *Sticht dich der Hafer?,* Wirst du übermütig (wie ein gutgefüttertes Pferd)?

22,8 *Ration*, frz., im Deutschen seit dem 17. Jh. in der Heeressprache üblich, zugeteiltes Maß, Anteil, täglicher Verpflegungssatz; aus lat. ratio: u. a. Rechnung, Rechenschaft; mlat. ratiō: berechneter Anteil.

22,21 *Krot*, Kröte, mhd. krot[te], kröte. Das Schimpfwort bezieht sich auf das giftige Speien der Kröte.

23,4 *Teixel überanander*, Fluch, bedeutet etwa: Teufel nochmal!

27,13 *Nihilismus*, eine geistige Grundhaltung, die bestehende Lehr- und Glaubenssätze, allgemeingültige Werte und Anschauungen ablehnt oder verneint; vgl. lat. nihil: nichts.

28,27 *Rabulist*, Wortverdreher, Haarspalter; lat. rabula: Zungendrescher.

29,16 *Fasson*, Form, Muster, Art, Zuschnitt; im 15./16. Jh. aus frz. façon entlehnt, das auf lat. factio (das Machen; die Eigenart, etwas zu tun) zurückgeht.

29,30 *jus gladii*, lat., Recht des Schwertes, d. h. die Gerichtsbarkeit über Leben und Tod der Untertanen zur Zeit der Leibeigenschaft.

31,28 *Mores lehren*, Anstand lehren, erziehen, zur Vernunft bringen; nach lat. mores: Sitten.

33,14 *Souper*, germ.-gallorom.-frz., anspruchsvolles Abendessen.

35,2 *Vogelphysiognomie*, Physiognomie, griech., äußere Erscheinung eines Lebewesens, insbesondere Gesichtsausdruck.

35,12 *Dejeuner*, lat.-vulgärlat., frz., Frühstück.

35,13 *Pirutschaden*, festliche Wagenfahrten innerhalb eines Parkgeländes.

35,30 *requirieren*, etwas auf gewaltsame Weise beschaffen, wegnehmen; hier: zwangsweise zur Arbeit heranziehen; von lat. requirere: verlangen, erfordern.

40,25 f. *Heiducken*, Haiduken, ursprünglich Bezeichnung eines ungarischen Volksstammes, dann eines leichten Reiters, schließlich eines Bedienten in der Tracht dieses Stammes; um 1700 durch den Wiener Hof vermittelt.

41,36 *Exekution*, lat., Vollstreckung eines Urteils, Bestrafung, Hinrichtung.

42,10 *Dignitäre*, lat.-frz., Würdenträger, eigentlich Würdenträger der katholischen Kirche; vgl. lat. dignitas: Würde, Ansehen, auch Ehrenstelle.

42,29 f. *Les adieux de Chloë*, frz., Der Abschied der Chloë; Chloë: antiker Name, in der Welt der Schäferspiele üblich, auch ein Beiname der Ceres, einer Fruchtbarkeitsgöttin.

43,17 *Auditorium*, Zuhörerschaft, Hörsaal; lat. audire: hören.

43,18 *Racine*, Jean Baptiste (1639–99), französischer Tragödiendichter des strengen Klassizismus.

43,25 *Equipage*, frz., herrschaftliche Kutsche, Luxuswagen.

43,37 *Lakai*, herrschaftlicher Diener in Livree; um 1500 frz. laquais als ›Fußsoldat‹, vermutlich aus dem Spanischen und Türkischen.

44,20 *embrassieren*, veraltet für umarmen, küssen; vgl. lat. brachium: Arm.

44,33 *Subsistenzmittel*, veraltet für Lebensunterhalt; lat. subsistere: standhalten, aushalten, gewachsen sein.

45,4 *une fausse sortie*, frz., ein falscher (schlechter) Abgang.

45,13 *Sugillation*, blutunterlaufene Stelle; vgl. lat. sugillatio: der blaue Fleck (vom Schlagen).

45,31 *Fatalität*, Verhängnis, Mißgeschick; lat. fatalis: schicksalhaft, verhängnisvoll.

46,16 *Delinquent*, seit etwa 1600 Verbrecher, Übeltäter, Angeklagter; lat. dēlinquere: etwas versehen, verschulden.

51,16 *stützig*, stutzig, frühnhd. und mundartlich für widerspenstig, störrisch, ursprünglich wohl auf Pferde bezogen, Ableitung von Stutz, mhd. stuz: Stoß.

57,15 *on a ses ennuyeux comme on a ses pauvres*, frz., man hat solche, die einen langweilen, wie man seine Armen hat (im Sinne von: beide sind unvermeidlich).

Inhalt